"LET ME SEE IF I HAVE THIS RIGHT," SHE said. "You'll help me with my problem if I'll help you with yours. You'll find out who's been terrorizing me if I sleep with you. Do I have it right?"

He shook his head. "Not quite. I'll help you whether you sleep with me or not. When we make love, it will be because it's what you want too. I don't consider sex as a competition or as a way to pay off a debt."

"But I'm not attracted to you." She spoke with as much force as she could muster.

He kept her gaze locked to his by silently challenging her, knowing she would respond to a dare. "I'm not alone in this, Silver," he said softly. "We've always struck sparks off each other. We've tried to extinguish them by snapping at each other, but that hasn't worked. We need to allow the attraction to burn out. It's time to put an end to this."

Silver had never felt so alive, so frightened, so exhilarated, so apprehensive in her entire life. Her mind had ceased to function, leaving only explosive sensations. When he lowered his head, she strained to meet him, her lips parting in anticipation. She'd wondered for too long how he would taste.

WHAT ARE *LOVESWEPT* ROMANCES?

They are stories of true romance and touching emotion. We believe those two very important ingredients are constants in our highly sensual and very believable stories in the LOVESWEPT line. Our goal is to give you, the reader, stories of consistently high quality that may sometimes make you laugh, sometimes make you cry, but are always fresh and creative and contain many delightful surprises within their pages.

Most romance fans read an enormous number of books. Those they truly love, they keep. Others may be traded with friends and soon forgotten. We hope that each LOVESWEPT romance will be a treasure—a "keeper." We will always try to publish

LOVE STORIES YOU'LL NEVER FORGET
BY AUTHORS YOU'LL ALWAYS REMEMBER

The Editors

STRANGE
BEDFELLOWS

PATT
BUCHEISTER

BANTAM BOOKS
NEW YORK · TORONTO · LONDON · SYDNEY · AUCKLAND

STRANGE BEDFELLOWS
A Bantam Book / May 1994

*If you would be interested in receiving protective vinyl covers for your
Loveswept books, please write to this address for information:*

> *Loveswept
> Bantam Books
> P.O. Box 985
> Hicksville, NY 11802*

ISBN 0-553-44332-1

Published simultaneously in the United States and Canada

*Bantam Books are published by Bantam Books, a division of Bantam Dou-
bleday Dell Publishing Group, Inc. Its trademark, consisting of the words
"Bantam Books" and the portrayal of a rooster, is Registered in U.S. Patent
and Trademark Office and in other countries. Marca Registrada. Bantam
Books, 1540 Broadway, New York, New York 10036.*

PRINTED IN THE UNITED STATES OF AMERICA

OPM   0 9 8 7 6 5 4 3 2 1

PROLOGUE

At age seventy, King Knight thought he'd learned most of the lessons life had to teach. However, thanks to his only daughter, he was discovering one more—don't celebrate a victory until the last battle has been fought. The previous skirmishes involving finding wives for his three sons had made him overconfident. Knowing Silver, he should have been gearing up for a full-fledged war.

At the moment he couldn't even do that. He didn't know where she was. How in the world was he supposed to arrange a romantic encounter for his daughter if he couldn't find her?

King debated using a private detective, as he had when he was investigating possible wives for two of his sons. He hadn't thought that would be necessary with Silver, since he knew the potential groom.

King had personally chosen John Lomax to take over as chief executive officer of Knight Enterprises for the simple reason that John was a tough, intelligent, honest man. He had walked through fire and had survived, although he had a few scars. Underneath his solemn exterior was a man with decent values and deep feelings. Those qualities were part of the reason King had chosen him as his daughter's husband. Any man who became involved with Silver would have to be especially strong to combat her stubborn independence.

Another reason had persuaded King that John was right for Silver. King had witnessed the sparks that ignited between them the few times he'd seen his daughter with John. The attraction between them was mutual and fiery, even though Silver and John went to great lengths to pretend otherwise. So far, circumstances had kept them from doing anything about it. King was going to change that.

Just as soon as he found Silver.

He glanced at the door of his study to make sure it was closed securely. After listening intently for the sound of his housekeeper's firm footsteps, he opened the lower right drawer of his desk and took out a silver flask containing a fine Irish whiskey. Uncapping it, he poured a dollop into the steaming cup of coffee Alvilda had brought in a few minutes ago. He quickly returned the bottle to the drawer, covering it with several old ledgers. Not everyone understood the need for medicinal spirits, especially his housekeeper, who had taken over as his conscience after his wife died three years earlier.

As he sipped his laced coffee King's thoughts returned to his daughter. In some ways, Silver had always been a mystery to him. Aside from being female, which in itself confused a mere male, she always seemed to feel everything more, to react more strongly than any of his sons, to expect more from herself than anyone else did, to suffer more when things didn't work out the way she thought they should. Part of her drive and ambition was due to being the youngest child and the only girl. Thanks to his perceptive late wife, King was aware of Silver's need to prove herself, although no one was forcing her to except herself. Myra had understood their daughter's competitive nature and had taught Silver the importance of balance in her life. Ambition was admirable, but shouldn't be more important than personal relationships with friends and family.

Lately, King had had the disquieting feeling that something wasn't quite right in Silver's life. The previous month she'd arrived at Knight's Keep along with her brothers for his seventieth birthday, and had taken part in the teasing and joking that always took place when they were all together. His sharp artist's gaze had caught glimpses of strain in her eyes, though, and he had occasionally heard an edge in her voice during her brief visit.

His attempts to talk to her since she'd returned to New York had been frustrating. Her replies to the faxes he'd sent on his new fax machine had been brief, with the excuse that she was busy and would call him when she had more time. During the last week, she hadn't answered any of his faxes at all. All he got when he phoned her apartment was her blasted answering machine. She hadn't returned any of his calls in two days. He could feel it in his old bones that she was in some kind of trouble.

A sudden thought had him narrowing his eyes as he gazed off into space. He'd been racking his brain trying to come up with an idea of how he could bring John and Silver together. Considering John was in Kentucky and his daughter lived in New York City, he had been having difficulty figuring that out.

He smiled. Silver had inadvertently provided the excuse King needed to contact John. King was going to ask his CEO to locate her.

His smile broadened as he visualized the muscle clenching in John's strong jaw when he heard what King wanted. The younger man wasn't going to like King's request one little bit, but he would find Silver.

ONE

John Lomax tapped his fingers impatiently on the steering wheel as he waited for the traffic light to turn green. Inanimate objects seemed to have it in for him this morning. Now it was a traffic light. Earlier, his alarm clock had stopped during an electrical storm and had gone off forty minutes later than usual. From then on, it had been one mishap after the other, including nicking himself shaving and dropping a bar of soap on his toe in the shower. He'd even had to leave his apartment without so much as a sip of life-sustaining coffee. It didn't give him much hope for the rest of the day.

A car horn blasted behind him. Glancing into his rearview mirror, John scowled at the impatient driver. The traffic light hadn't changed to green yet, so the line of cars couldn't go anywhere. If John had to make up a list of all the things he disliked, he would put hitting red lights at every intersection number one, and idiots who honked their horns before the light changed as number two.

The stoplight finally changed to green, and John coasted his car behind the stream of vehicles ahead of him until he had to brake at the next traffic light. To add to the overall dismal mood of the day, raindrops the size of marbles began to drop onto his windshield.

He'd almost begun to think he was jinxed or cursed, but he didn't believe in good or bad luck. He felt everyone should take the blame or the credit for whatever happened to them. Occasionally some things were out of a person's control, but the way they reacted to the situation wasn't.

Like Silver Knight. His hands tightened on the wheel as her image formed in his mind. She could twist his gut every time he thought about her, which was too damn often. He only saw the blasted woman twice a year, yet she was the first thing he thought about when he awoke in the morning, and he saw her face when he closed his eyes each night.

Forgetting her was out of his control, but staying out of her life wasn't.

The six-year journey to find peace of mind after his partner had been shot had been long and difficult, but John had finally become the master of his own fate. Luck didn't have a damn thing to do with it.

When he saw that no one was parked in his reserved parking space at the Knight Enterprises building, he began to have hope for the day after all. That elation evaporated when he arrived at his office on the top floor and discovered his secretary wasn't in. Normally, having a member of his staff on sick leave was only a minor inconvenience. Having Olive out was closer to a disaster, if the day was going to continue the way it had started. Olive could always be counted on to cushion any catastrophe and untangle any knot.

Fifty-five-year-old Olive Branch was his right arm, his eyes, and his ears; she was a walking encyclopedia, filing cabinet, and computer whiz all wrapped up into a plump package. She could easily take over his job, but he would be hard-pressed to take over hers. She'd been with him since the first day he'd taken over the reins of Knight Enterprises, and John hated the thought of putting up with a substitute even for a day.

The timid woman seated at Olive's desk seemed to be ready to jump out of her skin. He was aware he had the reputation of coming down hard on people who made stupid mistakes. He was also fair and nonjudgmental. He rarely suffered fools gladly, but he did give second chances if they were deserved. This wouldn't be the first temporary secretary who looked like she'd rather be assigned to clean the rest rooms with a toothbrush than work for him.

"Good morning," he said with as much warmth as he could muster. "You're replacing Mrs. Branch today?"

The woman gulped nervously. "Yes, sir."

"What's your name?"

"Edna Pole, sir."

"Has anybody given you any instructions about what you're supposed to do?"

"Whatever you tell me to do, Mr. Lomax."

"I'll let you know," he murmured, trying to keep his impatience out of his voice. He never had to tell Olive what to do. She always just went ahead and did it, keeping one step ahead of him.

"Yes, sir," Edna said, blinking like a faulty light bulb.

He walked into his office, running his hand through his rain-dampened hair. As he closed the door behind him he thought of the first time he'd ever been in this office. An Oriental rug had spanned the space between the door and a large mahogany desk that had seemed as big as his car. As he'd crossed the rug he'd felt as though he were walking a gauntlet with no idea of what he would find at the end. The person seated behind the desk had been King Knight, the man who'd given him a reason to keep going when his life had stopped abruptly.

Something out of place on the new dark green carpet caught his eye. He nearly lost his grip on his attaché case when he realized what the object was. It was a woman's shoe. He blinked, then looked again. A bright pink shoe with a two-inch heel was lying on its side near the leather couch. Raising his gaze, John spotted another shoe, this one dangling from the foot of a woman curled on her side facing the back of the couch. His gaze slowly ran over shapely legs, lingering on the soft swell of her hips.

His breath hitched in his throat. He'd seen that delectable rear end before. Almost afraid he was right, he let his gaze trace the straight line of her spine until he reached the black satin swath of hair held by a colorful scarf at the base of her neck.

He closed his eyes for a few seconds, then opened them again. She wasn't a mirage, nor was he dreaming one of his numerous fantasies about her. He was wide-awake, and she was real.

Silver Knight, the daughter of the owner of Knight Enterprises, the woman he'd wanted for longer than he could remember, was asleep on his couch.

He walked over to his desk and carefully placed his case on the floor. Leaning back against the desk, he crossed his arms over his chest and one ankle over the other as he stared at the sleeping woman.

His survival instincts were screaming at him to run before she woke up, but he knew it wouldn't do any good. A corner of his mouth twisted as he admitted it had been too late for evasive action the first time he'd met her. Lord, she'd only been fourteen, all legs and smiles and endless energy that had made him feel ancient at the ripe old age of twenty-six.

Now at thirty-nine, he was supposed to be older and wiser and more in control of his male urges.

And fish liked to be caught on a hook, he thought cynically.

His gaze took in the bright pink silk blouse tucked into the waistband of a navy-blue skirt that had worked itself up to above her knees. A matching navy jacket and a shocking-pink purse had been dropped at the other end of the couch. Whether in casual or business attire, Silver managed to convey her love of bright colors.

John debated waking her. This was his office, not a hotel, and he had work to do. Just then the phone on his desk rang. Silver didn't jerk, jump, or change her steady breathing. That worried him almost as much as whatever reason she had for being there. Several scenarios came to mind to explain such deep exhaustion. She could be ill, tired from a late night on the town, suffering from jet lag, or hung over. He dismissed them all. Unless she'd changed a great deal, none of those situations would apply to Superwoman.

He reached for the phone and gave instructions to the temporary secretary before she had a chance to speak. "Whoever it is, take a message and hold the rest of my calls."

John hung up the phone and walked slowly to the couch. Kneeling down, he touched a spot just under her ear. Her pulse beat strongly and regularly under his finger. He jerked his hand away when she made a soft purring sound, as though she was aware of his touch.

And liked it.

John stood up abruptly and put some distance between them before he did something incredibly stupid, like touch her the way he'd wanted to for what seemed like forever. As he neared his desk he heard her make another sound and, against his better judgment, turned to look at her. She evidently wasn't so deeply asleep that his touch hadn't registered somewhere in her sleep-fogged brain, disturbing her rest.

She had rolled onto her back, and some of the material of her shirt had caught underneath her, causing the front to draw tightly over her breasts. A button at the base of the V-neck opening had slipped loose, exposing an edge of delicate white lace against the gentle slope of her left breast. He was surprised by her choice of underwear. For a woman who was a walking rainbow, she was wearing a tame piece of feminine apparel.

Her delicate features were composed in sleep; her eyes, a deeper blue than her brothers', were closed. The resemblance to her beautiful mother would grow over the years instead of diminishing, her grace and charm becoming more compelling with age.

John closed his eyes and struggled to think of the quarterly stock figures he'd been studying the night before. Usually he found numbers fascinating, especially before he'd brought all the facets of Knight Enterprises into a healthy set of black figures. The CEO who had preceded him, the man King had appointed before he'd gone to live in England, had nearly run the company into the ground. John gave up and opened his eyes. Tallying the gross and net advances for the company wasn't taking his mind off the woman on his couch.

He doubted if anything short of a raging fire in his wastebasket would. Maybe not even then. Lord knows, he thought about her far too often as it was. And that was when she was hundreds of miles away.

He stepped around his desk and sat in his

leather chair. The desk wasn't much of a barrier between them. Barbed wire would have been better.

He wasn't in the mood to debate with Silver at the moment, and if he woke her, they would argue. Over the years the protective banter they'd eased into at first had developed into downright antagonism. John couldn't imagine why this occasion would be any different.

For the next thirty minutes John went through the motions of studying the promotion ideas the publicity department had come up with to advertise a specialized mail-order catalog that was scheduled to be launched in May. Since he'd been involved in the conception of the catalog, he should have been able to concentrate on the PR plans with some enthusiasm.

It didn't work. He was vitally aware of every breath, every slight movement Silver made the whole time. Which was why he knew exactly when she started to awaken.

He could have done without the soft sounds she made as she stretched out her legs and moved her arms. The rustle of fabric sliding on the leather couch and gliding over her body gave him a few bad moments too.

Even asleep, the darn woman could drive him nuts.

Something was pulling her out of the peaceful darkness, Silver realized through a sleepy haze, and she resisted. It had been so long since she had felt secure enough to close her eyes for even a brief period of time, and she wanted to make it last a little longer.

She ran her hand over the cushion near her right hip and frowned when her fingers touched warm leather instead of cool cotton. Her mind finally clicked into gear and registered that she wasn't at home in her own bed. Slowly opening her eyes, she saw a wall painted forest green where white wallpaper with small gold fleurs-de-lis was supposed to be.

With full consciousness came the realization of where she was. And why.

She glanced at the slim gold watch on her wrist to check the time. John would be coming to his office any minute now. She could easily envision the smirk on his face and imagine the type of snide remark he would make if he found her sprawled on his couch.

Sliding her feet to the floor, she sat up quickly and started to stand, but she stumbled over her own shoe that was lying on the floor. Her arms flailed around for several seconds until she managed to catch her balance.

She was bending down to pick up her shoe when a masculine voice drawled, "Been walking long?"

Her fingers tightened around the shoe. She took her time turning to face the man sitting behind the desk, silently cursing her timing, her disheveled appearance, and most of all John Lomax for making her feel like she was fourteen again. This wasn't how she'd planned their meeting. She wasn't supposed to look like she'd been sleeping in her clothes, her hair mussed, her makeup probably all over her face except where it was supposed to be. The impression she'd wanted to make was that of the grown-up, professional woman she was, not the awkward, sassy teenager she had been.

She was always defensive with him to counter the attraction she felt every time she saw him. Or thought about him. Evidently, absence had not made him any fonder of her.

It was especially galling that he looked like he'd just stepped off the pages of *Gentlemen's Quarterly*. His white shirt was immaculate, his silk charcoal tie conservative, his light gray suit emphasizing the muscular spread of his shoulders. His dark blond hair looked as though it had been combed by his fingers, its length a little longer than she remembered. She would call his features more rugged than handsome, his reserve and quiet power as much a part of him as the color of his eyes. She detected a few more lines at the corners of his dark brown eyes, the only indication she saw of the passing years on his tanned face. On most people, those minor grooves would be called laugh lines. Since she had never seen John smile or laugh, she attributed his to age.

She wasn't surprised to see that his gaze was as unnervingly frank as ever.

"Hello, John," she said as calmly as she could. "Do I need to introduce myself or do you remember me?"

"I know who you are, Silver," he said dryly. "It's been a while, but you aren't the type of woman a man forgets easily."

She didn't take his comment as a compliment. Their last meeting still unnerved her, and she hoped it didn't show in her voice. She'd been in Raleigh to attend a meeting of the board of directors of Knight Enterprises, act ing as King's proxy. Almost immediately after she had arrived at the building, there'd been a power failure. She and John had been alone in the dimly lit conference room while they waited for the power to be restored and the other board members to join them. She didn't think she'd ever forget the way he had looked at her as they'd sat in almost complete silence, smiling faintly whenever she challenged his intense stare with one of her own. It had been the only time in her life when silence had been louder than noise.

"The last time you saw me was five months ago at the board meeting. Since you said maybe ten words to me, even though we spent an hour or so alone waiting for the rest of the board to join up, I wasn't sure you did remember me."

"It would be easier to forget the one and only hangover I've ever had than forget King Knight's charming daughter. And it was only twenty-five minutes that we were alone together."

"It seemed longer," she murmured. But then, reality always seemed out of kilter when she was with John. She wasn't sure if it was because of the distance he put between them, or her constant battle to ignore her powerful attraction to him. "The one time I was early for a board meeting was the same day you arrived before everyone else."

"Some would call it fate."

She didn't miss the irony in his voice. "I see the months since I last saw you haven't done much to mellow your line of chitchat."

He leaned back. Resting his elbows on the arms of the chair, he steepled his fingers. "I decided to hell with growing old gracefully. I'm going out kicking and screaming."

"You make it sound as though the end isn't that far off." She was able to do two things at the same time, she congratulated herself. Put her shoe on and give John a hard time. "You're only thirty-nine, John. Not ninety. Lighten up."

He raised a single eyebrow, his only reaction to her knowing his correct age. "I might try it if I had the slightest notion what that meant."

"It means lighten your attitude, don't be so literal, so serious. A smile would be a nice start." She tilted her head to one side and stared at him. "Do you know I've never seen you smile? I bet that event would be worth the price of admission."

"I'll let you know if I decide to take it on the road."

She glanced around the room that used to be her father's office. "I've always wanted to ask. Whatever happened to the huge mahogany monstrosity King used to hide behind?"

John shrugged. "I haven't the faintest idea. Hopefully, it's gone to the same place as the Oriental rug that used to stretch from here to the door."

"That rug was a gift from a wealthy sheikh who wanted to show his appreciation for the portrait King painted of his prize stallion. The rug probably cost a fortune."

"The rug had big yellow chrysanthemums all over it, Silver. It had to go." He leaned forward, resting his forearms on the top of his desk. "Silver, are you going to voluntarily tell me why you're in Kentucky sleeping in my office instead of in New York dazzling Wall Street, or are you going to make me work for the answer?"

"I'll get to it," she said crossly. "I'm a little nervous."

"You?" he scoffed. "A thirty-foot python wrapped around your neck wouldn't make you nervous. You'd just slap it and tell it to behave itself."

It was irritating to hear him describe how she would react in a given situation. Especially when he was right.

"Would you accept being tired as an excuse for not being my usual calm, collected self?"

He shrugged again, implying he didn't care one way or the other. "I didn't know the stock exchange was open twenty-four hours a day now."

"Says one workaholic to another. I haven't had any sleep for over thirty hours," she said defensively. "But it isn't because I've been working. I drove here straight from New York and decided to make use of your couch while I waited for you to arrive. And to answer your next obvious question, I still have the set of keys to the building King gave me before he and my mother moved to England."

Scowling, John asked, "Why would King give you a set of keys to Knight Enterprises? Do you plan on making a move for my job?"

"Who knows why King Knight does anything? He gave keys to each of my brothers, too, along with shares in the company. Knowing King, it was a symbolic gesture to show us he wasn't getting rid of the family firm entirely. It was his way of easing his conscience about leaving the helm of Knight Enterprises.

Even though he's still on the board of directors, he's the first in three generations to abdicate responsibility to someone out of the family."

"He told me once that he expected his father and grandfather would be turning over in their graves because he'd handed the firm over to an outsider. His grandfather was always adamant about Knight Enterprises remaining a family-run business."

"You can relax. The last thing I want is your job." Her chin shifted up a notch. "Not that I couldn't do it."

"Of course," he agreed. "Now that we've established why you *aren't* here, let's work on why you've graced Knight Enterprises with your presence."

Even though he hadn't offered, she sat down in the straight-backed leather chair in front of his desk. Now that she was there, she wondered what had possessed her to come to see this arrogant man. When she'd paced the floor of her apartment after the latest break-in, her first thought had been to go to John Lomax for help. Considering she had three older brothers who would drop whatever they were doing to come to her aid no matter where or when, it was extremely odd that the first person she'd thought of was a man she tried to avoid. A man who didn't bother hiding the fact that he considered her a royal pain in the butt.

She should have taken more time to think things through before rushing off to Kentucky, she decided now that it was too late. Her priority had been to find a place where she would be safe. That would be wherever John was, so she'd thrown a few things in a bag and driven from New York to Raleigh, Kentucky. After a couple of hours of sleep on his couch, she realized she'd made a mistake.

"Decisions made at midnight aren't necessarily the ones we should take seriously in broad daylight," she said with a rueful smile.

"Meaning?"

She moved forward in her chair prior to standing up. "Meaning I shouldn't have come here. It was a spur-of-the-moment thing. I should have given it more thought."

John's gaze lowered to her hands. She was clenching the arms of the chair so tightly, her knuckles were white with the strain. Coupled with the shadows in her eyes that he suspected had nothing to do with lack of sleep, it finally dawned on him that Silver was genuinely worried about something serious. He'd been so preoccupied with controlling his reaction to seeing her again, he hadn't noticed the strain in her features.

"What's wrong?" He hadn't meant to sound so harsh. She flinched as though he'd slapped her, and he felt about two inches tall.

"Nothing you can help me with." She stood up. "I'm sorry I bothered you."

"Sit down, Silver," he said quietly. "You're here now. Tell me what's bothering you."

Judging by her glare, the commanding tone of his voice grated against her nerve endings. "I felt," she said, "as though I'd been folded, spindled, and mutilated before I got here. I don't need to be crushed any further by your heavy-handed attitude."

John sat back in his chair, studying her expression. He'd never seen her like this before, nervous, edgy, and flustered. Self-preservation had a tug-of-war with concern and lost the battle. For King's sake, he would find out what her problem was.

"Sit down, Silver. Now that you're here, you might as well tell me what's on your mind."

She stared at him for a few seconds, as if searching for any sign that he was simply humoring her, then she sat down.

She didn't immediately begin explaining, so John decided to get the ball rolling by asking a question.

"Let's go back to the time of midnight when you made the decision to come here. Were you in your apartment?"

She nodded.

"Were you alone?"

He was surprised to see her shudder.

"Yes."

"Did you get an obscene phone call?"

"No."

"Did someone follow you home?" This time she shook her head. He was beginning to lose what few ounces of patience he had left. "Did someone mug you? Rape you? Burglarize your apartment?"

The questions fired at her in rapid succession ignited her temper. "You're not a cop any longer, John. Stop interrogating me."

"Then get to the point. Tell me why you're here."

She hesitated, licking her lips as if trying to find the courage to talk. John tried to keep his mind off the sight of her pink tongue nervously stroking across her lips. Aside from the fact that his heart was beating like a trip-hammer, he was having problems with the knowledge that she really was nervous. It was a side of Silver he'd never seen before, or even considered possible for her or any of the other members of her family. One thing that had always impressed him about the Knight family was their supreme self-confidence. Silver seemed to have left hers back in New York.

"Save us both some time, Silver. I'm not in the mood to play twenty questions."

Silver almost walked out the door. He was so damn arrogant, opinionated, and blunt to the point of rudeness. But he was also tough and strong physically, mentally, and emotionally, the qualities she needed right now.

Feeling as though she was about to make a gigantic fool of herself, she took a deep breath and plunged ahead. "Even though we see each other once or twice a year at the board meetings, I don't think you really know much about me other than what King might have said. Since I'm his only daughter and he usually exaggerates, what you've heard about me has probably been a fairy tale or two. You'll have to take my word for it that I'm not the type of person to conjure up demons just for the heck of it."

"I know," John said, "that you are remarkably intelligent and can crunch numbers with the best of them on Wall Street, although you hate to have people think of you as only a brain. You usually have a sharp sense of humor, but it seems to have stayed in New York this trip. Your father has pointed out that you have a rather nasty independent streak from having to compete with three brothers. You like bright colors and you hate asparagus. That's about it. To answer your question, I would say you would be the last person to conjure up demons. So?"

She took a deep breath as though she were about to jump out of a plane without a parachute. "Someone is trying to make me believe I'm crazy."

TWO

John stared at Silver for a full minute, as if not sure he'd heard her correctly. "This is not exactly earthshaking news," he drawled at last. "From what I've seen of your family, you're all a little nuts. What makes you think someone is trying to make out you're due for the loony bin?"

"You have such a way with words, John. It absolutely amazes me that you never went into politics," she said irritably. "I *know* someone is trying to make me doubt myself and my sanity. This is some kind of crazy game, and I don't want to play. I want you to tell me how I can find out who is behind all the things that have been happening to me so that I can stop them."

"What things?" he asked.

Silver couldn't help wondering if she was wasting her time. John had that tolerant tone of voice that made her think of a grown-up patting a child on top of the head to placate her. She was here now, she told herself. She might as well stick to her original plan.

"One day the gas gauge on my car would register full, then the next time I used it, the indicator would be almost on empty, even though I'd only driven maybe twenty miles. Before I could fill the tank, the gauge read full again. Things were moved around in my apartment although the door and all the windows were always locked. Groceries have been delivered to my apartment that I've never ordered. Food items would be in my refrigerator, then be gone the next day. I set my alarm for six o'clock, and sometimes it would ring an hour earlier because it had been reset."

"Those incidents are irritating, Silver," John said patiently, "but they happen to people all the time. Everyone is absentminded at some time or other. Just this morning I was late because the electricity had gone off during the night and my alarm went off later than it was set for."

"That isn't the same as being set ahead of

the correct time. An electrical failure wouldn't affect the alarm in reverse."

"You probably pushed the wrong button when you set the alarm and didn't realize it. I can't see where any of the things you've described are all that horrible for you to get so upset about."

"If I was the klutzy or absentminded type, I'd agree with you." She looked down at her hands clasped in her lap. "There are just too many things happening that don't make sense. Since I'm not responsible for them, somebody else has to be. I've tried to think rationally and logically about all the odd events that have taken place during the last month, but I can't come up with a single reason why someone would purposely set me up for the loony bin, as you so elegantly put it. Too many odd incidents are happening for them all to be coincidences. The only logical conclusion is that someone is determined to scare me, and they're doing a good job of it."

"That's your answer."

"What's my answer?"

"You aren't crazy. You're paranoid. Stress can do odd things to people. It sounds to me as if you need to ease up on your work schedule and on yourself."

"Thank you for taking me so seriously," she said tightly.

"Exactly what do you want from me?" he asked. He'd been unable to keep the edge out of his voice.

"I mistakenly thought you might help me. I was hoping you might put some of your past experience as a policeman to use by advising me how I can find whoever is playing around in my apartment."

"I can't help you, Silver," he said flatly.

She met his gaze, her chin raised. "You mean you won't."

He shrugged. "Whatever. Perhaps all you need is to take a vacation and relax. After you've had some time off, you'll find the mishaps have stopped."

"You think," she said, her voice deceptively quiet, "everything I've told you is just my imagination?"

"It's easy to imagine all sorts of things when a person is overworked." He pulled a notepad toward him, wrote something on the top sheet, and tore it off. Reaching across the desk, he handed it to her. "Give this guy a call while you're here. I know him through the police force. He might be able to help you. If he can't, perhaps he can recommend a colleague in New York."

Disappointment bit a large chunk out of her confidence. Glancing at the paper he'd given her, Silver read the name he'd written, and the man's title. John's handwriting was clear and neat, easy to read and to understand. So was the reason he'd recommended this man.

"A doctor?" she asked as she folded the paper carefully several times. "Your idea of helping me is to recommend a doctor? Let me guess. He's a shrink." She paused, waiting for him to deny it. When he didn't, she compressed her lips and said bitterly, "Thanks for nothing."

John didn't move to stop her when she got to her feet and crossed the office to the couch. He was going to get his wish. She was going to leave.

Still, his conscience gnawed at him. "He's a psychologist and a friend of mine, well-known and respected. He can give you some tests to prove you aren't crazy. Isn't that what you want to hear?"

She grabbed her jacket and purse from the couch, then made a strangled sound of irritation when she accidentally dropped her hand-bag and some of its contents fell out onto the carpet.

She scooped up her belongings and tossed them back into her purse. "Why waste the doctor's time? I've just proved I am crazy by coming to you for help."

John watched her walk toward the door. Now that she was leaving, he felt an odd reluctance to let her go.

"Drive carefully back to New York."

For a few seconds she looked at him, her eyes more green than blue, her expression blank. She opened the door. "Good-bye, John."

He prepared himself for hearing the door slam. Instead, she closed it quietly behind her. He should be feeling satisfied and relieved that he had gotten through the meeting with her relatively unscathed and without making a fool of himself by doing something insane, like pulling her down on the couch under him. His imagination had given him some bad moments over the years, but his fantasies always paled next to the real thing. Damn, he wanted her. He had been forced to remain behind his desk so she wouldn't be able to see how she affected him.

He had wanted her to leave, he reminded himself, so why was he feeling guilty? Maybe it was the way she'd looked at him when she'd read the doctor's name, as though he'd just slapped her. He'd expected her to be angry, would have even welcomed it, but the hurt she hadn't been able to hide was haunting him now. The strong, willful Silver Knight he could resist. Not easily, but he managed. He wasn't so sure he could withstand the appeal of the vulnerable woman who'd just left his office.

He'd done the right thing, he told himself. Whatever she thought was going on in New York was only her imagination or coincidence or due to stress. He couldn't afford to become entangled in her life. She could cost him his peace of mind.

Caring for someone, letting them into your life, only led to pain. He'd learned that lesson the hard way. Standing over the coffin containing his partner, who was also the son of his closest friend, John had vowed to live a life free of personal involvement. Silver Knight was a serious threat to his self-imposed exile.

He stared at the door, unable to prevent a niggling doubt about the cavalier way he'd treated Silver. What if she wasn't imagining things? What if someone was actually trying to play with her mind? Or worse, might attempt to hurt her physically when the thrill of the game was no longer enough? He knew better than most how dangerous a large city like New York could be. As a cop, he'd seen man's inhumanity to man on a daily basis. It wouldn't be unheard of if some nut was stalking Silver for the simple joy of making her life miserable.

Dammit, he cursed silently. She had no right to ask him for help in the first place. She had three brothers and undoubtedly a number of friends in New York she could go to with her problems. He was out of the "protect and serve" business.

Unfortunately, he didn't seem to be out of the infatuation business. No matter how many times he told himself to forget her, she stayed in his mind day and night like a haunting dream. Hearing about her from King before and after the quarterly board meetings was hard enough. When she occasionally showed up as King's proxy, she played havoc with his mind, even seated at the opposite end of the conference table from him.

The last time they'd met, when they'd sat alone together, he had had to fight the enormous temptation to pull her into his arms and kiss her with fourteen years' worth of desire. He'd finally acknowledged to himself that his feelings for Silver were not going to fade away eventually. She was too deeply embedded in his mind to be extracted by simple discipline and wishful thinking. Wanting Silver Knight came under the heading of aiming for the stars and ending up with an empty sky. She was beautiful, intelligent, and completely out of his league.

Still, he watched her intently whenever he saw her, soaking up her smile, her voice, and the way she looked. That last time they were together, he had realized he was never going to get her out of his system. What he didn't know was how he was going to live with that knowledge.

With ruthless control, he returned to the paperwork on his desk.

Two hours later, he pushed back his chair and stood. With luck, the temporary secretary had figured out how to operate the fancy German coffee machine Olive had insisted on buying. He certainly could use a cup of the strong brew.

The phone on his desk rang before he'd taken two steps. He walked back when he saw that the button lighting up was his private line. Not many people had that number. He wondered if Silver had decided to try again to approach him for help. Giving up wasn't part of her makeup. Or at least it hadn't been before.

The deep male voice on the line sounded as though the speaker was in the next room instead of on the other side of the Atlantic Ocean.

"Glad I caught you in the office, John," boomed King Knight.

"Where else would I be?"

"Since I'm never sure if I've figured the time difference between England and Kentucky correctly, you could have been home snoring in bed."

"I don't snore."

"How do you know? Just because none of your bedmates have complained doesn't mean you don't rattle the windows."

John didn't bother explaining that he had never spent an entire night with any of the women he'd been involved with. Actually there hadn't been that many women, and he'd never even been tempted to stay for breakfast. Sleeping with a woman seemed more intimate than the sex act itself.

"Are you calling to discuss my sleeping habits or was there something else you wanted?"

King's voice changed abruptly. "I'm concerned about my little girl, John," he said seriously. "Something is going on with her. She hasn't answered my phone calls or fax messages the last couple of days, which isn't like her. I contacted the firm she works for and was told she wasn't expected back for quite some time. When I pushed for more information, I learned she's taken a leave of absence. She's in trouble, John, and she also seems to have disappeared."

John closed his eyes as a flood of guilt washed over him. "She's here, King. I saw her a couple of hours ago."

There was a long pause before King asked if she was all right.

"She's fine." At least physically, John added silently. "She has a few problems she wants me to help her with. It's a bit complicated to go into on the phone, but—"

"There's no need for details. As long as she's with you, I won't worry about her. I have faith in you, lad. You'll take care of whatever problem she has."

"King—"

"I won't fret any longer. I appreciate you putting my mind at ease, John. I know you won't let anything or anyone hurt her."

Knowing he'd done exactly that himself, John changed the subject by asking King about his latest painting commission. King had done what many men dreamed about and few had the courage to do. He had taken off his gold cuff links and rolled up his sleeves to become a full-time equine artist in England. His portraits of horses were extremely popular, and King had never regretted his decision to leave Knight Enterprises in John's hands. John knew King still missed his wife, who had passed away three years ago, but all in all, King Knight was a happy man.

However, John was well aware that there was one more goal the older man hoped to reach in his lifetime. He wanted to be a grandfather. When King had mentioned the desire for grandchildren the last time John had seen him, John had wondered if King was setting himself up for a major disappointment. He was just approaching his seventieth birthday at that point, and his four children were single, unattached, and apparently in no hurry to change their lives.

John and King talked a few minutes more

before King said, "You take good care of my little girl, John. You know, I wouldn't mind if she was the first of my children to provide me with a grandbaby."

Something in King's voice sent a warning alarm off in John's head.

"Don't go getting any ideas, King. There's nothing going on between me and your daughter, so don't go buying any baby booties."

"I have the greatest respect for natural phenomena like earthquakes and hurricanes. You and Silver have been like two volcanoes simmering under the surface the few times I've seen you together. All I have to do is wait for the explosion."

"King—"

"Keep in touch, John." The line went dead.

John stared at the phone for a few seconds before hanging up. He didn't like the reference King had made about a simmering volcano. It was too close to the way he felt when he was with Silver, as though his blood turned to molten lava. Hell, he thought. That's how he felt just thinking about her.

Suddenly restless, he shoved out of his chair and strode around the desk.

As he headed for the door he kicked something in front of the couch. Bending down, he picked up the object and saw it was a hotel key. Many hotels didn't use actual keys anymore, supplying guests with thin cards with holes in them instead. He knew of only one old, stately hotel in Raleigh that still used this type of key. The words *Ambassador Hotel* and a room number were stamped in gold on the brown plastic tag attached to the key.

The key must have fallen out of Silver's purse when she dropped it earlier. The Ambassador Hotel was one of the properties owned by Knight Enterprises and was where Silver stayed whenever she was in town. He shoved the key in his pocket and retraced his steps back to his desk.

The desk clerk at the Ambassador Hotel answered promptly after the first ring. Following John's request, he tried calling Silver's room and, a few minutes later, was extremely apologetic as he told John that Miss Knight didn't answer.

John punched out another phone number, the same one he'd written down for Silver that morning. His fingers rapped impatiently on the top of the desk as he waited for Peter Mantusco's receptionist to answer.

Three minutes later he replaced the phone and stared off into space. Then he pushed back his chair and headed for the door of his office again.

Silver hadn't called Mantusco, which didn't surprise him. She might be waiting until she returned to New York and would call someone there, but John knew he was only kidding himself. She wasn't going to make an appointment to see a psychologist. She would tough it out on her own.

At least he knew she hadn't checked out of the hotel. If she hadn't left within the last two hours, he reasoned, she probably wouldn't be leaving at all that day. Considering she had driven alone from New York, she was undoubtedly exhausted and would probably set out in the morning.

As he left his office he stopped at his secretary's desk, no longer interested in getting a cup of coffee. Edna Pole stared up at him with large brown eyes behind thick glasses. She looked like a frightened rabbit suddenly confronted by a large hungry eagle.

"Has a Miss Knight phoned to ask about a hotel key she might have left in my office?"

Edna Pole gave him a blank look. "No, sir."

"I'll be gone for about an hour, Ms. Pole. Take names, phone numbers, and messages

and I'll take care of everything when I return.
All right?"

"Yes, sir."

Lord, she was writing down what he said, he
marveled, watching as her pencil made squiggly
marks on a stenographer's pad. While she was
scribbling away he added, "Order flowers to
be sent to Mrs. Branch with a card wishing
her a speedy recovery. You can get her home
address from personnel."

"Yes, sir," she murmured. She obviously
didn't catch the double meaning behind his
directive.

John gave her a weak smile and left the
office. He made a mental note to ask personnel not to send Edna Pole up to replace Olive
when the older woman went on vacation. Miss
Pole was probably a very good secretary, but
she was too timid to be able to deal with his
often abrupt manner.

As he drove out of the underground parking area, he noticed the early-morning rain
had stopped. Not that rain would have made
him change his mind about going after Silver.
It was too late for turning back.

He knew all the reasons why he shouldn't
go to her. Unfortunately, none of them stood
up to his guilt at knowing he had hurt her.

While trying to protect his own feelings, he had unintentionally hurt hers. It didn't help to learn from King that she was obviously in more trouble than she'd let on. She'd only described a few odd incidents that had happened in her apartment. He vaguely remembered something about her car's gas tank, too, but he hadn't been listening very closely.

He'd practically thrown her out of his office instead, he berated himself. All because he was trying to protect himself. It was time for him to act his age instead of behaving like a frustrated teenager with an itch he couldn't scratch. For King's sake, he would investigate the mysterious problems she'd been having. Or thought she'd been having. That would be the extent of their involvement.

Two blocks from the hotel, John had to pull over as a fire engine sped by, its siren blaring a strident warning for cars and pedestrians to get the hell out of the way. His luck with traffic lights hadn't improved since that morning. As he stopped for the next red light another fire engine raced across the intersection in front of him.

Finally turning onto the street where the Ambassador Hotel was located, John was startled to see the two fire engines and other emergency vehicles blocking the street in front of the hotel. A ladder from the first fire engine stretched up to a window on the fourth floor. The window was broken and black smoke was rolling out of it. Remembering the room number on the hotel key in his pocket, John felt an icy sliver of fear race up his spine.

Silver's room was on the fourth floor.

Parking illegally, he slid out of his car and darted around an ambulance, two police cars, and one of the fire engines in order to get to the entrance of the hotel. A sturdy policeman stopped him with an outstretched arm as two paramedics exited through the wide glass doors, bearing a woman on a stretcher.

John was about to turn away, heading for a side entrance, when he caught a glimpse of raven-black hair surrounding a pale face smudged with smoke on one cheek. An oxygen mask had been placed over the woman's mouth and nose. A white blanket was spread over her from her shoulders to the end of the stretcher, where one pink tip of a shoe poked out.

John's breath caught in his throat. Her

eyes were closed. And she was so still. He felt a chill shudder through him at the thought of Silver being seriously injured. A sharp pain struck him in the chest as his mind took another step and considered the fact that she could be dead. He wouldn't accept that. He couldn't accept that.

"Silver," he murmured.

He ducked under the policeman's arm and ignored the officer's command to stay back. Approaching the paramedic closest to him, he demanded to know Silver's condition.

"I'm a friend of the family. Is Miss Knight going to be all right?"

The man nodded. "It looks like she took in some smoke, but she wasn't burned. We're taking her to the hospital to get her checked out more thoroughly, but she should be okay."

Walking alongside the stretcher, John grasped Silver's hand, which was lying on top of the blanket. Something loosened deep inside him when he heard her breathing slowly and deeply into the mask.

"Silver? It's John. John Lomax. Open your eyes."

She obeyed instantly, meeting his gaze. The expression in her eyes was oddly blank, as though a thin curtain had come down over her emotions. It was a look she might give a stranger.

He wanted to shake a response out of her. More than that, though, he wanted to hold her securely in his arms.

"What happened?" he asked, surprised to hear his own voice was husky, as though he, too, had inhaled smoke.

She raised the mask with her free hand and said hoarsely, "My imagination got the better of me again."

John's breath hitched as he realized what she meant. She had been in danger from a fire in the hotel. And she didn't expect him to believe her.

He was forced to release her hand when the attendants reached the back of the ambulance and maneuvered the stretcher through the opened double doors. Silver had closed her eyes again, effectively shutting him out. After asking the attendant which hospital they were taking her to, John stepped back so they could close the doors.

He stood in the street and watched the ambulance weave its way through the vehicles in the road, including his. The red light on top of the ambulance was whirling, but thankfully the siren hadn't been activated. Once he could no longer see the ambulance, John turned and walked quickly toward the hotel. He was going to find out what in hell had happened in her hotel room.

Two hours later John swept back a curtain around one of the cubicles in the emergency room and stepped inside. Silver was sitting on the edge of the examination table buttoning the front of her smudged bright pink shirt. Her hands and face had been cleaned, but the scent of carbon still clung to her clothing. A shapeless hospital gown was in a crumpled heap beside her.

When she looked up, her expression was one of polite inquiry until she saw who it was. Then she lowered her gaze to the front of her shirt, ignoring him completely.

He noticed her fingers were shaking. "I just talked to the doctor who examined you. He said he was releasing you."

Tucking her blouse into the waistband of her skirt, she kept her gaze lowered. "He told me the same thing. If you're here to take me back to the hotel, you wasted a trip. I had one of the nurses call a cab."

"I had one of the nurses cancel it."

She brought her gaze up to meet his. "Why

did you do that? I'll just have to call them again."

He shrugged. "Go ahead. I'll cancel it again."

"You can put your conscience on hold, John," she said with more than a degree of irritation. "You're responsible for my father's business, not his daughter."

"I'm not going to argue with you, Silver. I have your things from your hotel room in my car. You're staying with me."

"No. I'm not."

"I wasn't asking, Silver. I'm telling you. I talked to the fire marshal and the manager of the hotel. The smoke was from faulty wiring in the bathroom. It wasn't as dangerous as a fire would have been, but you could have suffocated. You can't stay in that room in its condition, and there are no other rooms available."

"Let me get this straight," she said slowly. "You believed the manager of the hotel and the fire marshal when they told you what happened, but you didn't believe me when I told you about the other things that have been happening to me. That stinks worse than I do at the moment, John."

"It wasn't a case of not believing you, Silver. I didn't want to get involved with you even for a short time."

"You got your wish. You don't have to get involved in my problems at all. Your instincts are better than mine. I didn't think you would still dislike me after all this time."

"Silver!"

"I'm going back to New York as soon as I pick up my car at the hotel. If you will leave my suitcase at the information desk, I'll get it after I phone for another cab."

John debated how much to tell her. She'd already had a big enough shock for one day, but she was going to have to know why she couldn't drive to New York right away.

Aside from the fact that he wasn't going to let her.

He stepped near her to help her with her suit jacket. "Silver, it's not possible for you to drive back to New York."

She slipped on the jacket, avoiding looking at him. "Of course I can. I told the police and the fire marshal everything I knew, which wasn't all that much."

"You haven't told *me* what happened."

"Now, why should I do that when you don't believe a word I say?"

"Don't push me, Silver. I'll push back."

She sighed heavily. "I was lying on the bed when I smelled smoke."

"You weren't asleep?"

"No." She gave a short laugh. "I was more in the mood to hit something than I was to sleep."

"Be glad you were so ticked off at me you weren't able to sleep. That might have saved your life. What did you do when you smelled the smoke?"

"When I saw it was coming from under the bathroom door, I called the front desk. Then I opened the door to see if I could do something to put out the fire."

"That wasn't too smart," he said roughly. The picture of her lying on a stretcher was still too vivid in his mind. "Even a five-year-old knows better than to open a door if there's a chance of a fire on the other side."

"I'm on a roll." Her mouth twisted into a rueful smile. "I've been doing a number of dumb things lately."

He let that go, knowing she included asking him for help among her list of stupid activities.

"Returning to New York today," he said,

"would be another 'dumb thing.' You're in no condition to make the long drive even if you could."

She gave him a sharp look. "What do you mean, even if I could? I told you I'm fine. I smell like a smudge pot, but I've been pumped full of oxygen and my lungs are clear. I haven't been burned, and there isn't anything further I can tell the authorities that would help their investigation. There's no reason for me to stay."

He turned her around to face him, tamping down his temper when he felt her stiffen. His fingers tightened on her shoulders as she tried to pull away from his grip.

"You can't drive to New York for the simple reason that you don't have a car."

Her eyes widened as she stared at him warily, as though he'd lost his mind and had no way of finding it again.

"Yes, I do. It's parked at the hotel." Her expression changed to a bleak acceptance when she saw his lips tighten into a firm line. Leaning against the examination table, she asked in a resigned voice, "What's happened to my car?"

"It's been trashed, along with four others

parked in the same row. A hotel parking attendant reported the vandalism while I was talking
to the manager."

"The manager explained to me he's had to
put on extra security during the last couple of
months due to vandalism and theft. There's
no proof that your car was the prime target.
Probably just bad luck, which you seem to be
experiencing a lot of lately."

"How bad is the damage to my car?"

"I had it towed to my mechanic, who will
check it out, but you won't be able to drive
it until some work is done. Some hoses and
wires have been ripped out of the engine and
the mechanic thinks sugar was put in the gas
tank. We'll know the full extent of the damage
in a day or so."

John wanted to hold her until she lost the
haunted look that had appeared in her eyes.
Knowing she wouldn't welcome his touch
caused a frustration unlike anything he'd ever
felt before.

With abrupt movements, Silver shoved the
sleeves of her jacket up her forearms, as though
preparing for a fight. "Send me the bill for
whatever repairs your mechanic has to make.
I'll call your secretary tomorrow and give her
the address where I'll be."

"That won't be necessary. She knows where I live." He looked her up and down. "You ready to go?"

"I'm not going to your apartment, John," she said firmly. "Coming to Kentucky was a mistake from start to finish. I'm leaving."

"Didn't you hear what I said about your car? You can't drive it."

"There are such things as planes, rental cars, and buses, you know," she said as she glanced around, looking for her purse. When she found it on a counter behind the examination table, she slung the strap over her shoulder, ignoring the sooty handprint on the colored leather. "You can put your conscience back in the dark closet where you usually keep it. King won't blame you for whatever happens to me, if that's what you're worried about. I don't plan on telling him or anyone else how I made a fool of myself by coming here in the first place. The fire wasn't your—" She made a startled sound when his hand closed around her upper arm. "Let go of me."

He was drawing her out of the cubicle. "Not in this lifetime," he said, "so you might as well stop fighting."

She struggled against his grip. "I never realized you had a hearing problem, Lomax. Dammit, let go!"

They were now in the busy emergency room. Hospital personnel and patients turned their heads to stare at them.

Lowering her voice, she hissed, "I'm not staying with you, Lomax."

"You seem to be under the impression you have a choice."

A nurse with a clipboard stopped their progress out of the emergency room by presenting Silver with some papers to sign to make her release official. As she folded her copies of the various forms and stuffed them in her purse, Silver could feel the tension emanating from the man standing close beside her.

Short of causing a scene in the emergency room, she was at a loss as to how to get rid of John. She had no illusions about why he had come to the hospital to check on her. It wasn't that he was worried about her personally. He was there for King's sake.

Weighing her options didn't take very long. According to John, she couldn't drive back to New York in her own car. The thought of making that long trip again had her dismissing the idea of renting a car. Her clothing smelled of smoke and her hair carried the odor as well. Since John said he had her belongings in his car, she decided to go to his apartment to take a shower and change clothes. Then she would figure out what she was going to do.

Adjusting the shoulder strap of her purse, she lifted her chin as she faced him. "All right."

"All right, what?" John asked suspiciously.

"I'm accepting your offer."

He let out the breath he wasn't aware he'd been holding. "As if you had a choice," he murmured.

He kept his hand firmly on her arm as they left the emergency room even though she was no longer resisting him. He would like to know why she was suddenly being so cooperative, but didn't ask. It was enough that she was going with him of her own free will.

It was so much easier than throwing her over his shoulder and carrying her to his car.

THREE

Over the years Silver hadn't given much thought to where John lived. Still, her last guess would have been an old-fashioned three-story brownstone located in an older section of town. Similarly styled brick buildings lined the narrow street. Many windows boasted lace curtains and flower boxes, already filled with the season's first blossoms. The sound of violin music drifted down from an open window across the street.

Silver had the feeling she'd stepped back in time to a softer, gentler era. Manhattan with its crowds, traffic, and fast-paced lifestyles suddenly seemed part of another world.

John parked in front of a building that had the house number carved in cement above the double-door entrance. As usual, his expression gave nothing away.

"This is where you live?" she asked.

"In one part of the first floor. There are three other tenants."

When he opened his car door, she did the same, stepping onto the broad sidewalk in front of the stately old residence.

An elderly woman wearing a blue calico housedress and a white-bibbed apron was seated on the top step. A young girl sitting beside her was happily losing a race to keep up with a dripping ice-cream cone. When the child smiled, she exposed a gap where two front teeth had once been.

The older woman raised a hand in greeting when she saw John. "Hilary and I made some chocolate-chip cookies, John. Would you like some for you and your friend?"

John lifted Silver's suitcase from the trunk of his car and joined Silver on the sidewalk. "How about it?" he asked her. "Would you like some freshly baked chocolate-chip cookies?"

"I can't remember the last time I ate home-made cookies," she said to the woman as she walked up the steps. "Thank you. I would love to try yours."

John's neighbor rose slowly, obviously

painfully, bracing one hand on the wrought-iron banister. The woman's gaze roamed over Silver's soiled clothes, but she refrained from asking Silver what had happened to her. "I'm Freda Christian and this child covered in ice cream is my son's youngest daughter, Hilary."

Silver clasped the woman's fragile hand. "How do you do? My name is Silver."

The little girl looked up with wide blue eyes, staring curiously at her. "Silver is a strange name."

For the first time that day Silver smiled. "That's true."

"That's funny, having a name like a crayon."

"There's a shiny metal called silver too. A long time ago people used to wear silver suits of armor. I think that was more what my parents had in mind when they chose my name. My last name is Knight, spelled with a 'K.' "

"You mean like the men who wear clanky stuff and point long poles at people? Not like when the sun goes down and it gets dark?"

Charmed by the child's logic, Silver said, "That's right, Hilary. Unfortunately, there aren't any knights in shining armor any longer."

Hilary frowned. "Where'd they go?"

"Like the dinosaur, they became extinct."

The little girl made a face. "I wouldn't like them if they stink."

"Good girl," Silver replied, her gaze shifting briefly to John, who was standing on the step below her. "A woman should always stick by her principles, especially when it comes to men."

Ignoring the ice cream dribbling over her hand, Hilary glanced at the suitcase in John's hand, then back at Silver. "Are you having a sleep-over at Uncle John's?"

Silver looked again at John. She could tell by his blank expression that she was on her own.

"It's more like a changeover, Hilary. As you can see, I got dirty today, and I need a bath and clean clothes. Uncle John offered to let me get cleaned up at his place."

The girl's grandmother made an indulgent scolding sound as she examined Hilary from head to toe. "That sounds like a good idea for you, too, young lady. I swear, you have more ice cream on you than in you."

As Silver followed John up the remaining steps she heard Hilary say, "You aren't supposed to swear, Grammy. Daddy says it's not nice."

John caught Silver's amused smile as he held the door open for her. "I'm not really her uncle."

"I figured that out for myself when I remembered my father saying you had no family." Stepping inside the tiled entryway, she saw a hallway leading straight ahead and stairs on the left leading to the next floor. "Which direction is your apartment?"

He gestured toward the hall. "Straight ahead. The first door on your right."

When she reached the appropriate door, she stepped to the side so John could unlock it. After he pushed it open, he waited for her to go inside.

Silver felt oddly reluctant to enter his apartment, although if he asked her why she wouldn't have been able to tell him. As she stepped over the threshold her first impression of the living room was of dark stained wood and forest-green walls. The sofa and two chairs were upholstered in an off-white fabric with wide dark green stripes. Two hunting prints were hanging side by side above an antique rolltop desk. Against another wall were two bookcases crammed full of books, current best-sellers in their color-ful book jackets among older leather-bound classics. Their worn spines indicated the generous supply of literature was not just for appearances.

The absence of a television set implied John either didn't have the interest or the time to watch television, or else he had a set in his bedroom. There wasn't a single knickknack, any personal photographs, or any live plants, as there were in her own apartment, yet the room had a quiet comfort about it that was inviting.

"I like your home, John," she said. "It suits you."

John looked around the room and wondered what she saw. He hadn't spent a lot of time choosing his furnishings. He'd gone to a couple of stores, saw what he liked, pointed, and paid.

When he'd made the decision to bring Silver to his apartment, he hadn't given any thought to how it would affect him to see her there. The very air in the room seemed to change, to vibrate with the current of attraction that sizzled in his veins. His home was never going to be the same now that she'd been there, he realized too late.

"This building and I have a lot in common," he said. "It's weathered a few storms and has stood the test of time without collapsing. We both have also mellowed with age."

Silver could have disputed his last statement, but she let it go. "How long have you lived here?"

He hesitated briefly. "I bought it the day after King offered me the job of CEO."

She noticed the way he'd paused before answering. "The apartment or the whole building?"

"The building."

She tilted her head to one side. "You don't find it easy to talk about yourself, do you?"

He shrugged. "Not that many people ask me personal questions."

Silver had a few questions she would like to have asked him, like how a cop from New York had become acquainted with her artist father and ended up heading King's large corporation. He didn't give her a chance to ask him.

Stepping around her, he carried her case into a room off the hall. She followed, thinking that he certainly knew how to end a conversation. He simply walked away. She stopped in the doorway of the room and watched him place her suitcase on a luggage rack at the foot of a double bed.

After glancing at the white walls, dark green drapes, and green-and-white geometric-pattern bedspread, she wondered if she should reconsider her decision to return to New York immediately. John's guest room was attractive, comfortable, and had the added benefit of being safe, since no one knew where she was. Her apartment had become a nightmare of unexplained incidents, but here with John, she wouldn't have to worry about facing another unpleasant surprise. That thought almost made her change her mind about leaving Raleigh right away. Almost—until she remembered his attitude in his office. His automatic response had been to decline to help her. After the smoke incident, his conscience must have kicked in. He didn't want to have to tell her father that King's one and only daughter had come to him for help and he had turned her away. But John had arrived at the hotel as she was being carried out, she remembered. He couldn't possibly have known she had run into another problem.

So why had he come to the hotel?

John's voice brought her back to the present. "There's only one bathroom, so we'll have to share. It's next door to your room. My bedroom is across the hall."

She walked over to her suitcase and snapped open the latches. "Would you mind if I use your shower now? I'd like to wash off this smoke and put on clean clothes."

"When I packed your clothes, I noticed they all smell like the things you're wearing. They're going to have to be cleaned. There's a robe hanging on the back of the bathroom door you can put on."

"I can't live in a bathrobe until a cleaner gets around to my clothes." Especially not his, she thought.

"Separate what needs to be dry-cleaned and what can be washed. I've got a washer and dryer here, so you can have something to wear in an hour or so." Again, he forestalled any comment from her by walking away. When he reached the doorway, he looked at her over his shoulder. "I'll be in the living room making some phone calls if you need anything."

"Aren't you going back to your office?"

John didn't answer right away. His attention had been drawn to the scrap of nylon and lace she had taken out of the suitcase and was holding in one hand. Lord, the panties were black and almost transparent. His fingers clenched and unclenched at the thought of sliding his hand between the delicate fabric and Silver's warm, soft skin.

When he spoke, his voice was rougher than he intended. "It's too late."

Silver frowned as he stalked out of the guest room. She'd once heard her father tell her brother Michael that John Lomax ate, drank, and slept Knight Enterprises. Knowing that, she couldn't understand why he would say the middle of the afternoon was too late to go back to the office. According to King, John normally worked twelve-hour days, seven days a week.

If John did return to work, she would be able to just leave. She could write a note with instructions about her car, a brief thanks for the use of his apartment, and an apology for the trouble she'd put him through.

Coming to Kentucky had been a lousy idea and an indication of how rattled she'd become. She needed to get out of John's life as soon as possible and get back to her own. With that in mind, she started searching through the suitcase for something to wear that didn't reek of a Girl Scout camp cookout. She came up empty-handed. John hadn't exaggerated. Every single item smelled of smoke. The thought of putting on the grungy clothing and wearing them all the way back to New York didn't appeal to her at all. Her departure from Raleigh would have to be delayed until some of her clothes were washed.

She had to wash her hair three times to get the smoke and grime completely out of the thick strands. With a bar of sandalwood-scented soap, she scrubbed her body and face ruthlessly until she was satisfied that all remnants of the smoke were eradicated.

After using a thick towel to dry off, she slipped on the black silk robe hanging behind the door. She tied the sash around her slim waist and rolled up the sleeves three times as she pondered the discovery that John's robe was made of black silk. She would have thought he was more the terry cloth or corduroy type. Or a towel simply wrapped around his hips rather than any robe at all. That thought conjured up a picture of a clinging damp towel draped low on his body, his chest and long legs bare. She knew he would feel solid and firm under her hands, his skin smooth and warm.

A familiar scent clung to the silk. Growing up with three brothers had given her a familiarity with an assortment of men's colognes, but the brand of this particular scent escaped her.

She raised her arm to roll one of the sleeves

another turn. The scent was stronger as she held up her arm, and she realized the elusive fragrance was on her own skin. A shiver of awareness had her rubbing her hands over her arms as though to wipe away the fragrance. It wasn't a cologne, it was his soap. Her skin now held the same scent as John's because he had rubbed the same bar of soap over his body as she had only minutes ago.

She shook her head as if to clear away the feeling of intimacy her thoughts had created. Great, she thought. As if she needed anything to remind her of John. Now she carried his scent on her skin.

She wrapped a towel turban-style around her head when several forays into drawers and cupboards didn't turn up a hair dryer. She didn't recall seeing her own dryer in her suit-case. The last time she'd seen it was in the hotel room. She'd set it on the dressing table off the bathroom when she had unpacked. John had evidently skipped that area of the smoke-filled room.

She walked down the hall to the living room to ask him if he had a hair dryer. Her thick hair would take several hours to dry naturally and would end up looking like a large chunk of staghorn coral.

Halfway down the hall, she heard his voice and slowed her step when he said her name.

John was agreeing with something the other party on the phone was saying. "I know. Believe me, Nick, if I could find another way, I would." After a short pause, he continued, "No, I'll contact you if I have to go there. I just wanted to give you a head's up so you'll be halfway prepared if I have to call you." A few seconds later he added with a brief laugh, "Hell, I'm in more danger than she is, and it will only get worse the longer she stays here."

Her bare feet made no sound on the carpeted floor, but John somehow sensed she was in the room and turned. His fingers had been rubbing the back of his neck, but when he saw her, he slowly lowered his hand.

He also ended his conversation. "Get back to me if you find something, Nick. You can reach me here or at the office."

He continued to look at her as he hung up the phone, his gaze flowing over her with an intensity that unnerved her.

She lifted a hand to the towel coiled around her wet hair. "I couldn't find a hair dryer. Do you have one?"

He shook his head. "I'll borrow one from my neighbor upstairs." He glanced at the phone, then back at her. "Aren't you going to ask who I was talking to?"

"No," she replied. "I only came out here to ask about a hair dryer. Your phone conversations are your own business."

"I'll tell you anyway. Nick Archer is a friend I knew when I was on the force. He's doing some initial inquiries in your apartment building." He held up his hand when he saw the look of mutiny on her face. "He'll be discreet. No one will know who instigated the investigation. He's only going to ask a few questions."

"What is he going to ask my neighbors? If they know the crazy lady on the tenth floor?"

"He'll try to find out if they've had any similar problems, to see if anyone in the building might be the guilty party."

"Most of the tenants are hardworking people trying to balance their careers and marriages. I don't know any that I've met who would have the time or be the type to play games with me."

"If that's true, they'll be eliminated as suspects. It's a place to start." He paused as his gaze became more intense. "The danger I was referring to on the phone has nothing to do with my getting hurt physically because of your situation."

She didn't understand why he was so intent on explaining the phone conversation. "I didn't think it did."

"I'm more concerned about something else, but I don't think you're ready to hear about that yet. How about if I apologize for not taking you seriously in my office? Will that do?"

"There's nothing like a good old three-alarm fire to make a believer out of someone," she murmured.

He frowned. "You're still ticked off at me, aren't you?"

When she realized he wasn't going to let the subject go, Silver walked over to the sofa and sat down. She curled her bare legs under her, tugging his robe down to cover them, and leaned back.

"I'm more angry with myself than I am with you. I was wrong to expect you to wave a magic wand and make all my problems disappear. I should be the one apologizing to you." She glanced around the living room, then looked back at him, watching as he tugged his tie loose from his collar. "I've disrupted your work and invaded your home. That isn't what I had in mind when I decided to come see you."

"Why did you come to me, Silver? Why not one of your brothers?"

"They wouldn't be able to be objective because they care about me. You don't. Emotion would interfere with their investigating, while you would approach the problem without any personal feelings getting in your way. There's also your previous experience in police work. You would know the right questions to ask, how to advise me on what I should do to find out who is behind all the tricks, and how I could prevent any more surprises."

John frowned again. Hearing her say he didn't care about her irritated the hell out of him. He cared too damn much.

"Why me, Silver?" he persisted. "You could have gone to the police or to friends in New York if you didn't want to notify your brothers. You didn't have to drive all the way to Kentucky. Why me?"

Crossing her arms in front of her, she slipped each hand into the wide sleeves of the robe. "I told you. It was late at night when I left, and I wasn't thinking too clearly. There's nothing like being frightened and alone in the middle of the night to make a person do dumb things."

John asked again. "Why me, Silver?"

She launched off the sofa and paced the floor, her arms still shoved in the sleeves, the robe trailing after her like a bridal train. "Just let it go, John. It doesn't matter."

"Silver," he said, a thread of steel in his voice, "it matters. Why me?"

She stopped pacing and whirled around to face him. "All right," she said tightly. "Next to my father and my brothers, you're the only other person I trust. It doesn't make sense why I would feel that way when you've made it clear I'm not your favorite person, but it's true. Even though I knew you dislike me, I felt nothing would harm me if I was with you. At the time, feeling safe was what I wanted more than anything. To feel secure, to be able to close my eyes and go to sleep without being afraid someone was going to enter the apartment."

"Your theory didn't work out too well, did it? You weren't safe in your hotel room."

"You weren't there either." She rubbed her upper arms. "I hate this. I've always made such an issue out of my independence, and I'm acting like a big baby afraid of my own shadow."

"Which is another reason you chose to come to me for help instead of your brothers.

You don't want them to think there's something in your own life you can't handle."

"You might be right." Her smile held a trace of self-mockery. "Being the only girl and the youngest, I've always felt I had something to prove. If I contacted any of my brothers, they would drop whatever they were doing and fly to help me—and then they would tease me the rest of my life about how I need a man to take care of me. They're worse than King about trying to get me married off."

"Speaking of King. He called after you stormed out of my office. He was worried about you, said you haven't returned his phone calls or answered the faxes he's sent."

Puzzled, she replied, "I haven't received any fax messages from him and he hasn't left any messages on my answering machine."

"It must be your gremlins again. King said he'd done both."

"What did you tell him?"

John smiled at the wary note in her voice. "I told him you were here."

"Did you tell him why?"

Shaking his head, John said, "He never gave me the chance. He came up with his own reason, and I let him run with it. I didn't think you wanted him flying over on the Concorde if he knew you were disturbed by uninvited guests in your apartment."

She took a deep breath and let it out slowly. He saw her expression of relief quickly replaced by apprehension. It had probably occurred to her how her father would interpret her visit to Raleigh.

"What did you tell him?" she asked.

"I didn't get a chance to say much of anything. He came to his own conclusions and said he wouldn't worry about you since you were with me."

"I knew it," she muttered. "King made you feel responsible for me. That's why you came to the hotel in the first place, isn't it? Because King asked you to take care of me. He thinks we're involved with each other. You should have told him how you allotted me ten minutes of your valuable time before sending me back to New York."

A full minute ticked by as they stared at each other. Then John held out his right hand. "Come here."

She frowned at his hand. "Why?"

"You've come this far. All the way from New York. Take another couple of steps."

She walked slowly toward him, stopping a foot away. Lifting her chin, she met his gaze with a steady, defiant expression in her eyes.

His fingers closed around hers, and he slowly, relentlessly drew her against him. He heard her make a small sound of surprise, then felt her slender frame conform to the hard planes of his body.

"This," he said in a low voice, "is what I should have done when you were in my office this morning instead of pushing you away."

He bent his head and touched his mouth to her throat, just below her ear. Her soft intake of breath hastened his own breathing. The feel of her against him was nearly too much.

"You're wrong, Silver," he murmured as he raised his head to look at her. "I don't dislike you. What I don't like is the way you make me feel."

Silver's mouth went dry. Pressing her palms against his chest, she was immediately aware of his heart thudding strongly under her hand.

"You've always acted as though you couldn't stand me," she said.

"Think about it, Silver. Lusting after the daughter of one of the few men I respect isn't something I'm very proud of. I've wanted you since you were a teenager."

Usually quick to comprehend most things,

Silver had to struggle to understand John's calm pronouncement.

"You've been so cold to me all these years," she asked, "because you hated being attracted to me?"

His mouth curved in a self-mocking smile. "Hate's a bit strong." He stroked his hands over her shoulders, his fingers gliding over the silky fabric covering her upper arms. "This morning I automatically shut you out, hoping out of sight would be out of mind. Call it a reflex action. It's what I've been doing since I met you."

"Then why did you want me to stay now? Nothing has changed. I'm still King's daughter."

"When I saw you on that stretcher," he said, his voice husky, "before I knew you were all right, when I thought I'd lost you, I realized how foolish I'd been to waste so much time."

She was still perplexed. "Exactly what are you saying?"

"You need my help, and I need to get you out of my system. With a little luck, we can both accomplish our goals during the next week or so."

Silver stared at him. She'd been propositioned before, but never as though she were a dose of distasteful medicine to be taken for a cure.

"Let me see if I have this right," she said. "You'll help me with my problem if I'll help you with yours. You'll find out who's been terrorizing me if I sleep with you. Do I have it right?"

He shook his head. "Not quite. I'll help you whether you sleep with me or not. When we make love, it will be because it's what you want too. I don't consider sex as a competition or as a way to pay off a debt."

"But I'm not attracted to you." She spoke with as much force as she could muster.

He kept her gaze locked to his by silently challenging her, knowing she would respond to a dare. Slowly, with deliberate pressure, he let his fingers flow over the curve of a breast, smiling faintly when he heard her sharp intake of breath. Caressing the soft feminine mound, he struggled with his swiftly rising need as he felt the tip of her breast harden against his palm. His hand absorbed the shiver of reaction in her slim body when he brushed his thumb over it.

"I'm not alone in this, Silver," he said softly. "We've always struck sparks off each other. We've tried to extinguish them by snapping at each other, but that hasn't worked. We need to allow the attraction to burn out. It's time to put an end to this."

His touch clouded Silver's mind and a-roused her senses. She tried to take a step back, but all that accomplished was to tighten his hold on her. Feeling oddly breathless, as though she'd been running a long race, she closed her eyes. When she opened them, she met his gaze again and became mesmerized by the stark need in his dark eyes.

"I won't sleep with you just so you'll help me," she said.

"Good. I don't want a martyr in my bed. I'll find out what's going on with all the scare tactics. Our becoming lovers is separate."

Silver had never felt so alive, so frightened, so exhilarated, so apprehensive in her entire life. Her mind had ceased to function, leaving only explosive sensations. When he lowered his head, she strained to meet him, her lips parting in anticipation. She'd wondered for too long how he would taste.

He didn't accept her invitation. Instead, she felt his hot, moist mouth on the sensitive area between her neck and her shoulder. Unable to prevent a sound of pleasure from escaping, she let her head fall back. As badly as she wanted his mouth on hers, she didn't want him to stop what he was doing. His hands clenched and released, stroked and caressed. His lips and tongue feasted on her skin. But not on her mouth.

The sheer intensity of his need vibrated through her, making her moan. She'd never been touched so beautifully, so blatantly sensually. She felt as though her skin was on fire, and she trembled with the force of her response. She suddenly had a desperate urge to discover the feel of his skin against her mouth. Shivering in reaction, she pressed her parted lips against his strong throat. He tasted like sin and salvation, like hope and despair, like raw emotion and gentle comfort. Like need, passion, and desire.

An odd satisfaction swept through her when he lifted his head and looked at her with a barely tamped-down desire heating the depths of his eyes.

"Are you involved with anyone in New York?" he asked, his voice rough with arousal.

She could manage only to shake her head. Speech would have to wait until she found some air in her lungs. Desire was writhing through her body, weakening her with its power, yet strengthening her in a way she couldn't explain to herself, much less to John.

"You're involved with me for however long it takes," he ordered. "Do you have a problem with that?"

"Yes," she answered, smiling weakly. "About a hundred doubts and a million questions, but at the moment I can't think of one."

He ran his thumb across her moist mouth. "I want the lights on when we make love the first time."

Her lips parted slightly, and her breath lodged in her throat.

Before she could speak, he released her. "I'll go ask Ginger upstairs if you can borrow her hair dryer. Maybe climbing all those steps will work the same as a cold shower."

After he left, Silver remained in the middle of the living room. She wrapped her arms around her waist to hold in the warmth his body had imprinted on hers.

She closed her eyes against the rush of sensations flowing through her bloodstream as she relived the explosion of emotions he'd ignited. He'd said *when*, not *if* they made love, and she had done nothing to make him think otherwise.

She'd come to Kentucky to look for the

answer to a problem. It looked like she had acquired another one, a very large problem, and its name was John Lomax. His admission about wanting her had stunned her, but had also made her admit the reason for her own antagonism was the same as his. The attraction had always been there, an invisible current flowing between them. She could see that now.

She shivered uncontrollably as she recalled the feeling of his hot mouth on her skin. John had given her a glimpse of what lay ahead for them—if she agreed to an affair.

He hadn't even kissed her properly, and she was a jumble of jagged nerve endings and sensual cravings.

She smiled. John had found a way to take her mind off her other problem. When he touched her, she thought only of him.

FOUR

John not only brought his neighbor's hair dryer back with him, he brought the neighbor. It took Silver just a few seconds to see that he hadn't had a choice. The small woman swept into the apartment like a mini-tornado, talking and walking at a fast clip.

Silver didn't even have time to be self-conscious about wearing John's robe in the middle of the afternoon. If John's neighbor noticed, she didn't appear to think anything of it. Silver hated the thought that finding a woman wearing John's robe was a regular occurrence.

Silver thought the woman's cinnamon-colored hair could have been created by an electrical charge, its tightly coiled curls sticking out from her head like a fiery bush. Silver caught a glimpse of white denim overalls and a yellow T-shirt draped on a petite frame just before her hand was grabbed and shaken like a pump handle.

"I am so pleased to meet you finally, Silver. Do you mind if I call you by your first name? I feel I've known you a long time, so it doesn't seem right to be so formal. I'm Ginger Wallis, by the way." She pointed up at the ceiling with her free hand. "I live upstairs, but I'm fairly quiet, so I shouldn't bother you. I usually go barefoot, so you won't even hear me clumping around."

Silver regained possession of her hand about the time she recovered from the burst of energy that had exploded into the room. "The man who lives in the apartment above mine in New York plays a cello in an orchestra and practices every chance he gets. I'm sure you won't bother me at all the short time I'm here."

Ginger glanced at John. "But I thought—"

"I told Ginger about the fire in your hotel room." John handed a hair dryer to Silver. "She's going to the dry cleaners this afternoon and has offered to take your smoke-damaged clothes with her."

Silver didn't want to have to wait a day

or two for her clothes to get cleaned. "That's kind of you, Ginger, but I'll take care of it. Most of my clothes are washable, and the rest I can get cleaned when I get back to New York."

"Who knows when that will be?" Ginger said as she started walking down the hall. "We'll get your clothes sorted out now and that will be one less thing you have to do. You can do the washable items here and I'll take the rest to Chino's cleaners down the street. Which room is your stuff in, the spare room or John's room?"

John answered for Silver. "The spare room."

Ginger stopped at the doorway of the spare room and looked back at John with one brow raised and a question in her gaze.

Knowing Ginger was perfectly capable of putting her curiosity into a blunt inquisition, John leaned down to speak softly into Silver's ear. "It will be easier to let her have her way than make a big deal out of it. I can always send your things on to you later."

When Ginger suddenly smiled, Silver realized how it had looked with John's head bent down to hers as though they were having an intimate conversation. Oddly enough, she felt as though they had. His warm breath had caressed the sensitive skin just below her ear, and she could feel the heat of his body.

Irritated by her instant response to his nearness, she walked toward the spare room as Ginger slipped inside it. How had things gotten so turned around in such a short time? All she'd planned to do was to change her clothes in John's apartment before heading back to New York. Now a strange woman was taking her clothes away.

This was not going the way she'd thought it would.

She found Ginger staring down at the open suitcase on the bed. "Whew. I can smell the smoke," the other woman said, grimacing with distaste. "That must have been some fire."

"Actually it was only smoke. I don't think there was a fire."

"One thing I learned as a teenager was where there's smoke, there's always fire." Ginger picked up a piece of delicate silk. "I hope the odor comes out of these things. Maybe I should just take all of it to the dry cleaners. They have special stuff that can clean anything from skunk spray to baby do-do."

"I'm sure with a little soap and water, they'll be like new." At least Silver hoped so.

She didn't even have anything to wear to go shopping for other clothes.

She took the suit she'd worn to John's office and another jacket out of the suitcase. Using the theory that it was easier to go with the tide than try to swim against it, she handed the clothing to Ginger.

"Ginger, could I ask you a question?"

"Sure. Go ahead." Shifting Silver's clothing so it was farther away from her sensitive nose, she waited for Silver's question.

"How do you know about me? You said you'd heard so much about me, you felt you knew me. I'm curious how that happened."

"I think the first time," Ginger said without hesitation, "was one night when Gary and I dropped in to see if John had a sleeping bag we could borrow for the weekend. It was on a shelf in his bedroom closet. While he got it, I looked around his bedroom and saw your picture on the bedside table."

"John has a picture of me?"

The other woman nodded. "Naturally, having a snoopy nature, I asked who the woman in the picture was."

Still reeling from learning John had a picture of her in his bedroom, Silver managed to ask, "What did he say?"

Tilting her head to one side, Ginger replied, "He said you were every man's fantasy."

Silver frowned in puzzlement. "What did he mean by that?"

Ginger shrugged her slender shoulders. "Beats me, unless he actually meant you were his fantasy. That's how I took it anyway. Your name also came up several times while we were thinking up the 'Chivalry Is Dead' game." Ginger's smile was kind, the expression in her eyes knowing. "I think he liked talking about you."

More to herself than to Ginger, Silver murmured, "All this time I thought he couldn't stand me."

Aside from raising a brow in silent disagreement, Ginger let Silver's comment go and walked to the bedroom door. "I doubt if John has the type of washing powder you need for those delicate underthings, so I'll bring some down with me before I go to the dry cleaners." By this time her quick pace had taken her into the living room, with Silver following at a slower pace. She asked John, "Do you still want me and Gary to come over tonight or do you want to cancel the session now that you have a houseguest?"

John had forgotten about the previous arrangements he'd made for the evening. Having company would definitely be the smarter way to spend the evening than being alone with Silver. It would also be a refined form of torture. But he had some ground to make up that he'd lost by refusing to help Silver that morning.

Nothing like seeing a woman being carried on a stretcher to make a man realize his stupid pride wasn't worth a pinch of salt when it came to preserving his life. And that's what Silver had become. The best part of his life. He had made excuses to himself in the past that his feelings for her were purely simple lust. Wanting to sink his body into hers was an important part of his deep involvement with her. But not all there was.

His desire to stay uninvolved didn't matter next to his desire for her. She was under his skin and embedded in his heart.

Ginger jarred him back to the present. "Silver would be a perfect guinea pig," she said. "We need to try the game on someone who doesn't know the rules and has to start from scratch. It'll be the first time someone who isn't familiar with the game plays it. I remember you telling me that Silver was the most intelligent woman you know. She'd be perfect."

Silver glanced at John, her eyes searching his for clarification. She started to ask him why he had mentioned her to his friends when she saw his faint smile, the amusement glittering in his eyes. She was so surprised to see both minor miracles, she waited too long to ask her question, and he spoke first.

"You're right," he said to Ginger, though his gaze was on Silver. "She is perfect." He turned to Ginger. "You and Gary come over around seven as usual. Is it my turn or yours to order the pizza?"

"Yours." Ginger grinned at Silver on her way to the door. "See you later."

The air in the room seemed to settle back to normal after Ginger left. Normal for them, however, Silver thought, meant a sizzling current surrounding them.

"Is she always like that?" she asked John, a hint of awe in her voice.

"If you mean is Ginger usually like a windup toy whose spring is wound too tight, then yes, she's always like that. Gary is just the opposite. Says maybe four words an hour." He tilted his head to one side and studied her. "As much as I'm enjoying the sight of you wearing my robe,

I'd rather you wore something else when Gary arrives with Ginger. He's crazy about Ginger, but he's still a man. I'll show you where the washer and dryer are so you can wash something to wear."

She held up the hair dryer. "I'd like to dry my hair first."

"All right. I have a few more phone calls I can take care of while you're doing that."

When she returned to the living room twenty minutes later, the first thing Silver noticed was that John had changed from his suit to casual clothes. She'd still been hoping he'd go back to the office and she could leave, but it wasn't likely he would walk into Knight Enterprises wearing jeans and a wine-colored polo shirt.

The moment she stepped into the room, he finished his conversation and hung up the phone. He glanced at the bundle of clothing in her arms and jerked his head in the direction of a doorway that led to a formal dining room, then a compact kitchen. Following him, she discovered the utility room was beyond the kitchen.

Silver's contribution to the task of washing her clothes was to sort them. When she'd hurriedly packed in New York, she had included a number of casual outfits—slacks, a pair of jeans, sweaters, shirts, enough clothes to get her through a week. Seeing the amount of clothing she'd brought made her wonder if she'd subconsciously thought of staying longer in Raleigh than a day or two.

She didn't even blink when John picked up a handful of panties and bras, putting them in a separate pile to be washed later with Ginger's soap. Exhaustion was dragging at her, making the simplest movements difficult. Blow-drying her hair had sapped what little strength she had in reserve. She caught herself swaying and leaned against the frame of the door.

John held up a piece of dark jade silk with thin straps. "What's this thing?"

She blinked to focus on the item he was holding. "It's called a teddy. I think its original intention was to drive men crazy, but I usually wear it under jeans and a sweater because it's comfortable."

"It's the same color as the sheets on my bed," John muttered. As he let it fall through his fingers onto the pile of dainty underwear, he promised himself he'd someday see the provocative bit of lingerie on Silver's slender body. And then take it off her.

Closing the lid of the washing machine, he

turned to look at her. She was leaning heavily against the door frame, her eyes blinking slowly like a drunken owl's. He swiftly crossed to her in two strides and swept her up into his arms.

She made a startled sound. "What are you doing?"

"You've had a busy day, little girl. It's time for you to take a nap before Gary and Ginger come over tonight."

"Don't call me that," she complained as she let her head fall against his shoulder.

"Call you what?"

"Little girl," she mumbled. "My brothers always used to call me that. They still do sometimes."

John turned sideways to carry her through the bedroom doorway. "The last thing I want you to do is put me in the same category as your brothers. The term was more for my benefit than yours anyway."

"I'm causing you a lot of trouble, aren't I, John?" she said after he'd laid her on the bed.

"Like no one else ever could," he agreed, smiling down at her. "But I can handle it."

"I can still go to a hotel."

The lower part of the robe had fallen open,

exposing a great deal of her left thigh. He sat down on the edge of the bed and adjusted the robe so it covered her all the way down to her feet.

"No, you can't," he said. "You've been recruited, remember. You heard Ginger. She wants you here to be a guinea pig tonight."

"She also said she felt she knew me from things you've said about me."

"Your name might have come up a time or two."

"Why?"

"You'll understand later."

"What exactly will I have to do tonight?"

He saw the way she was struggling to keep her eyes open and heard the drowsy tone of her voice. Unable to resist touching her, he let his fingers brush back the hair around her face. Her eyes closed, and he continued stroking her hair.

"Don't worry," he said. "It's nothing dangerous or embarrassing. Ginger and her boyfriend have invented a board game and are hoping to develop it into something that will sell to a manufacturer. She wants you to try it out."

Silver opened her eyes and met his gaze. "We're going to play games?"

"Only the one Ginger and Gary have invented. You and I aren't playing games."

"What are we doing?" she asked seriously.

"I can't speak for you, but I plan on finding out why I haven't been able to get you out of my mind for fourteen years."

She sucked in her breath, obviously astonished by his words.

"I know," he said. "It came as quite a surprise to me too. You've been a tantalizing vision in my mind for too long, Silver. Are you going to run away from me or stay, knowing what I want from you?"

For a few seconds she continued to look at him, the shock gradually leaving her eyes. Then she closed them. "I like the works on my pizza, except for anchovies."

Relief left him feeling light-headed for a moment.

"I'll keep that in mind." He continued running his fingers over her hair. "Go to sleep, Silver. You need to rest."

She took a deep breath and let it out slowly. When he lightly touched her cheek, she turned her head and brushed his palm with her lips as she said his name.

"I'm still here," he said. Whether her lips

caressing his palm was an accident or not, his heart rate soared.

"That's what I want to know," she murmured. "Will you be going to the office while I'm taking a nap?"

"I won't leave," he said quietly. "You're safe."

"I knew I would be."

He continued to stroke her hair because it seemed to soothe her. It had the opposite effect on him, but he kept it up until he was sure she was completely asleep. When he eased off the mattress to stand up, he watched her carefully for any sign of disturbing her, but her eyes remained closed, her breathing slow and even.

The shadows under her eyes were more obvious now that she'd washed off her makeup, making him wonder just how long she'd been fighting her demons by herself. Something dark and dangerous coiled deep inside him at the image of her lying awake and frightened each night in her apartment.

He thought of the last thing she'd murmured before falling asleep. He hadn't given her a reason to trust him, yet she felt safe with him. She had somehow sensed he would keep anything from harming her.

And he would, he promised her silently as he stood over her.

Turning away, John walked out of the room. He had another phone call to make, this one to Knight's Keep in England. It was going to be interesting to see how King took the news that Silver was now living with him.

John let Silver sleep as long as he dared. Gary and Ginger marched to a different drummer in every aspect of their lives except for one: they were always on time. By six-thirty, John had finished washing, drying, and folding all of Silver's clothes, even her delicate bits of silk and lace after Ginger had dropped off the special soap.

Laundry was a chore he usually put off until he was down to his last pair of clean socks. Washing Silver's clothes had been an oddly intimate undertaking he had enjoyed. He'd learned something about her in the process. For a woman who preferred bright colors on the outside, she chose soft sensual hues for the sexy lingerie she wore next to her skin.

It made him wonder about the real Silver Knight she kept hidden behind the bold independent front she presented to the world.

As he perused her selection of clothes, he knew she wouldn't like to spend the entire evening wearing his bathrobe any more than he wanted another man to see her in it. She was a curious mixture of innocence and sophistication, he was discovering. She would be able to carry off wearing a bathrobe several sizes too big in front of strangers if she had to, but behind her social smile, she would be cringing.

John frowned. Where had that analysis come from? he wondered. Since when was he an expert on Silver Knight? He didn't know the answer to that question, but he did know he was right about Silver's feelings about parading around in his robe in front of Gary and Ginger.

He could only guess how long it would take her to get ready. Thirty minutes was all she was going to get.

Entering the room he now considered hers, he said softly, "Silver?"

His intent was not to startle her awake. He accomplished his goal. She wasn't alarmed one bit. In fact, she didn't blink an eye or move an inch.

He made as much noise as possible opening and closing dresser drawers as he put the laundered clothes away, then said her name again, this time a little louder.

No response.

He walked over to the bed and stared down at her. Her eyes were still closed, her long lashes resting gently on the soft skin he longed to touch. Sometime during her nap, she had rolled onto her left side and was facing him. The front of the robe gaped open enough for him to see the soft swell of her naked breast. He also had a tantalizing view of a bare leg from the top of a rounded thigh to a small foot.

"Wake up, Silver," he said, aware of the pleading note in his voice. "Don't make me touch you, sweetheart. I used up my share of good intentions earlier."

"What good intentions?"

He nearly jumped out of his skin when she spoke. Her eyes were still closed, her voice husky with sleep. "When I carried you in here, I didn't stay."

She opened her eyes. "Was that why you kissed me everywhere but on my mouth? Good intentions?"

"I left a lot more out than your lips. There were a lot of other good parts I left untouched."

"Do you put yourself through these tests of restraint for all your houseguests?"

"No one has ever stayed here before."

"In this bed or in your bed?"

"Neither. You're the first." And only, he added silently.

He turned back to the dresser and shuffled through the clothes he'd just put in the drawer. Returning with a handful of clothing, he dropped them on the bed. "Gary and Ginger are going to be here in about twenty-five minutes. It certainly won't bother Gary if you spend the evening wearing my robe, but it will bother the hell out of me, so get dressed."

Silver didn't have to attempt to hide her smile. John whirled around and stalked out of the room. His rude manner didn't bother her. Her brothers had given her plenty of experience with ruffled male egos. She had learned it was better to leave a man's bruised pride to heal on its own than to try to smooth it over.

She looked down at the clothing he'd dumped onto the bed. A silver pair of stirrup pants and a loose-fitting red cotton sweater that was decorated with multicolored leaves scattered all over the front. He had neglected to give her the usual assortment of underclothing. She shivered at the thought that he might have excluded panties and bra on purpose. He had made no secret of the fact that he wanted her. She could wish he hadn't been so blunt and hadn't pronounced his intentions so soon, but that wasn't his style. He wasn't the type to beat around the bush. He was more likely to attack it and trample it under his feet.

Gathering the robe around her, she retied the belt and went to the dresser. Her clothes were folded and tucked into the drawers in an orderly fashion. She no longer had the excuse of not having anything to wear for her return trip to New York. It wasn't too late to rent a car or to find out when the next flight was. She could make her apologies to Ginger and Gary, thank John for everything he'd done to help her, then simply leave.

That's what she should do, which was why it was odd that she picked up a white silk bra and matching panties instead of packing everything back into her suitcase. Glancing around, she realized her suitcase wasn't even in the room. Evidently John had taken it somewhere to air it out. It didn't matter. She wasn't going to need it.

As she dressed she rationalized her change of mind about leaving. She could use a complete night's rest, she told herself, to make up for the many evenings when the slightest sound had kept her awake and unable to go back to sleep. Staying another night would also allow her time to think about the offer John had made to help her. And to consider what he'd said about exploring the attraction between them.

If she left now, she might never know the full extent of the magic he created within her. Yet if she stayed, she could possibly be opening herself up for the most devastating pain she'd ever experienced. She'd become obsessed with John Lomax the first moment she'd seen him, she admitted. He'd often appeared in her adolescent dreams, and had remained in her thoughts when she had outgrown the childish infatuation for an older man. She realized now that she had compared every man she'd ever dated with the image she had of John Lomax, and no man had ever been able to compete fairly with that.

She'd been astonished to learn she had been in his thoughts all this time as well. And thrilled that he hadn't been able to forget her either. She wondered if she should take the chance and explore the mysterious attraction that arced between them like an electrical charge.

And possibly start a relationship that could change her life forever.

If she didn't stay, she would never know whether her feelings for John were real or a figment of her imagination.

Having made the decision, Silver felt as though a heavy weight had been lifted off her shoulders. She walked out of the bedroom to begin what could be the most important phase of her life.

Four hours later, Silver stood beside John as Ginger and Gary got ready to leave John's apartment. Gary, a tall, exceptionally thin man who reminded Silver of a young Abraham Lincoln, was holding the box containing the game "Chivalry Is Dead," which they had been playing most of the evening.

Silver was still grinning as John closed the door after they'd departed. She put her hand to her side, which ached from laughing.

John glanced down at her. He was pleased to see the haunted shadows in her eyes had been replaced by amusement. "If everyone reacts the way you did to the game, they have a best-seller on their hands."

"If any of the manufacturers turn them

down, I think Knight Enterprises should undertake the financing. It is the most outrageous concept of a board game I've ever seen. I could have continued playing all night."

"I got that impression after you coaxed us into playing it a third time." He started walking toward the kitchen. "Do you have room for some ice cream after four pieces of pizza?"

"That sounds good." Following him, she said with mock indignation, "It's not polite to notice the amount of food someone eats."

"When you grabbed the last piece as I was reaching for it and nearly took off two of my fingers, I was bound to notice how many slices of pizza you were chugging down." He opened the freezer. "What kind of ice cream do you like?"

"What do you have?" She approached the freezer and peered inside. "Good Lord, John! There must be ten different containers of ice cream in here."

He shrugged. "I like ice cream. How about a banana split?"

"On top of four slices of pizza?"

"I only had three. You snitched the last piece, remember? Anyway, there's always room for ice cream."

Temptation came in many forms, she reflected. This one was safe enough to give in to. "All right. I'll have a banana split. What can I do to help?"

He started taking cardboard pint containers out of the freezer, setting them on the small rectangular table in the middle of the kitchen. "There are an assortment of toppings on the bottom shelf in the cupboard near the wall. You can put them on the table while I get the other stuff we'll need. Spoons are in the drawer next to the sink."

A few minutes later Silver sat down opposite John at the table. Along with all the ice cream, there were six jars of different syrups and a pressurized can of whipped cream. Silver peeled two bananas, and John sliced them lengthwise and placed them in two long oval dishes. After a few minutes of deliberation, she chose three different kinds of ice cream, and he scooped out a generous portion of each and placed them on top of her banana. While she poured chocolate and strawberry syrup over vanilla, mint chocolate chip, and rum-raisin ice cream, he heaped ice cream into his own dish.

He added a dollop of whipped cream to the top of hers, then his own. Remembering one more necessary ingredient, he fetched a small jar from the refrigerator. Plopping a maraschino cherry on top of her whipped cream, he declared her banana split ready to eat.

"Gary ate the last of the peanuts, so we'll have to do without," he added as he handed her a spoon.

For a few seconds Silver just looked at the overflowing dish in front of her. "If I manage to eat all this, I won't be able to walk."

"No problem." His eyes met hers, humor and a barely banked heat glowing in their depths. "If I can't lift you, I'll drag you off to bed."

"My hero," she drawled as she dipped her spoon into the middle scoop of vanilla ice cream. "Do you really have a picture of me beside your bed?"

He frowned. "Ginger has a big mouth."

"Does that mean she was telling the truth?"

"You're welcome to take a look for yourself."

"I think you just answered my question. I'll take a chance and ask another. Why?"

"I like your face."

"That's no answer."

"It's the only one you're going to get."

Exasperated, she said crossly, "I bet you're

the one who came up with the section on the game board that had to do with rescuing the dragon from the nagging fair maiden."

"I also contributed the part where the blue knight and the red knight go play golf instead of fighting over the wench."

Silver licked whipped cream off her spoon. "Ginger said you were the one who suggested they turn the tables on the usual knight-in-shining-armor theme when they first got the idea of creating a board game. I didn't realize you were so cynical about the state of affairs between men and women."

"I would call it being realistic, not cynical. Women have always had it easier than men when it comes to the courtship ritual. I thought it would be fun to turn the tables and give the guys a break for a change."

"Women have it easier than men? You've got to be kidding. If a woman is attracted to a man, it isn't easy waiting and hoping he'll eventually get around to asking her out. This might be the nineties, but men still have the predominant role in any relationship."

"A man takes a big chance when he asks a woman to go out with him," he stated as he stuck his spoon into the rich chocolate at one end of his dish. "She could refuse him, which is hard on the ego. If she agrees, then he has to go through the ritual of wining and dining her as he debates with himself whether to push for an invitation to come in for coffee and whatever else she might offer at the end of the evening."

"Are you saying that a man doesn't enjoy the wining-and-dining part? That his main reason for taking a woman out is to end up in her bed?"

"Sex isn't the only thing a man wants from a woman, but it's an important part of any relationship," he said, concentrating on his ice cream as though they were talking about the weather.

"That's why it isn't easier for a woman than it is for a man when they date. A woman has considerably more at stake than a man when she agrees to spend time with him."

He looked up. "How do you figure that?"

"Most women won't sleep with a man just because he bought her dinner or took her to a movie. Women can buy their own meal and pay for the movie themselves. But by refusing to have sex, she takes the risk of never seeing the guy again, which can hurt if she really cares about him. Yet if that's all he wants her for, she would be better off without him and has to tell him that, knowing he might reject her."

"What if the woman wants the man as much as he wants her?" he asked casually. "Does she shake his hand at the door on general principle, or invite him in?"

Silver couldn't tell if John was simply stringing her along or genuinely wanted to know her opinion. "We're getting off the subject. We were discussing how dating isn't any easier for a woman than it is for a man."

"There's an easy solution to the question of how difficult it is for a man to ask a woman out on a date."

"There is?" she asked, caution in her voice. "How?"

"You could reverse the roles by asking me for a date."

Silver stared at him, the ice cream on her spoon forgotten. "You want me to ask you to go out with me?"

"It's one way of showing you how difficult it is to approach someone knowing there's a fifty-fifty chance they could refuse your invitation."

"That wouldn't be a fair test. You'd refuse me just to show me how it feels to be turned down."

A hint of a smile softened the firm shape of his mouth. "Try me."

She leaned back in her chair. "All right." She sighed heavily. "Would you like to have dinner with me tomorrow night?"

He didn't give her an answer immediately. Her nonchalant attitude gave way to doubt, then wariness. He really was going to refuse her.

Finally, he said, "I can arrange to be home around six o'clock. If you make dinner reservations for seven, we'll have time for a drink first."

Although he sounded completely serious, she detected a note of amusement in his voice. He was enjoying the reversal of roles, so she decided to take hers a step further.

"It would be more appropriate if I pick you up at your office at six-thirty."

His eyes gleamed with wry humor. "All right. It's a date."

Silver stuck her spoon into her ice cream, her mind spinning ideas for the following evening. She would show him a night on the town he wouldn't forget for a while.

FIVE

John paced in front of his desk. At the end of each lap, he glanced at his watch and swore under his breath. It was only six thirty-two, but he couldn't get the thought out of his head that Silver was going to stand him up. He had been deadly serious when he had agreed to have dinner with her, but maybe she thought he'd been joking.

Now he wished he'd gone into her room that morning to confirm their plans for the evening instead of letting her sleep. It hadn't been entirely for her sake that he'd passed her door without opening it. Sharing a midnight snack was fairly impersonal compared with walking into her room while she was in bed. Resisting her when she was sitting across the table from him, gleefully digging into her ice cream, had been difficult enough. It would have been impossible if he had seen her tempting body relaxed in sleep, her hair spread out over the pillow.

He watched the second hand mark off another minute. Dammit, where was she? If she couldn't make it, the least she could have done was call and let him know. As he continued to pace he realized his thoughts were probably the same as any woman's who was waiting for a man. His clever little plan had backfired on him, and he was at a loss as to how to proceed if she failed to show.

He could go home and pretend nothing was wrong. She might expect him to be angry at being stood up, but he could let her think he'd only been joking about the date in the first place.

If she was there. She could have gone back to New York easily enough. He gritted his teeth at the thought of returning to his apartment and finding her gone.

If she had left, he was going after her.

The invisible line that had been stretched between them over the years had been crossed, and there was no going back to their neutral corners.

The intercom on his desk buzzed, and he stabbed the button. "What is it, Olive?"

"Miss Knight is here, Mr. Lomax," his secretary announced, her voice shaky as though she was trying not to laugh.

"Send her in," he ordered, relief flooding over him.

He leaned against the front of his desk and kept his gaze locked on the door. He could have sat down in his chair, pretending to be busy and unaware of the time, but he dismissed that thought as soon as it appeared. He wasn't going to play games with Silver just to salvage his pride. He had been waiting for her, plain and simple.

The door opened, and she walked in. His heart rate quickened and his breathing nearly halted when he saw her. She was wearing a purple dress made from a velvet-type material with a halter top that fit like a soft glove from her breasts to her waist. The full skirt flowed over her hips and ended midcalf, revealing purple heels on her small feet. She'd evidently gone shopping that day. He would have remembered packing a dress like that along with her other clothing from the hotel room.

A matching shawl run through with silver

threads was draped over one arm, and in that arm, she cradled a bouquet of brilliantly colored tiger-lilies. In her other hand, she held a box of candy covered in gold foil.

Her eyes were no longer clouded with fatigue. He felt a great deal of satisfaction in knowing she'd been able to sleep the whole night without fear. At least he'd been able to provide her with the safe haven she'd needed so desperately.

This was the way she should be, he reflected; vibrant, her unusual blue-green eyes gleaming with humor instead of shadowed by tension.

His mouth went dry as she walked toward him, her slender hips swaying with a subtle grace with every step she took.

Playing her role to the hilt, Silver let her gaze roam over his gray suit, immaculate white shirt, and dark teal tie. "You look very nice this evening, John. Are you ready to go?"

"Are those for me?" he asked, glancing at the flowers and candy.

Stopping in front of him, she offered the five-pound box of candy that had cost her a small fortune.

He tugged off the ribbon and lifted the lid, then whistled softly at the array of expensive chocolates nestled in their fluted paper cups. He picked up a piece and held it out to her.

"I'll share," he offered, his gaze on her mouth.

She started to reach for the chocolate, but he ignored her hand and extended the piece toward her mouth. When she parted her lips, he held it and she bit into the rich chocolate and caramel. Then he popped the other half into his mouth, his gaze locked with hers. The expression in his eyes made the gesture strangely intimate, and she felt her insides melting as quickly as the chocolate in her mouth.

Setting the box on the desk, he drew her closer by settling his hand at her waist. When she was standing between his thighs, he glanced down at the exotic orange blooms that were brushing against the front of his shirt.

"No one has ever given me flowers before," he said softly. "They're beautiful. Thank you."

Silver was moved by the note of awe in his voice. "I was going to buy roses until I saw these. They seemed more fitting to the occasion than the normal type of flowers."

"I don't know much about flowers. What kind are these?"

"*Lilium tigrinum.*"

"Thanks a lot," he drawled.

She smiled. "Tiger lilies." She glanced around his office. "I should have brought a vase for them. They should be in water."

Without allowing her to move away from him, he reached back with his free hand and pressed the intercom. "Olive, do you have a large vase for flowers?"

"Yes, sir. Would you like me to bring it in or wait until you're ready to leave?"

"Bring it in now."

Returning his attention to Silver, he murmured, "I haven't thanked you properly for the chocolate or the flowers or even said hello."

He bent his head and touched her lips with his. "Hello, Silver."

"Hello, John."

The door opened behind her, and she started to step back. John refused to let her go, however. Glancing past her, he said, "Set the vase on the desk, Olive. Then you can leave for the day. I won't be needing you for anything else."

The secretary didn't bother hiding her amusement. "Are you sure, Mr. Lomax? It looks like you have your hands full at the moment."

"I'm sure, Olive. I prefer handling this particular project personally."

"I got that impression." Chuckling, Olive said, "Well, good night, then. It was a pleasure seeing you again, Miss Knight. Please give my best wishes to your father."

"Thank you, Mrs. Branch. I will. Good night."

Once the door was closed behind his secretary, John took the flowers from Silver and stuffed them in the vase, which Olive had partially filled with water. Even without careful arranging, the blooms fell into an attractive cluster. He set the vase on one corner of the desk where he would be able to see them clearly while he was working.

"I could get used to this," he said.

"To women bringing you candy and flowers and taking you out to dinner?"

He shook his head. "To you bringing me flowers. The candy is optional." He placed his other hand at her waist. "So where are we going, Miss Knight? I hope you've chosen a restaurant that has good food. I didn't have any lunch."

"It will be a surprise for both of us. Ginger recommended the place. Are you familiar with a restaurant called Giovanni's?"

"Never heard of it. But if Ginger recommended it, the food will be excellent. That girl loves to eat."

Silver clasped his wrists with the intention of removing his hands, but he turned them over and threaded his fingers through hers.

One of them had to remember where they were. "We're going to be late for our reservation if we don't leave soon, John."

"In a minute," he murmured. "I told you I was starving. I think I need an appetizer to tide me over."

He bent his head and kissed her, his hunger for more than food obvious in the way he savored her mouth. Silver felt the tension in him as he held their clasped hands against her hips instead of drawing her into his arms. It was as though he needed the distance between their bodies, only their hands and mouths touching, in order to keep control of the situation.

She felt like she was standing in quicksand when he slanted his mouth over hers, deepening the kiss by parting her lips and delving inside. Her fingers tightened on his hands as pleasure pulled her under a shimmering surface into a sensual world she'd never visited before.

All too soon John lifted his head and looked down at her. His gaze was direct, his lips moist. "I told you I was starving."

"But an appetizer isn't going to satisfy you, is it?"

"No. Not much longer." He paused for a few seconds. "Unless I'm reading more into your response than you meant, I'm not the only one who wants more."

"John," she began, wondering how she could make him understand. "I'm not going to lie and say I'm not attracted to you."

"But?"

"But getting involved with you would only complicate things even more than they are already. I would be taking advantage of you by using you for the security I need right now. That wouldn't be fair to you."

"Shutting me out is more unfair than letting me in, Silver. The problems you're having in New York are a separate issue, which we'll take care of in the next couple of days. Whatever this is between us won't go away just because you want it to."

She smiled wanly. "I was afraid of that."

Releasing one of her hands, he trailed a finger down the side of her face. "You came to me because you trusted me to help you. Now

I'm asking you to trust me with yourself. I will do my damnedest not to hurt you in any way when we become lovers."

Silver was aware he'd once again said when, not if they became intimate. She also noticed he hadn't made any promises other than not to hurt her. He wanted an affair, not a long-term commitment. What she had to decide was whether that would be enough for her.

"I've known you for fourteen years, yet I really don't know you at all," she mused aloud. "Going to bed with a stranger is something I thought I would never do."

He drew her toward the door of his office. "You know more about me than most people do. I'll show you my blood-donor card to prove I'm healthy, if it will make you feel better. And when you walk me to my door tonight, I'll invite you in for coffee and we'll neck on the sofa for a while." He gently pushed her through the doorway. "Then you can tell me which bed you're going to sleep in."

"You'll leave the decision up to me?"

He punched the button for the elevator. "King once mentioned that growing up with three older brothers has made you dislike anyone telling you what to do. Sometimes you carry the independent thing a little too far, but in this case, I'll let you run with it. It's your choice. You know what mine is."

Stepping into the elevator, she turned toward him. "What if I would rather you took the initiative and dragged me off to your bed?"

"We've reversed roles for the evening, remember? It will be up to you to seduce me if you want me."

John recognized the light of challenge that appeared in her eyes, and felt both relieved and thrilled. He had found the right approach with her, and now all he had to do was wait. He just hoped he wouldn't have to wait too long.

Since she was without her own transportation, Silver had rented a limousine for the night. The driver took a few wrong turns before he located Giovanni's on a side street several blocks from the city limits of Raleigh. The area was clearly not a part of town the driver frequented.

The small Italian restaurant made up for its lack of a respectable address by offering an attractive decor and an astonishing array of food. The tables were covered by spotless white tablecloths, and a candle and small arrangement of fresh flowers decorated each table. Lighted aquariums were built into several walls, fish in varying sizes and species swimming around tiny shipwrecks and strands of seaweed. The air was heavy with the odor of oregano, mouth-watering sauces, and garlic.

Their waiter introduced himself as Guido. If his hair and bushy mustache had been white instead of gray, Silver mused, and if he had a beard, the plump man would have made a terrific stand-in for Santa Claus. After he rattled off the specials in rapid Italian and received blank looks in return, he laughed, his generous stomach jiggling just like a bowl full of jelly. Then he explained in broken English what each dish consisted of in vivid detail.

After taking their dinner order, Guido appeared puzzled when Silver reached for the wine list he had presented to John. She chose a bottle of one of their finer red wines to go with the veal scaloppine John had ordered and the eggplant parmigiana she had asked for herself. The waiter shrugged, then waddled away from their table, shaking his head and mumbling to himself in Italian.

While they ate their appetizer of sautéed red and yellow peppers and sausage, John asked Silver why she was on leave instead of working.

"How do you know I'm on leave?" she asked, then answered her own question. "King called my office, didn't he?"

"He was worried about you when you didn't answer his calls, so he did a little checking. Your office said you were on temporary leave. Why?"

She picked up a bread stick and broke it in half. "Tremaine, Darcy, and Tremaine are moving their offices to Japan. I'm not sure I want to go with them."

Panic surged through John at the thought of her going halfway around the world. "There are other financial consultant companies you could work for."

"That's part of the problem. I could go with another firm or even start my own business. I'm not sure I want to do either."

He'd thought her work was important to her. Now she seemed to be saying she didn't want to continue with her career.

"What is it you'd rather do?"

She waved the half a bread stick in a dismissing motion. "It doesn't matter right now. I also took some time off to settle the problems at my apartment."

His curiosity was aroused, but he shelved it for now. "Tell me again what's been going on."

Ah, Romance...

Don't you just *love* being in love? And what could be
more romantic than you and your special someone sunning
on the beach in exotic Hawaii, holding hands, listening to the
pounding surf ... or strolling arm and arm around London,
hearing Big Ben strike midnight as you toast each other with
champagne ... or slipping out of a casino to walk along the silky
beaches of the Caribbean on a warm, moonlit night?
Sounds wonderful, doesn't it?

WIN A ROMANTIC INTERLUDE
AND $5,000.00 CASH!

What's even *more* wonderful is that **you could win** one of these
romantic **14-day vacations for two**, plus **$5,000.00 CASH**,
in the Winners Classic Sweepstakes! To enter, just affix the vacation
sticker of your choice to your Official Entry Form and drop it in the mail.
It costs you nothing to enter (we even pay postage!) — so ***go for it!***

FREE GIFTS!

We've got **six FREE Loveswept Romances** ready to send you, too!

If you affix the FREE BOOKS sticker to your Entry Form, your first
shipment of Loveswept Romances is yours absolutely FREE. Plus, about
once a month, you'll get six *new* books hot off the presses, *before they're
available in bookstores.* You'll always have 15 days to decide whether to
keep any shipment, for our low regular price, currently just $13.50* —
that's 6 books for the price of four! **You are never obligated to keep
any shipment**, and may cancel at any time by writing "cancel" across our
invoice and returning the shipment to us, at our expense. There's **no risk**
and **no obligation** to buy, *ever.*

**SIX LOVESWEPT ROMANCES ARE ABSOLUTELY FREE AND ARE
YOURS TO KEEP FOREVER**, no matter what you decide about future
shipments! So come on! You risk nothing at all — and you stand to gain
a world of sizzling romance, exciting prizes ... and FREE LOVESWEPTS!

*(plus shipping & handling, and sales tax in NY and Canada)

Don't miss out! It's **FREE** to enter our sweepstakes ... plus you'll receive six fabulous Loveswept romance novels absolutely **FREE!** You have nothing to lose — so enter today.

Good luck!

She described once more her fluctuating gas gauge. Then she told him about the groceries she hadn't ordered that had been delivered to her apartment. When she'd contacted the supermarket, she'd been told the groceries had been bought at the store, and the buyer had given her name and address to the delivery person.

"It wasn't even the kind of food I usually eat," she added.

"What kind of food had been sent?"

"Mostly junk food. Cookies, candy, chips, soft drinks. That type of thing."

He smiled. "No ice cream?"

"Sorry, not a lick."

"What did you do with the groceries?"

"I left them in the box and shoved it under the kitchen table. Bit by bit, package by package, the food started disappearing, and I wasn't eating any of it."

He nodded. "What else?"

As she described more incidents, Silver was aware that John was listening to every word she said with an intensity that had been missing the previous day. This time he was taking her seriously.

"Can you think of anyone who might have a grudge against you personally or professionally?" he asked when she finished. "Any jealous ex-girlfriends of guys you've gone out with? Someone who got passed over for a promotion you were given? How about a man who was miffed after you turned him down when he asked you out?"

She shook her head. "I rarely date, so that eliminates a scorned lover. I'm usually too busy working to have any sort of social life. I admit there is a certain amount of competition in the financial consultant business, but everyone I work with has just as many clients as I do."

"Silver," he said patiently, "there has to be a reason why someone is harassing you. A fairly strong reason. They've gone to a lot of trouble to terrorize you."

"I honestly can't think of anyone who would hate me so much."

"You're an intelligent woman, Silver. You know the world is made up of all kinds of people. Hate is only one motive behind the cruel things people do to one another." He noticed the portly waiter was headed toward their table and lowered his voice. "Take it easy on this guy. He doesn't seem as eager to jump into the nineties as I am."

Guido approached with the bottle of wine Silver had ordered. He started to pour a sampling of the wine into John's glass, but John stopped him and nodded in Silver's direction.

Guido's mustache drooped as the waiter frowned at the departure from normal procedure. He stepped over to Silver's side of the table and poured a half inch of the red wine into her glass. He gave an abrupt nod after she sipped the wine and gave her approval. Once he had filled both their glasses, the confused waiter set the bottle onto the table and walked away. A short time later he returned with their salads, steaming plates of food, and a basket of hot garlic bread.

He served Silver first, giving her a look that dared her to insist he reverse the usual courtesy by waiting on John before her. She glanced up at him and smiled. John grinned when he saw Guido blink, then respond as any male under the age of eighty would, by returning her smile with one of his own. His expression softened as he asked if there would be anything else.

Silver ruined his restored jovial mood by saying, "Please give me the bill when we're finished, Guido."

The waiter gave John a beseeching glance. Then his expression cleared when he came up with a reasonable explanation for Silver's odd behavior. "Is this your birthday, sir?"

"As a matter of fact, it is," John answered. "But that isn't why the lady will be paying. The times are changing for us mere males, Guido. We have to move with them or get left out. She asked me out to dinner and even brought me flowers and a box of candy."

Appeased, Guido said, "This is very nice that your *amore* give you such a gift." He smiled at Silver, clearly forgiving her for her unusual behavior, then hurried off to the kitchen.

Silver leaned forward. "Is today really your birthday?"

"Why are you so surprised? I was born just like anybody else. It happened to have been forty years ago today."

"Why didn't you say anything?"

He shrugged and reached for a slice of garlic bread. "It's not that big a deal."

"Of course it is. We could have done something special."

He looked at her. "We are doing something special."

The soft tone of his voice and the warmth

in his eyes melted the last ounce of resistance she'd held on to. "I meant I would have given you a gift."

"You already have." When she gave him a puzzled look, he clarified, "You gave me your trust." He reached over and covered her hand with his. "That's more important to me than any tie or pair of cuff links wrapped up in pretty paper, Silver. I'll do whatever I have to to make sure I never let you down."

She lowered her gaze to his hand clasping hers. His touch was having the usual effect on her, and this time she didn't bother to hide it. Looking at him again, she said seriously, "I'm more afraid of letting you down. I've never been involved in an affair before. I could disappoint you." She ran her tongue over suddenly dry lips. "That's what you were talking about earlier, wasn't it? Having an affair?"

"For starters," he drawled, his words as cryptic as his smile. "I want you very badly, Silver. I have for years, which is why I was always so cool toward you. I'm tired of lying awake at night wondering what it would be like to have you under me in my bed."

Silver felt as though there suddenly wasn't enough air in the room. "Then what?"

He stared at her. "You're twenty-eight years old, Silver. Don't tell me you don't know what will happen when we go to bed together. What kind of question is that?"

Blushing, she plodded on into unfamiliar territory. "A fairly intelligent one from my point of view. What happens after we become lovers?"

"Dammit, Silver," he said tightly. "This isn't the time or place for me to describe all the things I want us to do together in bed. Thinking about it is difficult enough. Talking about making love to you in detail will drive me crazy."

"That's not what I meant," she answered in a voice as shaky as her whole insides. "I've never had an affair before. I was only curious how long it's supposed to last."

"There isn't a set of directions for this sort of thing. I have no idea how long an affair with you will last. Why are you thinking of the end before we even begin?"

She shrugged. "My practical nature, I suppose. I just realized I know the answer to my own question, though. Our relationship will last until I return to New York."

He shook his head. "You're wrong. You'll be returning to New York tomorrow."

Leaning back in her chair, she sighed. "Well, that was the shortest affair in history. You changed your mind rather quickly, didn't you?"

"The affair is still on. I'm coming with you."

SIX

Had it only been three days ago when she'd sat in John's office and asked for his help? Silver asked herself as the taxi pulled up in front of her apartment building. She certainly had gotten more than she asked for, the most astonishing thing being John's proposition. He had made it clear exactly what he wanted with her. An affair, not happily-ever-after.

Even more amazing was, she had agreed. Whatever had happened to her independent attitude? she wondered. What about standing on her two capable feet without the assistance of her father or her brothers?

Walking beside John to the elevator, she thought about the previous evening after they had returned to his apartment.

Once inside, she had expected him to take her in his arms and kiss her, to begin the affair he was supposedly so eager for. When he made no move toward her, she asked him if he'd like a cup of coffee. He shook his head and looked at her for a long moment, leaning back against the door. She waited for him to say something, to do something. Anything.

After what seemed like a lifetime, he stepped around her, loosening the knot of his tie as he walked toward the phone.

"You'd better get some rest, Silver. Our flight leaves at eight in the morning," he said matter-of-factly with his back to her.

She watched him pick up the phone receiver, completely mystified by his cool manner.

Who would he be calling at this hour? she wondered. "I take it the date is over."

"It looks like it." He began to punch out numbers. Raising his head, he met her gaze, his own unreadable. "Thanks for the flowers and dinner, Silver." A wry note entered his voice and he gave her a crooked half smile. "You've certainly made this a birthday I won't forget for a long time."

Confused by his abrupt dismissal, she said lamely, "You're welcome. Good night."

As she walked down the hall toward the

spare room, she heard him say, "Nick? Yeah, it's me. What have you found out?"

She stepped into the room and closed the door. Nick was the person John had contacted in New York to do some research for him. He hadn't wasted any time calling the man the moment he walked in the door, she thought with a great deal of irritation. If this was John's idea of the way to handle an affair, she didn't think much of it.

It wasn't until she lay in bed alone that she remembered the roles had been reversed for the evening. John had practically given her a script. It had been up to her to seduce him when they returned to the apartment.

He hadn't changed his mind about wanting her, she finally realized. He had waited for her to make up her own mind. When she had made no move toward him, he hadn't pushed or pouted. He had simply accepted her decision.

The rat.

She flopped over onto her stomach and punched the pillow. Growing up with her brothers hadn't helped her understand the workings of the male mind as much as she'd thought.

But then, at the moment, she didn't understand her own.

The following morning, they flew to New York. During the flight, John didn't talk much. When the seat-belt sign went out, he opened his attaché case and spent the entire flight going over computer readouts. Silver tried very hard not to be annoyed by his lack of attention. Her practical nature understood his need to attend to business. Instead of being irritated, she told herself, she should be grateful he was willing to drop everything and fly to New York with her.

She'd be less irritated, she realized, if she could get the thought out of her head that he was going to New York because he felt obligated to help King Knight's daughter.

Perhaps if they had made love last night, she would be more sure of him and his motives that morning. Then again, maybe not. She had never felt so unsure of herself. Or more sure of what she wanted. She wanted John Lomax.

After a harrowing ride in a taxicab driven by a man who spoke little English, they arrived at Silver's apartment building. It had none of the charm and personality that John's had, but it was what she'd called home for four years.

John wouldn't allow her inside her apartment until he had looked around first. He set their cases down in the foyer and pointed to where she was standing in the doorway.

"Stay there. I'm going to look around."

While he checked out the small kitchen, bedrooms, and bathroom, Silver looked through the stack of mail she'd taken out of her mailbox in the lobby. The bill for her car insurance and a postcard from her brother Ryder were mixed in with advertisements and charity solicitations. She was about to discard a white envelope with the junk mail when something about it made her examine it more closely. Her name and address were printed on the back in pencil, the handwriting resembling a third-grader's. There was no stamp.

"What's that?"

She turned to John, who was standing next to her. Handing the envelope to him, she said, "This was in my mailbox. It's been hand-delivered."

"There probably isn't a hope in hell there will be a fingerprint on it we can use." He took her wrist and drew her toward the couch. Standing in front of the coffee table, he released her wrist and told her to put the envelope on the table.

After she did, Silver sat down beside him and watched in fascination as John unfolded a slim blade from a small knife he'd taken out of the front pocket of his jeans. He picked up a pencil she'd left lying beside a crossword-puzzle book and used the eraser end to hold the envelope in place while he slit it open. A single piece of paper was inside. John pried the note from the envelope using the pencil eraser and unfolded it.

Silver leaned forward and read:

Where have you gone? You don't need to run away. I stopped him from playing those tricks on you. He was just having a little fun and didn't mean you no harm.

The child-like printing changed slightly at the end, the letters more crooked, the lines heavier, as though the writer were pressing down with considerable pressure.

I miss you. Please come back.

The note was unsigned.
John read through it twice. He didn't

attempt to maneuver the letter back into the envelope.

"Do you have a plastic bag I can put these into?"

Silver got him one from the kitchen. Handing it to him, she asked, "The note creates more questions than answers, doesn't it?"

He carefully inserted the envelope and note into the plastic bag. "I'll give this to Nick to test for fingerprints, but I have a feeling NYPD won't have a record of them on file."

"Why not?"

He held the bag out to her. "Take a whiff."

She bent her head. Her eyes widened as she recognized the smell. "Peanut butter?"

"That was my guess too. I think we're dealing with a couple of kids. Any idea who?"

She sat down heavily on the couch. "I know some of the children who live in the building, but mostly only to say hi in the elevator. Up until several months ago the two kids from across the hall used to come over once in a while, especially Tina. She was a quiet little girl, ten, maybe eleven years old, who used to look at me with eyes that seemed too big for her face. Her brother is fifteen, maybe sixteen, very protective of her." She laughed briefly. "And overly confident about his attractiveness to women."

John frowned. "Did he make a pass?"

"I never let it get that far." Something in John's expression made her add, "I think the family has moved. I haven't seen Tina or Ronnie for a month or so."

"I'll check them out anyway."

The thought of Tina being interrogated made Silver defend her. "A ten-year-old girl wouldn't be driving my car, John."

"I didn't say she would."

"Then why check up on her?"

"The note said he or she stopped someone from playing more tricks on you. The incidents don't necessarily mean someone's intentionally trying to give you a bad time. They could all be completely separate from one another. On the other hand, a sixteen-year-old might be tempted to take a spin in your sports car. Would he know where you keep it parked?"

"I don't know. I suppose he could have seen me. I keep it in a car park just two blocks from here."

"I'll have a chat with him too."

"But—"

"You asked for my help, Silver. I can't do anything for you if you tie my hands."

"You're right," she murmured. She stood up and walked over to the wide windows to open the drapes. She was going to have to trust John to treat Tina gently. Remembering the young girl's innocent blue eyes and quiet manner, she doubted if John would be able to be anything but kind to the child.

The light coming through the window highlighted Silver's black hair, and John had to force himself to stay where he was. Touching her was not an option. After last night, he wasn't sure when it would be. When they'd returned to his apartment, she'd calmly said good night like a polite houseguest and had gone to bed.

To get his mind off his desire to show her how it would be between them, he forced himself to take in his surroundings. Her taste in furnishings wasn't all that different from his, he noticed. Even the coloring was similar. Dark wood tones and shades of deep green. There wasn't a single sign of the cold contemporary chrome and glass that he disliked, or flowery Victorian ruffles that made a man feel he had stepped into a fussy dollhouse.

The curved sofa and two matching chairs were a jade green, the two occasional tables painted white. Crowding the porcelain lamps on the tables were dozens of framed photographs in varying sizes. A large Oriental rug covered a generous portion of the wooden floor, and leafy green plants filled a corner of the room.

Spotting a glass-enclosed display case against one wall, he walked over to it. The case was as long as his rolltop desk, although only half as wide. Inside was an assortment of glass, metal, ceramic, and wooden figures of knights in armor. Some were astride horses, others were standing alone with lances or swords in their hands. Most of them were no taller than five inches. Two were about ten inches tall. All were incredibly detailed.

Silver saw what had caught John's attention and joined him in front of the display case. "On my sixteenth birthday, my brother Michael gave me the knight bearing a flag with a coat of arms printed on the fabric." She opened the glass door to remove a silver statue situated in the middle of the others. She held it out for John to examine. "Michael thought every girl should have her own knight in shining armor. He said they were hard to find these days. Until I found one of my own, he would give me a substitute on my birthday."

"I know how old you are, Silver. There are more than twelve knights here."

"I've added to the collection and some have been given to me by friends."

He took the figure from her, studying it. "Being a knight couldn't have been very easy. People expected them to solve all their problems and save the world. They were sent out on impossible quests and occasionally to fight battles they hadn't a hope of winning. They were only men with faults and imperfections like anyone else, but somehow people forgot that."

"Are you speaking from experience?" she asked, thinking of his years as a policeman.

"No," he said with a short laugh. "I don't look good in a suit of armor."

"You wore a uniform, though. Some people consider policemen knights in blue."

"Being a cop is a lot of things," he said with a cynical twist to his mouth. Putting the knight back into the case, he carefully closed the door. "Cops are ordinary men who do the best they can with the job they've been assigned. Most of them aren't in it for medals and glory."

"That sounds similar to what you just said about knights. Many men wanted to become knights to follow a quest or chase a dream. What was your reason?"

John met her gaze. "For joining the force?"

When she nodded, he answered, "I didn't have anything better to do at the time."

Silver recognized a closed door when she saw one. She might have left it alone if they'd still been snapping at each other as they had in the past. But he had changed their relationship by wanting to become intimate with her, and she wouldn't give herself to a stranger.

She took several steps away before turning back to look at him. "Flip answers to personal questions are allowed if you want to maintain a distant relationship with someone, John. It doesn't work if you want to get closer."

"Are you saying you need my life story before you'll go to bed with me?" he asked, his dark eyes challenging her.

"I've only been with one other man, John." She saw a muscle in his jaw tighten at her admission. "I'm neither bragging nor complaining, just explaining why I haven't immediately fallen into your bed. Peter and I had known each other a long time, though not as long as you and I. Peter and I were friends first, good friends, sharing our thoughts, our dreams, our problems while we were in business school. We both got jobs here in New York, and we stayed close, partly because it's so hard to make friends in this city. Eventually, we became lovers."

"I don't want to hear this."

"Well, that's too bad because I need to say it and you need to hear it. Peter and I were great friends, but something was missing in our relationship after we became lovers. I thought perhaps it was because we hadn't made the final commitment. We ruined a good friendship by pushing ourselves further than we should have gone."

"That isn't the way it is between us. Damm-it, Silver, the air around us practically crackles like firecrackers whenever we're even in the same room together."

"I know that. I also know why last night didn't end the way you thought it would. I finally realized why I couldn't make the first move you said I would have to make. I'm desperately attracted to you, John, but I can't make love with you when I barely know you. I'm not made that way. You can call me repressed, a prude, or whatever word you want to use. I'm discovering I'm more old-fashioned than I thought I could ever be. I can't go to bed with a stranger. I think more of myself than that."

John walked away from the display cabinet, stopping in front of the window. He stared out at the city without really seeing it. "There are parts of my life I don't like to talk about, Silver. Not even to you. There are things I don't like to remember. I can't even promise to tell you sometime in the future." He glanced at her over his shoulder, a faint smile shaping his mouth. "Parts of my life you wouldn't want to know about. It isn't that I don't trust you. Maybe I want you to think of me as a knight in shining armor without knowing how tarnished that armor was at one time."

Silver took in the straight, stiff way he was standing with his hands curled into fists at his sides. Even though he hadn't let her into his past the way she'd hoped, he had explained why he found it difficult to talk about himself. He had opened that closed door a crack. Perhaps with patience, she would get him to open it all the way. For now, it was enough.

Before she could respond, he turned to face her, his fists still clenched. He looked like a man preparing himself for a battle, she thought. He didn't realize she'd already surrendered.

His gaze never wavering from her face, he said, "I might never be able to be the man you want, Silver. I could tell you what I thought you wanted to hear, but I won't do that just to get you into bed with me. I don't know if I'll ever be able to give you all the bits and pieces of my life that you seem to want. Either you want me and are willing to take me the way I am, or not. It's up to you."

The first step toward him was the hardest to take. The following ones were easier. She stopped in front of him and placed her hands on his chest. She could feel his heart pounding hard. Looking up at him, she saw a wary defensiveness in his eyes.

"You are the man I want, John. It's always been you. That's why Peter never had a chance."

He made a sound that seemed to come from the depths of his soul and pulled her into his arms. He kissed her with a startling desperation, as if he was barely able to restrain the desire he'd suppressed for what seemed like forever. His hands were unsteady as he caressed her, his breathing ragged.

Breaking away, he buried his lips in the hollow of her throat. "It will kill me if this is a dream."

"If it is," she murmured, "we're having the same dream."

John lifted his head so he could see her face. Cupping her head with his strong hands, he kissed her temple, the corner of her mouth, her eyelids. "I don't know how much longer I could have waited for you, Silver."

Silver held nothing back. "Don't wait." Now that she had thrown caution to the winds, she was eager to know the full extent of John's desire. "Please, John. I've wanted you so badly for so long."

He groaned deep in his chest. "I might not be sane after this."

Standing on her toes, she wrapped her arms around his neck as he lowered his head to take her mouth with a hunger that shook her. Responding to John's urgent touch and erotic assault on her mouth was as natural as the tide rising and falling. Nothing in her life had prepared her for the powerful need he drew from her, yet she found it was remarkably easy to give herself over to his passion, and even easier to meet it with her own.

She was vaguely aware of movement. His arm had tightened around her waist, lifting her off her feet as he walked toward her couch. His weight pressed her down into the cushion, his insatiable mouth never leaving hers.

Her legs tangled with his, her body becoming restless and demanding as his kisses became deeper, prolonged, and intimate. She felt one of his hands slide under her lower body, holding her still as he moved his hips against hers. She made a yearning sound deep in her throat when she felt his arousal pressing against the juncture of her thighs.

"John," she breathed.

"I know," he murmured against her mouth.

Her whole body shuddered with expectation and reaction when he slipped his hand under the waist of her stirrup pants and panties. With a single smooth movement, he swept them both off her hips and down her legs, then discarded them with a flip of his hand.

His fingers caressed the inside of her thighs, and she gasped when she felt his hand close over the center of her femininity. She arched her back and clutched at his shoulders as she sought relief from the spiraling tension curling through her.

She felt a momentary coolness over her breasts and realized he had opened the front of her white poet's shirt. A few seconds later she was aware he'd found the front closure of her bra and had unclasped it. His hips ground into hers as he broke away from her mouth to transfer his hungry caresses to her breast.

Silver cried out as sensation after sensation crashed through her body.

John didn't remove her shirt, nor did he take off his own. He didn't want to take the time. With fingers made clumsy by haste, he unbuttoned his shirt, then unfastened his belt and his pants. His gaze never left her as he shoved off his pants and briefs after taking a foil wrapper from one of his pockets.

He lowered his long frame onto her again, partially covering her. Sliding an arm under her shoulders, he brought her breasts against his chest. His other hand found her hip, her thigh, then her moist heat.

He heard her quick intake of breath and looked into her eyes. "Do you have any idea what it does to me when you respond like this?"

She shook her head, her hair moving against the cushion beneath her. "I only know what I feel when you touch me, as though I'm going to shatter unless you hold me together."

Her words were as seductive as her body, and he felt his control slipping away. "Come with me," he said as he parted her thighs with his knee. "I've never been where we're going. Hold on to me, and we'll go together."

She raised her hips, and with a groan, he accepted the silent invitation and sheathed his aching body in hers. He closed his eyes and absorbed the wave of sensations washing over him. For a moment he didn't move. None of his expectations compared with the real thing. He had never felt anything like this, as though he would splinter into a thousand pieces of pleasure, and yet so much a part of another person, he felt they were one.

He had no idea how long he would have stayed locked with her and not moving if she hadn't sighed softly, her breathing ragged because of his weight pressing her into the cushions of the couch. Her inner muscles clenched around him when she sighed, and his control snapped like a dry twig.

Silver clung to the only reality in her life at that moment as John began to move against her and then with her in a rhythm as old as time. She wasn't aware of the marks her nails were leaving on his skin any more than he was. She was only conscious of John and the rapturous tension spiraling through her.

He slid a hand under her bottom to tilt her hips upward, and she cried out his name as he delved deep, deep inside her. Closing her eyes, she saw thousands of pinpoints of light and fell into them.

John had never seen anything more beautiful than Silver's dazed satisfaction. He whispered her name, his voice strangled as he reached for the ultimate pleasure and found it within her.

SEVEN

John had no idea what time it was when something woke him from the soundest sleep he'd had in a long time. Silver was sleeping close beside him, her breathing deep and slow. She'd fallen asleep in his arms, exhausted after making love with him a third time. Three times, he marveled with male satisfaction. Each time they'd loved had been more incredible than before, leaving him doubting whether he would ever get enough of her.

He opened his eyes and was staring at the ceiling of Silver's bedroom when he heard a noise. It sounded as if someone was dragging a chair across a linoleum floor. Then he heard a jumble of voices, music, and canned laughter.

Someone had turned on Silver's television set!

His years of police training had him tensing, ready to slip into the living room and collar the intruders. But Silver was nestled against him, her head on his shoulder. Until he knew what was going on, he didn't want her waking up and possibly blundering into trouble.

He'd managed to get his arm out from under her when she sleepily asked, "Where are you going?"

"The bathroom," he whispered. "Go back to sleep."

"Okay," she murmured as she rolled onto her back.

He levered his legs over the side of the bed and stood up, his gaze on her. Her eyes remained closed, her breathing slow and natural.

Until he took a step and rammed his toes into one of the legs of the bed.

The sound of a foot crunching into the hard wooden bed support woke Silver. And possibly the people in the next apartment, she thought. It had seemed that loud to her. If they had managed to sleep through that, the succinct swear word that John barked should have jarred them awake. Silver sat upright and held the sheet over her bare breasts while she stared at him.

"John?"

He didn't answer her. He was limping toward the door, and in the light from the moon and the street lamps, she could see him flinch when he put weight on his left leg.

"John, are you all right?"

"Never better," he grunted, not pausing. He had his hand on the doorknob when they both heard the slamming of a door.

Silver switched to a kneeling position, her gaze shifting to her closed bedroom door. "What was that?"

"I don't know," he answered. "I'll go look. You stay here."

Still limping, John opened the bedroom door and slipped out into the hall. He hugged the wall and peered around the corner into the living room. The television screen was showing a black-and-white comedy show, but no one was watching it. The room was empty. An opened sack of potato chips had spilled out on the coffee table near two opened cans of soda.

Hearing a soft rustling sound behind him, he automatically reached to the small of his back. Considering he was buck naked and his gun was in the drawer of his bedside table in Raleigh, the gesture was completely worthless. So was ordering Silver to stay put, he discovered.

"Dammit, Silver. I told you to stay in the bedroom."

Silver continued buttoning his shirt, which had been the first piece of clothing she'd come across when she'd gotten out of bed. "I'm going to get some ice for your foot." She stepped past him and stopped abruptly. On the television screen Lucy and Ethel were trying to keep up with a conveyor belt carrying chocolate bonbons past them at a fast clip.

"Please tell me you couldn't sleep and have been watching television," she said.

"When would I have had the time? I've been in bed with you, remember?" he said curtly. "We've had some uninvited guests." He walked over to the set and shut it off. Glancing at the chips and soda cans, he added, "whoever it was certainly made themselves at home."

"Someone's been in here tonight while we were sleeping?"

"It looks that way." He turned on the light in the kitchen and glanced around, then he walked over to the front door.

"John?"

"There's no sign of forced entry. It looks like our midnight intruders have a key. If Nick can't get any prints off the soda cans, he might find some on the door."

"John," she repeated, a little louder this time.

"What?" he asked impatiently.

"You aren't going out in the hall, are you?"

He glanced at her. "I was thinking about it. That's where the bad guys went. Although they're probably long gone by now."

"I just thought I should mention that you aren't wearing any clothes."

He smiled briefly. "I noticed that." He gestured toward the kitchen. "Why don't you check and see what else they might have disturbed in the kitchen while they were taking the chips and sodas."

"They evidently brought the sodas. I didn't have any."

"If you think they've touched something, leave it until I take a look at it."

"What will you be doing while I'm in the kitchen?"

"I'm going to call Nick."

"At this hour?"

John paused on his way to the bedroom. "Yeah. I want him to come here early. If I wait to call him in the morning, I might miss him."

"I don't want to involve the police, John. I just want this to stop."

"Nick's still with the force, but this will be an unofficial visit."

"Why?"

"There isn't any proof of a crime having been committed. There is no forced entry, and a bag of chips and two soda cans aren't much in the way of evidence."

"At least now you know I was telling the truth."

"I didn't need any proof to know that." He scowled down at his foot. Two toes were beginning to swell. "I believed you." He looked up. "Why do you think I came with you to New York?"

"To sleep with me?"

He shook his head slowly. "We still have a long way to go if you think that's the only reason."

Silver wanted to ask him where he thought they were going. And how far and for how long. Instead she said, "I'll get some ice for your foot."

"I don't need any ice," he grumbled.

"You might not, but your foot does."

He scowled at her, and she struggled with the urge to laugh. It wasn't easy, but she managed to keep her amusement to herself. None of her brothers liked to admit they suffered any pain either. When it was unavoidable, like a broken arm or a case of the flu, they became borderline children. It was going to be interesting to see how John dealt with what she suspected was a broken toe or two.

After Silver ducked into the kitchen, John walked awkwardly into the bedroom and picked his jeans up off the floor. The heavy denim material dragged over his swollen, throbbing toes when he tugged the jeans on. He looked around for his shirt until he remembered where it was. Recalling how appealing Silver looked wearing it, he wasn't about to ask for its return.

He didn't plan on having his clothes on all that long anyway. There were several more hours before daylight. He would prefer to spend them with Silver in her bed. And not just so he could make love with her again. The intimacy of sleeping with someone had never appealed to him until he'd slept beside her. Even asleep, he'd been aware of her breathing softly on his skin, her slender body curled against him.

For the first time in six years, he didn't feel the hollow loneliness that had been his companion since his partner's funeral. Silver filled the emptiness.

Glancing around the bedroom, he looked for his suitcase. Then he remembered that he'd set both their suitcases just inside the front door when they arrived. Unless the midnight intruders had taken them, that's where they still were.

If tonight's visitors were the same people who had been causing Silver's sleepless nights, they weren't too sharp. Two suitcases standing by the door would imply the person who lived there was either coming or going. Any self-respecting burglar would have had the sense to check the bedroom first. Of course, any self-respecting burglar probably wouldn't have settled down for a couple of hours of TV watching before heisting the damn thing. That was only one of the things that didn't make sense.

Sitting on the bed, he pulled the bedside phone closer and dialed a number he hadn't forgotten in all the years since he'd left the force.

A man answered on the third ring, his sleep-soaked voice as much of a threat as what he said. "This damn well better be important."

"It is, Nick. The friends I was telling you

about have paid a visit to Silver's apartment tonight. I want you to bring your kit with you and dust the place this morning before you report in."

"Lomax?"

"In person and in New York. We arrived yesterday, but evidently our visitors didn't know Silver had returned. They were making themselves at home, watching television and having a little snack in the living room while we were sleeping in the bedroom."

"Cheeky little devils, aren't they." After a long yawn, Nick said, "It doesn't sound like these guys are pros, John. Taking prints is going to be a waste of time. It sounds more like kids."

"That's the way I figure it too, but they've been scaring Silver, and that has to stop. Whoever is hopping in and out of her apartment has to be keeping an eye on the place. Apparently they have a key, since there was no indication of forced entry. They knew she was gone before, but evidently didn't notice when we arrived."

"Is there a way they can see into the apartment?"

"There's a fire escape outside the living-room window. From there, they couldn't see that we were in the bedroom. We'll be able to tell from the size of the prints whether or not they are kids. If they are, we can use the prints to scare the hell out of them."

Nick agreed. "How are you going to find these kids? They know Silver is home now. They probably won't be back."

"That didn't stop them before. As long as they don't know I'm here, they might continue their midnight visits."

"And if they don't?"

"I'll have to get creative."

Nick yawned again, then said, "I'll be there around eight. I suppose it would be asking too much if you had coffee waiting for me."

"I'll see what I can find in her cupboards. Try to be light on your feet when you get here, Nick. I don't want our friends to see you coming or going. I'd rather they thought Silver was alone."

"Gotcha."

After John hung up the phone, he glanced at the rumpled sheets on the bed, sighed heavily, and walked out of the bedroom. Silver had cleared away the chips and sodas, and was walking toward the couch with a plastic bag filled with ice in one hand and a hand towel in the other.

"A bag of cookies is missing," she said, "and the bag of chips is from the stash under the table. Evidently, they've made themselves at home on other nights since I've been gone."

"That's why I'm going to check out your little friends across the hall. Everything points to kids using your place for a clubhouse."

The cubes of ice clattered together as she wrapped the towel around the bag. "I told you I don't think Tina and Ronnie still live there. I haven't seen them for some time. Although they could be avoiding me. I got the impression a couple of times that their mother didn't like it when they talked to me."

"Did you ever invite them in when you were here?"

"A few times. Ronnie helped me carry some bags of groceries from the lobby. Once Tina had scraped her knee on the sidewalk and I brought her up here to patch her up. She said her mother wasn't home."

"Not exactly in the running for parent of the year, is she?"

"I've never met the woman, even though we've been neighbors for a couple of years."

"In the morning, I want you to make a list of everyone who has been in your apartment in the last six months."

"You think someone's made a copy of my apartment key?"

"Either that or they are good at picking your lock." He walked around the end of the couch and inadvertently caught his battered toes in the fringe of the Oriental rug. He clamped his jaw shut on the first curse word that came to mind.

"John, stop being so stubborn. Sit down on the couch and put your foot on the cushion."

He was beginning to enjoy Silver fussing over him. As a rule, he didn't think much of the idea of being pampered. Not that he could recall an occasion when he had been. Having Silver fretting about him was different, though. Everything with Silver was different. Over the years he hadn't even come close to imagining what it would be like to make love with her. It was like expecting a satisfying meal and experiencing a lavish banquet instead.

He sat down on the couch. The front of the shirt Silver was wearing gapped open when she bent down to lift his injured foot onto a cushion, since he made no move to do so himself. His thoughts were elsewhere.

"Couldn't we do this just as easily in bed?" he suggested. "We would both be a lot more comfortable."

She shook her head. "I don't want to take the chance this plastic bag might leak and get the bed wet."

Silver set the ice bag onto the top of his foot, making sure the ice wasn't directly on his swollen toes. After trying to position the lumpy bag several different ways, she lifted his foot, sat down, then rested his foot on her thigh. She gently placed the bag of ice over his toes.

"It's cold and probably a little uncomfortable, but the ice will take away some of the pain and swelling."

"First flowers and candy, now this. You're spoiling me, Silver."

"I'm simply taking care of you because you won't do it for yourself."

"I've been taking care of myself most of my life. A little broken toe is not a big deal."

It was the first time he'd ever said anything about his past. It wasn't much, and Silver wanted to hear more. She sensed she would understand John better if she knew more about his past—the people, places, and events that had shaped the boy into a man.

To counter the coldness of the ice, she placed her palm on the top of his foot. "A broken toe isn't much compared to your other injuries." He gave her a puzzled look, and she added, "You have a scar on your left shoulder and another just above your waist on your right side." She smiled when he frowned. "It's impossible to keep such things hidden when you remove your armor."

"I'm not one of your gallant knights, Silver," he said in a clipped voice. "I have those scars because I made dumb mistakes."

"I see." And she did, oddly enough. She sensed that John was harder on himself than anyone else would be. What he considered mistakes she saw as examples of the dangers police officers faced, signs that John had placed himself in harm's way in order to battle crime.

John stared at her hand that was lying on top of his foot as he waited for the inevitable questions about the scars. Damned if he didn't feel the current of heat from her hand all the way up his leg. After several minutes went by in silence, he raised his gaze to her face. She had leaned her head against the back of the couch and was staring off into space.

"Well?"

Turning her head, she met his gaze. "Well, what?"

"Aren't you going to ask me how I got the scars?"

"Do you want to tell me?"

He frowned. "Hell, no."

"Then why should I ask?"

He sat up, nearly dislodging the ice bag. "Aren't you even a little curious?"

"Yes," she said seriously. "I'd like to know more about you. I realize it isn't possible to know everything about someone else, but I would like to know how you feel about certain things." She paused, then continued. "Like me, for instance. But I'm not going to push and prod and nag for that information, or for anything else I want to know about you. I'd rather you told me because you want me to know."

"And if I never do?"

"Then I'll never know, will I? You have a right to your privacy, the same as anyone else, John. While we're together, I'll try to remember that and not ask personal questions."

He should have been relieved. She was saying all the things he thought he wanted to hear. He was off the hook about making any commitments, or having any soul-searching discussions, or exchanging opinions, past experiences, and hopes for the future. He'd never been very good at that kind of stuff.

But something she had said irritated the hell out of him. What did she mean *while* they were together? That sounded pretty damn temporary to him. As he stared at her it occurred to him that a brief affair was all she expected from him, because he'd never given her any indication he wanted anything else. Did he want more? he asked himself. Hell, yes.

He lay back down, resting his head on his bent arm. "If you could ask me one question that I promised to answer, what would it be?"

Without hesitation, she said, "I've always been curious about how you got to know my father. Whenever I've asked King, he's simply said that you saved his life once. I always thought his answer was overly dramatic, which isn't all that unusual for him, but he's oddly reticent about giving me any details. *That* is unusual. He likes to milk every ounce from any juicy story, but in this instance, he always just changes the subject. I've never understood why, any more than I ever understood why he always made a point to see you every time he came to New York, and why he appointed you CEO."

"More than that," John said, "I know you resented your father inviting me to dinner or to the opening at a gallery featuring his paintings whenever he came to New York. He also included half the free world, but I was the only one you seemed to object to seeing. Why was that?"

"You were the only one I had a crush on."

He stared at her. "You were rude because you were attracted to me?"

She smiled. "Teenage girls experiencing their first infatuation rarely make sense," she explained philosophically. "You were going to tell me how you met my father."

John took a deep breath to force himself to relax. Staring at the ceiling, he said, "King happened to be in the wrong place at the wrong time. You know that sheikh who gave your father that Oriental rug as thanks for the painting King did? Well, while the sheikh was in New York the police got a tip that an assassination attempt was going to be made. My partner and I were among the officers assigned to protect him. We were stationed outside the Plaza Hotel, where the sheikh was staying, standing near the entrance. A limousine was parked out front waiting to take the sheikh and your father to the art gallery that had framed the portrait King had painted of that horse. Everything had been checked out—the hotel, the gallery, King, the limousine service, the works. But somewhere between the garage and the hotel, a switch had been made with the limousine. Just as your father, the sheikh, and the sheikh's entourage were all starting down the steps, the limousine windows were lowered and automatic weapons were pointed in the group's direction. Before the assassins were able to fire, I threw myself at the sheikh and King, knocking them over. My partner called for backup, yelled at the other civilians to get down, and discouraged the group in the limousine by firing at them. That was it."

That was it, Silver repeated silently. He had literally thrown himself in the path of the bullets if the assassins had fired their weapons. She got a knot in her stomach just thinking about the danger he'd placed himself in.

"Knocking someone over," she said, "and later going to work for them has to involve more than simple gratitude. King wouldn't hand Knight Enterprises over to you no matter what you had done for him if you weren't qualified."

"He looked me up a day or so later. I think it was the year you were all moving to England to live. You and your mother had left that morning. King had some stuff to take care of, so he was going to follow in a few days. When he contacted me, he said he wanted to shake the hand of the man who'd saved his life. He also proceeded to drink me under the table that evening." John grimaced. "Somewhere between the second drink and my taking him back to my apartment to sleep it off, we became friends."

"That must have been before he was diagnosed with arthritis. He can't drink alcohol now because of the type of medicine he takes."

"I rarely drink that much either. Thanks to your father, I suffered my one and only hangover. The next morning King noticed a stack of books on the kitchen table, where I studied for the classes I was taking at night school. When he found out one of the courses I was taking was business management, he said to contact him if I ever decided to leave the force."

"And you did?"

He shook his head. "I don't know how he found out I had resigned, but one day he called me at my apartment and offered me a job with Knight Enterprises in Kentucky. I grabbed the chance to get out of New York, not even bothering to ask him what kind of work I'd be doing. I wanted out of the city, but I didn't like the idea of starving. Moving to Raleigh was the solution. I certainly hadn't expected to become the chief executive officer. I was a cop with a couple of degrees. The ink was still wet on my master's. I tried to tell King I wasn't qualified, that I had no experience. We compromised. I took the job at a reduced salary. When I felt I deserved it, he hiked up my pay to what it was supposed to be."

Silver removed the ice bag and set it on the coffee table. "How do your toes feel now?"

He levered his leg off her thigh and stood up. "I have another ache that needs your tender, loving care." In a smooth, easy motion, he bent down and picked her up. "There's still a few hours left before dawn. Let's go back to bed."

"I'm not sleepy."

"Who said anything about sleeping?"

She wrapped her arms around his neck. "Watch where you're walking this time," she warned. "I used up all the ice that was in the freezer."

EIGHT

If there was a minimum weight limit for a policeman, Nick Archer barely made it. Yet he ate more food than Silver and John combined. A scant few inches taller than Silver, Nick made up for his lack of height by having a surplus of energy and enthusiasm that would make John's neighbor Ginger seem to be standing still.

John handed Nick a mug of coffee the minute he arrived, and Nick sipped it while he dusted the front door, the refrigerator, the television, and around the living-room window for prints. When he finished, he joined Silver and John in the kitchen for breakfast. His dark gaze immediately honed in on the plates of scrambled eggs, bacon, and hot biscuits Silver had just set on the table.

"Put her under house arrest, Lomax. Cuff her and read her the Betty Crocker rights instead of the Miranda version. She has the right to cook three square meals a day. She has the right to invite me over for every one of them."

"I get the picture, Nick." John glanced at the cards Nick had placed on the table. "So, what did you find?"

Nick waited to answer until he'd cleaned his plate and heaped on seconds. With the knife he'd been about to use to butter a biscuit, he pointed out a clear set of prints he'd taken from the door.

"By the size of the prints, they were made by children or small adults. I'd go with kids. You said nothing has been taken. Any burglar worth his salt would have seen the value of some of Miss Knight's furnishings, especially the silver and gold figurines in that glass case, and helped himself."

John agreed. "I think a couple of kids have been using Silver's apartment as a clubhouse, where they can get away from parents and have a grand old time."

"He's not absolutely sure," Silver interjected as she poured more coffee into their cups. "John is guessing it's the children across the hall, but he doesn't have any proof."

Splitting another biscuit apart, Nick slathered on enough butter for two. "Silver, you are not only facially gifted, you could put my dear sainted mother to shame in the kitchen. These biscuits are terrific."

"Which dear sainted mother is this one?" John asked. "The one who ran a bookie joint or the one who sang with the Dixieland Trio?"

Grinning, Nick said, "She did both. She also baked a mean biscuit. So, Lomax, what's the plan? How are you going to catch these desperadoes?"

"What makes you think I have a plan?"

"You always have a plan." Turning his attention to Silver, Nick explained, "No one could come up with a plan of action quicker than Lomax. The captain would have him back just like that"—he snapped his fingers— "if John ever changed his mind about trading in his pin-striped suits for his detective shield."

Silver saw a muscle in John's jaw clench. Redirecting the subject back to the original problem, she asked, "What's your plan?"

John crossed his arms over his chest. "How are you at video games, Silver?"

"I doubt I could beat a ten-year-old. Why?"

"You're going to buy one. We'll leave the empty boxes in the hall for a while to give our little friends a chance to see them and be tempted. Then we'll make a big show of going out for the evening. When we come back, we'll nab them."

"What if you're wrong and it isn't the kids across the hall? What then?"

"We go on to Plan B."

"Which is?"

"I'm hoping it won't come to that." Mainly because he didn't have a Plan B. He pushed himself away from the table and proceeded to clear off the dishes.

Silver remained seated, finishing her coffee. One of the things she was learning about John was his willingness to help with mundane chores. Her brothers used to have some of their biggest arguments over whose turn it was to do an assigned task around the house. Even though they'd always had household staff, their mother had been adamant about all her children knowing how to do various domestic chores.

John saw something that needed to be done, and he went ahead and did it. He hadn't made a big deal out of washing her clothes in Raleigh, nor had he seemed to expect profuse thanks from her. That morning, after helping her make the bed, he'd set the table while she cooked.

Nick handed his plate to John. "So you two will be taking care of purchasing the video-game stuff today. Right?"

"Right," John said. "I'll hook it up to the television in the living room, play it loud enough for the neighbors to hear a few games, then Silver and I will pretend to go out for the evening."

"If we do catch them," Silver said, "I don't want them carted off to Juvenile Hall like criminals. They haven't done anything except for drinking a few cans of soda and eating some junk food that they apparently bought. I just want them to stop coming to my apartment."

"They've scared you silly," John argued. "You've lost sleep and were frightened enough to drive all the way to Raleigh to ask for my help."

"Which makes me look really idiotic considering it's only children who've been causing all the problems."

"All I want is to get them to stop their midnight visits. I certainly won't hurt them in any way. They might not even be aware they've frightened you so much."

Nick cleared his throat to get their attention. "I'll be leaving now if you can't think of anything more you want me to do."

John shook his head. "You've been a big help, Nick. Thanks. I might need you in uniform for the final showdown."

"Whatever it takes. I'll see you two later." At the door, Nick gave Silver a broad wink. "I don't know whether I should wish you luck with Lomax or shoot straight for offering you sympathy."

"How about good-bye?" John drawled.

Sighing deeply, Nick made a mock bow. "Thanks for the breakfast, Silver. I'm leaving a sadder but fuller man."

The two men exchanged looks, then nodded.

Silver waited until Nick had left before turning to John. "There's something more behind Nick's willingness to help a friend, isn't there? He's really going out of his way for a minor crime."

"When it comes to kids, there are no minor crimes. If Nick can stop a kid from stealing hubcaps, maybe the kid won't graduate to stealing cars." He started walking back to the kitchen. "Do you want another cup of coffee before we go shopping?"

"Who stopped you from stealing hub-caps?"

"Duff Mariner."

John stopped suddenly when he realized what he'd said.

"Who's Duff Mariner?" she asked.

John turned and walked back to her. "Leave it alone, Silver. I could make something up and satisfy your curiosity, but I don't want to lie to you. Just let the past go. It doesn't have anything to do with us." He kissed her lightly, then took her hand. "Let's get this shopping over with."

He was wrong, Silver thought as she stood beside him in the elevator. Why was it so difficult for him to see why he needed to tell her what had happened to him in the past? She had so many questions. What had made him quit the police force? Why didn't he want to talk about Duff Mariner? Those years had been a pivotal time in his life, and until he could share them with her, she would feel he didn't fully trust her.

Or that they would never move beyond an affair.

Once outside her building, she expected John to hail a taxi, but instead he took her arm and began to walk. Evidently, she'd been mistaken about his toes being broken, since he had managed to put on his shoe and didn't limp when he walked.

They browsed around some of the sidewalk displays they came across, with John occasionally stopping to examine antique toys.

When she saw how carefully he held a replica of an old fire engine and how thoroughly he studied it, she asked if he'd had one like it when he was a child.

He put it down. "I didn't have any toys."

She glanced up at him. He was serious, she realized. "What did you play with then?"

"The streets," he replied, looking off into the distance. "There's always something to do on the streets of New York."

She grasped the piece of his past to add to the others she was collecting. So far, the picture she was getting was of a lousy childhood.

They strolled along for another block, Silver occasionally glancing in windows. When they reached a bakery, she paused, mentally going over the food in her kitchen. Not noticing she'd stopped, John kept walking. She was about to call to him when someone grabbed her arm.

"Don't move, lady," a voice rasped in her ear.

"John!" she cried instinctively.

John whirled around, his heart nearly stopping when he saw a thin, scruffy teenager was holding her. "Take it easy, Silver," he said as he walked toward them. "What do you want?" he asked the mugger.

"Your money and hers."

"Tough. You aren't getting any."

Silver stared at John. He might have been holding a conversation with someone he knew fairly well.

The teenager didn't like his answer. "Look, buddy. I'll hurt your lady if you don't hand over some bread."

"You hurt her and you're a dead man. Now, let her go and we'll let you go."

Silver saw John flick a glance in her direction. And he winked! That was all the warning he gave before he moved with incredible speed, jerking the teenager's arm away from Silver and slamming him into the front window of the bakery, his hand held high against his spine.

"Hey, take it easy, man," the punk whined.

"Shut up," John snapped. "Silver, are you all right?"

"I'm okay."

A clerk from the shoe store next door ventured out, a pair of shoelaces in his hand. "Would these help?"

John didn't plan on tying up his prisoner. Instead, he strong-armed him into a small alley between the shoe store and the bakery. He bent his head down and spoke to the mugger too quietly for Silver to hear what he was saying. Whatever he said, though, made a definite impression. The kid's face paled and his body started shaking.

Suddenly John released him, and the teenager took off. John joined Silver, calmly taking her arm as though nothing violent had just happened.

"Did you need to get something at the bakery?" he asked.

"A loaf of fresh bread appealed to me a minute ago. Now I seem to have lost my appetite."

"We'll buy some anyway."

After buying bread and muffins, they continued down the street, and Silver asked John why he hadn't turned the kid over to the police.

"He didn't have a knife or a gun. He was just bluffing his way through a holdup that was probably his first. He was more frightened than you were."

"He certainly was after you talked to him. What did you say?"

He looked down at her. "You don't want to know. Hopefully, it's enough to persuade him that crime doesn't pay." He turned toward the entrance of a store. "We should be able to find what we want in here."

Slightly bemused, Silver followed him into the store without further comment. He was treating the whole incident casually, so she tried to do the same.

As they wandered around the store Silver quickly realized she and John had different ideas about the kind of video game they were going to buy. She had in mind something that made a few bleeps and blonks to get the neighbors' attention. John's intention was to practically buy out the electronics section of the store.

Then she remembered he'd had no toys as a child, and started piling even more games onto the counter.

After John unpacked the games in her living room, the hallway outside her apartment was barely passable. If Tina and Ronnie peeked out of their door, they would have to notice the empty boxes and figure out what had been in them.

John had checked the names on the mail-boxes in the lobby and "Burns" was listed on the apartment across from Silver. Tina and Ronnie's mother still lived in the apartment. They had no way of knowing if her children were there or not.

John had the control box hooked up to the television in the time it took for Silver to make coffee and put the fresh muffins on a plate. He was putting a game cartridge into the machine when she brought a mug of coffee to him. Music started along with the game, and she saw a funny little man jump over mushroom-shaped creatures. Then he hopped on top of one of the mushrooms and she saw that John had earned some points.

Sitting on the floor beside him, she asked, "How do you know how to play this?"

"Directions." His gaze remained on the screen. "They're on the coffee table. I glanced through them while you were in the kitch-en."

She picked up the booklet and proceeded to give John instructions on how to play the game, even though he didn't want them. Her instructions were either a couple of seconds too late or said with so much excitement, he didn't understand what she was telling him to do. She began to gesture with her hands, brushing against him, driving him nuts.

After he lost his last man, he tossed the control aside and tumbled Silver over onto her back. Leaning over her, he growled, "You made me lose. Now you have to pay a forfeit."

"How did I make you lose?" she asked, her heart racing as she felt his weight pressing her into the carpet. "You weren't paying attention to any of my advice, so why is it my fault you lost?"

John pushed away from her, taking the time to close the drapes. He wanted to tempt the neighboring kids with the video game, not educate them with the facts of life.

Coming back to Silver, he lay down on top of her again. Lowering his head, he nuzzled the soft skin of her throat. "You are a powerful distraction." His teeth nipped her soft earlobe, then his tongue left a moist trail down her neck. "I'd much rather play with you than a miniature plumber."

"Is that what that figure is supposed to be?" She slid her arms over his shoulders and back, reveling in the feel of his hard body. "Do you think I'm an easier opponent than the little plumber?"

"There's no contest." His voice lost its

teasing tone when she tilted her hips into his aroused body. "In this case, we're both winners."

He kissed her, and the world spun away. Silver met his desire fully, eager to experience the whirlwind of pleasure she knew she would find in John's arms.

He purposely slowed her down, wanting each moment to last. He wanted to imprint her scent, each touch, every taste into his mind. He'd wanted her for so long, he needed to savor every moment with her.

As he smoothed his hand over her, he realized she somehow sensed his wishes. Her body moved slowly against his, inciting and exciting him in a slow burn. Her lips followed the path her hands made as she unbuttoned his shirt. He groaned deep in his throat when he felt her fingers on the fastener of his jeans.

She was going to drive him crazy, but he didn't care as long as she went with him. He set out to make sure of it.

The barriers of clothing were swept away along with his wishes to prolong the loving. His mouth was voracious, his hands demanding and urgent. Desire writhed through him and into her until he could no longer wait to claim her fire.

His arms clamped her to him as he rolled onto his back.

Silver stared down at him, suddenly lost in the blaze of primitive hunger reflected in his eyes. Her gaze locked with his when she raised her hips and took him inside her.

He whispered her name, and it was the last thing Silver remembered as she fell into the flames burning between them.

The bait was in place, but for the next two days there wasn't a single nibble. They left the apartment with a great deal of noise in the evenings, but none of the little traps John had set had been disturbed when they returned.

Silver enjoyed the evenings with him, going to see the *Phantom of the Opera* at the Majestic Theatre and a two-hanky movie the next night. There were no other incidents like the attempted mugging, although the city at night held dangers she didn't like to think about. With John, it didn't matter. She was safe with him in the city he seemed to know too well.

Silver was aware that John couldn't stay in New York indefinitely, although he didn't seem impatient when nothing happened. He used her phone, her fax, and her computer to keep in contact with his office a couple of hours every morning. She could hear the printer running occasionally and the low rumble of his voice.

By the end of the third day, she had cleaned every surface of her apartment, had baked a batch of peanut-butter cookies, and had run out of things to do. John was holed up in her spare room with the computer. She had taken a plate of cookies and a cup of coffee to him an hour earlier and had received an abstracted grunt of thanks in return.

Since it looked like a working day for him, she decided to go to the grocery store. She had never been very good at sitting around doing nothing, so she took a jacket out of the closet.

As she was slipping it on, she jumped in surprise when she suddenly had assistance.

John's hands settled on her shoulders after he turned her around to face him. "Where are you going?"

"To the grocery store."

He reached past her into the closet and took out his own jacket. "I'll go with you. I could use some fresh air."

"Let me know if you find any," she murmured. "You don't have to come with me if you have work to do. The store is just down the street. I go there all the time."

"And this time I'm going with you."

She grinned. "I know why you want to come. We're almost out of ice cream and you want to make sure I get all of your favorite flavors."

"That too," he agreed. "But mainly I want to see that you don't run into any ambitious young men who have designs on your delectable person."

"And to think I've survived in New York without you for the last four years."

"It boggles the mind," he said easily, and opened the door for her.

As she stepped into the hallway, the door opposite opened. Silver caught a glimpse of large blue eyes and a wisp of blond hair just before the door started to shut.

"Hello, Tina."

The door remained open a couple of inches. Silver felt John's fingers around her hand, but he didn't speak.

"I've missed seeing you, Tina. I thought you might have moved away."

"I go to school."

"Of course, I forgot that." The door didn't move so much as an inch either way.

"Who's he?" The little girl's eyes darted to John.

Silver gave the answer John had told her to give if anyone asked about him being in her apartment. "He's working on my computer."

The door opened enough for Tina to stick her head through the opening. "I didn't break it," she said defensively.

"I never thought you did." John again squeezed her hand, and she proceeded cautiously. "I just purchased one of those video games that are so popular. I'm not very good at it, but maybe you'd like to try it—" The door was shut suddenly, and Silver finished her sentence lamely: " . . . sometime."

John directed her toward the elevator and punched the button. Silver looked up, surprised at the expression on his face.

"You look like the cat who's just helped himself to a whole bowl of cream. I don't see anything to be so smug about."

"That's because you weren't standing where I was. Does her brother, Ronnie, have hair that sticks straight up about three inches in front, making him look like a bad brush?"

"Yes. Why?"

"He was standing behind the door while

you and Tina were having your little chat. We'll see if he takes the bait while we're out of the apartment."

They stepped into the elevator, and she asked, "And if he doesn't take the bait while we're gone?"

"Then we wait longer."

"John, I know how difficult it's becoming for you to run Knight Enterprises from here. We're not going to be able to wait indefinitely for the kids across the hall or whoever it might be to pay another visit."

"Trying to get rid of me?" he asked carefully.

"You know better than that."

"No," he said. "I don't." He took her arm. "One of these days maybe you'll get around to telling me."

"I'll tell you anything you want to know," she offered, hoping it would give him the same idea. "I'm the chatty one in this twosome. You're the sphinx."

John maneuvered her against the back wall of the elevator. He touched the side of her neck with his lips, smiling when he heard her gasp.

"Do you have any idea how it affects a man when a woman responds to him like you do?"

"You've given me a few hints during the last couple of days," she said weakly. On impulse, she reached up to trace the line of his curving mouth. "I've also caught glimpses of a smile a few times. I wasn't sure you knew how before."

He wasn't either. For the last six years he hadn't had much to smile about. Until Silver.

The elevator stopped and he drew back a little. Looking at her, he felt another smile curve his lips. "Would an independent woman of the nineties be insulted if a man told her she could make a sphinx smile?"

"Not this one."

He placed his hand at the back of her waist when the doors slid open. "I don't know why, but it's true."

Silver felt her insides warm with the knowledge that she made him happy. He didn't realize it yet, but hopefully someday he would. Lord knows, he was becoming extremely important to her own happiness.

NINE

The piece of paper John had left partially resting on the video game's control pad had been removed by the time John and Silver returned with the groceries they'd purchased. Silver had been skeptical about such an obvious ploy, but John had pointed out to her that these two kids were not the most professional of burglars. They hadn't noticed two suitcases inside the door the first night they'd arrived from Kentucky.

Now that she knew who had been responsible for the various pranks, she was hesitant about scaring them in order to get them to stop.

"They're only young kids, John. Couldn't we just talk to their mother and have her stop them? Threatening them with Nick in uniform, fingerprints, all seems a bit strong since they haven't taken or broken anything."

"What they're doing is wrong, Silver. They have to learn that. Not only are they breaking and entering, they frightened you to the extent that you drove all the way to Raleigh to get help. This can't go on."

"That bothers you more than the breaking and entering, doesn't it?"

"That they scared you? Hell, yes. No one does that and gets away with it. The only reason I'm not being harder on them is because what they did brought you to me. And remember, we'll be doing them a favor by showing them they can't get away with this. If they get away with breaking into someone's house, they're going to think they can get away with something else. Take it from someone who's been there. One stolen apple, then two. Next the cart."

"Scenes of your misspent youth, Lomax?"

"Something like that," he said with a faint smile. "While you were wrapped in cashmere and lace and being pushed in a pram by your English nanny, I was one of those tough kids on the street corner with a cigarette hanging out of the corner of his mouth and a chip on his shoulder a mile wide."

"So you were a tough guy, were you?" She slipped her arms around his neck, pleased when he responded by placing his hands at her waist. He wasn't evading her this time. "You've come a long way since then."

He suddenly lifted her in his arms and carried her toward her bedroom.

"So have we," he murmured against her mouth. "And we're going further."

As much as she wanted to hear more about his past, she willingly fell into the realm of passion between them, hoping he would reveal more another time.

That night they made a lot of extra noise leaving the apartment again. Just outside the door, for the benefit of anyone listening, Silver loudly asked John if he had the keys, adding that they were going to be late getting home. Their little act didn't cause the Burnses' door to open, but they went through with their planned charade anyway.

They ate at a small restaurant where the food had to compete with the decor and lost. Not that it mattered. They both paid more attention to their watches than to their meal. More than that, though, they were together. That was everything.

The agreed-upon time came as they were about to order coffee. John tossed money on the table and took Silver's arm to escort her out of the restaurant.

They had almost reached the door when John's fingers tightened painfully around her arm and he suddenly stopped walking. Silver glanced up at him and saw an expression on his face she'd never seen before. She was reminded of the look someone might have if he'd just seen something he wanted badly but couldn't have.

She followed the direction of his gaze and saw an older couple sitting at a table. Silver guessed the woman to be in her late fifties. Her face was pale, her smile wan, yet her eyes revealed an odd hope Silver couldn't begin to understand. The man beside her sat stiffly in his chair, his faded gray eyes staring at John as though he were an apparition.

Just as abruptly as he had stopped walking, John started again, drawing Silver along with him. They had taken only two steps when the woman got to her feet, nearly tipping over her chair in her haste.

"John. Please don't leave."

She had spoken quietly, but John stopped as though she'd shouted his name. For a few seconds he stood rigid, his head slightly bowed.

Uncertain what was happening, Silver placed her hand on his arm and stepped closer, letting him know she was there.

It took the older woman saying his name again before he reacted.

He slowly turned and faced the woman, who was still standing near the table. "Hello, Martha," he said. His gaze slowly slid to the older man. "Duff."

The man pushed his chair back and got to his feet with an effort, then extended his hand toward John. John stared at the man's hand as though it were a foreign object he wasn't sure he should take.

"John." The man's voice was hoarse with emotion. "It's been too long. Please."

Maybe it was the pleading note in the man's voice that got through to John, or perhaps the look of entreaty in his eyes. Whatever the reason, John finally raised his hand and clasped Duff's.

For several seconds both men stared at each other, then simultaneously released their grips.

John broke the tense silence in his typical

blunt manner. "Does this mean you no longer blame me for Paul's death?"

The older woman gasped, and the man looked shocked, as if John had just shot him.

"Blame you? Why . . . why would you think . . . ?"

"You turned your back on me at Paul's funeral," John answered, "as though you blamed for me his death. I understood and stayed away. Are you saying we should forget all that as though it didn't happen?"

The older man shook his head. "You mis-understood. I didn't turn my back on you that day. I couldn't face the sight of his casket that you were standing near. I've been to too many funerals for fellow police officers and friends. Burying a son is one of the hardest things I'd ever had to do, and I admit I did not do it well."

John stared hard at the man, seeing his anguish but not the blame he had believed was there. All these years, he thought with regret. He felt the heavy weight he'd been carrying around lifted from his conscience. Still, he felt compelled to ask, "Are you sure this is what you want, Duff?"

The man nodded abruptly. "I was wrong, but so were you. I should have made it clear we never blamed you for Paul's death, and you shouldn't have disappeared from our lives without giving us a chance to explain. But that's all in the past. Let's leave it at that and go on from here."

"From losing your son? I don't see how we can."

Martha put her hand on John's arm and said quietly, "We lost two sons when Paul died. We buried him and you disappeared. We can't change the past, but we can do something about the present and possibly the future." She lifted her hand to his face and smiled. "Come home, Johnny."

At her familiar, once-loved touch, all his good memories of the Mariners swept over him, blotting out—for the moment—the more recent pain-filled ones. He stepped forward and wrapped his arms around Martha. When he finally raised his head, his voice was husky with emotion. "Do you still fix a pot roast every Friday?"

"Yes," she said, her eyes brimming with tears, happy tears. She glanced at Silver, who was standing just behind John. "You're welcome anytime, and you're welcome to bring your friend. I always have plenty."

John held out his hand to Silver. When she

clasped it, he drew her forward. He slipped his arm around her waist and held her to his side.

"This is Silver," he announced as though her last name wasn't necessary. "Silver, this is Duff and Martha Mariner."

The names clicked instantly in Silver's mind. Paul Mariner, she knew, had been John's partner when he'd been on the police force. She filled in the blanks, the few she had, and smiled at Paul Mariner's parents. Duff was the policeman who had taken John off the streets.

"It's a pleasure to meet you," she said, shaking hands with them both.

"We need to get going," John said.

Disappointment clouded both Duff and Martha's expression until he added, "We'll come over Friday night if that's all right with you."

Like magic, their forlorn faces lit up like bright candles, and they let them go without further complaint.

Outside, John kept Silver at his side and raised his free arm to summon a cab. Within seconds, one pulled to the curb. During the drive, John remained silent, his hand grasping hers tightly.

Silver finally spoke when they were in the elevator. "We could have stayed if you'd wanted to, John."

"I know." He applied pressure to the small of her back when the doors slid open. "It was enough."

She thought about his words as they walked down the carpeted hallway to her apartment. The tense minutes in the restaurant seemed to have lifted an intensely heavy burden from his soul.

She wondered if he would ever tell her what had happened to cause the pain between him and his partner's parents. He was so damned reticent about himself, except physically, and she was becoming impatient to have all the walls torn down between them.

When they reached her door, he held up his hand to stop her from putting her key in the lock. He listened for a few seconds, then gave her a crooked smile. "Mario is trying to save the Princess."

Not knowing what he was talking about seemed to be the way things were going that night.

"Good," she said, making it sound as though she knew what he meant.

He chuckled and kissed her lightly, almost

playfully. She realized he was actually enjoying this.

He grinned at her. "Let's get this out of the way."

He opened the door and pushed her inside, following closely behind her.

When they exploded into the living room, the two kids who had been sitting in front of the television jumped up, accidentally bumping into each other in their panicked rush to be anywhere but where they were.

Ronnie tried to protect his sister, jerking her behind him and causing her to spill the bag of jelly beans she clasped tightly in her hand.

John latched onto the front of Ronnie's shirt and pushed him toward the couch.

"Sit," he ordered. "Both of you. Sit down."

He only had to glance at Tina for her to plop down beside her brother, her frightened gaze going to Silver as though pleading silently for her help.

John clicked off the video game and the television, then stood in front of them, his legs spread apart, his hands clamped on his hips.

He directed his gaze at Ronnie. "Explain what you're doing here."

The teenager's spiked hair stabbed the air when he jerked up his head. "We haven't done anything wrong."

John counted off a series of offenses, starting with breaking and entering and ending in car theft. It was an impressive list.

"I didn't steal Miss Knight's car," Ronnie said, taking exception to that charge. "I only used it."

"Without her permission. It's picky, but that means the car was stolen."

"I put gas back in it a couple of days later when I got the money," Ronnie said defensively.

"I bet you don't even have a driver's license. Another offense."

Ronnie's gaze settled on the stylishly torn knees of his jeans, and he picked at a couple of threads. "I'm only fifteen." His head came back up. "But I'm a good driver. I learned on my grandfather's farm. He let me drive his tractor. I never hurt Miss Knight's car."

Silver stepped over to stand beside John. "Why did you take my car, Ronnie? And please don't say you had a hot date."

Ronnie remained stubbornly silent, but Tina turned her wide blue eyes on Silver. "He went to look for our mom, Miss Knight.

He didn't have any money for taxis, so he had to take your car."

The whole story came gushing out with Ronnie defensive to the last and Tina weepy and apologetic. Their divorced mother occasionally didn't come home from work, sometimes for a couple of days at a stretch. Other times she brought men friends home and told the children to play in the lobby or hall for several hours, and usually late at night. Instead, after Ronnie discovered that the key to their apartment worked in Silver's lock if jiggled just right, they would slip into her apartment. They knew she was usually in bed by eleven, and Tina admitted she liked knowing Silver was there, that they weren't completely alone.

John looked down at the pair. "You might not have meant to, but you scared Miss Knight when things happened in her apartment she didn't understand."

All eyes stayed on John as he went to the phone and made a call. A few seconds later he said, "Nick, we caught the kids who've been bothering Silver." After a brief description of the two criminals, John said abruptly, "Right. I'll bring them in." When he hung up, he looked at the two by now badly frightened kids.

"Let's go. I'm taking you to the police station."

"You can't arrest us," Ronnie said. "You aren't a cop."

"I was and a friend is. Now, either move of your own free will or I'll help you and you won't like it."

They moved.

Silver started to follow, but John shook his head. "You stay here. Nick and I'll handle this."

"But—"

"I'll be back as soon as I can." He cut off any further protest she was about to make. "It has to be this way. Trust me."

Since she did trust him, she nodded. "All right. I don't like it, but I'll stay here."

As she watched him leave the apartment with her two young neighbors, Silver felt immense relief that her nightmare was over. More importantly, she could devote all her energy to John now. She decided not to wait any longer to hear about John's past. It was time to force the issue, to ask him to allow her into his past. Meeting the Mariners seemed to have settled a painful part of his life. She wanted, needed him to share this important part, to share himself with her.

Silver had fallen asleep on the couch by the time John returned. He saw she had changed into a silky nightgown and robe. Her shiny black hair was spread out across the cushion, and one hand lay on her stomach while the other was curled beside her face.

She was so incredibly beautiful, he thought in a possessive rush. And his.

He hunkered down and let his fingers play with a lock of her hair as he enjoyed the privilege of looking at her as long as he wished.

And that was forever.

As her hair curled softly around his finger, he realized he would rather face ten hoods in a dark alley than let Silver go. She had been a part of his life for fourteen years and hopefully for the rest of it as well.

He was just going to have to make sure she remained with him.

Even though she was sleeping soundly, he took the chance of waking her by slipping his arms under her to carry her to bed. He would have left her on the couch if there had been room for him beside her. Since there wasn't, he was taking her to bed. His nights of sleeping alone were over.

She opened her eyes when he lifted her to his chest. "You're home," she said simply.

He held her closer. "Now I am."

"What happened to Ronnie and Tina?" she asked as he carried her to the bedroom.

He laid her on the bed. "I'll tell you all about it in the morning."

She pushed herself into a sitting position as he began to unbutton his shirt. "I can't wait until tomorrow."

He shucked off his shirt, but left his jeans on and sat down on the bed. "I've always known you were a demanding woman, Silver Knight. A lesser man would be too intimidated to take you on. Lucky for you, I'm not."

"Are you going to tell me what you did with those children or not?"

"I guess I'm going to have to if I want any sleep tonight." He jerked his head in the direction of the neighboring apartment. "Nick delivered them to their mother along with a severe warning about leaving them alone and that charges could be brought against her for neglecting her children. At the police station he scared the hell out of the kids by booking them. It was unofficial, since you weren't pressing charges, but they didn't know that. They had their mug shots taken, were fingerprinted, and placed in a holding cell for a while before Nick took them home."

"So it's over?"

"It's over if they don't break into your apartment again."

"I wasn't sure at first that the way you were handling the situation was the right way. Then I realized you knew exactly what you were doing because you'd been through something similar."

He reached for her hand. "The problem with getting involved with a smart woman is staying one step ahead of her."

"My parents walked side by side. That's the way it should be and rarely is."

"And if that's the way it's going to be for us, I'm going to have to spill my guts. Is that it?"

"I don't have to know everything about you, John. I'm not giving you an ultimatum. You can tell me about the situation with the Mariners or not. I don't have to know your past, but I want to understand."

After staring at her slender hand, he shifted his position to sit beside her, leaning against the head of the bed. He took possession of her hand again.

"Duff was the policeman who took me off

the streets. He really busted me and ran me through the mill at the station, leaving me in a holding cell for about twenty-four hours with some drunks and a couple of hard-core bad guys. I had plenty of time to enjoy the fun and thrills of being locked up. Then he gave me an alternative to the streets by taking me to his home. Martha gave me a bar of soap with instructions to wash the grime of the streets off my skin. It took a bit longer for the real stain of my life on the streets to wear off. I stayed with them and went back to school."

"Where were your parents?"

"I was living with an uncle after my parents were killed in a car accident when I was eight. His idea of parenting consisted of leaving a couple of bucks on the kitchen counter for food. I fell in with a rough crowd and probably would eventually have been dead or in prison."

"If it hadn't been for Duff Mariner."

He nodded. "I owe him a great deal . . . and I paid him back by getting his son killed."

She could feel the tension in his hands enfolding hers. "Tell me what happened."

"Dammit, Silver!" he exploded, dropping her hand and sliding off the bed. "I hate to even think about that night."

He walked to the window and stared out at the lighted city. Silver waited. She debated going to him, but some inner instinct made her stay where she was.

John slid his hands into his back pockets, his gaze remaining on the New York night. "Paul was the Mariners' only child. He grew up hearing about his father's great career on the police force and decided to follow in some pretty big footsteps. After he came out of the academy, he was assigned to be my partner. I think Duff pulled some strings, but I never asked him. Paul was a raw rookie with more guts than good sense. One night we got called to a convenience store that was being robbed. We stopped the robbery and were handcuffing the perps when Paul got stabbed. He had neglected to pat down his suspect, and the guy had a knife. It was over in seconds, and I couldn't do a damn thing to stop it."

And the guilt was lasting a lifetime, thought Silver.

"How many suspects were you covering?"

"Three." He turned and smiled faintly. "I appreciate the defense, Silver, but he was my responsibility."

She slid off the bed and walked across the floor to him. She didn't touch him yet.

"He was his own responsibility, John. What kind of a policeman would he have made if his partner always had to do his own job and Paul's too?"

John turned to her and placed his hands at her waist. "So loyal," he said, shaking his head as though he found her response utterly amazing. "Even a tarnished knight doesn't make a difference to you, does it?"

"If you had taken Paul's death lightly, then you would be tarnished deep inside. You've made your peace with the Mariners. Don't you think it's time to make peace with yourself?"

He drew her into his arms and held her against him for a long time. Silver slipped her arms around his waist and silently soothed him with her nearness and support.

Finally, John loosened his hold and cupped her face in his hands. "I didn't think it was possible for me to love you more than I have over the years. I was wrong."

Her sudden gasp was muffled by his mouth covering hers in a devastatingly intimate kiss. Before she was given a chance to say anything, she was carried back to the bed and lowered onto the sheets. John lay down beside her and again staked his claim on her.

Silver was swept into the heat and passion

willingly, his glorious words reverberating through her, filling her with a joy unlike anything she'd ever felt. He loved her!

Her hands impatiently worked their way between their bodies to the clasp of his jeans.

John broke away from her mouth to look at her. He didn't speak. He couldn't. He was so full of her, yet not enough. He needed to lose himself in her warmth. As long as he had her, he would never be cold and alone again.

When she made a sound of frustration as the clasp of his jeans proved stubborn, he smiled into her eyes.

Less than a minute later all of their clothes had been swept away and nothing was between them except a deep hunger being fed by touch and taste. John was relentless as his hands incited, his mouth ravenous as he drove her and himself to impossible heights.

When he finally filled her, he heard her cry out his name, and he fell into the abyss of love for this wonderful woman.

Silver held on and toppled into the fiery aftermath.

TEN

The phone rang early the following morning, and as it happened to be on his side, John answered it.

"Lomax?" a male voice shouted. "What the hell?"

John blinked twice and tried to climb out of the sound sleep he'd been in. "King?"

"Hell, yes. Silver's father, in case you happened to have forgotten. What in blue thunder are you doing in her apartment in what I think is the middle of the night over there?"

"Well, I was sleeping until the phone woke me. What do you want? Silver's asleep."

After a few sputtered words that could have gotten him disconnected by any fussy telephone operator, King finally said, "Have you ever heard about marriage? What in hell are you doing in bed with my daughter?"

Silver showed signs of waking. Lowering his voice, John said, "You don't really expect me to tell you, do you?"

Apparently King detected the humor in John's voice. He sputtered some more, then said, "I expect you to marry my only daughter, dammit. If you don't after—"

"King, if you'll listen—"

Silver's eyes opened. She turned her head and saw John holding the phone away from his ear.

"Who is it?" she asked.

"Your father. He wasn't expecting me to answer the phone. For once, he knows what time it is."

She groaned and covered her head with her pillow, then removed it when she heard John say her father's name twice in an attempt to enter into a conversation that was momentarily one-sided.

Silver threw off the covers and dove for the phone, yanking it from John's hand. "King, shut up!"

That worked. "This comes under none of your business," she went on. "Why are you calling?"

John frowned in puzzlement as she suddenly laughed and said, "You're kidding. That's great. Of course I'll be there."

She listened again, then said, "I don't know. I'll ask him."

"Ask me what?" John said.

She pressed the fingers of one hand to his lips to silence him. He couldn't resist kissing those fingers, then licking them. She scowled at him, and he chuckled.

Finally, she said into the phone, "I don't know if he knows how to play chess, and I don't care. I love you dearly, Dad, but in this one instance you're going to have to butt out." Her eyes widened and she gulped. "Grandchildren?" She wouldn't meet John's gaze. "I'll phone when I know more."

Leaning across John's chest, she slammed the receiver down before burying her flushed face in her hand.

John took away her hand. "Grandchildren? Is there something you should be telling me?"

"Not if it's about being pregnant. King said he's getting impatient for some grandchildren. Michael is getting married next week. That's what King wanted to tell us. Michael can fulfill King's dream for a grandchild and leave me out of it."

John propped himself against the head of the bed and gave her a strange look. "Why? Don't you like children?"

"I love children, but I don't plan on having any just because my father wants a grand-child."

"Are you having doubts about my ability as a father, considering the way I was brought up?"

She stared at him as though he'd lost his mind. "I think you'd be a wonderful father. It's four in the morning. Why are we talking about children at this particular moment? King wants me at Michael's wedding next week and wants you to come, too, considering . . . well, considering."

"Considering I'm sleeping with his daughter? If you're going, so am I."

Silver bit her lip, wishing this conversation was taking place after she'd had a full night's sleep.

"I'm not sure that's such a good idea."

He looked at her, completely stupefied. "Why not?"

She didn't care for the tone of his voice. "After tonight, you know darn well my father will hound you about marrying me. It would be awful for you."

"Since that's exactly what I'm planning to do, I don't see the problem."

Silver sat up so abruptly, she nearly toppled off the bed. John grabbed her and lifted her onto his lap. Because of the coolness of the room, she'd slipped her nightgown back on before falling asleep, and he had to tug the skirt out of his way so he could place his palm on her bare thigh.

"Why are you so surprised?" he asked. "I love you, remember? I want you in my life. Dammit, you are my life."

If that was a proposal of marriage, it needed work, she thought abstractedly.

"This might be the nineties, but a woman still expects to be asked. At least I do."

His hand cupped the side of her face, compelling her to meet his gaze. "Silver Knight, I have loved you for what feels like forever. We're going to spend the rest of our lives together. For the children's sake and King's, and your brothers, we should make it legal. Will you marry me?"

She stared at him. "You're serious!"

"I've never been more serious in my life."

She bit her lip. "I haven't told you why I'm dithering about the decision to go to Japan with my company."

"I'd rather hear the answer to my question first, but go ahead and tell me."

"For a supposedly independent woman, it's not easy for me to admit I'm not the ambitious, career-hungry woman I'm cracked up to be."

"You don't have to work if you don't want to, Silver. That's up to you."

She looked down at her hand nervously pleating the edge of the sheet. " Lately, I've been thinking of my mother's life, how happy she was to simply be there for King and for my brothers and me. She was warm, caring, fun, strict, but not too stern. I know she used to worry about my competitive nature when I tried to keep up with the boys."

"Exactly what are you getting at, Silver? I told you it doesn't matter to me if you want to work. As long as you're home every night with me, I won't complain."

"That's just it." She raised her head to look at him. "I don't think I want to work in an office juggling figures, phone calls, and people's money. I want to bake cookies and raise babies. I've discovered I'm more like my mother than I thought."

He trailed a finger along her jawline. "She

was a beautiful woman and so are you. I don't have a problem with you staying home to raise our children. Now, are you going to answer me or do I have to ask again?"

She flung her arms around his neck. "Yes. I'll marry you so my brothers and my father won't nag you forever."

"I appreciate that," he drawled. "I was sort of hoping for another reason from you, though."

She smiled into his eyes. "I love you, John Lomax. I think I have since I was fourteen, but nothing like the way I do now and not even close to how much I will tomorrow."

His eyes gleamed with satisfaction just before he kissed her.

Silver met his need with her own, and their loving took on a new, exciting quality now that their lives were going to be forever linked by the unbreakable bonds of love.

Because of their late night, they slept longer than usual. When the phone rang again, John seriously debated throwing the damn thing across the room. Since it was Silver's phone, though, he answered it after one ring so she wouldn't be awakened.

As he listened to his secretary his gaze went to Silver. She remained asleep beside him, her glorious hair tousled by his hands and by sleep. If it were up to him, he would never let her out of his sight again.

Finally, he said quietly, "I'll let you know in an hour, Olive."

He quietly hung up the phone and eased his long length out of bed without waking Silver. Within minutes he was in the shower.

An hour later Silver woke to find herself alone. After slipping on a robe, she went searching for John. The first thing she saw when she stepped into the living room was John's suitcase sitting on the floor. He was seated on the couch talking on the phone. When he hung up, he turned to see her scowling at him.

"And to think I get to see that lovely smiling face every morning once we're married."

"Why the suitcase?" she asked, ignoring his attempt to tease her into a smile.

He stood and walked over to her, taking her hand and drawing her back with him to the couch. "We need to talk about that." He urged her to sit, then sat beside her. "Olive phoned about an hour ago with a problem I have to handle in person in Raleigh. My first thought was to make reservations for two and take you back with me, but since we're leaving for England in four days, I realized you might want to tie up loose ends here before we leave."

"Loose ends?"

"There are a few practical matters to take care of, such as telling Tremaine, Darcy, and Tremaine to send you a postcard from Japan. Such as deciding what you want to do with this apartment. Such as packing for the trip to England and later to Raleigh."

"It sounds like I'm going to be busy. So I'm moving to Raleigh?"

"Would you mind? It would be one hell of a commute from here if you wanted to stay in New York."

Silver brushed her hair back from her face. "Do they need an ex–financial consultant in Raleigh?"

"I do," he said.

Almost as soon as John left, Silver realized how accustomed she'd become to having him in her apartment, in her bed, in her daily life. The next two days seemed to creep by, even though she was busy every waking minute.

She had the locks changed as John had

ordered, gave her final notice to Tremaine, Darcy, and Tremaine, and got rid of everything she didn't plan to take to Raleigh.

John's nightly phone calls were indecently long, for he was as unhappy with their separation as Silver was. Business matters were taking longer than he'd hoped, and he didn't see how he could get away until late Thursday. Their plane reservations to England were for Friday afternoon, leaving from New York.

By Wednesday evening, Silver had reached the end of her endurance. For an extremely independent woman, she was chagrined to realize how much she needed to be with John.

She tossed her plump organizer book, which she'd lived with the last couple of days, into one of the boxes to be shipped to Raleigh and grabbed the phone.

Early Thursday morning, John was standing in front of his bathroom mirror lathering the lower half of his face when he heard someone rapping on his front door.

Cursing succinctly under his breath, he grabbed his black robe and slipped it on as he walked to the door. Ginger was the only person he knew who would be pounding on his door at seven in the morning. He only hoped he had what she wanted to borrow, although if it was food, she might be out of luck. He'd eaten stale sandwiches on the run the last couple of days in order to get everything done. He was even out of ice cream.

He thought of Silver as he threw back the lock, wishing with every fiber of his being that she would be the one knocking on his door. Why should now be any different? he groused as he yanked the door open.

For a few seconds he simply stared at the woman standing in front of him. She was dressed in a brilliantly colored Hawaiian-print shirt, which included every color of the rainbow and a few extra. Metallic-blue slacks toned down the outfit, but not by much.

"Silver?"

"Oh, good! You haven't forgotten me. Can I come in?" She gave his robe a once-over. "I don't mind that you're not dressed for company."

John lunged.

Silver laughed.

She threw her arms around his neck when he lifted her off her feet and across his threshold. He kicked the door shut without letting go of her. The desperate way he was feeling, he might never let her go again. The pine-scented lather on his face was cold and frothy against her skin when he kissed her with relentless hunger.

He finally raised his head, his eyes glittering with love when he looked down at her. He grinned when he saw her face had more of his shaving cream on it than his did. Using the towel around his neck, he gently wiped her face, then his own.

"What are you doing here?"

"You might want to sit down for this." She took his hand and drew him over to his couch.

His fingers tightened around hers. "You better not have changed your mind about us, Silver. I love you, dammit. We belong together."

"I love you too, which is why I wanted to give you a whole day to think about marrying me in England on Saturday instead of waiting until later. Actually, it was King's idea. I phoned the Mariners. Luckily, they both have passports and are thrilled to be invited. All I have to do is call them back. I've made reservations for them on the same plane we'll be on just in case you said yes. Not only is Michael getting married, but Ryder and Tyler and their prospective brides are tying the knot at the same time. King thinks we should join them. What do you think?"

"I think I'm in a lot of trouble with King Knight as a father-in-law, but I don't have anything against making you Mrs. Jonathan Xavier Lomax as soon as possible."

"Xavier might do it," she teased. "But since my middle name is Morgaine, I don't have a lot of room to criticize, do I?"

"Not much. I forgot I'll be joining the Knights of the Round Table."

"A daunting prospect, but I will make it up to you by loving you for the rest of your life."

He kissed her again. "You got a deal, as long as I don't have to wear a suit of armor when I marry a Knight. It would make for a noisy honeymoon."

"No suit of armor, although I can practically guarantee King will insist on a tux." She laughed at the face he made. "I'm giving up a trip to Japan. You can wear a tuxedo for a few hours."

"For an independent woman, you're giving up a lot. Are you sure being with me is what you want?"

She grew serious. "The past three days

have shown me how empty my life is without you. Nothing is as important as being with you. The rest is trimming. You are the foundation."

John lifted her in his arms and carried her to his bedroom. For the first time since taking over Knight Enterprises, he was late for work.

EPILOGUE

King fussed with the formal tie he'd attempted to fold and knot, his irritation making it worse.

"Damn nonsense," he muttered, yanking one end in order to start all over again. When there was a rap on his dressing-room door, he grumbled, "Come in."

The door opened and his daughter walked in. She took one look at him and understood the problem.

"I'll tie that for you", she said.

His cranky mood disappeared instantly. "Is everybody in place?"

She nodded. "The boys and John are lined up like gorgeous penguins in Mother's rose garden waiting for you to escort all of us brides there. For once, the sun has decided to shine, and all the guests are seated. I was sent to hurry you along."

He gazed lovingly at his daughter, who was wearing her mother's wedding dress. He touched a bit of lace surrounding her neck.

"I wish your mother could have been here today."

"I know, Dad. We all wish she could have been here too." She put the finishing touches on his bow tie. "I like to think she's with us in spirit."

He smiled. "You look very much like her, especially in that dress. You also look happier than I've seen in a long time. It's in your eyes and the way you smile. The man I chose for you makes you happy. That pleases me." His smile widened. "You know how I like being right."

She rolled her eyes. "We all know. And remember what we all agreed last night, Dad. You were an excellent matchmaker, but you're going to leave the procreation of your grandchildren to us. You promised no more interference."

He looked affronted. "I wouldn't think of it. As long as you all get on with it. From all the hand-holding, kissing, and disappearing acts going on around here, though, I don't think I have a thing to worry about. I have great faith in nature taking its course."

Silver slipped her arm through his and walked with him to the door. "Even though you felt you had to give fate a little push by matching your children with their mates."

"It turned out perfect. You met Emma, Cassidy, and Hannah last night and saw how your brothers wouldn't let them out of their sight." He ushered her through his bedroom and into the hall, her long skirt swishing softly with each step. "If I waited for you kids to get around to pairing off, I'd have been too old to play with my grandchildren."

"You'll never be too old, Dad." Silver stood at the top of the stairs and saw her future sisters-in-law gathered in the foyer waiting for her and King.

Alvilda, King's housekeeper, was in her element, fussing and murmuring, "Oh, dear," over and over as she brushed out a wrinkle and adjusted a flower in a bouquet.

Like Silver, Cassidy Harrold was wearing her own mother's wedding dress for her marriage to Michael. Silver knew she would be wearing denim almost perpetually once they returned to his Montana ranch, but not today.

Emma Valerian, Tyler's bride, wore a dress

made of satin without an ounce of lace, the simple style emphasizing her slender frame and stunning eyes.

Hannah Corbett—whom Silver had called a brave woman for taking on her stubborn and pushy brother Ryder—was wearing a white leather dress trimmed in beads and with long fringe brushing against her doeskin moccasins, in keeping with her Native American heritage.

A few minutes later, the four women walked across the grass toward the decorated arbor in the rose garden, where four men were lined up waiting for them.

Once the vows began, King had to clear his throat as emotion nearly overwhelmed him. A chapter in his family's life was ending and another was beginning. He glanced around the grounds of Knight's Keep. Soon there would be children's laughter filling the air. Bringing his gaze back to the wedding ceremony, he smiled as his sons took their brides' hands and John clasped Silver's hands. The sun glinted off gold rings slipped onto fingers.

King began to look forward to the expensive champagne he'd ordered for the reception, hoping he could sneak at least a sip to toast the finest work he'd ever accomplished.

If he could get all of his children married off, he could certainly figure out how to secure a bit of bubbly.

He glanced over at his housekeeper, who was crying quietly into a handkerchief. She looked up and frowned at him as though she'd read his mind.

He sighed silently and turned his attention back to the wedding. Applause rang out as the couples kissed.

King smiled and murmured, "And they lived happily ever after."

THE EDITOR'S CORNER

Summer is here at last, and we invite you to join us for our 11th anniversary. Things are really heating up with six wonderful new Loveswepts that sizzle with sexy heroes and dazzling heroines. As always, our romances are packed with tender emotion and steamy passion that are guaranteed to make this summer a hot one!

Always a favorite, Helen Mittermeyer gives us a heroine who is **MAGIC IN PASTEL**, Loveswept #690. When fashion model Pastel Marx gazes at Will Nordstrom, it's as if an earthquake hits him! Will desires her with an intensity that shocks him, but the anguish she tries to hide makes him want to protect her. Determined to help Pastel fight the demons that plague her, Will tries to comfort her, longing to know why his fairy-tale princess is imprisoned by her fear. Enveloped in the arms of a man whose touch soothes and arouses, Pastel struggles to accept the gift of his caring and keep their rare love true in a world of fire and ice. Helen delivers a story with characters that will warm your heart.

The heroine in Deborah Harmse's newest book finds herself **IN THE ARMS OF THE LAW,** Loveswept #691. Rebekah de Bieren decides Detective Mackenzie Hoyle has a handsome face, a great body, and a rotten attitude! When Mack asks Becky to help him persuade one of her students to testify in a murder case, he is stunned by this pint-sized blond angel who is as tempting as she is tough . . . but he refuses to take no for an answer—no matter how her blue eyes flash. Becky hears the sorrow behind Mack's cynical request and senses the tormented emotions he hides beneath his fierce dedication. Drawn to the fire she sees sparking in his cool gray eyes, she responds with shameless abandon—and makes him yearn for impossible dreams. Deborah Harmse will have you laughing and crying with this sexy romance.

FOR MEN ONLY, Loveswept #692, by the wonderfully talented Sally Goldenbaum, is a romance that cooks. The first time Ellie Livingston and Pete Webster met, he'd been a blind date from hell, but now he looks good enough to eat! Pete definitely has his doubts about taking a cooking class she's designed just for men, but his gaze is hungry for the pleasures only she can provide. Pete has learned not to trust beautiful women, but Ellie's smile is real—and full of temptation. Charmed by her spicy personality and passionate honesty, he revels in the sensual magic she weaves, but can Pete make her believe their love is enough? **FOR MEN ONLY** is a story you can really sink your teeth into.

Glenna McReynolds has given us another dark and dangerous hero in **THE DRAGON AND THE DOVE,** Loveswept #693. Cooper Daniels had asked for a female shark with an instinct for the jugular, but instead he's sent an angelfish in silk who looks too innocent to help him with his desperate quest to avenge his brother's death! Jessica Langston is fascinated by the hard sensuality of his face and mesmerized by eyes that meet hers with the force of a head-on collision, but she refuses to be dismissed—winning Cooper's respect and igniting his desire. Suddenly, Cooper is compelled by an inexorable need to claim her with tantalizing gentleness. Her surrender makes him yearn to rediscover the tenderness he's missed, but Cooper believes he'll only hurt the woman who has given him back his life. Jessica cherishes her tough hero, but now she must help heal the wounds that haunt his soul. **THE DRAGON AND THE DOVE** is Glenna at her heart-stopping best.

Donna Kauffman invites you to **TANGO IN PARADISE**, Loveswept #694. Jack Tango is devastatingly virile, outrageously seductive, and a definite danger to her peace of mind, but resort owner April Morgan needs his help enough to promise him whatever he wants—and she suspects what he wants is her in his arms! Jack wants her desperately but without regrets—and he'll wait until she pleads for his touch. April responds with wanton satisfaction to Jack's need to claim her soul, to possess and pleasure her, but even with him as her formidable ally, does she dare face old ghosts? **TANGO IN PARADISE** will show you why Donna is one of our brightest and fastest-rising stars.

Last, but definitely not least, is a battle of passion and will in Linda Wisdom's **O'HARA vs. WILDER**, Loveswept #695. For five years, Jake Wilder had been the man of her sexiest dreams, the best friend and partner she'd once dared to love, then leave, but seeing him again in the flesh leaves Tess O'Hara breathless . . . and wildly aroused! Capturing her mouth in a kiss that sears her to the toes and catches him in the fire-storm, Jake knows she is still more woman than any man can handle, but he is willing to try. Powerless to resist the kisses that brand her his forever, Tess fights the painful memories that their reckless past left her, but Jake insists they are a perfect team, in bed and out. Seduced by the electricity sizzling between them, tantalized beyond reason by Jake's wicked grin and rough edges, Tess wonders if a man who's always looked for trouble can settle for all she can give him. Linda Wisdom has another winner with **O'HARA vs. WILDER.**

Happy reading,

With warmest wishes,

Nita Taublib

Nita Taublib
Associate Publisher

P.S. Don't miss the women's novels coming your way in June—**WHERE SHADOWS GO,** by Eugenia Price, is an enthralling love story of the Old South that is the second volume of the *Georgia Trilogy*, following **BRIGHT CAPTIVITY; DARK JOURNEY,** by award-winning Sandra Canfield, is a heart-wrenching story of love and obsession, betrayal and forgiveness, in which a woman discovers the true price of forbidden passion; **SOMETHING BORROWED, SOMETHING BLUE,** by Jillian Karr, is a mixture of romance and suspense in which four brides—each with a dangerous secret—will be the focus of a deliciously glamorous issue of *Perfect Bride* magazine; and finally **THE MOON RIDER,** Virginia Lynn's most appealing historical romance to date, is a passionate tale of a highwayman and his lady-love. We'll be giving you a sneak peek at these wonderful books in next month's LOVESWEPTs. And immediately following this page look for a preview of the terrific romances from Bantam that are *available now*!

THE NEW YORK TIMES BESTSELLING NOVEL

DECEPTION
by *Amanda Quick*

"One of the hottest and most prolific writers in romance today . . . Her heroines are always spunky women you'd love to know and her heroes are dashing guys you'd love to love."
—USA Today

**NOW AVAILABLE IN PAPERBACK
WHEREVER BANTAM BOOKS ARE SOLD**

Winner of *Romantic Times*
1992 Storyteller of the Year Award

Patricia Potter

Nationally Bestselling Author
Of **Notorious** and **Renegade**

RELENTLESS

*Beneath the outlaw's smoldering gaze, Shea Randall felt
a stab of pure panic . . . and a shiver of shocking desire.
Held against her will by the darkly handsome bandit,
she knew that for her father's sake she must find a
way to escape. Only later, as the days of her captivity
turned into weeks and Rafe Tyler's fiery passion sparked
her own, did Shea fully realize her perilous position—
locked in a mountain lair with a man who could steal
her heart . . .*

The door opened, and the bright light of the
afternoon sun almost blinded her. Her eyes were
drawn to the large figure in the doorway. Silhouetted by the sun behind him, Tyler seemed even
bigger, stronger, more menacing. She had to force
herself to keep from backing away.

He hesitated, his gaze raking over the cabin,
raking over her. He frowned at the candle.

She stood. It took all her bravery, but she stood,
forcing her eyes to meet his, to determine what was
there. There seemed to be nothing but a certain
coolness.

"I'm thirsty," she said. It came out as more of a challenge than a request, and she saw a quick flicker of something in his eyes. She hoped it was remorse, but that thought was quickly extinguished by his reply.

"Used to better places?" It was a sneer, plain and simple, and Shea felt anger stirring again.

"I'm used to gentlemen and simple . . . humanity."

"That's strange, considering your claim that you're Randall's daughter."

"I haven't claimed anything to you."

"That's right, you haven't," he agreed in a disagreeable voice. "You haven't said much at all."

"And I don't intend to. Not to a thief and a traitor."

"Be careful, Miss Randall. Your . . . continued health depends on this thief and traitor."

"That's supposed to comfort me?" Her tone was pure acid.

His gaze stabbed her. "You'll have to forgive me. I'm out of practice in trying to comfort anyone. Ten years out of practice."

"So you're going to starve me?"

"No," he said slowly. "I'm not going to do *that*."

The statement was ominous to Shea. "What are you going to do?"

"Follow my rules, and I won't do anything."

"You already are. You're keeping me here against my will."

He was silent for a moment, and Shea noted a muscle moving in his neck, as if he were just barely restraining himself.

"Lady, because of your . . . father, I was 'held'

against my will for ten years." She wanted to slap him for his mockery. She wanted to kick him where it would hurt the most. But now was not the time.

"Is that it? You're taking revenge out on me?"

The muscle in his cheek moved again. "No, Miss Randall, it's not that. You just happened to be in the wrong place at the wrong time. I don't have any more choices than you do." He didn't know why in the hell he was explaining, except her last charge galled him.

"You do."

He turned away from her. "Believe what you want," he said, his voice indifferent. "Blow out that candle and come with me if you want some water."

She didn't want to go with him, but she was desperate to shake her thirst. She blew out the candle, hoping that once outside he wouldn't see dried streaks of tears on her face. She didn't want to give him that satisfaction.

She didn't have to worry. He paid no attention to her, and she had to scurry to keep up with his long-legged strides. She knew she was plain, especially so in the loose-fitting britches and shirt she wore and with her hair in a braid. She also knew she should be grateful that he was indifferent to her, but a part of her wanted to goad him, confuse him . . . attract him.

Shea felt color flood her face. To restrain her train of thought, she concentrated on her surroundings.

Her horse was gone, although her belongings were propped against the tree stump. There was a shack to the left, and she noticed a lock on the door. That must be where he'd taken the weapons and where he kept his own horse. The keys must be in his pockets. He strode over to the building and picked up a bucket with his gloved hand.

She tried to pay attention to their route, but it seemed they had just melted into the woods and everything looked alike. She thought of turning around and running, but he was only a couple of feet ahead of her.

He stopped abruptly at a stream and leaned against a tree, watching her.

She had never drunk from a stream before, yet that was obviously what he expected her to do. The dryness in her mouth was worse, and she couldn't wait. She moved to the edge of the stream and kneeled, feeling awkward and self-conscious, knowing he was watching and judging. She scooped up a handful of water, then another, trying to sip it before it leaked through her fingers. She caught just enough to be tantalized.

She finally fell flat on her stomach and put her mouth in the water, taking long swallows of the icy cold water, mindless of the way the front of her shirt got soaked, mindless of anything but water.

It felt wonderful and tasted wonderful. When she was finally sated, she reluctantly sat up, and her gaze went to Tyler.

His stance was lazy but his eyes, like fine emeralds, were intense with fire. She felt a corresponding wave of heat consume her. She couldn't move her gaze from him, no matter how hard she tried. It was as if they were locked together.

He was the first to divert his gaze and his face settled quickly into its usual indifferent mask.

She looked down and noticed that her wet shirt clung to her, outlining her breasts. She swallowed hard and turned around. She splashed water on her face, hoping it would cool the heat suffusing her body.

She kept expecting Tyler to order her away, but he didn't. And she lingered as long as she could. She didn't want to go back to the dark cabin. She didn't want to face him, or those intense emotions she didn't understand.

She felt his gaze on her, and knew she should feel fear. He had been in prison a very long time. But she was certain he wouldn't touch her in a sexual way.

Because he despises you.

Because he despises your father.

She closed her eyes for a moment, and when she opened them, a spiral of light gleamed through the trees, hitting the stream. She wanted to reach out and catch that sunbeam, to climb it to some safe place.

But there were no safe places any longer.

She watched that ray of light until it slowly dissipated as the sun slipped lower in the sky, and then she turned around again. She hadn't expected such patience from Tyler.

"Ready?" he asked in his hoarse whisper.

The word held many meanings.

Ready for what? She wasn't ready for any of this.

But she nodded.

He sauntered over and offered his hand.

She refused it and rose by herself, stunned by how much she suddenly wanted to take his hand, to feel that strength again.

And Shea realized her battle wasn't entirely with him. It was also with herself.

SUSAN JOHNSON

Nationally bestselling author of **Outlaw** and **Silver Flame**

SEIZED BY LOVE

Now available in paperback

Sweeping from the fabulous country estates and hunting lodges to the opulent ballrooms and salons of the Russian nobility, here is a novel of savage passions and dangerous pleasures by the incomparable Susan Johnson, mistress of the erotic historical.

"*Under your protection?*" Alisa sputtered, flushing vividly as the obvious and unmistakable clarity of his explanation struck her. Of course, she should have realized. How very stupid of her. The full implication of what the public reaction to her situation would be left her momentarily stunned, devoured with shame. She was exceedingly thankful, for the first time since her parents' death, that they *weren't* alive to see the terrible depths to which she had fallen, the sordid fate outlined for her.

Irritated at the masterful certainty of Nikki's assumption, and resentful to be treated once more like a piece of property, she coldly said, "I don't recall placing myself under your protection."

"Come now, love," Nikki said reasonably, "if you recall, when I found you in that shed, your alternatives were surely limited; more severe beatings and possibly death if Forseus had continued drugging you. Hardly a choice of options, I should think. And consider it now," Nikki urged amiably, "plenty of advantages, especially if one has already shown a *decided* partiality for the man one has as protector. I'm not considered ungenerous, and if you contrive to please me in the future as well as you have to this date, we shall deal together quite easily."

Taking umbrage at his arrogant presumption that her role was to please *him*, Alisa indignantly said, "I haven't any *decided* partiality for you, you arrogant lecher, and furthermore—"

"Give me three minutes alone with you, my dear," Nikki interjected suavely, "and I feel sure I can restore my credit on that account."

Her eyes dropped shamefully before his candid regard, but she was angry enough to thrust aside the brief feeling of embarrassment, continuing belligerently. "Maria has some money of mine she brought with us. I'm not in *need* of protection."

"Not enough to buy you one decent gown, let alone support yourself, a child, and three servants," Nikki disagreed bluntly with his typical disregard for tact.

"Well, then," Alisa insisted heatedly, "I'm relatively well educated, young, and strong. I can obtain a position as governess."

"I agree in principle with your idea, but unfortunately, the pressures of existence in this world of travail serve to daunt the most optimistic hopes." His words were uttered in a lazy, mocking drawl. "For you, the role of governess"—the sarcasm in his voice was all too apparent—"is quite a pleasant conceit, my dear. You *will* forgive my speaking frankly, but I fear you are lacking in a sense of the realities of things.

"*If*—I say, if—any wife in her right mind would allow a provokingly beautiful young woman like yourself to enter her household, I'd wager a small fortune, the master of that house would be sharing your bed within the week. Consider the folly of the notion, love. At least with me there'd be no indignant wife to throw you and your retinue out into the street when her husband's preferences became obvious. And since I have a rather intimate knowledge of many of these wives, I think my opinion is to be relied upon. And as your protector," he continued equably, "I, of course, feel an obligation to maintain your daughter and servants in luxurious comfort."

"I am not a plaything to be bought!" Alisa said feelingly.

"Ah, my dear, but you are. Confess, it is a woman's role, primarily a pretty plaything for a man's pleasure and then inexorably as night follows day— a mother. Those are the two roles a woman plays. It's preordained. Don't fight it," he said practically.

Alisa would have done anything, she felt at that moment, to wipe that detestable look of smugness from Nikki's face.

"Perhaps I'll take Cernov up on his offer after all," she said with the obvious intent to provoke. "Is he richer than you? I must weigh the advantages if

I'm to make my way profitably in the demimonde," she went on calculatingly. "Since I'm merely a plaything, it behooves me to turn a practical frame of mind to the role of demirep and sell myself for the highest price in money and rank obtainable. I have a certain refinement of background—"

"Desist in the cataloguing if you please," he broke in rudely, and in a dangerously cold voice murmured, "Let us not cavil over trifles. You're staying with me." Alisa involuntarily quailed before the stark, open challenge in his eyes, and her heart sank in a most unpleasant way.

"So my life is a trifle?" she whispered, trembling with a quiet inner violence.

"You misunderstand, my dear," the even voice explained with just a touch of impatience. "It's simply that I don't intend to enter into any senseless wrangles or debates over your attributes and the direction in which your favors are to be bestowed. Madame, you're to remain my mistress." His lips smiled faintly but the smile never reached his eyes.

WILD CHILD
by Suzanne Forster
bestselling author of
SHAMELESS

"A storyteller of incandescent brilliance . . . beyond compare in a class by herself . . . that rare talent, a powerhouse writer whose extraordinary sensual touch can mesmerize . . ."
—*Romantic Times*

Her memorable characters and sizzling tales of romance and adventure have won her numerous awards and countless devoted readers. Now, with her trademark blend of intense sensuality and deep emotion, Suzanne Forster reunites adversaries who share a tangled past— and for whom an old spark of conflict will kindle into a dangerously passionate blaze . . .

"I want to talk about us," he said.

"Us?"

Blake could have predicted the stab of panic in her eyes, but he couldn't have predicted what was happening inside Cat. As she met his gaze, she felt herself dropping, a wind-rider caught in a powerful downdrift. The plummeting sensation in her stomach was sudden and sharp. The dock seemed to go out from under her feet, and as she imagined herself falling, she caught a glimpse of something in her mind that riveted her.

Surrender.

Even the glimpse of such naked emotion was terrifying to Cat. It entranced and enthralled her. It was the source of her panic. It was the wellspring of her deepest need. To be touched, to be loved. She shuddered in silence and raised her face to his.

By the time he did touch her, the shuddering was deep inside her. It was emotional and sexual and beautiful. No, she thought, this is impossible. This isn't happening. *Not with this man. Not with him . . .*

He curved his hand to her throat and drew her to him.

"What do I do, Cat?" he asked. "How do I make the sadness go away?"

The question rocked her softly, reverberating in the echo chamber her senses had become. *Not this man. Not him. He's hurt you too much. . . .*

"Sweet, sad, Cat." He caressed the underside of her chin with long, long strokes of his thumb. The sensations were soft and erotic and thrilling, and they accomplished exactly what they were supposed to, Cat realized, bringing her head up sharply. He wanted her to look up at him. He wanted her throat arched, her head tilted back.

No, Cat! He's hurt you too much.

"Don't," she whispered. "Not you . . ."

"Yes, Cat, me," he said. "It has to be me."

He bent toward her, and his lips touched hers with a lightning stroke of tenderness. Cat swallowed the moan in her throat. In all her guilty dreams of kissing Blake Wheeler—and there had been many—she had never imagined it as tender. She never had imagined a sweetness so sharp that it would fill her throat and tear through her heart like a poignant memory. Was this how lovers kissed? Lovers who had hurt each other and now needed to be very, very cautious? Lovers whose wounds weren't healed?

Age-old warnings stirred inside her. She should have resisted, she wanted to resist, but as his lips brushed over hers she felt yearnings flare up inside her—a wrenchingly sweet need to deepen the kiss, to be held and crushed in his arms. She had imagined him as self-absorbed, an egotistical lover who would take what he wanted and assume that being with him was enough for any woman. A night with Blake Wheeler. A night in heaven! She had imagined herself rejecting him, ordering him out of her bed and out of her life. She had imagined all of those things so many times . . . but never *tenderness*.

His mouth was warm. It was as vibrant as the water sparkling around them. She touched his arm, perhaps to push him away, and then his lips drifted over hers, and her touch became a caress. Her fingers shimmered over heat and muscle, and she felt a sudden, sharp need to be closer.

All of her attention was focused on the extraordinary thing that was happening to her. A kiss, she told herself, *it was just a kiss*. But he touched her with such rare tenderness. His fingers plucked at her nerve-strings as if she were a delicate musical instrument. His mouth transfused her with fire and drained her of energy at the same time. And when at last his arms came around her and brought her up against him, she felt a sweet burst of physical longing that saturated her senses.

She had dreamt of his body, too. And the feel of him now was almost more reality than she could stand. His thighs were steel, and his pelvic bones dug into her flesh. He was hard, righteously hard, and even the slightest shifts in pressure put her in touch with her own keening emptiness.

His tongue stroked her lips, and she opened

them to him slowly, irresistibly. On some level she knew she was playing a sword dance with her own emotions, tempting fate, tempting heartbreak, but the sensations were so exquisite, she couldn't stop herself. They seemed as inevitable and sensual as the deep currents swaying beneath them.

The first gliding touch of his tongue against hers electrified her. A gasp welled in her throat as he grazed her teeth and tingled sensitive surfaces. The penetration was deliciously languid and deep. By the time he lifted his mouth from hers, she was shocked and reeling from the taste of him.

The urge to push him away was instinctive.

"No, Cat," he said softly, inexplicably, "it's mine now. The sadness inside you is mine."

Studying her face, searching her eyes for something, he smoothed her hair and murmured melting suggestions that she couldn't consciously decipher. They tugged at her sweetly, hotly, pulling her insides to and fro, eliciting yearnings. Cat's first awareness of them was a kind of vague astonishment. It was deep and thrilling, what was happening inside her, like eddying water, like the sucking and pulling of currents. She'd never known such oddly captivating sensations.

The wooden dock creaked and the bay swelled gently beneath them, tugging at the pilings. Cat sighed as the rhythms of the sea and the man worked their enchantment. His hands *were* telepathic. They sought out all her tender spots. His fingers moved in concert with the deep currents, stroking the sideswells of her breasts, arousing her nerves to rivulets of excitement.

"Wild," he murmured as he cupped her breasts in his palms. "Wild, wild child."

And don't miss these spectacular
romances from Bantam Books,
on sale in May:

DARK JOURNEY
by the bestselling author
Sandra Canfield
"(Ms. Canfield's) superb style of writing
proves her to be an author extraordinaire."
—*Affaire de Coeur*

SOMETHING BORROWED
SOMETHING BLUE
by
Jillian Karr
"Author Jillian Karr . . . explodes onto the
mainstream fiction scene . . . Great reading."
—*Romantic Times*

THE MOON RIDER
by the highly acclaimed
Virginia Lynn
"A master storyteller."
—*Rendezvous*

OFFICIAL RULES

To enter the sweepstakes below carefully follow all instructions found elsewhere in this offer.

The **Winners Classic** will award prizes with the following approximate maximum values: 1 Grand Prize: $26,500 (or $25,000 cash alternate); 1 First Prize: $3,000; 5 Second Prizes: $400 each; 35 Third Prizes: $100 each; 1,000 Fourth Prizes: $7.50 each. Total maximum retail value of Winners Classic Sweepstakes is $42,500. Some presentations of this sweepstakes may contain individual entry numbers corresponding to one or more of the aforementioned prize levels. To determine the Winners, individual entry numbers will first be compared with the winning numbers preselected by computer. For winning numbers not returned, prizes will be awarded in random drawings from among all eligible entries received. Prize choices may be offered at various levels. If a winner chooses an automobile prize, all license and registration fees, taxes, destination charges and, other expenses not offered herein are the responsibility of the winner. If a winner chooses a trip, travel must be complete within one year from the time the prize is awarded. Minors must be accompanied by an adult. Travel companion(s) must also sign release of liability. Trips are subject to space and departure availability. Certain black-out dates may apply.

The following applies to the sweepstakes named above:

No purchase necessary. You can also enter the sweepstakes by sending your name and address to: P.O. Box 508, Gibbstown, N.J. 08027. Mail each entry separately. Sweepstakes begins 6/1/93. Entries must be received by 12/30/94. Not responsible for lost, late, damaged, misdirected, illegible or postage due mail. Mechanically reproduced entries are not eligible. All entries become property of the sponsor and will not be returned.

Prize Selection/Validations: Selection of winners will be conducted no later than 5:00 PM on January 28, 1995, by an independent judging organization whose decisions are final. Random drawings will be held at 1211 Avenue of the Americas, New York, N.Y. 10036. Entrants need not be present to win. Odds of winning are determined by total number of entries received. Circulation of this sweepstakes is estimated not to exceed 200 million. All prizes are guaranteed to be awarded and delivered to winners. Winners will be notified by mail and may be required to complete an affidavit of eligibility and release of liability which must be returned within 14 days of date on notification or alternate winners will be selected in a random drawing. Any prize notification letter or any prize returned to a participating sponsor, Bantam Doubleday Dell Publishing Group, Inc., its participating divisions or subsidiaries, or the independent judging organization as undeliverable will be awarded to an alternate winner. Prizes are not transferable. No substitution for prizes except as offered or as may be necessary due to unavailability, in which case a prize of equal or greater value will be awarded. Prizes will be awarded approximately 90 days after the drawing. All taxes are the sole responsibility of the winners. Entry constitutes permission (except where prohibited by law) to use winners' names, hometowns, and likenesses for publicity purposes without further or other compensation. Prizes won by minors will be awarded in the name of parent or legal guardian.

Participation: Sweepstakes open to residents of the United States and Canada, except for the province of Quebec. Sweepstakes sponsored by Bantam Doubleday Dell Publishing Group, Inc., (BDD), 1540 Broadway, New York, NY 10036. Versions of this sweepstakes with different graphics and prize choices will be offered in conjunction with various solicitations or promotions by different subsidiaries and divisions of BDD. Where applicable, winners will have their choice of any prize offered at level won. Employees of BDD, its divisions, subsidiaries, advertising agencies, independent judging organization, and their immediate family members are not eligible.

Canadian residents, in order to win, must first correctly answer a time limited arithmetical skill testing question. Void in Puerto Rico, Quebec and wherever prohibited or restricted by law. Subject to all federal, state, local and provincial laws and regulations. For a list of major prize winners (available after 1/29/95): send a self-addressed, stamped envelope entirely separate from your entry to: Sweepstakes Winners, P.O. Box 517, Gibbstown, NJ 08027. Requests must be received by 12/30/94. DO NOT SEND ANY OTHER CORRESPONDENCE TO THIS P.O. BOX.

SWP 7/93

ING FORWARD

LOOKING
FORWARD

By
GILLIAN TINDALL

ARBOR HOUSE   NEW YORK

F
TIN

N. 1

Library of Congress Cataloging in Publication Data
Tindall, Gillian
  Looking forward.

  I. Title.
PR6070.I45L6 1983   823'.914   84-24291
ISBN: 0-87795- 669-3

Prologue

One Sunday in the late 1970s, a day of uncertain rains and harassing wind, Joanna Webber, her husband Tom and their eldest daughter Kate, began clearing out Mary Denvers' flat near Baker Street.

They had talked of tackling the job in one day, but it soon became obvious that this was beyond their powers. There were too many cupboards to go through, too many drawers, too many files of paper, books, clothes, letters, saucepans, prints, blankets, gramophone records, photographs, pots of bulbs, spice jars, biscuit tins, bags of string and so much else—too many decisions to be taken. 'And it isn't even,' said Joanna, in the constricted voice which seemed the only way she could speak of Mary now, 'as if she was a hoarder. Not like some.'

She was referring to Tom's large family. In contrast, Mary had few people to bear witness to her life and its ending. Joanna, her nearest relative, was the child of a cousin.

'She kept things a bit,' said Tom. 'All the same.'

'I know. She liked to talk about not being sentimental, but I think that was sort of on principle. Expected, you know, in her generation for people like her.'

After a pause Tom said, in a soothing tone which irritated both his wife and his daughter: 'We could just take it all back to our house for the moment . . .'

'As I've already pointed out,' said Joanna, 'everything that is taken anywhere has to be carted down four flights of stairs and loaded into the car. And, when we get it home, where do we put it? We've already got a house bursting with stuff, as if you didn't know.'

'We don't *need* any more biscuit tins,' Kate stated. 'Or clothes pegs.'

Tom, who knew this, said irritably in his turn:

'All right then, leave the lot for the dealer. Like I said.'

'You can't ask a dealer in to buy the furniture if the place is still covered in packets of Daz and baking powder and whatnot—can you?'

'*I* don't know.' Tom went on dourly loading old medical text-books into a carton. 'Someone will be interested in this collection,' he had said with forced energy two hours ago. Now, Joanna could see, the idea that anyone might be interested in obsolete testimony was receding. The realisation that death is not an event but a permanent situation, and that the dead can only fade and fade from the lives of the living, was beginning to establish itself. The flat, with its orderly load of possessions, a pleasant setting which had been superficially so familiar to them, had abruptly transformed itself into an intolerable burden. On one hand Joanna found herself hating all these abandoned objects with which she was suddenly forced into intimacy—these folded jerseys, these racks of good quality shoes, that drawer of tumbled underclothes and rolled stockings which she had not yet brought herself to empty, these photograph albums full of dead people. Yet on the other hand she felt a respect for the things as a whole that made the enforced intimacy worse: her strongest desire, as she laboured, was *not* to dismantle the décor of Mary's existence, particularly in this hurried, exhausted way.

'Of course, a lot of this stuff must have been Lionel's too,' said Tom presently. He, in his turn, had come to an irresolute pause.

'Yes. But . . . he *really* wasn't a hoarder, you see. I once asked Mary—after he was dead, you know, and we were sitting having a chat about him—what his first wife had been like. She said she had no idea! Lionel hardly ever mentioned her and apparently didn't even have a photo of her. Mary was quite funny about it. She said that when they first got together she imagined it was deep-seated grief that made him

6

so unforthcoming, and it wasn't till she knew him better that she realised he really did not think about the past. To him it was just—over, and he didn't value it or worry about it and was a bit puzzled when other people did. Oh, he was the real rationalist, I think.'

'Then all those First World War letters can't be his family.'

'What letters?'

'You know. In the bureau drawer. You saw them too.'

'I saw one bundle. I didn't know there were lots.'

'Well there are. What the hell do we do with them?'

They looked at each other.

'Do they look interesting?' asked Joanna forlornly.

'Not particularly. I mean—it all depends if you are interested. In First World War letters, that is . . . We *could* just chuck them away.'

'Oh Tom, we can't possibly. Not after all this time—'

The plaster over Mary's living-room mantelpiece had cracked and come away when they had tried to detach the two decorative Breton plates that had always hung there. She said bleakly to her husband, who could not protect her against this disintegration, and who seemed for the moment a stranger:

'Can't we give them to the Imperial War Museum?'

'We can try, but I should think they may have more than they want already. So many families must have kept bundles of letters like that, and they would all have been coming to light in the last ten years or so.'

'Mmm . . . People become *more* dead, don't they, when the ones who remembered them have gone too. It must be odd now for all those young men who died at Ypres and Passchendaele and all those places, and who were so mourned, just *not being remembered* any more.' To forestall the expression of principled unbelief in personal survival that she could see settling on Tom's face, she added in the same taut, conversational tone:

'Oh dear, I wonder if perhaps we ought to clean these clothes before we send them to the old people's outfit. I mean, no one ever has all their clothes clean at once in the ordinary way, do they? And this was ordinary: when she went into hospital she never dreamed she wasn't coming

7

back quite soon; she'd bought in tins of soup, and eggs . . . She didn't know she was dying—'

'She must have known it was possible, Jo. A doctor like her. And she was over seventy-five.'

'She didn't know, Tom, she really didn't. She'd have said if she had. She wasn't afraid of death. She was a member of that voluntary euthanasia organisation. She'd always said she didn't intend to linger. But she didn't expect to die just like that, having a minor operation. You know what she was like—if she'd had any real suspicion she might not come back she'd have cleared the place up much more before she went into hospital. She wouldn't have wanted to leave it all to us. She was cheated. It doesn't seem right—' She heard her voice going thin and high with the unshed tears that had been with her for days, but was unaware that she had said, or felt, something like this in her life before: *why didn't you tell me you were going to die? Why have you left me like this?*

They found that their daughter, defeated by the contents of the kitchen, had retreated to the living room, where she was eating biscuits with an abstracted voraciousness and reading a novel whose mat, two-toned dust-jacket was still intact. It showed a hipless woman of the 1930s, poised beside a tree, one hand raised to her waved hair, while the silhouette of a man in evening dress loomed near. The title swam in delicate script above her—'*Oh Willow* by Dorothy Denvers'.

Joanna's mother.

'Are you enjoying that?' asked Tom.

'Not much. It's pissy. Full of people called Jeremy and Adrian and Marina fussing about things. Jeremy has just said—yes, here it is: "Oh my God, Adrian, are you sure?" And they keep lighting cigarettes at each other . . . Was my grandmother really considered any good in those days, Mum?'

'I don't know. I was brought up to believe so, but I don't think she published anything after I was old enough to take notice.'

'Oh. Why not?'

'I don't know. She just didn't.' Why indeed? That inflamed question had haunted Joanna's childhood. Increasingly, as the years accumulated, Dodie Denvers had answered it herself—'*Of course, bringing you up, I've simply not had the*

8

time . . . One has to make sacrifices for a child: you'll understand that one day . . . One can't have everything one wants in life, you know. Life does things to you. You'll find that out . . .' In unconscious defence Joanna clenched her fists.

Kate said: 'Something's written on the first page: "To Willie, from Dodie. Always." Always what, it doesn't say . . . Was that your Uncle Willie?'

'Yes, it must have been.'

'Do I remember him?'

'Shortish and bald,' put in Tom. 'Smoked cigarettes in an ivory holder. Mary used to invite him here with us about once a year.'

'Ooh yes, I know: he was the one whose book on oriental whatnot was all burnt up when the sun came through his paperweight and set fire to it! I never quite believed it—I mean, can a paperweight really act like a burning glass?'

'*I* never entirely believed in his great work on oriental porcelain,' said Joanna. In her head, very clear, she heard Mary's voice saying, with a hint of untypical maliciousness, 'So like poor Willie to pick on a subject none of us was in a position to check up on.' Tradition had turned Uncle Willie into a puppet figure, an official joke; it was a disguise to which, in his last years, he himself had seemed to subscribe.

Out of the corner of her eye she saw Kate collecting together several Dorothy Denvers novels and putting them on to the pile of books they had already set aside to take home. She had a sudden image of Mary's rôle by-passing herself, devolving on Kate, Kate who was barely in her teens but who was already beginning to show an impatient, half-formed desire to get the past in perspective and to master the future: Kate was a survivor.

For herself, at that moment, she longed only to leave the flat and run away down the echoing tiled staircase into the wet streets below. Not to abandon Mary's home but to leave it intact for ever, safe in memory. Through two open doors she saw the row of jam pots above Mary's kitchen sink. Each supported an avocado stone, carefully suspended on matchsticks, and several had begun to sprout. These jars she would, she knew, have to carry now to another district of London, slopping in a car, have to install them in her own kitchen, have to tend them, feel guilty if they failed to flourish, plant them out in pots if they did, protect them from the cats and the toddler and from slugs—intolerable. Her heart swelled, and tears began to trickle down her face.

In her variegated life, parts of which still frightened her so much that she never thought of them, Joanna had only consciously experienced love in a primitive way, as something indivisible from a physical relationship: love for a mother, a husband, a child. Yet now, belatedly, in her late thirties, she understood that she had indeed loved Mary, and wished, too late, that Mary had known it too.

In another house, twenty-odd years earlier, where Mary had been soberly and doggedly disposing of her cousin Dodie's belongings, Willie had come to stand in a doorway and had said:

'My dear, I really can't help you, much as I would like to. It's all far too *Time and the Conways* for me.' And he had gone away, leaving Mary to do the job on her own.

At the time, Mary had not protested, feeling that Willie probably had his own reasons, but later she had thought furiously how absolutely typical of Willie that was, the bland assumption that his own feelings took priority over any consideration of duty or kindness. After all, this pathetic litter of Dodie's life painfully recalled her own youth, too, just as much as Willie's—perhaps more. And how typical, too, that he should express himself in that tiresome, literary way, by implication converting real life, private, unassuageable grief and failure, into fashionable drama, distancing himself from people as always.

The real tragedy of things was not dramatic but slow, piecemeal, ignominious . . . A downwards spiral into darkness that, year by year, seemed unmomentous, but which acquired, in retrospect, a horrid quality of predestination. Looking helplessly round at the out-of-fashion high-heeled shoes, the encrusted jars of make-up, the bottles of homeopathic remedies, her heart bled for Dodie. Her throat constricted. In a sudden gesture she began to cram all the bottles into the waste-paper basket.

It was not till the last ten years of her life, when Lionel was gone and she herself was working less, that Mary speculated much upon the past. She supposed that this was usual: were not the elderly alleged to 'live' in the past, wearying those still engaged in the present by remembering the past 'as if it was yesterday', and at the same time regarding it as a place of safety, a cross between heaven and a tea-shop on a wet afternoon? But, on further reflection, she decided with relief that this was not, for her, true. The distant past did not seem in the least like yesterday to her, or yet like a refuge from today, but more like a series of uncertainly coloured picture postcards, clear but diminished in scale, like those hand-tinted ones you could still buy in village shops in the 1920s.

Beyond a certain age, she thought, early memories do not fade, no—but they transmute, becoming other, divorced from one's present self. One does not so much remember as remember remembering. The memory is long since fixed, in truth or distortion, framed and glazed with later associations and assumptions. In some cases it is simplified into a silhou-ette, a hieroglyph even. A certain tennis ball bouncing from a cricket bat across the sand and rolling into the water repre-sents many summers of childhood: one moment when Mother, in her black, caped coat, fumbled with her latchkey in the porch and said, 'Let's get these things upstairs quickly before the boys see them,' encapsulates all the Christmases the Boys spent in our house. But are these true images from my own experience or are they fuzzed by time, part of any-one's Edwardian childhood? I no longer really know.

Of course, when I think properly, I do remember all sorts of individual things about the Boys, some dear, some commonplace, some discreditable—but essentially, when I do recall them these days, what I see is a series of tableaux in which all three are together: edited, concentrated memory as in a memorial album. Like one of those white vellum books that bereaved families produced for private circulation after the Great War: pictures of dead young men in open-necked cricket shirts; poems or sketches by them; letters from their old housemasters.

Oliver. Roland. Nigel. Even their names sound elegiac, part of the great record against which the rest of our generation were constrained to live out our lives, not an

11

unseen presence but a constant motif of absence, a persistent lack. *They shall grow not old, As we that are left grow old . . .* But of what use is the shadow of a boy of nineteen to a woman of twenty-nine, thirty-nine, forty-nine?

That is finally over now as well. The women who spent the rest of their lives intimating that 'the men who would have been our husbands were killed in the First World War, you see', are now dying themselves; the parents who lost their sons are at last an extinct race. Even now, as I sit here in my flat in the 1970s, cautiously trying the Boys' long unspoken names on the empty air, they and their kind are passing at last from collective memory into history. Is that why I cannot really see them any more as part of my own personal memory?

Over fifty years. People used to tell one 'time heals': did they realise that time, enough time, in the end does this at the cost of removing the sense of the lost individual altogether, till grief itself becomes only a gesture, an outworn habit?

But even without the passage of so much time, the war itself, the '14–'18 war, distanced much, putting a great barrier between then and now, a kind of Berlin Wall across the landscape of time. On the far side of it everything, even the things we remember clearly, happened to other people, not ourselves—and this has been true for decades already. I have often and often heard people express it. By the mid-1920s, already, 1913 seemed inexpressibly remote, a mixture of Dark Age and Golden Age. It was a deformity of view, really, but a powerful and apparently very general one: perhaps we had to see the immediate past like that, in order to bear it.

Novels are customarily written going forwards, but that isn't at all how we usually view events. In reality the past, or our perception of it, is constantly being modified by subsequent developments. It is just a convention of fiction, as of psychoanalysis (another form of fiction, Lionel used to say), that things go on mattering in the same way for ever, bearing the same meanings for ever, people being the same for ever. It isn't true. Oh, *thank* God it is not true.

And yet Dodie, ah Dodie, still represents an everlasting present to me: she has not retreated into a symbol, a harmless husk of meaning, much as I might like her to. She is *there*, Dodie, still, as she always was. Sometimes, even now, if I wake in the night from the febrile sleep of old age, I find myself arguing with her, wanting to impress her, getting even with her . . .

Triumphing over the dead. What a shameful, pointless— no, worse than pointless—occupation. Clearly I am not nearly such a nice person as I and my friends tend to believe. Or as she believed. Oh Dodie! You, at any rate, still have the power to distress me, to annoy me, to touch me. Oh Dodie . . . What happened to you, to all the different yous? . . . A child-princess in yellow silk; a flapper with her lovely hair down her back; slim in black like one of the heroines of her own books . . . In that mustard-coloured costume with the gaping skirt-band the last time I ever saw her, munching cakes with her mouth open in that dim tea-shop . . . What happened? I still wonder.

PART ONE

WHEN MARY DENVERS WAS BORN IN ENGLAND IN 1902, her doctor father had been dead for seven months. He had succumbed to what was then still called enteric fever at a military post in a remote part of north-west India where he and his wife had been stationed, and his widow travelled home to have their child. She and her baby girl were established in a small, gabled house on a green near Tunbridge Wells—'small', that is, according to the upper-middle-class standards of the period—by the dead father's brother, Uncle George. In this characteristically generous act Uncle George had an ulterior motive, and this was characteristic of him too. He was only on leave in England, and was due to return to Calcutta, where he owned a large jute manufactory and other interests and where his wife and children were living. He and his wife May were conscious that within the next few years first Oliver and Roland, then Nigel, would have to be despatched back to England for their education. Someone would have to be found to take charge of them, and who better than 'poor Ellie', who henceforth would have no occupation in life—other than her own baby girl, of course?

So by and by Oliver aged eight and Roland aged six were sent off from Calcutta to Tunbridge Wells, leaving behind everything that till then had made up their lives. Like orphans of some natural disaster, they had to begin all over again. Somehow they survived the transplantation intact, managing, like many other children of their time and class, to suppress their homesickness and sense of loss down to the deepest levels of their being.

17

They attached themselves to Aunt Ellie and their 'new' little sister, at first warily, then with growing confidence. (They had a real little sister, in India, Dorothy, born the same year as Mary, but she had been abruptly lost along with everything else: her image was wiped from their minds, replaced by that of Mary.) During the term they were weekly boarders at a school which specialised in small boys from 'Indian families', but Roland confided to Mary later that boys at school hardly ever spoke of this background in common: perhaps to do so would have been too intimate and painful, compromising those masculine structures that little boys sent to live in institutions weave around themselves if they are not to perish. Only alone together in the holidays in Aunt Ellie's house did Oliver and Roland dare to speak of their lost land—of the heat of the day and the brain fever bird at night, of rides with the *syce* in the early mornings, of *chota-hazri* and the *khitmagar*: the power words of a fading tongue, the nursery Hindi that carried for both of them such potent nostalgia that they could hardly bring themselves to utter it. The letters that came regularly with Indian stamps, written on thin paper in handwriting neither boy could read easily, signed 'Your loving Mother' or 'Your affectionate Father', spoke briefly of these things, gave facetious little accounts of Nigel and Baby's doings, or confusingly mentioned people and places the boys did not recognise. The letters, though current messages from the lost land, seemed less real and significant than what existed inside their own minds, and by and by became objects of guilt because they used to lie around the playroom unread.

Then, when the precious memories were at last becoming insubstantial, shredding and altering like the mist dispersed by morning light on those rides with the *syce*, Nigel joined them. A delicate-looking child, driven almost distracted by the grief of separation from the places and people he had regarded as his, he suffered more openly than the other two had, wetting his bed, waking crying '*Ayah!—Ayah, qui hoa?*' India was made present again for Oliver and Roland: it had, they now understood, been there all the time, just covered over by other things. At night, in the room the three of them shared in the holidays, they used to talk about it, endlessly, inconsequentially, inventively, incorporating into it as time went on unlikely details from the books by Henty or Ballantyne or Kipling that they read or had read to them, till Aunt Ellie called up the stairs saying, 'Hush! You must be keeping each other awake.'

Mary could never remember a time before the Boys were there: she could not, therefore, speak of her earliest memories of them, they were almost as much part of the texture of her life as her mother was. But one of her first remembered perceptions was the puzzled realisation that Oliver, Roland and Nigel (as well as being Boys and Big) had some secret other place of their own to which they either could not or would not admit her, some mysteriously bright land like the one people sang about in hymns. Keenly possessive where her Boys were concerned, longing to share everything with them, she occasionally bothered at her mother about this:

'Mummy, will they go to India when they're grown up? Nigel says so, but Oliver isn't sure and Roland won't tell me.'

'Well, they may do, darling. It all depends what professions they take up. I suppose one of them will go into Uncle George's business, though I don't think it will be Oliver. He seems much keener on the Army.'

'Can I too?'

'What, darling, go into the Army? Hardly! Perhaps you could marry an Army officer.'

'No, go to India.'

'Oh well, I don't know about that.' Mary's mother had mixed feelings about India, a place with which she had never got on to terms; most of her brief married life had been spent there, but it was India that had robbed her of her husband. However, being a conscientiously fair woman—a trait enhanced by caring for other people's children—she added: 'Yes, perhaps you could, why not? Girls do, after all . . . Maybe Uncle George and Aunt May would give you a season out there.' *After all I've done for the boys they surely will feel they must do something for Mary.*

'What's a season?'

'Oh, you know, darling—going to dances, meeting young men, having fun. When you're eighteen or so.'

19

'When will that be?'

'Let me think . . . 1920. But you could have done the sum yourself, lazybones!'

It sounded improbably far off. Mary concentrated on trying to evolve with Nigel, who was nearest to her own age and the most amenable to Let's Pretend games, a fantasy about having their own house in India, complete with an elephant in the stables. But although Nigel would impart precious items of information about the place, and would sometimes even condescend to pretend with her, he was always slipping away from her—back to school on Sunday night, or off with the elder two, or simply to do a Boy thing like oiling his cricket bat or fishing in the pond on the far side of the green.

She yearned to be part of their world. Loving all three of them desperately, sometimes one the most, sometimes another, she spent her childhood struggling after them, hanging round on the fringes of their activities, eagerly running their errands, cleaning out the rabbit hutches for them as a lovely surprise (they didn't always notice), always the fielder in their interminable games of cricket. She was exhilarated for a whole day by a kind word from Oliver, cast down in the same proportion when Roland told her she was only a girl, or that she was too little to join in whatever they were doing, or simply that they did not want her.

She did not long to be a boy herself. (Occasionally, in later life, when boyish girls were everywhere and many of her colleagues were avowed feminists, she wondered why, and never quite found a satisfactory answer.) But she wanted to be indispensable to them. She wanted to be part of them—all three of them, indiscriminately.

As she and they grew older she realised that she could only marry one of them, and secretly began to give much thought to which one it should be. Nigel really seemed to like her the most, she thought, coming to her for company when the other two had left him out of something. But Oliver looked so nice in his cricket things now he was getting tall, and then again Roland, though sometimes the nastiest, could be the nicest as well and could draw so wonderfully, creating real objects for her out of flat paper: rabbits, houses, his own

20

brothers . . . The marriage question was a pleasurable, if insoluble, dilemma. She never mentioned it to the Boys, as, according to her mother, boys were not interested in such things till they became men, and not always then, and she knew that they would laugh at her. But in her own mind she took it for granted that her future husband would be one of the three; they would live in a nice house (perhaps on Ashdown Forest?) and she would lay his clothes out for him and cook all his favourite foods. No other possible course of life seriously presented itself.

1909, 1911, 1913 . . . First Oliver, then Roland and finally Nigel went off to Haileybury. They were all getting tall now. Stuck, it seemed, in childhood, two years younger than Nigel and a full six and a half years behind Oliver, she strained hard, when they came home in the holidays, to please and interest them. Before getting into bed at night she prayed to God to make her grow up quickly, so that they would not leave her too far behind.

During the summer holidays in 1914, to Mary's surprise, England went to war with Germany. She did not recall having heard plans for this before, but apparently other people had. Oliver, who was in the Sixth and would be nineteen at Christmas, told her that the 'German menace' had been hanging over them for years, and that it was on the whole a jolly good thing that matters had now come to a head. He was due to leave Haileybury the following summer—he had stayed on to be Captain of House—and was fretting that the war would all be over by then. Seeing him off to a school OTC camp in his uniform, she thought he looked lovelier than ever, and wondered why her mother seemed a little cross and sometimes absentminded at the sight of him so dressed.

Something else happened that summer which had more immediate importance for Mary than the war. Uncle George and Aunt May appeared from India, bringing with them the Boys' mythic little sister, Dorothy. They came down to Tunbridge Wells in a hired motor-car one Sunday. There were smells of joint, and hot dust, and petrol and rubber and the fresh roses Mary and Mother had picked for the vases, and the starch sticking prickly in the seams of a best white

21

broderie anglaise dress which Mary disliked because it was babyish. As they waited for the visitors near the white painted gate she felt on edge and obscurely anxious. She was wary of these strangers who, in theory, belonged more closely to the Boys than she did herself.

In particular, she was wary of Dorothy, enshrined for her as a fat, sun-bonneted infant in the arms of a dark nurse, in the little photograph on the Boys' dressing table, but now apparently transformed into a girl called Dodie, and twelve like herself. She had heard a certain amount of elliptic conversation about Dodie and her parents in recent years, round the Tunbridge Wells tea-tables where her mother's friends foregathered, and had gleaned the information that Dodie's parents were mysteriously to blame for keeping their daughter with them for so long. Apparently, once you were older than seven, India, like fairyland, did awful things to you: it was for your own good that you were sent Home as the Boys had been, and if you weren't, your skin was apt to turn yellow and you would become bad-tempered, fussy and rude to the servants.

'Like the girl in *The Secret Garden*?' suggested Mary to her mother. Because of the opening in India, and because of the way the girl (who was called Mary) eventually became friends with two boys who were not her brothers, it was one of her favourite books. She had managed to persuade Nigel to read it, though not the older two.

'Yes, just like. So if Dodie seems very spoilt we must just pretend not to notice and be very kind to her, but very firm.' Mary's mother, who was by nature the most indulgent and protective of parents, was conscious of the need not to 'spoil' her only daughter, and compromised with her affectionate nature by periodically giving Mary little lectures on the importance of her 'being independent' and 'learning to do things for herself', theories which Mary filed away in a mental compartment for future use without giving them another thought. Rooted, as only the child of a lone mother can be, in the knowledge that she herself was the centre of her mother's existence, she said:

'But perhaps Aunt May wanted to keep her little girl with her? As the Boys are here, I mean.'

22

'Yes, perhaps she did.' For some reason Ellie Denvers sighed, but maybe, thought Mary, it was because she was looking in the hall mirror as she spoke and was noticing again the way her upswept dark hair was going grey in front. Nice women did not then use hair dyes. With tired briskness, she repeated:

'Anyway, darling, you must be welcoming to Dodie but not stand any nonsense from her. Take her to your room and show her your things. She may be a bit shy of her brothers, not being used to boys.'

What neither Mary nor her mother foresaw was that Dodie was equally determined to be nice to *them*, and to put them at ease in the way she had seen her own mother doing for years at garden parties in Calcutta and Ootacamund. For what emerged from the large and glittering car when it finally drew up, with Uncle George jovial beside the chauffeur, was not the sallow, cross little 'Indian' girl of Mary's mental picture, but a young princess, glowing with apparent health and exuberance.

Her dark hair lay in fat curls down her back, tied at the side with satin ribbons that Mary would have thought babyish if they had not been so luxurious. (Mary's own hair was in sensible plaits.) Her short dress was of yellow silk with lace across the yoke, lace trimmed the matching yellow 'dolly-bag' she wore on one wrist, and her little shoes were the same yellow beneath her lacy stockings. Mary could only feel silently thankful, after all, that she herself was wearing her broderie anglaise rather than one of her usual brown or blue holland summer dresses. In its shape, Dodie's dress was like that of a baby, or a very expensive doll, and yet the whole ensemble, complete with bag and shoes, managed to give her the air of a Society beauty. Similarly, her manner was an odd mixture of infantile enthusiasm and adult turn of phrase. Far from being shy of her unknown elder brothers, she made what her father described with besotted amusement as 'a dead set at them'. She wanted, Mary saw, to charm and amuse and win them to the club of Dodie-admiration already founded by her parents. And Mary also saw, with a painful and suffocating emotion that was new to her, that, yes, they were charmed and amused. Especially Oliver, the eldest. It did not seem fair.

Late in the afternoon, when everyone had left (for Uncle George and Aunt May had taken the boys away with them for a holiday in Bournemouth), Mary's mother said:

'Darling, Uncle George and Aunt May are thinking of sending Dodie to a boarding school on the coast—it's called Bessemer. It's quite famous actually. Uncle George has offered to pay for you too. Isn't that kind of him? Such a good opportunity for you!'

The emotion that had lain there all the afternoon swelled in Mary's chest. Struggling with it, she said:

'I don't want to go to boarding school with Dodie. I don't like her.'

'Don't be silly, dear. I know she's a bit affected, but that's not surprising considering she's not used to the company of children near her own age, and underneath I believe she's a thoroughly nice little girl. I heard her trying to make friends with you after lunch [this was, to Mary's chagrin, true], and I'm sure that you and she could be nice companions for each other.'

'But I don't *want* to go to boarding school. I don't want to go away from here—from you—and everything—' Even as she spoke she knew it was useless. Not because her mother would insist on this school as such, but because, that afternoon, she had got her first whiff of the inevitable changes that were on their way, her first real intimation that 'growing up' was not something creditable you did yourself but something that happened *to* you. The state of childhood, which she had known to be temporary but had experienced as permanent, was coming to an end. At lunch they had spoken of the war, now two weeks old, and Oliver and even Roland had discussed it enthusiastically with Uncle George as if they were men already. She clenched her fists.

'I thought you would be pleased at the idea of boarding school,' said her mother uncertainly, prey to an inner struggle of her own. 'I don't really feel we should refuse . . .' After a moment she added adroitly:

'After all, darling, you'll be more like the Boys then, won't you? And I believe Bessemer has a very good curriculum and standard—you'll be doing all the same sort of lessons as them, Algebra and Latin and everything. Just think how much you wanted to learn Latin when you used to hear the Boys repeating declensions and those things! Well, now's your chance.'

After a silence, Mary said:

'Does Dodie want to learn Latin?'

'I've really no idea. I don't suppose she's been offered the choice.' It was not customary to consult children's wishes in 1914.

Mary knew about girls' boarding schools. She had read stories about them, and several girls from her day school in Tunbridge Wells had gone away to board. She knew that everyone was frightfully sensible in girls' schools, and played lots of games including cricket, and wore ties. The prospect was a little alarming but not entirely unpleasant. She said cautiously:

'I can't imagine Dodie at a boarding school.'

'Well, to be quite honest, darling, nor can I. I should think she would take longer than you to shake down and find her own level.' The phrase was brisk, but Ellie Denvers spoke it uncertainly.

'Perhaps Uncle George thinks it would be good for her?'

'If you ask me,' said her mother, with one of her sudden moments of frankness towards her young daughter that were to create a close friendship between them as Mary grew up, 'if you ask me, I don't think that Uncle George thinks much about these things at all. I don't believe George knows anything about girls' education—or boys', come to that, but of course for a boy it's all laid down. I imagine he's got this idea about Bessemer just because someone's told him it's one of the best schools for girls in the south of England, and George always likes to feel he's got the best of whatever's going. And Aunt May does everything he wants. Not that you or I should complain. In the circumstances.'

That autumn Mary and her mother paid a visit to the mansion flat in Kensington which the other Denvers had rented: Uncle George and Aunt May were not, after all, to

25

return to India just yet; 'because of the war' (which in some unspecified way had an encouraging effect on Uncle George's business) they were to remain in London. The idea of life in a flat struck Mary as luxurious in the extreme—the building was centrally heated, so the bedrooms and bathroom were as warm as the drawing room, an extraordinary indulgence— and also rather modern and daring. Dodie, needless to say, seemed to take the flat in her stride, only complaining, in her mother's voice, about the house-parlourmaid.

'She's so rude and cross, Mary. These agency servants have no loyalty, of course, they just work for money. I must say I *do* miss the darling servants we had in India. Though your Susan is awfully nice, isn't she? You are lucky.'

'*You are lucky.*' It was a great phrase of Dodie's. It worked on the hearers to mollify them and make them feel flattered and, against her will, Mary found it working on her.

They were taken to a large department store to buy their outfits for Bessemer: trousseaux so lengthy and complex that they might indeed have been brides embarking on a new existence. Mary, reared in an atmosphere of genteel financial restraint, reinforced by her mother's leaning toward an artistic simplicity, found the number and variety of the clothes they apparently needed overwhelming. Not only brown tweed skirts and flannel blouses, a special overcoat *and* a cloak, but a brown gym-tunic for games with its own special linen blouses and school crest, two brown wool dresses for evening wear, one 'neutral shantung' dress for best, one special Sunday dress which could, daringly, be blue *or* grey, one felt hat (with badge), one straw panama ditto, two berets, one umbrella . . . the list went on and on. And so many under-clothes! Both Mary's home-knitted vests and knickers and Dodie's expensive silk-edged equivalents must now be re-placed by 'regulation' wear, even if one was not a regulation shape. Mary was still small and thin for her age, and the chest-gussets in the new, stiff, ugly Liberty bodices would remain ironed flat for the moment. In the changing cubicle, where the servile middle-aged shop assistant constantly came and went with more garments, she noticed that Dodie's chest was already expanding to fit her Liberty bodice satisfactorily. Yet Dodie was only a few months older than she was. The suffocating emotion which she had not yet learnt to call jealousy swelled again within her.

In London that week they were taken to museums and to the Zoo and to tea in shops along with another cousin, a boy of Nigel's age called Willie, only son of Aunt May's sister. He was not, therefore, Mary's cousin, just Dodie's and the Boys', but Mary recalled him being brought to Tunbridge Wells several times during the Boys' holidays. She remembered him as a small, fat boy who wailed 'It's not fa-ir', each time he lost a game. She and the Boys were supposed to be kind, as otherwise he would get asthma. But it soon became apparent that Willie had his own power, as a divisive tale-bearer setting one cousin against another. Perhaps, Ellie Denvers had said forbearingly, he had found it hard because he was, unlike 'their' boys, such a muff at outdoor games. It was several years since Mary had last seen him, but he did not seem to her to have changed much, though he had developed glasses and a precise, adult manner of speech. He was a scholar at Winchester now and was said superfluously by Dodie to be 'very clever'; apparently much of his spare time was spent perfecting an elaborate board-game he had invented, a cross between Mah-Jong and Ludo but using soldiers as pieces. It was also the Boys' half-term: they came up from Haileybury for the weekend, and Uncle George, at his most paternally exuberant, had arranged for everyone to see *Charlie's Aunt*. Willie, who had seemed to laugh as much as everyone else during the performance, said on the way home that he thought it was 'common . . . a bit orf actually', which enraged Oliver and Roland; perhaps, when they thought of it, they would really rather have seen a more adult show anyway. They and Nigel retaliated by addressing him as Little Willie, which was not a kind thing to do in November 1914, since that was the nickname of the German Kaiser.

After they reached home Willie had asthma, which made Mary scornful and uneasy but seemed to excite Dodie's sympathy. Afterwards, in the much-draped bedroom they were sharing, she told Mary, in the special, hushed, grown-up voice she regularly used when imparting a piece of family information, that Willie was highly strung because

27

his father was behaving badly towards his mother—Uncle George and Aunt May were very angry with his father, it seemed.

'What sort of behaving badly?' asked Mary, puzzled, wondering if Willie's father were rude or untidy, or forgot to do things he had promised to do, as the Boys sometimes did. Reared in a home without a father, her own concept of marital relations was of the vaguest.

'Oh, _you_ know—' Dodie made a small face, copied from her mother, bent her head to shake out her nightdress as if it were a silk skirt, and added nonchalantly in her father's voice:

'Other women and so forth . . .'

Mary was not enlightened. But she perceived, not for the first time, that Dodie seemed to have some intuitive grasp of the nature of life which eluded her. Beside Dodie she felt a fool, and she resented it. Yet at the same time she could not help warming to Dodie's engaging personality, in which both impulsive child and adult woman seemed to co-exist. She was like the heroine of one of those school stories called _Patsy's First Year_, or _The Madcap of the Fifth_, who had gipsy blood or a pet frog or who saved the French mistress from drowning. When we get to Bessemer, Mary thought drearily, she will be popular. No one will want to talk to me, much.

But that winter Mary was ill, first with tonsillitis and then with pneumonia, and after Christmas Dodie departed to Bessemer on her own, with many tears, they heard. Mary's mother nursed her day and night. In later years, thinking back, it seemed to Mary that in those weeks her mother's hair grew much greyer—that she became, and remained, middle-aged then, while Mary herself also grew and changed in that brief space of time. As she lay convalescing, the previous summer and all the summers of childhood already seemed distant.

Oliver came to see her. He hadn't stayed at school the two more terms, basking in the pleasures and privileges of being Captain of Bartle Frere house before going up to Oxford the following September, but instead had left at Christmas and was for the moment living at home in the flat in Kensington and trying to get into the Army. He was finding it harder than he expected. The exhortations to enlist that had papered the streets of town for the last four months had been taken to heart by men of between eighteen and forty of all classes, all over the country, for many different reasons; their Country might Need them, but their country could not in fact process them as fast as they presented themselves, particularly the young officer-cadets like Oliver. He was impatient and physically restless, pacing Mary's bedroom.

'Isn't Uncle George cross that you've left school now?' Mary wanted to know.

'Not at all. He's absolutely with me on this—thinks I'm quite right to want to go. My Mamma's a bit fussed about it, of course. Thinks I might catch cold or something, out in France!'

'But you were going to go to Oxford.' Mary felt wistful about that. She had been looking forward to visiting him there.

'Oh well, I might still. After the war, you know. But I'm not too bothered about it, in fact. Roland's always been more of a swot than I have—perhaps he'll be the one to go.'

A few weeks later, when she was up and about but still feeling unaccountably tired and even weepy, he came again, elated, and told her that he was off to a training camp in the next few days and that after that he expected to go to France. He said:

'When I get posted over there, it would be nice to get lots of letters and things from home. Aunt Ellie says she'll write often. Will you write to a fellow too?'

'Of *course* I will,' she said, irradiated with love and admiration. How could he even think she might not write? But then he half spoilt it by saying indulgently:

'I asked Dodie, but she says she's no good at writing letters, little beast. I'm not surprised to hear it; her spelling's awful. She doesn't seem to have had any proper education in India—just some sort of govvy. I know it doesn't matter in the same way for girls, but she ought to be able to spell, at least, if she's going to be a lady. Perhaps this fancy nunnery she's going to will teach her . . . When are you joining her there, by the way?'

29

'In the summer now, I think.' She thought of adding, 'Please will you write to me there, it will be nice to get letters when I'm away from home too,' but it would have sounded silly, comparing her situation to his own. Anyway, he would have more important, grown-up male things to do there than write to her.

In the summer term at Bessemer she found Dodie, as she had expected, already ensconced in a circle of giggling devotees. In that closed and female institution, where the rôles of normal society had to be shared out among a much narrower range of people than usual, personal differences became exaggerated and stereotyped. Dodie, far from being masculinised, as some of the other girls were by the ties, the use of surnames and the no-nonsense style of the staff, seemed particularly feminine and kittenish. She was naughty, not in a disruptive or serious way, but with an officially recognised, jokey, bad-little-girl naughtiness that some of the mistresses obviously liked and even indulged. She whispered in morning assembly and drew mildly rude pictures in the margins of her rough book, and was repeatedly in detention for not learning Latin or French verbs. Her marks generally were bad; she did not, in fact, seem to be very clever, and this surprised Mary who had assumed that Dodie's acuteness and *savoir faire* would be marked by an equal ability at school work. Perhaps Dodie deliberately did not try but, if that were so, she was surprisingly persevering about it.

Once she had got over the long, private agonies of home-sickness and the bleakness of life in a renowned girls' boarding school compared with life at home, Mary found to her surprise that she herself seemed to be quite clever. New subjects like Latin and Chemistry, which had not been taught in her unambitious Tunbridge Wells day school, presented her with no problem. Tidy, willing and superficially adaptable, she fitted into school life: the staff liked her and, after a while, so did the other girls. She did not become well known or attract a fan-club like Dodie, but then she had not expected to. 'Try to get all you can out of it, darling,' her mother had said as she hugged her goodbye, and Mary, suddenly understanding that her mother's sadness at separation was even greater than her own and that from then on her mother would spend much of her time alone, took the words to heart. She settled down philosophically to school like a prisoner to his sentence—or a soldier to the duration of the war. It was indeed as if the war, originally just an excitement offstage, had now entered into her own life as an ordeal to be borne. Or like a long illness, from which one could only gradually hope for recovery.

1915 ached its way into 1916. The heating at Bessemer, never adequate for a building poised on a cliff overlooking the sea, was cut down to a tepid suggestion of warmth. You were allowed to wear mittens in class, as well as on the raw, rain-drenched playing fields, but chilblains were commonplace among both girls and staff. The food, never lavish either, became consistently unappetising and often insufficient. Cakes from home were the only material solace, greedily yearned over by all. Dodie received more food parcels than anyone else, and sometimes gave slices of cake or pie to Mary, particularly when other people were present; but they saw less of each other now, for Mary had been moved into a higher class whereas Dodie had not.

On cliff-top walks that bitter spring the long crocodile of girls passed by a pillared house which had become a convalescent home for what were always referred to as 'wounded Tommies'. Men lounged outside the gates on warmer days, sniffing for some hint of spring; men in overalls with crutches or with empty sleeves or with bandaged heads. Sometimes they whistled after the girls, and the mistress, chap-lipped and felt-hatted, would crossly urge her charges to walk on faster.

Mary would have liked to stop and talk. She felt sorry for the Tommies, many of whom looked no older than Oliver and Roland, and she divined that they were merely bored and lonely. But they were seen by Bessemer as a threat to the whole school ethic, an alarming and unwelcome hint of a world which the school gates carefully excluded. On the afternoon when, to the echo of strap shoes over wooden floors, it got about the building that Dorothy Denvers and two other girls had been caught straggling behind the crocodile, talking to the Tommies and *actually giving them sweets*, a thrill of horror went through girls and staff alike. Such a misdemeanour was far worse than naughty, it was *common*, and constituted letting down the school. As Dodie's cousin, Mary felt apologetic and censured herself. Yet, lying on her thin mattress that night, in the communal dormitory that smelt of soapy water and peppermint toothpaste, she felt again stirring within her a jealous admiration for Dodie, who was now officially in Coventry.

That summer, Mary was fourteen. Roland had reached his eighteenth birthday some months before, and both he and Oliver were now in France. The heroic gesture of enlistment which Oliver had been able to make had become, by 1916, a matter of obligation: it was said that in any case conscription was coming. The war had lost its glamour and its savour. On his last leave Oliver had not seemed to want even to talk about it.

Other girls, too, had brothers and cousins and even fathers at the Front, and every so often one or two would be sent for by the Head, and then everyone would 'know' and a small silence would descend on the classrooms and the dining tables. Sometimes the girls went home for a week or two, but more of them, as time went on, stayed at school, red-eyed and withdrawn or consciously brave according to type, indulged or avoided by their teachers and classmates. In that efficiently run institution no special arrangements could be made for them to mourn. So many men seemed to be dying.

During the slaughter that was later to be called the first battle of the Somme the school was in the midst of summer exams. Mary went through each paper competently with the surface of her mind; almost without realising it, her deeper thoughts were all elsewhere. People said that, on a still day, you could hear the guns in France. She was perpetually straining her ears.

When, in assembly on the morning of 5 July, her name and Dodie's were read out among several names of girls who were asked to come and see the Head, the shock was not that of an unexpected blow but of a horrible confirmation. It would be Oliver, because he was the eldest, Oliver who had been so brave and pleased when the war started, and to whom she had written a silly schoolgirl's letter last week, wishing she could say more things to interest him, Oliver who had carried her on the bar of his bike and given her piggyback rides long ago on picnics . . . She was weeping for him before they reached the Head's study.

It was not Oliver, but Roland. He had been in the Army four months, and in France less than six weeks.

That afternoon, Uncle George and Aunt May came and fetched Dodie from school and took her home with them. Mary only discovered this after evening prep. They had not, it seemed, thought to take her too, and had not even asked to see her. She understood now what her mother meant when she had said that George and May could be rather thoughtless sometimes . . . No one at Bessemer realised the exact situation, and she suffered her grief alone. Dead cousins officially rated no more than a brusque 'Sorry about your cousin, Denvers': you were not supposed to mind about them as you might a brother.

That evening too, by coincidence, was the moment she first began to bleed, or, in the antique school phrase presumably inherited from an earlier generation of governesses, 'became a young lady'. Of course she knew what it was: she was the child of a modern-minded mother. Yet in the restless, miserable night, disturbed by an unfamiliar ache and by a bulky cloth between her legs, she dreamed feverishly that she was bleeding for Roland, taking his fatal wound upon herself, *dying that he might live*, as it said in church. Passionately and consciously, feeling the blood seep from her, she gave up her life that his might continue. But the next day came, and a waking knowledge that he was indeed dead, dead, dead, returned to her like a more chronic sickness, and her dream seemed merely silly and a bit disgusting.

Dodie did not return to school that term, which was understandable, but she did not reappear at the beginning of the autumn term either. Mary had hardly seen her, or Nigel, in the summer holidays: they had been with their parents in Scotland. (In view of the war, holidays were now considered vaguely unpatriotic, but apparently Scotland counted as more moral than Bournemouth, and Aunt May was said to be 'in a poor way' which further excused the family departure. Mary and her mother passed a quiet, sad holiday alone at home.)

Only when term had begun again did Uncle George write to tell his sister-in-law that Dodie would not be returning to Bessemer. Ellie Denvers wrote to Mary:

> . . . It seems rather a sudden decision, but he and Aunt May have of course been hit hard by poor dear Roland's death, and I suppose that has altered their ideas. Uncle George is now saying that Aunt May needs a daughter to keep her company, and that he never approved of blue-stocking women anyway. (!) I must say, I can't feel he's doing right by Dodie and it seems rather a change-about after him being so all-for Bessemer two years ago, but that's Uncle George for you. I felt quite worried when I got his letter in case he might have changed his mind about paying your fees too (for you know, darling, we could never afford them without him) and I actually went over to the Fanshawes to ring him up on their telephone. But it seems he's quite happy to go on paying for you for the moment, which of course *is* generous of him. So, darling, you will be on your own . . .

Not till several years later, when she was in the sixth form and was the trusted confidante of one or two members of staff, did Mary discover by chance that Dodie's parents had been told it might be better if Dodie did not return to Bessemer. Because of her lack of work, together with the wounded Tommies incident, it had been felt that Dodie was 'not really a good influence in the school' or at any rate 'not quite the Bessemer type'. Floundering slightly, but old and confident enough now to query judgment (debating was encouraged in the Sixth), Mary suggested that surely the wounded Tommies episode had been harmless?

Well, yes, in itself perhaps . . . The housemistress visibly hesitated. 'There was the business about pilfering money too,' she said quietly. 'But perhaps you didn't know about that? My dear, as she is your cousin perhaps I shouldn't have

mentioned it anyway. These things are always difficult . . .
But, in the circumstances, we all felt Bessemer would be
better without her, and that the school could not give her
what it hopes to give its girls.'

Utterly taken aback, Mary managed to say:

'But—taking money you say? How odd. I mean, because
her family are actually quite wealthy. She's certainly never
lacked anything.'

'Surprising as it seems,' said the housemistress drily, 'she
is not the first gel like that I have known to pilfer. It doesn't
seem to have anything to do with need, in my opinion.' Then
she changed the subject.

Some time during the interminable middle years of both the
war and Mary's education Susan, the cook-general who had
been with them since Mary had been a small child, unexpectedly left. At least it was unexpected to Mary, who
came home one holidays to find Susan's friendly face absent
and, in her place, a silent Belgian refugee who seemed to
dislike Britain and everything pertaining to it. Surely, Mary
asked her mother, their own Susan had not gone off to make
munitions? It was other people's badly treated servants who
did that.

Her mother reassured her, adding that Susan would be
back again, she hoped. She had just gone to work for Aunt
May and Uncle George in London for a while.

'For heaven's sake, why? I know they're always carrying
on about the servant problem and how ungrateful These
Modern Girls are, but surely that doesn't mean we have to
lend them Susan?'

'Well, you see, darling . . . Oh dear. Well, as a matter of
fact it was quite kind of your Aunt May to offer to have her for
a bit. You see, poor Susan hasn't been entirely well.'

'In that case I should think Aunt May's the last person
she should work for. You know how Aunt May lies around
on sofas and expects to have everything fetched for her.
What's the matter with Susan? Why is London better for
her?'

'Poor Susan is going to have a baby,' said Ellie Denvers
bravely. She looked at her daughter and then, disconcerted

35

by Mary's expression of amazement, looked away again and searched for something in her workbox. After a minute she said:

'Susan will be better off in London, you see, because she isn't known there and can call herself "Mrs" and pass herself off to the tradespeople and so on as a war widow. There are such a lot of them now . . . Then, when her time comes, she can have the baby in one of the big London hospitals. Aunt May and Uncle George will arrange that for her.'

'And then she'll come back to us?'

'I hope so. I must say, I miss her. Germaine is so depressing.'

'And she'll bring the baby to live here?'

It was her mother's turn to look surprised.

'Why no, darling, that would hardly do. Since the whole point is that no one here in Tunbridge Wells should know anything about it.'

'But what will happen to the baby?'

'Well, Dr Barnardo's would always take it . . . Or perhaps the hospital almoner might find some nice family to adopt it. That would be much the best, of course.' Contemplating this possibility Ellie Denvers looked more cheerful, as if just imagining 'some nice family' were tantamount to finding them.

'But won't that be very sad for Susan? After all, it is her baby.'

'I know, I know.' Her mother wore the face of crumpled distress she wore when another Tunbridge Wells young man was heard to be missing in action, or when the gardener had to be asked to drown another litter of kittens, or when the puppy bought for the Boys had been run over. But, as on such occasions, she went on with conscious briskness:

'I'm very much afraid poor Susan ought to have thought of that before. You see, it really is very wrong—well, dreadfully thoughtless, anyway—to have a baby when you're not married. I must say, I'm surprised at Susan, she's always been so sensible before and she's hardly a young girl. I think that perhaps she thought the man would marry her, though she doesn't seem to have known him at all well . . . A soldier, of course. Goodness knows where he is now.' Inaudibly: 'I'm

36

afraid he deceived her . . .' More briskly: 'She's probably much better off without him.'

Much of this passed over Mary's head, and anyway the facts she had gleaned from Biology lessons about human reproduction suggested to her that you couldn't possibly *not* know someone well if you were having his baby. Disliking the feeling of being out of her depth, she said crossly:

'I don't understand at all. It seems perfectly silly . . . Why can't *we* adopt the baby? We've plenty of room. Now that the Boys—now that Oliver's grown up and Nigel doesn't need to come here so much because of having his parents back home.'

Equally crossly, sounding upset now, her mother answered:

'We can't possibly adopt Susan's baby. Don't be silly, Mary. I thought you were more grown up than that. I quite wish I hadn't told you.'

In the night Mary thought of Susan, and of babies, and wondered, painfully stretching her imagination in an attempt to understand, what it would be like to be carrying a baby inside you from which you must separate yourself as soon as it was born. It would be dreadful, she thought.

One night she dreamed that Susan's baby was born and had grown up unnaturally fast ('Of course the working classes do develop early,' she had heard someone say) and was now at the Front with Roland. They were both alive, but neither would return. They had been abandoned by their mothers. Both were angry about it.

Did Aunt May have dreams like that? she wondered the next day. But it was impossible to imagine Aunt May having dreams about anything.

Later that holidays Mary and her mother went up to town for lunch and a show, as it was called, with Aunt May, Nigel and Dodie; this had become a holiday ritual since Dodie had left Bessemer. She was currently attending a fashionable school in Kensington, where the emphasis was not on Latin and Chemistry and Higher School Cert. but on French, Elocution and Drama. There was of course no uniform. Her clothes were almost as expensive and sophisticated as her mother's, but she still wore her glossy hair in ringlets down her back with a large ribbon. Nigel called her 'our flapper', which seemed to please her but annoyed Uncle George and Aunt May. Mary thought she could guess why. There was a lot in the papers about flappers these days; it was smart to be a flapper—but they weren't perhaps, quite, ladies? They seemed to be a new kind of person invented out of the war, like the 'temporary gentlemen' they were photographed with at tea-dances, or like the 'wartime profiteers' Uncle George pontificated against at the lunch table over casserole of liver.

In the hall of the Denvers' flat Mary took both Susan's hands, delighted to see her, but Susan seemed embarrassed and quickly retreated to the kitchen regions. Hurt a little, Mary said to Dodie when they were alone together taking off their hats:

'Poor Susan—I *do* think it's sad for her.'

Dodie looked surprised: 'Oh, but the hospital will cure her, Mamma says. It's just a quite ordinary tumour, apparently. They should have a bed for her soon.'

It had never for one moment occurred to Mary that Aunt May should have concocted such a story for Dodie—and maybe for Nigel too? Without reflection, and with a sense of confused indignation on Susan's behalf, she hastened to enlighten her cousin.

Dodie made a disgusted face, screwing up her pretty nose as if at a bad smell. 'Honestly, Mary, *what* a thing to say! I thought it was me that invented stories, not goody-goody old you.'

'But it's true.'

'Of course it isn't! I mean—how could it be? Mamma and Dado wouldn't have her in the house if it was. I mean—it would be disgusting. Honestly, you are queer sometimes.'

In the face of an ignorance that yet seemed far more sophisticated and knowing than her own approach, Mary was silenced.

In November 1917 Oliver, by then a survivor of many battles and one minor wound, was killed at Passchendaele. Or rather, his name appeared on the long list of those who were missing, who had apparently been sucked down unseen—alive, dead or dying—into that countryside of mud that the name Passchendaele has come to mean. As the days without news lengthened into weeks, his family had to give his absence the name of death, but there was never one moment at which anyone could say conclusively 'Oliver is dead', and so Mary was not told what had happened till she came home for the Christmas holidays. Then she was angry with her mother as she had never been in her life and would never be again.

'Why didn't you tell me? Why did you let me go on thinking he was alive, when all the time he was lying there cold and decaying? How *could* you?'

'Darling, darling—'

'Did you think it doesn't matter what a schoolgirl thinks— that she's safe at school and doesn't count?'

But her mother now, at the words 'cold and decaying', was weeping too much to answer.

Incoherent in her grief, and in the anger of grief, Mary could not explain that she felt she had failed Roland and Oliver (but particularly, now, Oliver) by allowing them to die at all. Oh, if she had loved them even harder, thought about them even more, could that somehow have tipped a small balance of fate, far out across the battlefields? Intellectually she knew that it could not be so, yet she went on believing it.

It was also at that time that the first thought of one day becoming a doctor, a person of special powers who might actually be able to tip the balance in favour of a life, drifted across her mind. It returned at intervals, and finally, secretly, embedded itself. A famous old girl of Bessemer had founded a women's hospital. With the men away at the war, woman doctors were ceasing to be rarities . . . Affectionate and pliable as a child, Mary was slightly surprised herself to find this and one or two other novel ideas growing like tough roots within her. Adults who encountered her in the streets of Tunbridge Wells on her bicycle, with her plaits twisted into a jug-handle, sometimes thought her a little formidable in spite of her nice manners, and wondered if she were going to turn into one of those clever, modern women of which one heard so much in the papers these days.

The following year, the last of the war and the year in which she became sixteen and took Matric, Mary solaced herself by writing long letters to Nigel, to which he responded with short but prompt notes. She had always been closest to him, though admiring him less totally than his brothers. Just eighteen himself now, he had left school and was living at home in the grand new tile-hung house that the Denvers had bought near Esher when the Zeppelin raids began on London; he was learning to ride a motor-bike and waiting to go to Camp.

Although he said little about it directly, Mary knew him well enough to know that he dreaded the thought of his call-up, with a sick, continual dread unalleviated by the sense of excitement or courage or even self-sacrifice that had cheered his brothers. How could he feel otherwise, with both of them gone? Uncle George, transformed from a militaristic patriot into a bereaved father, was said to be trying to 'pull strings' at the War Office to have Nigel declared fit for home duty only, but there was no reason for this ploy to succeed. It was several years now since Nigel had outgrown both his air of delicacy and his shameful bed-wetting; too many parents of dead sons were attempting to save their remaining ones. What, censorious letters to the papers asked, of the parents of only sons? No one had excused their boys; they had had to make the supreme sacrifice, hadn't they? Well, then. The misery installed in homes rich and poor up and down the land did not, it seemed, breed generosity and compassion but an avid bitterness: the war must continue.

At the end of September 1918 Nigel conferred instant glamour on Mary, in the eyes of her school-fellows, by arriving unheralded at Bessemer one Sunday on his motor-bike. As he was in his new officer's uniform, and on embarkation leave, they were allowed one hour together on their own in the housemistress's sitting room.

Shy at first with each other in these unaccustomed circumstances, they tried various topics of conversation before falling back on reminiscences of their shared childhood. After a while Mary dared mention their pretend games about India, with a deprecating smile—because of course Nigel, as a boy, would have forgotten all about that, or anyway wouldn't want to be reminded. But, to her surprise

40

and pleasure, he seemed eager to talk about it, to recall with amusement the elephant and the pretend servants they had had. India itself, he said, as an actual memory had pretty much faded. He had, after all, been only seven when he had left . . . Oh, except that he had dreamed about it a little while ago. His parents had not been there, but Oliver and Roland had (he spoke their names bravely), and their old bungalow in Calcutta and everything—though that seemed, as the dream went on, to get a bit mixed up with the house in Tunbridge Wells. It had been a jolly sort of dream, though nothing much had happened in it as far as he could remember.

'I felt sad when I woke up and it was just a dream,' he said, his voice suddenly thickening, and he looked at the beige roses on the carpet, and fiddled with his swagger-stick till he dropped it with a clatter.

'Perhaps you really will go back to India one day,' she said, to distract him. 'Like we used to plan.'

He answered valiantly—his imminent departure for France had hardly been mentioned between them—that this was in fact on the cards:

'Father's hoping I'll go into the firm, and I really think I might. I mean, financially I'd be a fool not to. If so, I'd probably go to Calcutta, at any rate for a few years, to take charge of that end of the business. Father says this country's being ruined by—by the war, you know—and that once it's over the Empire's going to be the best bet, in the long run . . . Rather fun. I say—Mary?'

'Yes. What is it, Nigel? Tell me quick because Miss Pritchard will be back in a minute and I have to go and take horrible junior choir practice at three o'clock.'

'Mary—if I go out to Calcutta for the firm, why don't you come too? You'll have left school by then, I should think. To keep house for me, I mean. Do! It'd be fun being there together. Now that the others have gone—'

She thought of her secret idea about becoming a doctor, but she said warmly, 'Yes, that would be fun! Yes, I'd love to.'

'That's a deal, then,' he said. They beamed at each other awkwardly, both pleased. As an afterthought, he said:

41

'I suppose the grown-ups'll let us . . . But we'll be grown up ourselves by then, won't we?'

He left soon after, in his uniform as an officer and leader of men, on his motor-bike, admired by juniors goggling from the top dormitory. He had been accustomed from early days to traumatic departure—to England, to boarding school, now to France. She dreaded that she might never see him again; and she never did.

As it happened, he very nearly survived, for great Allied advances had been made during the summer, and most of the big battles were over. Yet, as if some relentless, bureaucratic pattern were still working itself mindlessly out in the last weeks before the Armistice, the news came on 23 October that he had died of wounds in a casualty-clearing station near Messines Ridge three days earlier.

As the family went for the third time through the rituals of mourning, it seemed to Mary that even their grief had, through repetition, become a poor, worn thing. It was as if the fate that had drained the colour and interest and meaning from life, by taking away the Boys, had robbed even pain of its sharpness. Everything, even sorrow, was diminished, made futile.

At Christmas George and May Denvers and Dodie were in Switzerland, where they had gone because May had 'broken down' in some unspecified way. Words like 'total collapse' and 'complete nervous prostration' were bandied about the family. Mary found herself with a mental picture of a broken, very expensive doll, its wax face cracked, its arms—still clad in real silk—detached from its padded torso. Everyone said it was only to be expected: the three sons all gone like that; the war had been a terrible thing but now at least there would never be another one. The boys had not died in vain . . .

That Christmas holidays Mary's mother was quite ill, with flu from the epidemic that was sweeping Europe in a bitter accentuation of tragedy, bereaving further the already bereaved, finding easy victims in those who had lost their reason to live. Together with Susan, now restored to her former place and respectability, and the local doctor's wife who was a close family friend, Mary helped to nurse her mother, and for the first time in her life felt entirely grown up and responsible. It ought to have been a good feeling, she thought, but it was a sad one. Sadness seemed everywhere these days, not as a sharp pain but more like a continual ache or burden. It affected, subtly, everything you thought, everything you did.

Dodie was reported to be 'very good' with her mother's nerves, and, later, to be having a 'gay time' in Lucerne.

The following Christmas, 1919, Mary had just left school. She already had her Higher School Certificate, and in a few months would be eighteen. The Head of Bessemer had wanted her to try for Oxford or Cambridge; in fact she had been pressing about it both to Mary and to her mother. But Ellie Denvers was adamant that they could not possibly ask Uncle George to pay for any more education, and Mary saw reluctantly that she was right.

Had she been a boy, Uncle George would almost certainly have regarded it as his duty to 'see the lad through' university or medical school, but that, of course, would have been quite different.

She did pluck up courage to write to Uncle George and ask him if she should not embark on some specific further training 'since I would rather earn my own living than be a burden to Mother'. In return, she received a hurt letter saying that she surely did not want to be a schoolmarm or a typist, did she? And that, 'Thank God the time has not yet come when my only niece has to turn-to in that way. I shall continue to assist your mother as I always have done, and, should anything happen to her one day—which God forbid—remember you always have a home with us. Until, that is, you marry, which I sincerely hope you will, as in my humble opinion that is still by far the best career for a woman, and I am thankful to say that Dodie feels as I do.' This infuriating communication ended with a magnanimous offer that Mary should spend her Christmas holidays with the Denvers, at the house they had rented in Cadogan Square, 'for the season', and that she should 'come out' there.

Dodie, it appeared, was 'out' already. Mary's mother said

43

with a gleam of humour that was rare with her these days that presumably that little minx Dodie had escaped so far out of her box in Lucerne that it had proved impossible to put her back in again.

Whatever Uncle George might say about war-profiteers it was evident that his own business had profited by the war. The house in Cadogan Square was unequivocally grand; there was even a butler. It was a pity, thought Mary, that the theatre parties and dances to which she and Dodie were escorted by a re-assembled Aunt May, superb in mauve, somehow did not quite live up to the surroundings. She was too inexperienced to grasp fully that in their new-found wealth Uncle George and Aunt May were attempting to 'crash' a level of society they had not hitherto entered, and were having only limited success. But she sensed an unease, a hollow loudness as in Uncle George's laugh, that perhaps echoed round life itself.

In prospect it all sounded so new and exciting. But, when the time came, most of the girls at dances were no different from the plainer and sillier ones at school, in spite of their expensive dresses; and most of the young men in tails and white gloves seemed to Mary to be versions of Cousin Willie, condescending and offhand when they danced with you or else very young, even younger than herself and Dodie, nervous seventeen-year-olds wearing their fathers' evening suits, boys who had been Too Young for the war . . .

It was being said that the 'flower of British youth' had died in France. Looking round at the ballrooms of Knightsbridge and Kensington, Mary could believe it.

Willie, though he was twenty now, had not been in the war. His asthma had excused him—or else someone had 'had a word' with someone at the War Office. Mary recalled, 'It's not fa-ir'. Now, it seemed, it was Willie who was not fair. According to Dodie, Uncle George disliked him in consequence. But nevertheless Willie, on vacation from Oxford, was frequently at their house and seemed to fill the rôle of official escort for Dodie. Perhaps it was because there was no one else.

If Nigel had been there . . . Or any of them. A new and

44

more worldly sense of loss was added to Mary's personal grief for them.

Would she ever again, she wondered in panic over the wastes of a polished floor, waltzing stiffly in the slack arms of a stranger, talk easily and naturally to any boy—any man—as she had done to Nigel, Roland and Oliver?

Dodie did not talk naturally to her dancing partners either, but then she did not try to; she giggled and flirted and told tall stories and played the fool in a way that made Mary curl inside. 'Ridiculous showing off' it would have been called at Bessemer, but some at least of the boys seemed not to mind. She was so very pretty. Sorrowfully, but with a dogged pursuit of truth, Mary registered in front of a cloakroom looking glass that her own 'quite nice' looks, her 'quite pretty' light brown hair and her 'neat' figure were as nothing compared with Dodie's downy loveliness. Yet it wasn't just skin or hair or eyes with Dodie; there was some inner glow there too, a message of excitement, something conspiratorial. She looked like a child with a secret, or the one whose birthday party it is. She had not put her hair heavily 'up' as Mary had; instead she had had it bobbed (explosions of wrath, followed by muttering indulgence, from Uncle George); it lay in a peak on the nape of her neck like black feathers so that you wanted to stroke it. Was she grown up?—Or not? What *did* she know? By her account, imparted to Mary in a whisper in the bedroom, as if Aunt May or Uncle George might be hiding behind the velvet drapes, she had met 'someone' in Switzerland with whom she was currently corresponding *poste restante*. A singing master. Married. It sounded to Mary an adult and alarming situation But two days later she heard Willie make a drawling joke about 'your dago suitor', and though Dodie had hit him with her handbag and tried to pull his hair she had seemed to treat it as a joke too. How seriously did she mean herself to be taken? Did she understand what was meant by 'playing with fire'? Impossible to tell.

But Mary, questing and guessing, ignorant of society but with her senses sharpened by loneliness and loss, half divined that Dodie represented a new kind of woman, made for the new decade and for what was already being called the

45

post-war world. Not what the last century had called a 'new woman': they were heavy and tweedy; there was sweat in their armpits and veins in their sensibly stockinged legs. They had been present for thirty years already; they had known their humanising disappointments and defeats. Well-preserved 'new women' had largely staffed Bessemer. Others had nursed soldiers in France or had driven vans or had worked on the land. But Dodie was really new. Somewhere, obscurely, during the war, people were intimating, a mould had been broken. Notions of commitment and high-mindedness, enduring love and even decorum had leaked away into the torn and bloody earth and out, with her little silver frock and her bobbed hair, had sprung Dodie.

On the last evening of the old year they sat, with Mary's mother and Willie, round the elaborately decorated table; the sustained and determined gaiety of the last ten days had spread a pall of unadmitted nervous exhaustion and biliousness over the company. Uncle George, who had consumed a good deal of claret already, Mary had noted, broke a particularly long silence by raising his glass ceremoniously and clearing his throat:

'I know—ah—in the Established Church we don't drink to the dead—to, ah, the fallen, I should say. That would be Papism. But, my dears, I should still like to drink a toast to youth and courage. At least it's something to have bred men, and three such fine ones . . . Even if they were called upon to give up their lives so soon.'

Tears trickled out of the corners of his bloodshot eyes. Mary, too deeply embarrassed to be moved by this spectacle, hastily raised her own glass to get the matter over. But, to her surprise, her mother was on her feet:

'George, I won't drink to that; it's not true. To be men, they didn't need to die. And they weren't men anyway, they were innocent schoolboys—'

'They gave their lives, m'dear.'

'They didn't have a chance to know what life was to give! And they didn't give—anything. It was all taken from them—*taken*, do you hear?' She collapsed in a passion of uncontrolled tears such as Mary had never seen her in—not

46

when the telegrams came, not through all her years of matter-of-fact widowhood.

A bleak insight into the real meaning of the words 'for ever' swept over Mary. This was for ever, this unhealed sore of regret and loss. People, she saw, were not equipped by nature to believe in 'for ever': feeling that the happy past must still exist and return in some natural cycle like the seasons, they talked in an unfocused way of 'consolation' and 'things being better by and by'. But it was not true. The truth was that something had been taken away which could not be replaced, and life would literally never be the same again. If God had ever been true, she found herself thinking in those seconds with a new, devastating objectivity, then He too had certainly died somewhere in France as well. Aghast at her own vision, she averted her mind from it.

But Aunt May was on her feet too:

'How dare you say that? My sons didn't go to the war because they had to—well, poor, dear Nigel may have—but Oliver and Roland went because they were brave, because they knew it was their duty to fight for King and Country. How dare you try to take that consolation away from me?'

'Your sons!' cried Mary's mother, beside herself. 'Your sons, indeed—you met them as strangers when they were big boys already. Who brought them up? Who taught them to wash and say their prayers and be polite to people? Who got Nigel out of wetting his bed, and went down to see the Head that time when Oliver failed his exams—*and* that other time when Roland was found cheating at Greek Unseen? Who nursed them when they were ill? Who *loved* them? Not you—'

'And was that my fault?' Aunt May shrieked, her bland face transformed and mottled, looking as if she would attack her sister-in-law physically. 'You took my sons away from me. Just because I was loyal to my husband. *You* didn't have to make that sacrifice, but I did—'

'Don't you dare say I've had an easier life than you! It's been hard, May, and I never told you all I spent on your sons, to give them treats and little things they needed—spent *gladly*, mind you, but—'

47

'And who paid for Mary's school, I should like to know—'

Mary, appalled, could only look from one woman to the other. It was Dodie who provided a diversion by drumming her heels on the floor and screaming, so that no one else could hear themselves speak.

'I read about hysterics in a book,' she confided to Mary afterwards as they fetched their cloaks—for they were going on to a dance. 'I thought I did it rather well, don't you?'

By that time the quarrel was officially over. The two women had wept, and patted each other, and had assured each other they had not meant what they had said. But Mary never forgot a word of it, and she suspected that no one else did either.

She felt shattered, and her head began to ache. She would have been glad to forego the dance to which they were invited that night, but did not like to say so, as Dodie, Aunt May and Willie seemed to be gripped by a hectic desire to behave as if nothing had happened; seeing the New Year in was a moral obligation.

They returned home at last to the solid, vibrating house, some time after midnight. Mary's mother, who had not accompanied them, had gone to bed: from Uncle George's study came the smell of his Trichinopoly cigars. Aunt May, who either conceived of Mary as much younger than Dodie or wished to, sent Mary to bed, while Dodie and Willie were still drinking cocoa in the dining room. But Mary, who had smoked a cigarette for the first time that evening, found herself, although exhausted, feverishly wakeful.

After a long time, in the course of which she was not even sure if she had slept or not, she got up and went softly to the next-door room where Dodie should have been sleeping. But the single walnut bed was still as the maid had left it hours before, with the silk cover turned down and the ironed lawn and lace nightdress spread out. What could Dodie be doing downstairs all this time? The small French clock on the mantelpiece said a quarter to two.

In her Jaeger school dressing gown she ventured barefoot down the carpeted flights. The servants would all be in bed by now and presumably Uncle George too: the door of his

48

study was ajar, lit only by the embers of a fire, and the big drawing room was in darkness as well. But from under the dining-room door came a dim light, as if the wall-lights over the sideboard were on.

As she lifted her hand to turn the handle someone screamed within the room, not loudly but as if with concentrated fear or excitement. It didn't sound like Dodie this time. Could it possibly be Aunt May—Aunt May and her 'nerves' again? Mary hesitated a long moment, but no further cry came. She went in.

At one end of the long, polished table, Aunt May, Dodie and Willie sat facing each other in the weak light. There was some sort of board on the table, like a raised tray, and for a moment Mary thought absurdly that Willie must have persuaded them—in the middle of the night?—to play that boring invented game he had been absorbed in when he was younger. At the end of the board nearest to Aunt May was what looked like a slanting stick, to which she held her fingertips with great concentration, while Dodie and Willie held the sides of the board. Then, seeing Mary, Willie pushed back his chair and sprang quickly to his feet. The board skidded away from him across the table, nearly skating off it, exposing a scribbled sheet of paper.

'What d'you want, Mary? We thought you'd gone to bed hours ago.'

But Mary scarcely heard him. Her eyes instead were on her aunt. Aunt May had not seemed to hear her come in. Although the board had slid sideways her fingers remained clamped to the stick—giant pencil or whatever it was—and she gazed at the scribbles on the paper with an expression of naked fear and fascination. When Dodie, like Willie, got up quickly and jogged her mother's shoulder as if to arouse her attention, Aunt May gave another tiny, breathless scream. She reminded Mary of Nigel, whom she had seen once or twice as a little boy stuck in a nightmare from which he apparently could not rouse himself. Or a woman whom she had once seen on a bus in Tunbridge Wells, having some sort of fit.

It was Willie who reached the door first and quickly shepherded Mary out into the hall.

49

'Willie, *what's* going on? Is Aunt May ill?'

'Sshh, keep your voice down. We don't want to wake your mother—or Uncle George, though he's probably blotto. No, she's not ill. We were just—trying something. Haven't you ever seen a planchette board before? *You* know. Spirit writing.'

Mary hadn't. Her immediate reaction was that it sounded the sort of thing housemaids went in for, but that reflection sounded so much like Aunt May herself in a normal state that she choked it back. Instead, she said lamely:

'I—I think the juniors tried it at school once, but with a tumbler and letters on bits of paper. I know the housemistress was annoyed with them and said it was unhealthy and so on . . . Willie, I'm sure Aunt May oughtn't to do it if it puts her in such a state. I've never seen her like that before.'

'Oh, we often do it with her,' said Willie casually. 'She wants to, so why not? Always be obliging when you can afford it, that's my motto. But Uncle George doesn't like the idea; that's why we do it late at night when no one else is about.'

'But—what for?'

Willie stared at her coldly. Perhaps he felt embarrassed, or even guilty, but he wasn't going to show it. He said:

'Why do you *think*, Mary? She's trying to get in touch with the dear departed, of course. With Oliver and Roland and dear little Nigel.' His tone offended Mary almost as much as the words he used. Trembling, and fully awake now for the first time, she said:

'What a horrible, disgusting idea, Willie. How can you let her do it?'

'Let her? She's my aunt, you little twit. How could I stop her?'

'Well, you don't have to egg her on. And I bet you are! You're a trouble-maker, Willie. Mother said you were when you were a little boy, and you still are—'

'Huh, thanks very much. Of course *you're* perfect, aren't you? A perfect little schoolgirl. A dear little prefect. With Matric.'

'Shut up, shut up,' she said desperately, putting her fingers in her ears. 'I'm not going to listen to you. I just know that—that the Boys were *real*. How can you use them to play a horrid, spooky, kid's game? . . . And how can Dodie, and their own *mother*—'

'*Do* keep your voice down, you'll wake the others.' Willie spoke more kindly now, as if recovering his self-possession. 'What do you mean, how can Dodie? As a matter of fact, it was all her idea in the first place. She met some people in that hotel in Switzerland who went in for it, apparently, and of course Dodie has to try anything that's going. And as for Aunt May, she's pretty hopeless anyway, isn't she? And any old way, *lots* of people are trying Spiritualism and so forth these days. Of course they are.'

'Well, I won't.'

'The war killed eleven million people, Mary. A million and a half in this country alone, they say. What do you expect?'

'But you don't believe in it, do you?' she said with certainty.

'Oh, my dear—' He waved a pudgy hand affectedly, as if he had a cigarette holder in it. 'I told you; I aim to please. To make up for not being dead or heroic or anything else of that kind . . .'

They heard Uncle George's door open, which was on the floor above. A landing light went on and at the same moment Dodie, eyes huge and dark, appeared in the doorway and said urgently to Willie:

'For God's sake, come and help me put it away.'

It was Mary who, hesitating, re-entered the dining room, where Willie was now hastily removing board and paper, coaxed her dazed-looking aunt to her feet and led her to her bedroom. On the landing, they encountered only a sound of flushing. Luckily Aunt May and Uncle George had separate rooms.

'Will you be all right now, Auntie? . . . You will go straight to bed, won't you?'

Aunt May sat on the edge of the high bed, legs dangling. Tears rolled down her once-pretty face that had been puffed and dried by years of Indian sun and made snail-tracks in her thick face powder. In spite of her smart violet evening dress she looked, Mary thought, like an old, beaten woman.

51

'He wrote a message to me, Mary,' she said. 'Oliver wrote to me, through the board. He said he was thinking of me. And last week Nigel had a message for me too, though I couldn't quite read it. They do come through, Mary, they really do.' Her voice was loud and toneless. It reminded Mary of people reciting the Creed in church. If Aunt May did believe, why did she need to affirm it like this? And why did it apparently bring her more distress than comfort? Gently, firmly, trying not to speculate too much tonight, Mary encouraged her aunt out of her tight layers of clothes and into her nightgown. Her body, the body that had borne those boys, was white and flaccid; it filled Mary with compassion, and with an obscure mixture of empathy and repulsion whose roots went deep. She had never seen a mature adult naked before, not even her own mother.

Afterwards, she slipped downstairs again to the dining room, which was in darkness. She felt about in the Benares bowl that served as a waste-paper basket and her hand closed on several sheets of paper crumpled together. She carried them fearfully away to the downstairs cloakroom to read in privacy.

The scrawls were mainly unintelligible, like large, loopy writing, only in imitation. But here and there an unmistakable initial letter was shakily formed—an O, an R or an N, and a few isolated, semi-legible words and phrases: 'think of you', 'best wishes', 'flowers' and 'gone ahead'. They seemed scattered at random over the sheets and not part of a continuous message. She tried hard to read more, turning the crumpled papers different ways, but there was nothing more to read.

With a sudden disgusted conviction she tore the sheets into small pieces and consigned them to the encased mahogany water closet.

Upstairs, she found Dodie's door ajar and Dodie calmly in bed, lying with her arms beneath her head.

'Dodie—you make that stupid board work, don't you? You and Willie.'

'Why on earth should you think that?' said Dodie in a small, cool voice, like a child determined not to admit it has broken something.

'Because *I'm* not a superstitious fool. Those messages poor Aunt May thinks she gets—you make them. Or Willie does. Or both of you.'

Dodie yawned elaborately: 'Have it your own way, dear.' Never had she sounded so like Willie. Till now, Mary had not perceived that the two cousins, in spite of their different physical looks and styles, were in some ways very much alike.

Mary went to her own bedroom, but an anger and distress, which she told herself was on Aunt May's behalf but was really on her own, kept sleep away from her. After some time she got up again and went softly to Dodie's door. It was open a crack. She pushed it wider. 'If you and Willie go on like this,' she had determined to say, 'you could drive Aunt May mad. Anyone can see she's not really well. And if she gets worse now it will be *your* fault. Some things *are* your fault, you know—'

But Dodie was either feigning sleep or was genuinely oblivious of the truth-teller at the door. And Mary's nerve failed her.

She returned to her own room and continued to lie awake till a grey light seeped from under the pelmets of the window curtains, and milk churns began to clatter in the mews behind the house. Something of what Willie had said rang desolately true to her. Looking into the empty night, it seemed to her she was looking out into an England where people had indeed been driven secretly mad by the war and had lost their way. All over England, perhaps over Europe too, in dining rooms and front parlours and back kitchens and chilly bedrooms, bereaved women were trying to reach through the thick dark to their dead. In the void, the planchette boards squeaked and scrawled, the tables bumped, the muttered evocations went on and on. But nothing, in truth, came in answer to them.

There was only time, and a great silence. It was a silence that was to take those who heard it most of fifty years to acknowledge, and many of them never did. They lived out their lives, lives so restless and so filled by minor triumphs and griefs, with this humming void at the back of their minds, and some knew it only when they were old and the knowledge had become irrelevant; and some never knew it at all.

Mary returned eventually from London, the Season and her 'coming out' officially over, to find her mother subdued and withdrawn. Tunbridge Wells seemed dreary after London, and to have too many people in bath-chairs. Mary spent much of the time gazing out of the window over the green, half thinking she was waiting for something, or someone, only to realise once again that nothing was due to happen and no one was going to come. She had always been much attached to her home, but she was profoundly relieved when, after she had been there a week or two, her mother said quietly to her:

'Dear, I've been coming to a decision: I think we should leave this house—move away altogether, in fact. We don't need so much space, just for the two of us, and it is so full of memories that I can hardly bear it any longer. Oh I know, I know, the Boys were growing up and would have gone away anyway, but I can't bear it any more, I tell you.'

She went on to say that she thought they should move to London. 'Nowhere as grand as Cadogan Square, I'm afraid, darling, or Kensington either. But I've been thinking about Brondesbury. It's said to be very nice and secluded, for somewhere so near in. Rosalind Fanshawe's sister and her family live there, and it does sound our sort of place . . . Or perhaps West Hampstead—your father's old friend Dr Gurney lives there. Would you mind very much?'

Mary discovered that she did not mind at all. Even the idea that she might mind seemed out of date. Her happy childhood in this house and on that green now seemed as remote and inaccessible as their Indian life had once seemed to the three boys, a Happy Land that could only be revisited in fantasy or in dreams. She was ready to forget it, to let it sleep. Indeed, she knew in her heart that she had no choice. Time was moving all the living on, rattling them inexorably through the weeks and months, towards next year and the next . . . Already there were fashions in clothes and hair the dead of the war had not known; already there were jokes in *Punch* which to them would be meaningless. How long it seemed already since Roland had gone. And even Nigel— not long ago she had looked forward with hopeless stoicism to a life of mourning which could never change. Yet change had insidiously and callously crept in. The final deprivation, she was discovering, is that the dead inevitably lose touch with the living.

PART TWO

When later in life Mary recalled those years of the 1920s, when she and her mother lived in a red-brick terrace in north London, they came back to her as a map; time and landscape fused. Behind their terrace, rising to the heights of Frognal and, above that, to the countryfied eyrie of Hampstead proper, were substantial houses, gardens with shady trees, networks of streets where tradesmen's carts called daily and where there was an evening paper round as well as a morning one. On the 'other side' towards Brondesbury the slopes were lower and the social rise less marked, but still there were quiet streets, space, white-capped servants, green sun-blinds and a tennis club. But down the valley in the middle, like a dark but noisy stream, ran the Kilburn High Road: dirty, crowded, without rest.

To Mary, who had recently read Compton Mackenzie's *Sinister Street*, it seemed pregnant with an alien life which had its own fascination for her. There the shops stayed open late on Saturday nights, selling off cheap the meat that would otherwise 'turn' over the weekend and that more prosperous households would disdain. There were stalls in cobbled side alleys, and a litter of cabbage ends and orange papers trodden into the black water of puddles; there, little girls in dirty pinafores pushed younger children in dilapidated prams; there, boys with boots that did not fit hawked newspapers, uttering throaty cries; there, ex-soldiers played the mouth-organ in the gutter, or sold matches or tin toys, or furtively begged. There, the life of nineteenth-century London survived.

Elsewhere the twentieth century was burgeoning: motors were commonplace, horses and carts were dwindling in numbers, tea-shops and dress-shops proliferated; so did picture palaces and underground stations. Bright new villas that could be run without a servant were beginning to cover the fields of Golders Green, Cricklewood and Wembley. But here in Kilburn High Road, shopping for her mother or on the way to change their library books at Arkwright Road, Mary saw the encrusted poverty and degradation of the old world still intact, and began to understand for the first time what people meant when they wrote of class and social unrest and 'the struggle of Labour'. She saw that she and her mother were privileged, protected from every form of real need. As time went on it began to bother her.

Yet, by the terms of their own society and their relatives, she and her mother were the 'new poor', as they jokingly agreed. It was a phrase much in the air in those years, and a perfectly acceptable if inconvenient thing to be—laudable indeed, in a way that to be 'new rich' was not. The cost of living had more than doubled since 1914. All over England a great, passive mass of people in Ellie Denvers' position, living on fixed pensions or annuities or on the proceeds of parental or grandparental investment in the decades of Victorian prosperity, found themselves now without the means to lead the kind of life they had been brought up to expect. To the war-induced grief of many was added a new bitterness, fermented over tea-tables ('can't afford to entertain properly these days, of course') where such new evils as death duties, the servant problem, jazz, short skirts, make-up, Bolshevism and the dangerous revolutionary spirit abroad among the working class were discussed with obsessional fear and distaste.

Others, like Ellie Denvers and her daughter, less prone by nature to resentment and more accustomed to fortune's reverses, quietly adapted themselves, moving into smaller houses, making do with a part-time servant, installing gas-cookers and geysers instead of the attention-demanding range, going shopping themselves, computing the cost of a bus or tram ticket against that of shoe-leather. 'Ellie's such a brave little thing,' Mary could imagine Uncle George and Aunt

May telling their friends deprecatingly. She knew, without anyone putting it into words, that their move to London constituted a social de-rating in many people's eyes. England, Stanley Baldwin had said, was its countryside. London might be the biggest city in the world, the 'heart of the Empire', but there was something intrinsically un-English and therefore rather common about city life, just as English gentlemen were the only real ones and well-born foreigners were just a flawed imitation of the ideal.

Mary, being young, healthy and, in spite of everything, eager for life, enjoyed the move to London, though she felt that their quiet routine hardly constituted 'life in the big city'. Long afterwards it both amused and annoyed her to hear the 1920s referred to by tradition as 'gay' or 'roaring'— 'They were not like that at all,' she told someone younger than herself long afterwards. 'At least, not for the great mass of people, including people like us. They were *desolate*, with the middle classes mourning their dead, and all those men back from the war with no jobs and nothing that they'd been promised . . . Looking back it all seems bleak, like a black and white film . . . And it seems typical that I had very dreary clothes then and didn't know how to wear them. But those years, the early twenties, were an important time for me, all the same. I was vegetating really—convalescing, perhaps. But I read an awful lot: Freud, Jung, Huxley, Lawrence, Siegfried Sassoon: there was a whole new generation of writers then whose ideas seemed to open new *worlds* to people my age . . . Not counting the more popular writers like Michael Arlen and Margaret Kennedy, that no one talks about any more.'

Dodie, she thought, would have given a different account of the 1920s. For Dodie undoubtedly had then what was called a gay time. The big house at Esher, with its elaborate tile-hanging and inglenooks, had also (naturally) a tennis court, and a double garage in which Dodie's own little blue Morris coupé nestled beside Uncle George's Daimler. Dodie, it appeared, could go where she liked, when she liked. Uncle George, in spite of his traditional ideas on women's rôle and his opposition to either his daughter or his niece having a job ('you're not shop-girls'), was infected by a hazy idea of precocity and advancement which made him rather proud of

Dodie's modern ways. In his trumpeted censures ('Tearing about . . . all these cars . . . young men in the house at all hours . . . using the place as an hotel . . . this fad for dancing . . . jazz and so forth . . .') Mary sensed a leaven of fatuous indulgence, a pleasure in that very irresponsibility and hedonism which he pretended to condemn.

In contrast, Mary thought Uncle George regarded her as too serious, dowdy, not his idea of what a girl should be; girls should frolic. On the Sundays when she and her mother were invited down to Esher (always referred to as 'the country' by Uncle George and Aunt May) for lunch and a tennis party, she would feel Uncle George's eyes upon her, predatory, faintly puzzled, a little angry even. Was he regretting all those fees he had paid? Did he suspect her of harbouring some secret plan of ingratitude which would show him up? Nervous of him, she did her best, joining in with the assembled young men and girls of Esher, who all (she told herself crossly) seemed to be called Buffy and Miffy and Bicky, and were hard to distinguish one from another. She played tennis energetically although it bored her; a childhood with the boys, followed by Bessemer, had fortunately given her a competence at ball-games. Dodie, by contrast, was hopeless at tennis, though she contrived to hide this under a display of not caring and egging her partners on to excel themselves. But Mary sensed it was no use: Uncle George did not really like or trust her. Particularly once she began to work for the Abandoned Mothers.

Looking back long afterwards, Mary came to regard her introduction to the Abandoned Mothers as a piece of intervention by fate for which she could only feel enduringly grateful. In retrospect she seemed to herself to have been so somnolent at that period, so unambitious, so oddly lacking in direction and unaware in her thoughts that she could not believe she would have found her own way to the Abandoned Mothers at all—and hence into her future life—had it not been for fate in the person of Dr Gurney, her father's friend from medical school days.

It was a little ironic that Dr Gurney should have been the instrument of so much. He did not—as he explained with lengthy circumlocutions to Mary and her mother over Sunday tea—entirely approve of the methods of the new charity that had been founded in the last year of the war. He was faintly disgusted that its headquarters should be near at hand in West Hampstead, thereby lowering still further the tone of that already descending area. Dr Gurney might not go as far as being content to see 'these wretched women' die on the streets, but he would have preferred it if they could have been saved in streets in a more distant and obscure part of London.

No, what had stirred his heart and conscience were the babies. Many more illegitimate children had been born during and just after the war: for 1919 alone, he said, the figure had been nearly forty-two thousand. He apologised to Mary for mentioning such things boldly, but he knew that she was a well-educated, modern-minded young woman who would not flinch from hearing a spade called a spade. To Dr Gurney, these hapless babies were the children of the war dead—'The men who fell at Mons and Marne, Mrs Denvers. In all conscience we *cannot* ignore them, or allow them to die from neglect. The country desperately needs all the young lives it has.' It was for the sake of these innocent young lives, and their supposedly dead and heroic fathers, that he had been prepared to over-ride his moral reservations and give his support to the new and struggling charity. To come to the point—Another slice of fruit cake? No? Sure? Another cup of tea then?—the charity was looking for a volunteer worker to help keep their files, draw up appeal lists, answer the telephone. They were looking for somebody well-educated and a *lady*. The usual type of secretary-typist, though she might be an excellent girl in her way, would not quite do. Most of the ladies already interested in the charity were, of course, married, which was why the charity had thought of looking for someone younger, someone whose education would perhaps have given her the will and competence to work, someone not too proud . . . In short, he ventured to suggest— Mary had at once come to his mind—Could he dare to hope? With Mrs Denvers' permission, of course. And it would, after all, be for the sake of the children. The new generation.

Dr Gurney was a widower. His only son had been so seriously injured at Gallipoli that his brain would never function again like a normal man's, and indeed he did not live at home in the unloved house in Hampstead but in a nursing home in the country. Mary knew this; 'poor old Dr Gurney', as her mother habitually called him, was a frequent visitor to their own small house. But not till she was years older did she hear that the doctor knew or believed that his son, before his mutilating wound, had fathered a child whom its grandfather would never see, and that it was the image of this unknowable child that powered Dr Gurney's desire to 'do something' for all those thousands of babies.

'There is no provision in English law for the adequate assistance of the mother of an illegitimate child in maintaining her offspring unless she can muster courage to bring affiliation proceedings against the father. The utmost she can then recover is a pittance of five shillings a week, upon which she must maintain, clothe and educate her child until it is 14 or 16 years of age. Should she lack courage for these proceedings, or fail to obtain the fruits of her successful action, her only refuge, in the great majority of cases, is the workhouse. If, in consequence, her child dies from lack of proper care or nurture, or unhappily at the hands of the desperate mother, the community is an accessory to its death and should be held equally accountable with the mother. To our disgrace, the law of England is punitive in principle and not protective or remedial.'

So ran one of the pamphlets Dr Gurney gave Mary to take home with her and 'consider carefully'. That night she asked her mother what had become of Susan's baby, and wondered at herself that she had not thought to ask before.

'Oh dear, yes, I'm afraid it died. I didn't mention it to you because you were so upset at the time.' Ellie Denvers wore her screwed-up face. 'Poor little thing. Susan put it with a foster-mother over at Bromley and everything seemed to be going nicely, but then it got ill when it was about six months old—infantile convulsions, I think—and it died. Poor Susan was so distressed. Not having been there herself, and wondering of course if the woman had cared for it properly . . . But I'm afraid it was really all for the best, you know. It would have been a dreadful financial burden to her for years.'

So it came about that Mary was installed for two and a half days a week in the first-floor room of a one-time vicarage near the Kilburn High Road, together with a desk, a telephone, two filing cabinets, a display of pamphlets and photographs, and a gilt-framed print of *The Age of Innocence* that hung forward from the picture-rail as if it would one day descend. Gradually her world which, without her fully realising it, had been an essentially solitary one since she had left school, began to repopulate itself with people who came to mean something to her. They included Mr Evans the general secretary, whose office was in the next room, Mrs Parsons, the friendliest member of the management committee, Mrs Levy, the bossiest, and Gladys Stone, who typed on the landing and kept an eye on the trickle of clients who appeared there to sit silently on bentwood chairs.

It took Mary a while to get over her private sense of shock on first encountering the clients—'our customers', as Mr Evans liked to refer to them when he was in a genial mood. Not because there was anything shocking about them, but because they were indeed so ordinary, exactly the sort of girls and women who served in shops and applied for jobs as cook-generals with proper references. A few of them, even, were educated; they spoke much like Mary herself, their hats were restrained, their unbuttoned coats were good quality, they did not have raw, work-worn hands or cheap cotton gloves, they did not call Mary 'Ma'am'. Seeing them pass through the office (Mr Evans or one of the committee conducted the actual interviews), Mary for the first time began to speculate on the nature of that private passion that could drive young women not unlike herself to commit such an irrevocable and disastrous deed. Had one been older during the war oneself . . . If someone she had—loved, very much, had made such an extraordinary request just before he left for the Front . . . ? But, even so, how did it begin, and how long did it go on? Was it not very embarrassing—and did it not hurt?

Her senses began vaguely to stir. But they lacked an object. Once or twice, waking in the night, surfacing from confused layers of dreams, she found herself with the sudden awareness that, after all, 'it' need not be embarrassing, and that if it hurt one would not even necessarily mind . . . But, in her waking hours, this perception eluded her again, for it was undirected; nor, in spite of her new familiarity with Freud and his theories of repression, did she connect what she had read with herself. Desire in her was dormant, like a daydream too rich and disturbing to risk dreaming, though it was not till long afterwards that she realised how untrue to herself this had been. Was it partly because of her education among all those women, she wondered? But she decided it was more as if, for years after the war and the successive blows of the Boys' deaths, she had not believed that the future was any longer there. The emptiness was not only outside her, but also within, in her unexplored self.

It only occurred to her long afterwards, too, that when Dr Gurney suggested she take on the work at the AMs he had either been more advanced than she had realised or else unusually innocent. For a number of Ellie Denvers' friends appeared disconcerted on hearing of Mary's new pastime, and the Denvers at Esher were openly outraged. Uncle George expressed himself forthrightly on the unsuitability of such an occupation for a young girl, and Aunt May backed him up with grave uncertainties about whom Mary might *meet* in such an organisation—'Really, Ellie, we've tried to do our best for her, but . . . I do hope at least she won't *talk* about it when she comes down here.'

'If only,' said Mary to her mother, 'she could see Mr Evans!' Mr Evans, the only full-time salaried staff except for Gladys Stone, was an ex-schoolmaster and a Methodist lay-preacher. The Abandoned Mothers, and the Methodist church half a mile up the road, were the twin centres around which his busy, self-abnegating life turned. Under his influence, the church had become a centre of social life and charitable care in Kilburn. Nearly every evening, it seemed, lights were burning in the church hall, and Mr Evans was a governor of several schools and sat as a magistrate and knew every shop-keeper and his family. Talking to him (or rather listening to him talk) Mary found her outsider's view of the Kilburn High Road, the mysterious 'city of dreadful night', habitat of alien lives, shredding away before this daylight

66

knowledge. In his tight black suit and his wing collar he was indefatigably polite to her, though occasionally in the very briskness and readiness with which he would answer a hesitant question from her she sensed a concealed dismissal, a hint that, however polite, he would not tolerate fools gladly. In spite of his sallow, formal looks there was something athletic about him. Muscular Christianity, she thought with an inward giggle.

Mary did not tell Aunt May about Mr Evans; but she let her know that a Lady Waters-Clarey was on the committee and a frequent visitor to the office, and this information mollified Aunt May as Mary had intended it to. Dodie, who had at first been inclined to scoff at the AMs ('Darling, how *dreary*'), had changed her mind too.

'Doing a proper job—even if it is only voluntary . . . Oh, I *long* to, you can't imagine, I get so *bored* here sometimes that I feel like doing something outrageous. Like taking off all my clothes on the Common and screaming! You are lucky, Mary.'

'You could find something to do without taking off all your clothes, surely!' said Mary, but thinking to herself that any regular occupation might interfere with Dodie's late nights and morning lie-ins.

'How can I—in Esher? I hate the country, I've decided.' She made a disgusted face. 'This morning Mrs Wainwright rang up wanting me to sell raffle tickets for the Conservative Club, and was quite cross when I said I was too busy. I ask you! It's as if all the time I know something is due to happen to me, and I wait and wait but it never does . . . I do wish we lived in London all the year. No, what I really wish is that I could have a dear little flat of my own there. Actually, you and I could share one, you know. Oh think, Mary, wouldn't it be lovely—?'

And she really does mean it, thought Mary, looking at Dodie's glowing, eager face. In her way she is nicer than me; she doesn't remember things—doesn't have reservations about people. It must be lovely to be her. No wonder she's popular. She said gently:

'It would be fun, Dodie. But I don't think I could leave Mother on her own for no reason, you know.'

'No, I know that really . . . And of course Father would

67

never stump up the money for me to have a flat of my own. He wouldn't trust me.' She giggled suddenly. 'He suspects Arnold of trying to seduce me as it is.'

The various Biffys and Rickys who had populated Dodie's conversation and the Esher tennis court now seemed to have receded before the presence of the mysterious Arnold, whom Mary had never met but of whom she had heard much. He was said by Dodie to have had 'a brilliant war record', though she was vague about its details, and he was now, like so many ex-officers in the 1920s, 'between jobs'. He lived with his mother at Maidenhead, and it was there, to a road-house near the river, that he and Dodie drove many evenings in Dodie's little blue coupé. Mary suspected that Dodie paid for many of the evenings too, for Arnold surely could not have much spending money at the moment and Dodie was not, Mary thought, venal or calculating. She envied them rather. It did sound fun.

Willie was now down from Oxford and also unemployed; but he possessed a modest private income and, being a man, he was allowed to live a separate existence in London of which he gave an account to nobody. At rare intervals he invited Mary out to a concert or a theatre. He took her to see the Diaghilev troupe perform and to Shaw plays at the Everyman in Hampstead. Willie was something of an intellectual (at least, he read books and referred to them familiarly) and on the basis of this Mary had managed to develop a slightly constrained friendship with him. She knew that he thought her part-time work insufferably earnest and that he vaguely despised all women anyway, but he introduced her to the poems of T. S. Eliot and to T. E. Lawrence's *Seven Pillars of Wisdom*; he had travelled on the Continent and spoke casually of Paris and Berlin, and she always returned home from an evening with him feeling alert and stimulated and dissatisfied.

She knew that he still saw a lot of Dodie and her family, so she asked him about the mysterious Arnold.

'A Jewboy,' said Willie dismissively, tapping ash from his cigarette.

'Really? Are you sure?' To Mary's innocent ears the phrase of the period conjured up an image of an oily, exotic-looking man who could not by any stretching of words be a gentleman, 'temporary' or otherwise. 'I wouldn't have thought Dodie would have liked someone like that,' she said. 'I mean, she's actually a bit—' She had been going to say 'snobbish' but then stopped, remembering the wounded Tommies and the Italian singing master in Switzerland, and wondered if this were in fact true. 'I mean, she's rather fastidious, I think,' she ended lamely—then wondered again why she thought this and indeed if it were true.

'Oh, he's not a bad chap—if you like that sort,' said Willie with the lordly objectivity of one above such tastes. 'Quite presentable and everything. I mean, he doesn't say "Beg pardon" or eat peas off his knife. He annoys our respected Aunt May by not knowing that gentlemen are supposed to use the downstairs cloakroom rather than penetrating to the upper reaches of the house, if you'll forgive my frankness, but I'd hardly regard that as a crucial test of social acceptability myself. He's getting on a bit, I'd say, and losing his hair, but—*il plaît aux dames*, I should imagine. I've really no idea, of course.'

'Dodie seems very—fond of him.'

'Dodie needs a husband,' said Willie shortly. He activated a little lever in his holder to remove a long cigarette stub from it (he always discarded his cigarettes half-smoked) and made a protracted business of extracting a new Turkish cigarette from his case and inserting it in the holder. Mary waited for him to say more. His previous remark seemed promisingly forthright—as Willie could be, occasionally.

'I mean,' he said at last, 'it doesn't do a girl any good to racket around the way she does. I know I sound like my respected uncle, but it's true. Dodie's like the girls Wells talks about in *Ann Veronica*: she's either too innocent for the life she's leading or—she soon won't be innocent enough to settle down with some worthy householder . . . Don't get me wrong, though. As a matter of fact I do think Dodie's quite innocent. For the moment.' He laughed self-consciously, that shrill, staccato laugh of his that was not an expression of humour but of a social nuance. Mary was aware that he was conveying to her some message which he would be offended if she questioned him about, but which she was nevertheless expected to receive. But she did not entirely understand. She said, laughing nervously herself because Willie made her feel awkward:

'I don't know about that. Dodie certainly seems sophisticated. No, that's not the right word. But she seems to have—some knack of living, knowing what to do at the right moment, and what to say to different people. As if she were more awake than most people. She makes me feel stupid often, I know.'

If she had hoped to be told that she did not seem stupid she was disappointed. Willie did not go in for compliments. Instead he sat frowning. He said after a minute:

'Dodie exploits people.'

'You mean—men?'

'Mmm. It partly *is* innocence, of course. She doesn't realise the effect she has on them. But she ought to. All you girls ought to. There are uglier words for it than "exploit", you know. And, if it comes to that, men can play at that game too . . . Men can turn quite nasty, you see. If pushed too far.' And again his high-pitched, mirthless laugh, like a parrot's shout.

Mary said uncomfortably: 'I don't know anything about that.'

'Don't you? Just as well. But bear it in mind. Believe your cousin-by-marriage who tells you so.'

Discrepant images knocked together in Mary's mind. Dodie at the last party they had been to together, flushed and exultant in a swirling short dress trimmed with daisies; other girls at dances, garrulously comparing notes in the crowded cloakrooms, smelling of scented powder and perspiration, avidly competitive under a veneer of giggles; the ill-looking girls who came into the office, twisting ringless fingers together, unable sometimes even to allude to the men whose children they were carrying in their swollen stomachs; D. H. Lawrence's men and women, a prey to dark impulsions; Willie, with his lank, Brylcreemed hair, his rimless glasses, his cigarette holder and his obscure yet vaguely menacing remarks. Did Willie ever—? Even to embark on the thought seemed obscene, and she thrust it aside, feeling herself blushing.

'Dodie's just a normal, very pretty girl,' she said, aware

70

that she was fighting for a viewpoint Willie had already undermined. 'It's normal for her to want to have—fun.'

'And what about you, little-Cousin-Mary?' he asked, glinting at her through his glasses. 'Don't you want to have—fun too? Or do you intend to devote your life entirely to good works among unmarried ladies?'

'Oh, I have fun sometimes,' said Mary hastily, in what she herself felt to be a silly schoolgirl voice. *Don't let him go all arch with me, don't let him, I can't stand him when he's like that, and I want to like him. He does at least take me to the theatre* . . . In an attempt to regain control of the situation, she said:

'Willie, this has been nice, but I think I ought to go home. I have to be up in good time in the morning.'

'Ah yes—the working girl.'

'If you like . . .' *Sneering beast*. 'And I know Mother will be waiting up for me and I don't want to keep her up late.'

'How *is* Aunt Ellie? Sorry to hear about her bronchitis.'

'Yes, it's been very tiresome this winter. Ever since that 'flu at the end of the war, you know, Willie, she's had this trouble, and of course the London fogs don't help. The doctor says it ought to improve when the warmer weather comes. I hope he's right.'

'Mary, old thing—may I say something to you?'

'Yes, of course . . .' What on earth? Much to her own discomfiture, she felt her heart thumping, till she was almost afraid Willie would notice it through her low-necked silk blouse.

'I do think you ought to use a bit more make-up. Perfectly nice girls—women—do now, you know. You're so pale, you need a bit more definition.' He contemplated her as if pretending to be an artist, eyes screwed up behind his glasses, small pink lips pursed. She almost expected him to whip out a pencil and measure her against it. She said defensively:

'You paint a bit, don't you, Willie?'

'I draw,' he agreed remotely. 'A bit.'

She waited self-consciously for him to finish.

'Buy yourself a lipstick,' he said definitively.

With historical neatness, the year in which the AMs' charity was founded was also the year in which the glamorous but obscure figure of Marie Stopes published *Married Love*. Three years later she opened her birth-control clinic in a drab London district, similar to Kilburn but further east. Within a year she had been attacked in print, and retaliated by starting a libel action against the book's author. The case came to court early in 1923, and at the AMs Mary heard it energetically discussed. Most, but not all of the committee members, she gathered, were in favour of Marie Stopes, and there was a certain amount of tension in the office. Kind, garrulous Mrs Parsons, whose husband was a consultant at Guy's, took it upon herself to instruct Mary:

'. . . the doctors are some of the worst offenders you know, my dear. They airily say to these poor women, "You mustn't have another baby, it will kill you," but they don't say a *word* to them on how to avoid one. And that silly old woman Miss McIlroy going about saying that the check pessary is harmful. Such nonsense! She knows perfectly well that women of our class have been using it for *years*. I have myself.'

'Isn't it a little uncomfortable?' Mary hazarded with interest. She had been wondering about that for a while, since the publicity surrounding the trial had enlightened her on the whole subject of contraceptives. Mrs Parsons, who was untidy and motherly, was an easy person to ask a question which, in prospect, would have seemed daring in the extreme.

'Not at *all*, my dear. I do recommend it to you . . . Oh, do excuse me, of course you're not married yet; you seem so sensible and old for your age that I always forget that. Yes—well, *when* you're married, my dear, and want to space your family nicely . . . After all, as my husband says, it's very much in the country's interest to produce good stock. How can we expect the race to do anything but decline when we let these poor women go on having six or a dozen children one after another like rabbits?'

Mary, at twenty-one, wasn't sure she liked being called 'sensible and old for her age'. Much of the time, it was true, she felt it. But that was not the same as wanting other people to see her like that. An empty future of monochrome, sensible adult years yawned momentarily before her, making her flinch—and, as abruptly, closed again. Mrs Parsons spoke so blithely of her marrying and having children. But was that

72

certain, or even likely? It was being said that the losses of the war had left over a million 'superfluous' women in England, and that this situation would last for a generation.

She remembered that she still hadn't bought a lipstick.

Gladys Stone, who had apparently overheard Mary's conversation with Mrs Parsons (lack of sound-proofing was a perpetual problem in their exiguous offices), was, to Mary's surprise and interest, inclined to take a more cynical view. Gladys was the youngest daughter of the man who played the piano in the picture palace down the road: she was about Mary's age, but while Mary had been learning hockey and Chemistry Gladys had been learning commercial shorthand during the day and how to 'deal with boys' in the evenings. She was brisk on the subject of male turpitude, seeming to regard all men as irresponsible, overgrown children.

'To my way of thinking, you see, Miss Denvers, a man doesn't respect a woman if he thinks she knows how to look after herself. That's what I've got against this birth control, you see.'

'But, Gladys, Marie Stopes is helping married women, not young girls going out with their best boys.' 'Best boys' was a patronising commonplace of Gladys' when chattering about her female friends and relatives.

'Oh, I daresay, but what's sauce for the goose is sauce for the gander, if you take my meaning . . . No, but what I mean to say, Miss Denvers, is, once you start telling people about these things, how are you going to keep it to married ladies, mmm? You can't, and that'll mean all the naughty girls will be able to do what they like with nothing to fear, and a lot of nice girls will become naughty girls what wouldn't otherwise because it will be just too easy—if you take my meaning.'

Forty years after, remembering Gladys with affection, Mary thought to herself that the girl had been perfectly right. In 1923, however, she rejected such a mechanistic view.

'Rubbish, Gladys. Nice girls wouldn't start doing what you suggest just because they could stop worrying about the consequences. And surely it's better all round if feckless women *don't* have babies?'

'Ah,' said Gladys, tolerant with primeval wisdom, 'you're like our Dad. He's got "faith in people" like you. Now me

73

and our Mum, we don't agree—begging your pardon, of course.' And she took out a compact to cover her pretty, peaky face with another layer of powder from a grubby swansdown puff. Powdering one's face in public, along with smoking, was one of the new, daring gestures. Mary had seen Dodie do it too. It infuriated Uncle George, as was no doubt intended. But then Uncle George seemed to thrive on indignation these days, as if he found the emotion comfortable and had lost touch with what his obscure anger might really be about, linking it arbitrarily now with this object, now with that. Currently he was conducting a furious correspondence with the Home Office and the *Morning Post* about the possibly deleterious effects of wireless transmission on the weather. What his views must be on Marie Stopes Mary could guess only too well.

She had assumed, without thinking much about it, that Mr Evans, like many churchmen, would disapprove of the birth-control movement. She would never have broached the subject with him herself, but one pouring wet evening when she was without an umbrella he offered to see her home, and in the course of the walk he made determined conversation that finally got round to the trial. Did not Miss Denvers feel it was crucial to the development of a healthy and happy society in the post-war world that Marie Stopes' work should be allowed to continue freely?

Mary reflected, and said that she did. She felt happy at discovering that her own mind was indeed made up on the subject. Cautiously, fumbling a little for words that should be discreet without being quite incomprehensible, she conveyed to him Gladys Stone's argument and asked him what he thought.

Mr Evans thought that Gladys' view was very prevalent among respectable girls of her type, and of course he sympathised with the moral feeling behind it—but he could not agree. No, indeed. He would in fact go so far as to say he thought the information and the assistance should be made available to *all*, without distinction. He could see—oh yes, he could see very clearly—the drawbacks and the evils that would result from this. But he had come over the years to think that the evils resulting from female ignorance and

74

helplessness were far greater. And of course, as Gladys said, you could not simultaneously withhold knowledge from one group and impart it to another. In this as in so many other, ah, political matters, the only way on was forward. 'But I'm afraid you'll be thinking me dangerously advanced, Miss Denvers,' he finished breathlessly, glancing at her under the umbrella.

'Oh dear,' she said after a moment. 'I don't know whether to say "not at all" or "never mind"!' She felt surprisingly at ease with him. He really was a nice man, for all his muscular jocularity.

'You may find this hard to believe,' he said, stopping suddenly and holding the umbrella further over her head while rain pattered on to his own bowler hat. 'But my dearest wish would be that scientific and social advances should one day make my job unnecessary—make the AMs no longer needed, I mean. Because every child would be a wanted child, called into being on purpose, a genuine child of love. Just think what an advance that would be, how life would be transformed.'

She was to remember his words, and the tone in which they were spoken—eager, awestruck, almost boyish with emotion—long after his unremarkable face had faded from her memory.

He invited her to come with him to a meeting in Islington on the night the trial ended with a confusing verdict that gave a clear victory to neither party. She accepted eagerly, then spent the afternoon regretting it. What on earth would they find to talk about on the long tram-ride there? Check pessaries? Hardly!

In fact they talked about politics: a General Election was due later that year, and there were hopes that Baldwin, who had not been a success, would be unseated. Mary and her mother were Liberals, favouring Mr Asquith: Mr Evans was a lifelong Liberal and supporter of Lloyd George, but he confessed that in the coming election he was planning to vote for the Socialist candidate.

'It's not that I'm pro-Bolshevik, Miss Denvers, don't think that. I don't approve of revolutions. But we've got to do something to break out of the spiral these men have got us into—this obsession with money and military power and doing the other fellow down. "Getting and spending, we lay waste our powers." High tariffs, indeed. Punitive reparations against Germany—as if the German *people* hadn't suffered as much as us and more. Huge sums of money spent on overseas garrisons when what we need here are jobs and homes . . . At this rate we'll be preparing the next war before we've recovered from the last one. Ramsay MacDonald was a pacifist in the war and suffered for it—but, you know, I'm impressed by him more and more.'

'They say it was the war-to-end-war,' said Mary bleakly. His grim vision of a continuing covert struggle was a new one to her.

'Please God it may have been, but I see little sign of it. Ah—except for the League of Nations. That at least is a step in the right direction. Something to build on.' And he talked enthusiastically about the League till they reached the Agricultural Hall in Islington.

Years later, the chief memory she was to retain of that meeting was of someone on the platform reading out with scornful emotion the libellous passage on which the trial had centred: '. . . the poor are the natural victims of those who seek to make experiments on their fellows. In the midst of a London slum, a woman who is a doctor of German philosophy has opened a birth-control clinic . . .' There was hissing, and someone called out 'Shame!'

Mr Evans said quietly to Mary: 'You see the point? This writer was trying to suggest by implication that Mrs Stopes has been guilty of "Hunnish practices". As if we are not all God's children in these matters. There are as many Christians in Germany as there are here, probably more. I deplore this anti-German feeling. It is patriotism grown rank and evil.'

Mary would have liked to have agreed with him but could not quite bring herself to do so. The idea that Germany represented some intrinsic evil and that it was against this that the Boys and the rest of the one and a half million had died fighting was still engrained in her imagination.

They left the hall in a great, slow-moving crowd. In the damp street, fog was making haloes round the gas-lamps. The queues at the tram-stops were so long they decided to walk down to Kings Cross and catch the Metropolitan Line from there. On the busy pavements, Mr Evans offered her his arm.

She said sincerely: 'That was so interesting. Thank you very much for taking me.'

'Miss Denvers—Mary—may I?—the pleasure has been all mine. It is both a delight and a privilege to be in the company of a young lady who is prepared to take an interest in things that matter. I'm hardly one of the Bright Young Things, Mary—certainly hardly young any more—and your candid, clear-sighted approach is all that I could wish in a woman.'

She was still digesting this pretty speech, and trying to think of a suitable rejoinder, when he asked her, lowering his voice slightly, if she had in fact read *Married Love*. No? Then would she allow him to lend it to her? Far from being a disgraceful work it was, he humbly believed, a beautiful book, which all men and women should read:

'As you know, Mary, I'm not married myself. Too busy a life, you see—so much always going on; and I had a disappointment in youth . . . I've always promised myself I would indeed get married one day, but it has to be to the right woman. Time has slipped by, perhaps you may feel I've left it too late . . . Anyway. Let me lend you the book. I happen to have a copy on me.' And he produced it there and then from his attaché case. It was tactfully covered in brown paper.

The next day she read it quietly in her bedroom. It was not, she felt, quite the book to sit with in the drawing room while her mother knitted opposite, for all that Ellie Denvers might not have objected. As she read, it was borne in on her that what she had listened to last night had been a veiled proposal of marriage. She finished the book slowly and thoughtfully, then went back and reread certain passages.

It was no good, of course. Impossible, in fact. It wasn't only that Mr Evans (or Eric, as she supposed she should call him now) was not her class. He had very little Welsh accent, not more than a vague intonation; he was an educated man—he had a degree from Manchester. His world was a universe away from that of Uncle George and Aunt May, and even a considerable way from that of Mary and her mother, but that would not have mattered had she loved him or felt she could love him. She would gladly have braved family surprise and displeasure for that.

But she did not love him. Not in the least. She could see now that he was eminently lovable; she sympathised with most of his ideas and admired his energy, his selflessness and his independence of thought. She sensed, rather than spelling it out to herself, that under his black-suited exterior was a heart and body capable of considerable passion, but—oh no, the very idea was preposterous! Not Mr Evans. With him it would certainly be—well, not embarrassing perhaps, but she flinched away from the thought.

She worried for some time about how to return his book to him without hurting his feelings too much. In the end a good idea came to her, and the more she thought about it the more she felt that the formula was not merely tactful but true. She handed him back the book when they were alone together in the outer office, and said how pleased she had been to have an opportunity of reading it since she was nursing an ambition to take a medical degree—'and for a woman doctor, of course, such a book is essential reading. Wouldn't you say, Mr Evans?'

After the slightest perceptible pause, during which his face seemed momentarily immobile, jarred, as if he had bitten on metal with a stopped tooth, he assented. He went on to add, with his usual energy, that if she should require any practical help with her plans he would be only too happy to oblige.

'But perhaps you really ought to talk to one of the doctors among our team, ah, Miss Denvers? Dr Green, for instance, or Mrs Parsons' husband—I'm always so pleased to see a young woman wanting to do something with her life,' he said in his most schoolmasterish way.

After that he never again attempted an intimate conversation with her but arranged for her to meet Professor Parsons and, when she began to have further coaching in Maths, took an interest in her progress and often explained points to her. Usually he called her Miss Denvers but occasionally, when they were out of the office, Mary, and once or twice he imparted to her some piece of information he thought she should know. It was in this way that she learned that Gladys Stone's eldest sister had died, three years earlier, of 'a certain illegal operation' and that that was how the family had become known to Mr Evans.

'But does Gladys know?' she asked aghast, thinking of Gladys' stance on birth control.

He paused a moment as if thinking, then said quietly:

'I think she must—don't you? Facts don't necessarily alter opinions, you know, in the way one feels they should.'

She was grateful to him, for his help and concern, and for something harder to define too. She felt that, through him and his feeling for her, she had learnt something, and was no longer quite the dim spinster that Willie and Dodie might imagine her to be. It was as if, in some unphysical way, he had touched and released something within her.

The Maths lessons were Professor Parsons' idea. She had taken Zoology and Chemistry in Higher School Certificate, and he felt that if she could offer Maths as well at this level there would be a better chance of a medical school accepting her as a pupil. Men who wanted to be doctors did not have to satisfy such stringent standards; but that, of course, was different.

These plans were still tentative and long-term. Where the money for medical school might come from Mary had no ideas. When at length she broached the subject her mother said that it 'might be managed' but, untypically, did not seem anxious to discuss it 'till the time comes'. The sense of vague but persistent impermanence, of moving into a future that wasn't there, that had hung in the air since 1918, was undispersed. Life was temporary, this much Mary understood. But she was annoyed when Dodie, in whom she had confided her ambition, expecting interest and sympathy, said:

'After all, Mary, wouldn't it be rather a waste? I mean, you'll probably get married.'

'Oh really, Dodie! I may well not—anyway, I think it's perfectly awful the way girls like us sit round waiting for men to come and marry us. We pride ourselves on not being Victorian, but are we all that different? One shouldn't let life revolve round waiting for a man to choose one. It's—it's degrading.'

'Oh, it's all right for you,' said Dodie miserably. 'You're different. You had a proper education. But what else can I do?' She burst into tears.

Mary reproached herself for raising the subject. She had known that Dodie was in a delicate, unhappy state of mind. She understood that the Arnold situation had reached a crisis, and had at first supposed that Uncle George had forbidden him to come to the house, or some similar Uncle George gesture, but apparently it hadn't been like that. From hints and half-conversations she gathered that Dodie had parted from Arnold 'because she felt it was better'. Perhaps Willie had been doing a little discreet proselytising.

Now, stroking Dodie's head as Dodie sobbed abandonedly, sprawled over Mary's dressing table, Mary said:

'Poor Dodie . . . were you awfully in love with him?'

Dodie's head jerked up: 'Who?'

'Why—Arnold, of course. I mean . . .'

'Oh, *him*.' There was scorn in Dodie's voice and, beyond it, a kind of fear. 'No, I certainly wasn't. I don't love him at all. I thought he was nice but he wasn't. I trusted him—and then it was just—awful . . .' Her words died on her lips. She stared into the glass, but Mary wasn't sure if she was looking at herself or at some frightening inner vista. Full of foreboding, she said:

'Oh, Dodie, did he—? That is—did you—?'

Failing to get a proper answer, she made an assumption and worried considerably about her cousin. Willie, it seemed, had been right. Dodie was being allowed too much freedom for her own good.

Uncle George and Aunt May's reaction to Dodie's tearful state was both illogical and typical, Mary thought. They sent Dodie to Paris for six months, to board with an impoverished countess in Passy who 'took in' girls of good family and introduced them to good society, 'Whatever that may mean,' said Ellie Denvers resignedly. 'I hardly think the sort of people Dodie is likely to meet will be Uncle George's cup of tea. However, that's so like him. He doesn't think things out.'

'If they're musicians and artists and Jews and people I

should think he'll have a fit,' said Mary. 'You know—like *The Constant Nymph.*'

'Oh dear! Well, as long as Dodie doesn't end up dying in someone's arms in a boarding house in Brussels . . .'

Dodie did not die, nor (as far as Mary could tell) did she end up irretrievably in anyone's arms. She merely came back with a new persona. Gone for ever was the enthusiastic, girlish, bubbling Dodie. Instead it was a languid, drawling, adult beauty who reappeared in London in the spring of 1925, her face veiled behind a clown's flawless mask of white and red make-up, her hair a small, sleek cap, her hands emphasised by new, red nails that seemed not to belong to her. She smoked heavily now, leaving in every saucer stubs which her glistening red lips had pressed, but the gesture with which she exhaled the smoke was a masculine one. She had acquired a number of mannish gestures, as attractive women sometimes do from the company they keep. She had a loose leather coat like a pilot's jacket, and stood around in it indoors with her hands thrust into its pockets, humming under her breath as if her attention were elsewhere.

'Willie chose it for me,' she remarked casually when Mary said how well the jacket suited her. 'Actually he does have quite good taste.'

'Oh yes—of course he was in Paris a lot of the time too, wasn't he? Did you see much of him?'

'On and off. You know our Willie'—she pronounced the 'W' as 'V'—'leads a rather *subterranean* existence. I went once or twice with him to parties in people's studios, and to the Bal Nègre. That sort of thing.'

'Goodness, what fun!' Mary tried not to feel too envious, or that it wasn't fair.

'Well—up to a point. The company was a bit *drear*, actually. I think Willie's One of Those.'

'You mean—?'

'I mean he's a nancy,' said Dodie shortly, lighting a fresh cigarette from the end of the last one. 'My dear, so many young men *are* these days. It's chic, you see. After all, marriage and all that is rather *vieux jeu*. Particularly now that no one who's possible can afford to get married any more.'

'Oh, really . . .' Mary struggled with a mental image of

Willie, posing as a Greek statue, and with the various other ideas contained in this designedly 'outrageous' statement. She said at last:

'But, Dodie, I don't think people *choose* to be homosexual, do they?' It was the first time she had actually uttered the proper word, she thought, but it turned out to be quite easy.

However, it appeared that this was exactly what Dodie thought: that one could adopt a style, a way of life, as a matter of decision and principle. What a silly, affected, French idea, said Mary, with mounting irritation. But Dodie had a crushing answer to that: she had, in Paris, 'decided' to become a writer. And, what was more, she had written a novel to show that she was serious, and actually finished it, and now a publisher she had met at a party was interested in it.

'I told you I felt something important was lying in wait for me,' she said triumphantly, showing a brief glimpse of the old, excited Dodie behind her mask of blasé worldliness.

Dodie's book was published in September 1925, and she could think and talk of little else. Nor, come to that, could Uncle George and Aunt May, though their preoccupation was ostensibly one of sustained concern and titillated moral shock, rather like the relatives of an illegitimate baby.

The book was called, shockingly enough, *Fruits of Experience*, but no babies appeared in it; instead the fruits seemed to be a kind of restless perversity on the part of the boyish heroine (Daphne) which led her to reject the honourable advances of man after man while pursuing—across London, Paris and finally the Scottish moors—a mysterious Other with whom (the reader was left to assume) Daphne had had her original Experience. The experience was not described or named, but English readers of that date were presumed to be able to fill the gap for themselves, and most of them evidently did, according to taste. The book created a small sensation on the literary pages ('Miss Denvers' alarmingly modern young woman is indeed a tragic figure of our post-war time . . .') and sold well. It was seriously discussed, as there was a certain amount of imagery in it taken from the classical myth of

Persephone, which Mary clearly remembered them 'doing' during the first year at Bessemer; Daphne had, it seemed, some time in her unrevealed past, descended (metaphorically speaking) into the Underworld with the God of those regions (the Underworld seemed to be Paris, but it was a little vague) and that was one reason why she subsequently wandered like a pale but expensively equipped ghost through the world of the day, unable to attach herself permanently to any of the ardent young men with broad shoulders and large incomes who yearned after her. 'I am transparent,' she said daringly two-thirds the way through the book, at the culmination of a particular crisis. 'A hall of glass . . . Men pass through me.' The remark was quoted in an undertone to one another by readers who found it deeply moving, and it became, briefly, famous. Near the end Daphne, in flight across Europe either with or from her God of the Underworld (it was not clear which) died under the wheels of a train, and the novel was therefore castigated from several pulpits as 'nihilistic', but a rather advanced bishop pointed out that such a tragic end was deeply moral and Boots' library decided to stock the book after all.

Unwillingly, Mary admired the work, not so much for anything it might actually be saying (for Daphne, when one came down to it, seemed a flimsy creature, and surely in real life all those men wouldn't have behaved quite like that?)— but for Dodie's unexpected sureness of touch and for the amount of contemporary fiction she must have read to produce such an expert synthesis.

Through that autumn Dodie was constantly on the move, solicited by journalists and tradespeople, invited by hosts she had hardly met, fawned on and cosseted by old acquaintances. In slithery little frocks of lamé or coppery silk she attended signing parties and receptions, first nights and openings, and frequently she made use of Ellie and Mary Denvers' house in which to change beforehand or spend the night after. Sometimes she even took Mary with her: to the more sober and female occasions.

Her drawling speech became rapid again. She still cultivated, when sitting, her new, conscious repose, like a vessel whose contents must not be spilled, but behind her mask of paint she seemed to glow with an inner excitement that was all the more potent for being suppressed. Her innate warmth now expressed itself in sudden gestures of generosity that touched Mary's heart, even though Mary knew Dodie could well afford them: the impulsive gift of a silver bangle that Mary had admired; her arrival one morning, unannounced, at the small house in West Hampstead, with her arms full of bronze chrysanthemums, sheaf upon sheaf of them.

'I couldn't resist them! The French think they're only for the dead—did you know that, Mary?—but I love them so. I wanted you to have them.'

And as they together filled all the vases the house could muster, she suddenly exclaimed:

'I feel so well, Mary! So much as if I could do anything. Anything . . . Did you know you can make people in the street smile at you just by looking at them?'

'*You* can, perhaps!' said Mary indulgently. Privately she did not think that Dodie, attractive and vibrant as she undoubtedly was, did look very well. She had got thinner during her winter in Paris, and thinner again it seemed during the last two or three months since her book had appeared. As a flapper she had been inclined to bemoan her pretty breasts as 'my enormous chest': now she evidently had no difficulty in suppressing her bosom into fashionable flatness; her wrists and ankles were birdlike and her bright, black, bird's eyes looked out from hollows. The plump, enchanting curve of her cheek had thinned. It was as if by some secret chemistry, at variance with her proclaimed happiness, Dodie had transformed herself physically into a simulacrum of her own haunted heroine.

She had many plans. She was writing another novel— 'altogether much bigger and more profound, Mary. It's about how the way we live now is producing a new race of people— there's never been a period like this before, you know . . .' She had been asked by Lady Rhondda to give a series of lectures to a women's organisation, and to write on morals for the *Daily Mail*. She was apparently—this considerably surprised Mary when Dodie told her—in correspondence with Freud, was planning a visit to Vienna and was learning German with this in mind. 'Foreign languages are easy, Mary, easy!

I discovered that in Paris. Why did no one ever tell me before?'

'They did, at school. You wouldn't learn the verbs.'

She was, Mary noticed at a dinner party, eating very little. (In the past, Dodie had always been rather greedy, with a weakness for rich, sugary food.) She also seemed to need much less sleep than she once had, much less than Mary herself: on the nights she spent in Hampstead she kept Mary up talking long past midnight, but was the same lively self again at eight the next morning when Mary felt tired and a little resentful.

Then, one morning in early December, when Mary had been going to meet Dodie at Peter Jones for Christmas shopping, Aunt May rang up, and this was followed later in the day by a call from Uncle George. Once more the words 'breakdown', 'nerves' and 'complete mental and physical collapse' reverberated about the family. But this time the subject of them was not Aunt May but Dodie.

There had been some sort of scene at a dinner party, after which Dodie had been lost for some hours, and had finally been found early the next morning walking alone in the rain, soaked to the skin.

Mary never got a full account of what had happened. Willie, who had been there, was laconic in his description. But he did say that Dodie had 'electrified' the other guests by talking to the table at large at the top of her voice for twenty-five minutes without stopping.

'What on earth about?'

'Herself and her own plans, very largely. You know that's the only thing that interests our celebrated authoress these days.'

Shocked at his callous tone—for it was obvious, on reflection, that Dodie had not been acting normally for some time—Mary said coldly:

'What on earth did people think?'

'Actually, I should imagine they thought she was squiffy.'

'And was she?'

'No. Dodie hardly drinks at all, you know. Not like some girls do these days. All that *âme damnée*, knocking-back-the-cocktails is a pose. She doesn't like the taste. No, she wasn't drunk. More—potty, I thought. To be absolutely frank, my dear.'

. . . '*It's as if all the time I knew something was due to happen to me . . .*'

Dodie spent some weeks in a nursing home and was presently reported by Aunt May to be 'her old self' again. *Which* old self, exactly? Mary wondered. After the initial drama the Esher Denvers seemed eager to play the whole matter down. Officially Dodie had just been 'doing too much', and had got 'overtired' and 'run down', and 'a good rest had set her back on her feet'. No one seemed anxious to reflect that Dodie's abnormal state had not been the result of Doing Too Much but its cause, and Mary stifled the thought as one best left unexplored—if Dodie were indeed all right again.

In the new year she was invited to accompany Uncle George, Aunt May and Dodie on a fortnight's recuperative holiday in Harrogate. She was not enthusiastic.

'Really, Mother, I don't see why I should go everywhere they summon me, just because they want me to keep an eye on Dodie. Yes, it *is* like that, you know it is. They think I'm Horatio in *Hamlet*—"Look to him, good Horatio"—and off I trot. Suppose I don't want to? And suppose the AMs can't spare me? We've got more and more work in the office these days.'

But in the end, defeated by her own nature, she went, still outwardly rebellious.

'I don't need baths or whatever it is we're going for. I'm as strong as a horse. *You're* the one whose health could do with attention, Mother.' Indeed, Ellie Denvers' 'bronchitis' now seemed to affect her winter and summer, a permanent condition of life.

'Nonsense, dear, I don't want to go to Harrogate. I've never liked hotel life. All those women carrying their hand-bags around indoors and dressing up for breakfast . . . Your Aunt May loves it, I've never understood why. You go; you'll enjoy it more than you think, you'll see.'

On a previous visit to Harrogate the Denvers had apparently stayed at the enormous Hotel Majestic where, before the war, foreign royalty had taken suites, but this time they stayed at the Cairn Hydro up the road—smaller and quieter and therefore on this occasion more suitable, according to Aunt May. It did not seem particularly small or quiet to Mary: you could hardly find a seat in its winter-garden lounge on sunny mornings, and its ballroom was crowded each night. It had its own baths in the basement, and each day she and Dodie took their 'treatment', presided over by a dictatorial little woman with a hunched shoulder, whose surgical boot echoed up and down the tiled floors like that of a jailer, commanding them to endure heat or a sudden cold plunge. Mary wondered what it must be like to spend your working life among naked or near-naked bodies when your own was irremediably twisted. Did the poor woman live with a corrosive envy of all that straight, fat pinkness, and was that why she was brusque and distant? Or had she, simply, long ceased to notice it?

Some of the women huddled shyly in bathrobes at the very brink of the plunge-pool, as if their flesh were unfamiliar and disconcerting even to themselves. But others, Mary thought, seemed to flaunt their unaccustomed nakedness as if an abandonment of conventional modesty were part of the whole experience, and as important to their health as the jets of water or the seaweed sitz-baths or the massage. She was a little surprised when Dodie reacted to these uninhibited women with some disgust:

'All that bare flesh, Mary . . . It's a bit horrible, don't you think?'

'No, why? It's just nature.'

'Well, I'm not keen on it. And that hair down there. Ugh! You must admit it would be much nicer if people didn't grow hair on themselves.'

Mary found nothing to reply to this. Body hair was not pretty, perhaps, but surely this wasn't the point? She glanced sideways at Dodie's own slight figure and registered that the recent transformation of it into fashionably boyish shape was more than just an effect of clothes. Naked, Dodie, though clearly female, did look somehow androgynous these days, as if she had managed by some effort of will to reduce her breasts and her inevitable pubic hair to mere appendages, not an essential part of herself. There came into Mary's mind the title of a French novel, published in the last few years to acclaim and scandal, and rumoured in England to be so indecent that it could not be translated: *La Garçonne*. That was what Dodie looked like. Yet surely experience (or whatever one chose to call it) should logically make a person more of a woman, not less? '*I am transparent. A hall of glass . . . Men pass through me . . .*' Yes, Dodie did seem in some way transparent, Mary thought, feeling deeply ill at ease in a subject which was clearly of central importance but of which she knew so little in practice.

Did Dodie possess a check pessary? Supplied perhaps by some faintly sinister foreign doctor? But, if so, on this crucial matter she was silent.

In the evenings, reduced by clothes to normality, they danced with the other hotel guests, and in particular with a young man called Walter Lambourne, whose family was in textiles, in Leeds, as he confided to them. He was a confiding young man, and after a few days Mary and Dodie knew all about his thriving business and his widowed mother's rheumatism (the reason for his presence in Harrogate), his sister, his sister's unsatisfactory husband, his own prowess at golf, his Lancia, the horse he had recently bought, and a number of other things. They were inclined to giggle together about the enthusiastic completeness with which Walter laid his life before them, and presumably before all his dancing partners. Still, they agreed, he was nice-looking, very attentive, obviously kind to old ladies and an excellent dancer. He expressed himself deeply impressed at the opportunity of talking to a 'real writer'; like Stanley Baldwin, of whom he approved, he was a great admirer of Mary Webb's *Precious Bane*.

Mary assumed that Dodie was his main interest, and that by dancing with her as well he was simply showing that he had been nicely brought up. It was therefore several days before it dawned on her that he was actually asking her to dance rather more often than he asked Dodie, and that he was seeking her company during the daytime as well. One night he led her out into the gardens, gallantly draped his tailcoat over her shoulders against the January cold and kissed her behind some gaunt, pruned rose-bushes with enthusiastic tenderness. She enjoyed it very much—he seemed so large and healthy and warm, in spite of having given her his coat—and she was a little anxious the following morning to reflect on the eagerness with which she had probably returned his kisses. But perhaps that was all right; he had certainly seemed as pleased as she was.

She did not mention the episode to Dodie, and in any case Walter Lambourne disappeared to Leeds to attend to his textiles. But the following Friday night he was back again and, once more, spent the evening dancing more with her. He also took her out into the garden again but, to her own surprise, she shivered so that he brought her back almost at once, full of concern that she might have caught a chill.

The following morning Mary woke up with a sore throat and cold coming: so much, she thought disgustedly, for all those supposedly health-conferring baths. Aunt May (who had refrained from treatment herself because she had previously found it 'too taxing') made a fuss of her and told her she should stay in bed; so she did, consuming the hotel's delicious invalid diet and desultorily reading a copy of *Precious Bane* she had found in the reading room. Its rustic passion seemed worlds away from textiles in Leeds, but perhaps that was what Walter Lambourne liked about it.

From below the sound of the band faintly reached her. She would have loved to be there with him.

On the Sunday morning she felt better, and got up. Dodie and her parents had gone to morning service, Dodie with particularly vermilion lips and her Parisian air of superior withdrawal. Mary wondered why Dodie did not decline to go altogether if she felt like that about it, but then Dodie, for all what Willie called her *âme damnée* airs, still seemed oddly subject to her parents' will; possibly her recent breakdown had served to draw her back into a childlike state.

In her heavy tweed coat and muffler Mary walked in the thin sunshine, unable to breathe properly but enjoying the tame beauty of the great greens with which the little town was surrounded. Eventually she reached the path between trees that led to Teevitt's Well. The cupola over it lay ahead through the lacy trees; I'll just walk to it, she thought, then go home.

Suddenly on the path before her, and walking briskly from the well, was Walter Lambourne. Disconcerted but pleased she hesitated, prepared to stop and talk. However, as if disconcerted himself and flustered, he merely raised his hat, greeted her and passed on.

She continued toward the well. As she reached it, a slight figure slipped between the pillars on the far side and began walking away as if feigning not to have seen her approach.

Gasping for breath, Mary eventually caught up with her.

'Oh, hallo!' said Dodie, turning round too quickly.

'What on earth are you doing here?'

'Well, if it comes to that . . . What are you? I thought you were ill in bed.'

'I'm not ill. I got up. I thought *you* were in church.'

'Well, I'm not,' said Dodie shortly. 'I draw the line at sermons.' She began absurdly to whistle.

Furious with this act, Mary said:

'You've been meeting Walter Lambourne, haven't you?'

'My, my,' said Dodie in a provoking little-girl voice. 'Are we jealous?'

Mary felt a choking sensation in her throat and chest which were not entirely connected with her cold. She could not reply. On the face of it, it was ridiculous. Was she just annoyed because Dodie, the sophisticated authoress of the year, was slipping out of church to indulge in hole-and-corner meetings with a Leeds textile manufacturer as if she were a shop-girl? No, of course not: Dodie's manners and morals were not her business. And she told herself that she wasn't in love with Walter Lambourne, didn't want him in any serious way. But he had seemed to like her enough to single her out and kiss her; that had been in its own way important and real. The idea that Dodie might have got him away from her, just for fun or experience or whatever it was Dodie sought, and might have been encouraging him to kiss her, to fall in love with her and God knew what else, was insupportable, unfair, agonisingly and permanently unfair . . .

She sought relief from her feelings in a few cold remarks on making oneself cheap. But she knew, as she did so, that she was being dishonest, covering a far more painful feeling with a veneer of civilised disapproval. She felt cheap herself, tainted by whatever it was that was being enacted here, and by her instinctive reaction to it.

Walking quickly side by side, exchanging fragmented and barbed remarks, they reached the hump-backed bridge that led over the Leeds-Harrogate branch line. On the bridge Dodie paused, and turned to face Mary theatrically.

'Have you finished? Because I don't at all want to walk along with you insinuating in my ear how nice girls ought to behave. I'm not a nice girl, in case you haven't noticed. I'm a writer. If you think your timid middle-class notions of propriety cut any ice at all with me then you've understood nothing about me, absolutely nothing at all. Don't you see, I have to be free. Free to live—free to die, if necessary. Of course you wouldn't know anything about that, with that grey little life you lead in Kilburn.'

Inside the pockets of her coat Mary clenched her fists so that the nails dug in. She heard a voice that seemed to belong to an uglier, older woman than herself:

'Then I'd rather have a grey little life, as you call it, than be a hall of glass like you. Yes, it is true—I thought that was just a poetic image you made your Daphne-woman say, but you *are* transparent. You get your colour from picking up things around you and making use of them. You make use of people too. It doesn't matter much when it's a cousin, like Willie or me, but it does matter when it's people like—like Walter Lambourne. You've got no character, Dodie—'

But Dodie didn't hear, because, at Walter's name, she had turned sharply and set off, and was now running across the green.

Unfair. Cruel. Over-reacting. She's only a pretty, highly strung girl, still learning about life, and what else can she do, bright as she is, but pick things up from other people? She had no education to speak of, no foundation for any coherent view of life; she's been spoilt and indulged since childhood, but not *loved*, not as you and the Boys were loved . . . You should be sorry for her, but you're so mean and jealous that you can only attack her. You're becoming a goody-goody spinster like she and Willie think. And she's been ill too, a breakdown, something very strange that everyone is anxious to cover over, and instead of trying to help her you jump on her. A fine doctor you'd make . . .

Mary's conscience nagged her all the way back to the hotel. At lunch in the huge dining room she looked so wretched and ate so little that Aunt May urged her back to bed again for the afternoon. But Dodie ate beef and Yorkshire pudding and gooseberry fool and chatted brightly about her stroll to Teevitt's Well as if she had been there on her own, and perhaps in a sense she had.

The rest of that winter turned into one of the worst periods of Mary's life. Or rather it seemed to her that an endemic sickness in life, which had been concealed and undiagnosed for a long time, found that moment to manifest itself. Events, trivial in themselves, had stripped off her defences, and the sickness was exposed in all its painfulness—a pain that was the worse for seeming, not grandly tragic, but squalid and commonplace.

Peering fearfully down the tunnel of years to come, she saw them empty. She had swallowed her grief for the Boys, and for the lost country of hope and plans they had represented to her, by going on feeling at some level inaccessible to reason that these bleak 1920s were simply a close season, a time of waiting, and that life, like the cycle of the seasons, would eventually renew itself. She knew that Oliver, Roland and Nigel would not return, but several times she had dreamed of them being (as in Nigel's own dream) in India, unreachable, but still in some sense existing.

Only now did she find herself consciously facing the possibility that there was no renewal. These past half-dozen years she herself had been subconsciously waiting for something new to happen, but perhaps nothing ever would—nothing important or transforming. Why, she asked herself, probing her pain in a masochistic attempt to discover how bad it was, should she expect anything more?

The Walter Lambourne episode, inconsequential and even ridiculous in itself, had, she felt, exposed her true position so that she could no longer ignore it. She had thought she had come to terms with the knowledge that the war had destroyed all those young men's lives: only now did she see how many female lives—not to mention potential children's lives—it had pre-empted as well. Yes, 'surplus' woman, that would be her role: a marginal, peripheral life, volunteer do-gooder; a maiden aunt making a conscientious best of things, the good sport taking her nieces and nephews (Dodie's children?) out for pantomimes and cream teas, the relation always on hand to clear up family messes because, after all, she didn't have anything else important to do, did she? And if, with the accumulating busy, empty years, she became a little withered and acerbic and set in her ways, no one would blame her. No one would care, anyway.

She suffered in double measure, partly from her sense of loss and waste but also from shame at finding that it came down to such an ignoble, age-old, female predicament. Nothing of the moderate, sane feminism she had imbibed at Bessemer and at the AMs could protect her against this. She even found herself fantasising at moments about Eric Evans, and wondering if he still . . . ? But their relations had taken on another pattern now. And in any case . . .

There was talk in the papers these days of the government extending the franchise down to women in her own age group. For the first time she tasted the bitterness of such hollow victories compared with her life's central deprivation.

As that winter wore into spring Mary, shut in her private misery, nevertheless became aware that a more general distress and restiveness were at work in other people's lives. The miners and the railwaymen had been threatening strikes for months: the newspapers she usually read called it 'class-warfare', but the *Daily Herald*, which Eric Evans brought into the office, called it 'social justice' and 'the fight for freedom'.

Mary was repelled by the hints of violence, and suspicious of those whom she suspected of being excited by the idea of revolution, but she saw the poverty and hopelessness that manifested itself in their office and which was visible up and down the Kilburn High Road, round the greasy stalls under the naphtha lamps, and drew her own long-term conclusions. By May, and the General Strike, her sympathies had settled on to the side of the strikers and were to remain there for much of her life. Three days before the strike was due to start she refused to speak to Uncle George, when he rang up urging them to 'join forces' with his family in Esher, where he was organising a patriotic volunteer force and stockpiling supplies of food. She could hear his voice booming, as her mother, with an expression of faint pain, held the telephone away from her ear; he sounded both peremptory and elated.

'It's no good, Mother. You go to Esher if you like, but I won't. He makes me too cross.'

'Oh dear, I'm afraid he's in his element in this sort of thing . . . You know, I often think that George doesn't have quite enough to do these days. So bad for him.'

In the middle of the strike Willie appeared on their doorstep; he had just arrived from Paris.

'How did you get up to London from Dover?' Mary enquired with interest.

'Got a lift from some chaps who were driving up to help with food deliveries and so forth. Good chaps—one was a stockbroker. Of course he's pretty worried about the effect this idiotic business is having on the world markets, and so am I. Bloody working class. Why can't they ever see beyond the end of their own stupid noses?'

'Perhaps it's because they haven't had the same educational advantages that you have, Willie,' Mary said in a small, deliberately annoying voice. He looked at her sharply, but apparently decided to let it pass. Like Uncle George, he seemed excited. The usual drawling and blasé Willie had been temporarily replaced by an almost enthusiastic young man, with a flushed face and a lock of lank hair falling over his forehead. Mary remembered that poor Willie had missed the war. She said, as she took his hat and scarf:

'Do you just happen to be in London? Or did you come over deliberately?'

'You bet I did.' He added self-consciously: 'Mustn't desert the old country in her hour of need, what?'

They drank tea, and Willie talked about his journey and the Stock Exchange. Meanwhile Mary marshalled her thoughts and got her courage up. Willie, after all, was not provincial or essentially stupid. He read books and he travelled. Surely

94

there was a level on which she could reach him? She said carefully:

'Willie, about this strike-breaking, patriotic service or whatever it's called. You've never worked, have you? Because you've got a good private income. Oh, don't get me wrong, I'm not *blaming* you, but—'

'I should think not, my dear!'

'—But have you any idea—any *idea*, Willie—what some of the working class earn? Not just miners and railwaymen. There are—oh, masses of people—far less well-paid even than that. I'm not talking about the unemployed but about men in responsible, regular work. They can't afford medical treatment for their wives and children, they don't even have—oh, the *decencies* of life—'

'My, my. Quite the little Socialist, aren't we?'

'Oh, I knew you'd jeer. But it's true, Willie. Surely, without necessarily approving of strikes, you can see that—'

'Have your little pals at the fallen sisters outfit been feeding you this stuff? You girls are so gullible. Dodie's just the same.'

'—They *aren't* all Red Revolutionaries. They're just ordinary bus-drivers and milkmen and people—'

'You make my heart bleed! Oh, come off it, Mary, use your intelligence. Can't you see all this sob stuff is just a front and the whole thing's being manipulated by International Communism? *You* are being manipulated, if it comes to that. I may not be one of the toiling masses you're so keen on, but I do get about and hear things, you know.'

'Of course. You would have the time to.'

'Don't you adopt that sneering, governess tone with me, my dear. You don't exactly earn your own living, do you? What paid for your famous education, may I ask, but private income? And where would you and your mother be now without the family money, which enables you to sit around indulging in good works and parlour Socialism? You know what? You girls make me sick. You're leeches, the lot of you. Po-faced frauds—'

After that they could only go on to quarrel bitterly, and at cross-purposes, until finally Willie banged out of the house, leaving Mary in tears of pure fury, with herself as much as with him, and his expensive silk scarf hanging in the hall.

They did not, as things turned out, see each other again to speak alone together for over thirteen years.

Among the assorted griefs that kept Mary sleepless for much of that night was the dawning conviction that, had the Boys lived, they too would have been cheerful, brutal strike-breakers, good chaps riding up to town to offer their services to King and Country and have a beano while they were at it, all men together.

PART THREE

IT HAD BEEN DURING THE COLD SPRING OF 1926 THAT MARY applied to St Jude's, her father's old medical school. 'Get your plans laid, my dear, get yourself accepted,' said Professor Parsons. 'Then you're in a stronger position to look about for the money. That's always been my principle whenever I've needed research funds.' And so she found herself, one day in early March, attending St Jude's for an interview. She had acted obediently, almost absentmindedly, going through the motions of realising an ambition that misery had for the moment driven from her heart. She answered the questions the admissions board put to her without nervousness; the interview somehow did not seem to have much to do with herself and her real preoccupations, and perhaps (she thought afterwards) that had helped her to give an impression of coolness and efficiency. Yet when, in a lull between postal strikes in May, the letter arrived telling her that there would be a place for her in St Jude's medical school in September she found after all that a pride and an excitement stirred within her.

'They did ask about money,' she admitted to her mother. 'I just said "family money", and they didn't ask any more. I know I shouldn't really have said that. You've always said that we couldn't ask Uncle George for any more.' She had been nursing an idea of borrowing some from Dodie, who had made a lot from *Fruits of Experience* and was always generous. But now it came to the point she found herself quailing. Had she not, after all, indulged in the greater luxury of speaking her mind to Dodie, even if Dodie herself affected to have forgotten all about it?

It was not, however, necessary to ask anyone. After some hesitation, her mother explained:

'Darling—you know that one of my reasons for moving here to this little house was to save money? Well, I don't think I ever explained to you quite what I was saving it for. The fact is, I felt worried about what might become of you when I'm gone. Anyway, in the end, on Dr Gurney's advice, I took out quite a big life insurance. I've been able to pay the premiums by economising, you see (and of course you've helped me in that), and I've felt that it would be *something* for you, years and years ahead . . . But darling, if you really feel that becoming a doctor is the thing you want to do with your life then we could cash the policy and use that for your fees.'

The thing you want to do with your life. Further elucidation hung, unnecessary, in the air between them. Women doctors were known as 'dedicated'. They dressed in severe, sensible clothes and enjoyed (if they were lucky and worked hard for years) a status and an income which was denied to ordinary women. They did not need dowries or marriage settlements; they could hardly expect to have marriage as well as a career. One could not, after all, have everything.

Mary said that that was what she wanted. It would have been more truthful to say that she felt this was merely the best of several daunting alternatives, and that she must do *something* with her life. But that would have distressed Ellie Denvers and spoilt her pleasure in her daughter's success. Mary never said it and, in time, as her life as a doctor took her over, she ceased to feel it.

One year of first MB doing more Chemistry and Zoology and also Botany and Physics. Two years of second MB doing Anatomy and Physiology. Two major exams during that time and, on the second MB, countless tests and vivas. Hours and hours spent in the medical-school library, in her room in West Hampstead or walking round the heath, memorising lists and charts and set descriptions. Hours and hours too in the Anatomy laboratories in the basement of St Jude's, where, among a smell of formaldehyde and chalk, cut with occasional whiffs of cabbage and gravy from the kitchens across the yard, she and the other forty students in her year dissected the dead, grey, cool flesh that was to be the basic material of their trade. Here, among disembodied legs, arms, hands, feet, thoraxes, stomachs, wombs, genitals, spines, jaws and knees, was their introduction to humanity. Of real human beings, upstairs in the wards and crowding into the Out Patients, suffering pain or distress or nausea, breathing, eating, defecating, sweating, bleeding, laughing, crying, they saw nothing. In these first three years of training they did not touch a single living patient.

It presently became apparent to Mary that there were several kinds of medical students. There was the substantial coterie of young men who were following in their fathers' footsteps and who would probably take each exam at least twice. They groaned exaggeratedly over the rote-learning, but most of them were secure in the knowledge that a place in a comfortable country practice lay waiting once they had hauled themselves over the minimum necessary hurdles. Apart from them, there were the ones who seemed interested in scientific knowledge for its own sake. They memorised lists of parts and functions with an enthusiastic obsessionalism Mary recalled from Roland with his birds' eggs collection and Oliver with his stamps. They seemed to enjoy dissection, she thought, in the way they enjoyed tinkering with the second-hand cars they bought and parked in the roads near St Jude's; she concluded that this must be a masculine approach, for the handful of women on the course, including herself, all seemed to fall into a third group. This group had little interest in facts or techniques as such, and simply regarded the acquisition of these as a necessary but formidable chore before they might be allowed to confront what really interested them—the patients.

Secretly Mary knew that she herself probably had even less of the scientific attitude of mind than most of the students. At Bessemer she had done as many Arts subjects at Matric as Modern ones; she had known herself to be one of those good all-rounders who will tackle anything competently but have no outstanding talent. She managed now to keep up with the acquisition of knowledge that was required of her simply because she had a good verbal memory and was conscientious. But it was obvious to her after a few months' labour that she would never be the sort of doctor who makes a 'valuable contribution to original research'. Her suitability for the profession, if any, she concluded, could only lie in her interest in people; and for the moment people were denied to them.

It was a hard and unrewarding grind, but it was not an unhappy time. Mary enjoyed the company in the lectures and the dissecting rooms; it was like regaining the sane, enclosed world of school. And by the time she was on her second MB she had begun to make some friends—something that she had not done for years, unless you counted Mrs Parsons, who was so much older than herself, and Mr Evans who was—Mr Evans.

One of the few other women in her year was a dark, elegant girl called Olive Shapira who, like herself, was several years older than the mass of young male students fresh from public school. Olive had studied music in Paris before the conviction that she actually wished to be a doctor had finally, as she put it, caught up with her. She was the daughter of a well-known surgeon, and lived with her family in a grandly furnished house off Eaton Square. Mary did not especially envy Olive this background of wealth, but she was intrigued and attracted by the cosmopolitan flavour which she sensed there for the first time—a whiff of unorthodoxy underlying the surface decorum; pictures in the house by Klimt, Kokoschka and Marie Laurençin that were presents from the artists themselves, German-speaking uncles in the wine trade who came and went in the echoing hall and embraced each other on meeting and parting, even telephone calls to Paris and Vienna without anyone apparently regarding this as unthinkably extravagant.

What made Olive still more remarkable, in Mary's eyes, was that she was unofficially engaged to a houseman at St Jude's called John Hershey. He was a barrel-chested young man with legs not quite long enough for his body and an engaging, crumpled face. He played rugby with the hearties on Saturday afternoons and sang funny songs at the medical school Christmas party, but he also collected eighteenth-century prints of London and shared Olive's interest in music. Mary liked him, too, very much indeed, but eventually wondered aloud to Olive whether they could realistically hope to get married if she were serious about a career in medicine?

'Oh I think so, eventually, yes,' said Olive carefully. In spite of her family's flamboyant life-style, she was rather a serious person on the surface, cautious in her statements.

'But could you ever hope to get a job as a married woman?' A few years earlier—Mary remembered it clearly: it had been soon after she had gone to work for the AMs—a Dr Mialls-Smith had been dismissed from her job as medical officer to a London borough because it was discovered she had got married during her summer holiday.

'In a hospital, no, not a hope,' said Olive. 'But you see John wants to go into general practice. Somewhere in London, probably, with a partner or two. So, once he's established, I could fit myself into his firm as the lady doc. Awfully useful, you know, a lady doc around to see the shy schoolgirls and the expectant mums. Of course, we'll have to hold off for years, till I've managed to qualify, and I really ought to qualify in Midder too. Oh dear! Roll on autumn 1933—'

'You'll be—what? Thirty then.'

'Yes. Ancient. But it can't be helped. And John seems quite sanguine about waiting. Well, it'll take him that long to get properly established himself, I should think.'

'Do you mind very much?' said Mary shyly, for Olive, though frank in some ways, was rather a private person. 'Mind having to wait so long, I mean? I should think that, once one had met someone one—one loved, it would be quite hard . . .'

'Oh Mary,' said Olive, rolling her eyes slightly, 'I just feel *so thankful* for what I've got—for the situation, I mean, without craving for anything more yet. I feel we've been so lucky to find each other, when you think of all the odds against it and all the people—perfectly nice, sincere people, I'm not jeering—who settle for marrying just anybody, whether they particularly suit or not. And the extraordinary thing is that John's had masses of girls before me, whereas I never really thought about getting married at all, and yet soon after we first met we both just seemed to know "This is it". And think how unbelievably lucky for me that he's one of the same lot. Because, although religion doesn't mean that much to me, it's something . . . I don't think I could have easily married out. It would have been like doing violence to something . . . Besides upsetting everyone at home, of course. But although John doesn't care tuppence about it he does have a perfectly respectable Jewish family, and we'll be able to bring up our children as their grandparents would wish them to be. Sometimes, you know, I wake in the night and wonder what I've done to deserve such a blessing. Why me?'

'Oh—why not you?' said Mary. 'That's the only proper answer to the question "Why me?" isn't it?' She herself was familiar with the question in her own mind, but for a different, sadder reason.

In the summer of 1929 Mary passed her second MB—or, as she believed, scraped through by luck and a blinkered concentration on facts, topped up in the last days before the oral with short-term cramming that left her feeling weak mentally and physically. There was no denying, she and Olive agreed over a private, celebratory lunch at a small French place in Soho: these last three years had been an ordeal.

'And, in a way, an awful waste of living,' said Olive critically. 'Just think of all the things we've *not* done and *not* been interested in meanwhile. All sorts of things have been going on and we've missed them. The Flapper Vote, for instance. Once, in my impulsive girlhood, I would have been quite excited about that but, my de-ah, old and grey as I now am . . .'

'And the Labour government coming in,' said Mary, thinking guiltily that the last time she had really taken a close interest in what was happening in England, let alone in Europe, had been during the General Strike three years earlier. Without Eric Evans' influence her nascent Socialism had faded; most of her fellow medical students tended to conservative views, a fact by which she had been innocently surprised.

'And all the books we haven't read and the plays we haven't seen,' said Olive. 'I still haven't read *All Quiet on the Western Front*. And there's no excuse for me, with my connections.'

'Nor have I . . . We did get to *Journey's End*, though, didn't we?'

'Yes,' said Olive, 'thanks to John standing in a queue for us, we did get to *Journey's End*.' She looked at Mary with compassion. The play, the most talked about that year, showed young officers living and dying in the trenches. One line in particular had reverberated through the West End audiences and hence round England in widening ripples of shock and recognition. It ran simply:

'It all seems a bit silly—doesn't it?'

This bald truth had taken ten years to be voiced. Already the war was supposed to be 'old history', almost a subject of derision to the new generation of young men who had missed it; something near to a taboo was attached to the survivors, particularly if they talked too much about it or had not made a satisfactory life for themselves. Yet this supposedly discarded topic was only just beginning to surface into drama and literature, and as it did so its continuing potency was unmistakable. How long would it go on having its traumatic effect under the surface of people's lives? Mary wondered. Another sixty years, until everyone who remembered it was dead? Looking into her own heart, it seemed possible. She had been profoundly moved and distressed by the play, and had found herself suddenly crying at the restaurant table afterwards—here in this same restaurant—weeping with awful, embarrassing tears that seemed to rise and rise from some source below her conscious mind.

John Hershey and Olive had appeared concerned but unsurprised—less surprised than she was herself, she had thought with muddled wonder through her tears. They had each held one of her hands tight and had mopped her face with their napkins as if she had been a child. Then the three of them had gone back to John's digs, and she had talked to them about the Boys and cried some more, and John had played grand opera to them on his wind-up gramophone and had given them apricot brandy. They had all ended up quite cheerful. The next day, apparently, John had had a little trouble with his landlady because he had had 'two young persons in his rooms so late'.

'I explained to her,' John reported cheerfully to Mary,

'that there's safety in numbers. I mean, I'm hardly likely to seduce you and Olive together, am I?'

John's outspokenness, thought Mary, made him easy to talk to. Olive was more reserved, but there was still a directness about her to which Mary responded most gratefully. Would she have found herself able to cry openly after *Journey's End* had she not been with two such people? Only now, in their company, did she realise the extent to which her own English family, in varying ways, avoided explicitness as far as possible. Yes, even Mother, so sensible and calm and honest compared with Uncle George and Aunt May and Dodie and Willie, even Mother avoided a lot of topics, Mary thought. That, perhaps, was part of the conscious matter-of-factness with which, as a widow, Mother had faced the world; a number of things which were possibly matters of profound importance (like, indeed, having no husband) were awarded a place of unimportance as if that were the only proper way of dealing with them. In unthinking emulation, Mary had adopted this approach to life herself. Now, reflecting on many things, she was not sure that it was, in the long term, a tenable one for her.

A new sense of the terrible deprivation at the centre of her mother's life, a deprivation brought about by fate but also by resignation and a kind of cowardice disguised as endurance, welled up within her. She felt a rush of agonised sympathy which yet had a spume of censure to it. Surely individual life and endeavour need not be over because one was widowed at thirty? She was within sight of thirty herself.

She was, in any case, worried about her mother these days. Ellie Denvers' health had continued to deteriorate. She pretended herself that this was not so, and Mary only realised it, with a small shock, when she compared her mother's present state with the way she had been, say, at the same season two or three years earlier. Ellie's intractable 'bronchitis' had for some time occupied their own doctor and various specialists. The last specialist to whom Mary had accompanied her mother had used the word 'emphysema'. Ellie had seemed pleased and even relieved to have a new name by which to refer to the breathlessness of which she attempted to make light, but Mary of course looked the condition up. She also asked one of her tutors about it, pretending it was an objective query. She did not like what she was told.

Sometimes, seeing her mother crouched over the fire, gasping and gasping in the attempt to draw air into her sclerosed lungs, Mary felt that this insidious suffocation, this death in the breast, was like a dreadful symbol of Ellie's life. And even she herself, the one loved person who remained to Ellie, was stealthily growing away from her now, moving on to other relationships, other things, while Ellie was left stranded in her disability, an enfeebled and shrunken version of the all-important person she once had been.

But the sheer practical care of Ellie further encroached on Mary's time and energy, providing another insulation, in addition to her medical studies, against events in the outside world. That September, with relief and renewed enthusiasm, she and Olive embarked on their three years of clinical studies; at last they were allowed on to the wards, and bodies became real once more. So absorbing did she find this new situation that when the Wall Street crash occurred in October, bringing the rest of the world's stock-markets down with it, she was barely conscious of what had occurred. Not till Christmas, on a duty visit to Esher where she now rarely went, did she hear Uncle George's flushed and frightened predictions of things to come. He spoke, as he often did, of the 'menace of Bolshevism', then, almost in the same breath, of the conspiracy of international financiers, who had 'made a packet' out of speculation and then 'got out just in time, leaving the little man to pay the price'. Evidently, in this context, Uncle George, in spite of all those jute mills and his substantial Esher home, regarded himself as one of 'the little men'.

When she had been younger and more at his mercy she had got her own back on him secretly by telling herself how well he fitted Baldwin's remark years ago about 'hard-faced men who look as if they've done well out of the war'. But she had to admit to herself that Uncle George, red faced and coarse though he might look these days, was not hard: there was, indeed, as her mother had always implied, something intractably innocent about George, which both redeemed him and made him all the more awkward to deal with.

He was also, she now noticed, consuming large amounts of wine and spirits. Late at night his heavy snore could be heard from his study, where he ostensibly went to 'look at papers'. Mary mentioned this to her mother, who said resignedly:

'Yes, I know. He's been doing that for years.'

'Doesn't Aunt May try to stop him?'

'Well, it sounds an awful thing to say, but I don't think she really notices. You know Aunt May's always rather lived in a world of her own, even before . . . And now she's taken up this Coué business I don't think she'd thank me for mentioning George's habit to her, do you?'

Mary agreed. If Aunt May really believed (like Coué, whoever he was) that the problems of life could be solved by repeating to oneself daily, 'Every day, in every way, I am getting better and better,' then at least this cult seemed innocent of harmful potential. Unlike that earlier pre-occupation with Spiritualism.

Mary also registered that Aunt May did not seem to have noticed Ellie's state of health. At any rate no reference was made to it. With the legacy and example of two such parents, it was surprising that Dodie noticed as much as she apparently did. And yet, as soon as Mary had formulated the thought, she decided it was unfair. Who could say how much less Uncle George would now be drinking, how much more aware of reality Aunt May would now be, if their sons had not been wiped out? Ten years earlier she, like her mother, had been inclined to belittle the bereavement of these absentee parents whose boys had been brought up by others. Now she began to see that this very fact might make the blows of death all the more destructive to them.

Dodie was no longer living in Esher, though she still went down for long weekends, when she lay in bed recovering from London and being cosseted by the whole household. She had at last achieved her ambition of 'a dear little flat'. It was a studio near Primrose Hill, up an iron staircase, with a blue front door at the top—and Dodie had filled it with tubular steel and glass furniture and cubist canvases painted by a friend to whom she referred as 'Pete', and whom Mary assumed must be her new young man.

She had produced two more novels (*The Inconstant Moon* and *The Arch and the Shadow*) and her first, *Fruits of Experience*, had been turned into a play. To her embarrassment, Mary had not seen it; she had not accepted Dodie's invitation to the first night because it had been the evening before a Pharmacology paper. She had intended to go and see it later on, when her exams were over; but the play, in spite of having Edna Best in the lead, had come off rather more quickly than anyone had expected.

If Dodie had been disappointed by the play's reception she had not shown it. She seemed to have fallen in love with the theatre, confiding in Mary, with an intimacy now rare between them, that actors were 'such very special people . . . somehow different and more alive than ordinary people. They live with their feelings closer to the surface, of course. They are intensely honest, actually.' When at length she invited Mary to a party at her flat, almost everyone there seemed to be, in one way or another, connected with the stage. Standing uncertainly on the rim of the crowd, which packed Dodie's small living room well beyond comfort or even space in which to breathe, Mary saw what Dodie meant about feelings close to the surface—did everyone kiss *everyone*, or was there some more complex hierarchy she had not yet grasped?—but the honesty of which Dodie spoke was not apparent to her.

Mary had not come unaccompanied, and realised this had been a mistake. When she had received Dodie's telephone invitation she had felt that she did not want to appear as the spinster cousin with no escort, and had boldly asked Dodie if she might bring someone with her. She had derived satisfaction from the slight hesitation of surprise that had come before Dodie's airy, 'Of course. The more the merrier!'

The person in question was a fellow medical student, a solid, dark, good-looking young man called James, a Lowland Scot. Over work, an undemanding friendship had developed between them; he was a deft, methodical student, whose superiors thought well of him. He had taken her to concerts several times, and once to lunch with his mother and sister at the Trocadero. She liked him, and regretted rather (it *was* nice to have someone around whom people took to be your young man) that she could not feel more fervently towards him.

A few times, saying goodnight to her, he had kissed her. She had felt then confusedly that if he had done so with more passion and application, making use of his strong young body rather than subtly withdrawing it from her, she could have responded much more. But he acted with too careful a restraint: there was something finicky and sentimental about his kisses, and about the things he said at these times, which seemed to have been learnt for the occasion—at any rate they did not square with his everyday, matter-of-fact personality. She tried telling herself that he was just too nicely brought up; but there was something in him at these times which chilled her.

However, he was extremely presentable, and she was pleased to have him come with her to Dodie's. Very soon she wished she had come alone. The party was much noisier than she had thought it would be. Dodie was too busy to take much notice of them, and everyone seemed to know everyone else. On her own, in her one inconspicuous 'good' black dress, Mary felt that she could have slipped between the crowds unobserved but observing, and could have derived some pleasure and interest from that. But, with James on her hands, she could not melt into the shrieking wall of people, and she hung apologetically by his side, incapable of either making conversation to him (how ridiculous, anyway, to come here to do that!) or abandoning him.

James, for his part, was ill at ease, and showed it. In the world he came from, clearly, women did not wear so much make-up nor hang so on men's shoulders calling them 'darling'. Nor did men wear green shirts or long hair nor fall publicly asleep on divans, as one portly man had done. James was not at all amused (though Mary was secretly) when a stout middle-aged woman, with a shock of grey hair and dangling amber beads, surged up to him and declared that he had the perfect profile and would make a marvellous model. 'I can't see your body under all that gent's suiting, but I'm sure it's marvellous too,' she declared loudly with a girlish loucheness that might have been fetching twenty years earlier but was now grotesque. James, with his perfect profile, nevertheless wore the look of a disgusted camel, and started backwards when the woman patted his arm. People standing round laughed at him, in his role of unwilling stooge; evidently this was just Pete doing her familiar act. Yes—Pete. For this sagging, proprietary mother-figure was, it turned out, the creator of the cubist daubs that decorated the room, and that Mary had assumed must be the work of a lover.

Caught between her old loyalty to Dodie and a newer loyalty to James, she endured a most uncomfortable party. The remainder of the evening they spent in a cold and under-populated German restaurant in Baker Street, where James—who had drunk a certain amount at the party in self-defence—so far forgot himself as to monologue about what he would expect from 'the sort of girl one might marry'.

'I'm not a prig,' he kept saying, 'but—' Until Mary began to decide that he was indeed a prig, and to wish fervently that she had never brought this wretched evening on herself.

The next day Mary rang Dodie up to thank her. She and James had slunk from the party without saying goodbye, and she could not rid herself of the habit of good manners. Dodie said, in her most affected and infuriating voice:

'Darling, *who* was that divine-looking but *wooden* young man you had in tow? Pete said he jumped a mile when she laid a hand on him, and Viola said he lectured her on drains or something dreary . . . Honestly, sweetie, we must find you someone a bit better. I'll have a lovely dinner party soon.'

But if Dodie did give a 'lovely dinner party' Mary didn't get to it, for, towards the end of the winter, Ellie Denvers' condition worsened perceptibly. She became bed-ridden, and Mary's life narrowed down to a clock-haunted round of hospital and sick-room, sick-room and hospital, with little energy or inclination to look beyond the next lecture, the next invalid's meal of fish and junket to be prepared, the next night of strained, light sleep, ears perpetually open for a movement in the next room.

'Clinical experience', as her present stage of training was called, was not, in any case, particularly easy, though it was varied and interesting. You were attached for a period of

111

weeks or months to this or that consultant and his 'firm' of junior doctors, as general dogsbody and note-taker. As soon as you had got to know the ways of the consultant and his speciality you were likely to be moved on somewhere else. That spring Mary was attached to a famous gynaecologist who had beds in St Jude's—all the consultants were men in private practice who gave their services to the hospital for nothing—and this one did not disguise the fact that he regarded hospital patients as inferior. More specifically, he had the reputation of despising women: Mary did not like to speculate on the motivations that had brought him into Gynaecology. His particular speciality was an operation for prolapse of the uterus, which—it was murmured among the junior doctors—involved stitching the poor creatures up so short that further risks from activity in that area would be at an end for them anyway.

Mary had been warned in advance that he always singled his women students out for insulting remarks however careful they were not to offend, but still it was an unpleasant shock the day he said to her in the theatre—

'Stand over there, Miss Thingummy. You'll be no use there, of course, but at least you won't get in my way.'

She meekly went where she was told, but anger possessed her. Later that day she had a lecture to attend, one of a series on Morbid Pathology given by a visiting physician who was not on the staff of St Jude's. She liked this tall, slightly worn-looking man, who seemed to care about the students and to take trouble to ensure they had understood him, but today she fluffed an answer to a question, then failed to hear when he addressed her again because her seething mind was concocting retributive fates for the gynaecologist. After the lecture Dr Stanhope stopped her by the door.

'Is something the matter, Miss Denvers? You don't seem yourself today. Tired, perhaps?'

His direct, slightly abrupt manner, with a hint of north-country intonation behind the educated style of speech, disarmed her. Uncharacteristically, she said: 'I'm not tired so much as furious'—and went on to explain why.

Dr Stanhope nodded his head sympathetically but without apparent surprise. When she had finished, he said:

112

'That particular individual you mention is notorious. There's nothing you or anyone can do about it, I'm afraid. You'll just have to bear it, and contain your spleen—as one often has to in life.' And he bestowed a sudden, awkward smile on her, as if to indicate that he knew this remark might sound sententious.

On another occasion, after he had set them a test, he said to her again in the corridor:

'You getting on all right, Miss Denvers? You look a bit washed out. Not more concealed anger, I hope?'

'Oh—no. No, I suppose I am a bit tired. No worse than anyone else, though . . . Oh dear, was my test paper that bad?'

'Your test? Oh no, it was quite good actually, as far as I remember. No, it's just that someone mentioned to me—Dr Leary, I think it was—that you have a sick mother on your hands.'

'Oh—Oh, I see. Yes. I've been taken off Gynae. I'm attached to Dr Leary at the moment . . . It's a nice change, I find him very helpful.'

'Yes, he's a kind man. Anyway, we were chatting the other day and he mentioned to me that he thought you had a lot on your plate. I'm sorry. In this life it's so often the women who get landed with all the responsibility, isn't it? If you were a young man, now, no one would expect you to nurse the sick at home as well as here.'

This had not occurred to Mary. She was so accustomed to the tacit understanding at St Jude's that women medical students must do everything the men did, but better and more efficiently if they were to be acceptable, that it had never occurred to her that anyone might make allowances for her. Dr Stanhope's gratuitous concern almost overwhelmed her. But she just said:

'I'm all right. We manage. In any case—'

'Yes?'

'I think—our GP thinks—that Mother will have to go into a nursing home soon. Either that, or a nurse in the house, and we don't have the servants that a nurse would expect—'

'I see,' he said quietly. 'I see. I'm very sorry. If there's anything I can do . . . Do you have money problems about a nursing home? Don't be shy, tell me. I know about these things myself.'

'My uncle and aunt will pay, I think,' Mary said painfully, embarrassed a little by his own lack of embarrassment. 'I mean—I think they'll have to—'

'I'm very sorry,' he said again. 'Please let me know how things go. I mean it.'

That summer Mary and her mother had a sober little holiday in Brighton, paid for by Uncle George, who was loud in his certainty that this would 'put Ellie on her feet again'. Walking behind the hired bath-chair, feeling like the dowdy paid companion she was sure she looked, Mary thought: this cannot go on much longer. And knew the guilty sadness of longing for a loved person to die. Beyond that, she did not yet look.

Ellie Denvers died, with the first autumn chills, more suddenly than the doctors had predicted. When Mary returned to St Jude's again after the funeral, rejecting offers from Esher of a 'good rest in the country', she looked for Dr Stanhope to let him know, telling herself it was because he had been so kind. Someone had told her that he was a widower, that his wife had died of pernicious anaemia not very long ago, leaving a young child. She felt that he was someone who would understand the daunting strangeness of loss, without—unlike George and May—making a great fuss about how she would now 'manage'. Even on their brief acquaintance she had felt that he believed in women students and in her and her career. But no external Path. lectures were in progress at that time, so Dr Stanhope was not visiting the hospital.

She was twenty-eight years old, alone and free. There must be something to be said for such a situation, she told herself. With the help of Dr Gurney, she sold the house in Kilburn and most of its contents. As the insurance policy had been cashed to pay for her training, she had inherited little money from Ellie, and felt she needed to realise all she could. Uncle George had renewed his expansive 'you always have a home here with us' offers, but seemed put out when she explained that if, instead, he would continue to subsidise her until she was fully qualified, that was what she really needed. She gathered, obliquely, that the jute business was not what it had been, and also that Uncle George had lost quite a bit this last year on the stock-market, but she ignored these hints and persevered politely with her request. I must be getting hard, she thought, with a dim amusement, seeing herself from the outside. Yes, tweed skirt going baggy, hand-knitted jersey, flat heels because of the long hours in hospital on her feet, plaits pinned up round her head, white coat hanging carelessly open—the archetypal lady doctor. In a few years people would be calling her a 'tough old bird' and patients would be confiding, 'Doctor doesn't stand any nonsense, you know.'

With her mother gone she felt a need to try to look at herself a lot these days. It was as if a mirror that had always been there, and which she had taken for granted, had been removed, leaving her disorientated. Who was she? There was no Other there to tell her—to define her. She had several good friends among the students, and Olive and John were attentive and spoiling—but they had each other. She was alone.

Homeless, and wanting to leave Kilburn and its associations without moving too far off, she rented a room in the Camden Road. It was a large ground-floor room with double doors in the middle, a sink in a cupboard, a view of a sooty tree-hung garden at the back and the traffic in the wide road at the front. The room was noisier than she had expected it to be, but she got used to it, and the place was convenient for the trams, which ran down to Kings Cross and the hospital. It wasn't the traffic she minded.

It wasn't the Holloway prison for women just over the road either, or the proximity of Seven Sisters Road, which seemed to scandalise Dodie:

'Darling, it's practically a slum! Think of *Sinister Street* . . . Are you sure you'll be safe there at night?' (It would have scandalised the elder Denvers too, but Mary did not describe the location exactly to them, knowing that they would never bother to visit her.) No, what she found, to her shame, that she really minded was coming back tired in the evening and knowing that she would find everything exactly as she had left it in the morning on her hurried way out—her dressing-gown over a chair, her books and papers undisturbed on the table, the saucepan still in the grate beside the gas-ring with the dregs of milky coffee in it. She, well-educated, free, modern, independent Mary Denvers, who in another eighteen months of unremitting work would be a real doctor, found that she minded terribly, desperately, having no one to come home to.

The feeling did not strike her all at once; it accumulated gradually, as the distraction and amusement of arranging her new room and buying it pictures began to wear off, and a repetitive sameness and quietness settled on her evenings. Choosing and preparing exactly the snack she wanted for supper, without reference to anyone else, was fun at first but presently began to revolt her. It was so self-centred. Greedy . . . Unnatural. Yes, she decided as the dreary winter neared its end, unnatural was the word for her whole new life. She might be 'fulfilled' all day at the hospital doing things for people, but to have no one any longer to do anything for at home made her feel as if, at some fundamental level, she no longer existed.

She thought tentatively of sharing a flat with another woman. But could she embark on what would inevitably be an intimate life with someone, just because they were vaguely suitable and she did not like living alone? She might find herself stuck for ever like that, pigeon-holed in people's minds: two stout old girls with a comfortable routine, splendid, dedicated professional women. Backbone of British society . . . Doing *The Times* crossword together at night over their shared Welsh rarebit and homemade gooseberry fool. Two surplus women making the best of things. Awfully loyal to each other . . .

No, no, she would not accept that defeat of the heart. Not yet—

In March, she and several others of her year were sent to a fever hospital on the eastern outskirts of London to learn that branch of medicine. It was not uncommon for students on such attachments to catch things from their patients, and Mary sickened with what was tentatively diagnosed as para-typhoid. She spent two and a half weeks in that same hospital as a patient, huddled under the red blankets, woken before dawn by nurses manically bent on getting the patients washed and all the bed-corners neat before the day-shift came on duty. It had been, she decided later, a salutary experience, but not one to raise the spirits. Given leave to convalesce, she went weakly to stay at Esher where, to her amazement, Aunt May seemed to have developed a bee in her bonnet about the desirability of a 'cool season' in India for her.

'It would be so nice for you, dear. So much better for you than all this unhealthy medicine. I'm sure some of our old friends in Cal, the Beazleys or the Hammonds, would have you for a bit . . . If we paid your passage out, of course. You could always pay us back later . . . Don't you think so, George?'

But Uncle George looked discomfited and muttered about times not being good and anyway India not being what it had been, what with these damned riots and that fakir in a dhoti. At this Aunt May continued blithely:

'But George, in the long run it would be an investment for her, don't you see? . . . India is *such* a marriage market.' She smiled, as if with a girlish satisfaction at her own worldliness.

Enraged at having her own deepest longings and fears played back to her in this grotesque form, Mary said very coldly:

'Aunt May, doesn't it occur to you that I have a career? And that, in my position, I *need* a career?'

'Now don't get nasty, dear, I'm only thinking of your own good. That's just the trouble with you modern career women, as everyone says: you tend to get just the tiniest bit embittered . . . Don't look so offended, Mary, I'm just telling you for your own good.'

Dodie, who was down for the weekend, said nervously to Mary afterwards without any of the affectedness that was usual with her these days:

'Sorry Ma was so awful to you. You mustn't take any notice of her.'

'I don't,' said Mary, a shade more firmly than was polite.

'It's me she's really getting at,' said Dodie, in a sudden rush of confidence. 'She's upset because I'm not married and she thinks I ought to be. So she takes it out on you.'

'Perhaps *you'd* better go to India, then,' said Mary, laughing, her anger dispersing. Dodie had always—almost always—been able to get round her.

Dodie rolled her eyes:

'My dear, can't you just imagine it! Callow subalterns under a tropical moon saying "Gosh, fancy you writing books. You must be awfully brainy" . . . Ma can't understand my life and attitudes at all. She thinks my friends are *decadent.*'

'Well . . .' said Mary, thinking that in the past Dodie had seemed to try quite hard to give that impression herself.

'She doesn't understand that it's possible to live a free life on principle—that it's absolutely essential, in an adult relationship, that people shouldn't tie one another down. And all that disgusting obsession with *possessions* that overcomes people when they marry—all that renting cold little houses in South Ken or somewhere dreary and filling them with twin beds from Heals and housemaids and nannies and prams . . . Actually, though,' she added, with one of her descents into childish candour, 'with people so off marriage I'm not surprised the government are getting fussed about there not being enough babies. I mean, even with my married friends one infant is absolutely *all* they can afford. It's called "committing race suicide", isn't it? I can see it happening, I really can.'

'I can't,' said Mary promptly, thinking of the packed obstetric clinics she had attended, of the worn-out women who appeared in Out Patients with strings of dirty, peaky children. 'I think all that about "race suicide" is just propaganda from the anti-birth-control lobby.'

'Oh, do you?' said Dodie vaguely, as if she had never considered this aspect of the matter. 'Oh well, I suppose it's a matter of class, really?'

'Yes. I think people are genuinely worried that mothers of—of our class—are not producing enough children while the least fit parents are producing so many. *That*, of course, is one of the reasons it would be a good thing to get birth control more widely used.' It was many years before Mary and her contemporaries found it necessary to question the innocently genetic basis of their stance.

118

She had wondered a little herself, several times, that Dodie had not married by now, even transiently. She was sure in her own mind that Dodie, in spite of her advanced airs, was not really the woman to value permanent independence. How impressionable she still was, and how prone to hero-worship! Nor, come to that, had she ever shown any noticeable aversion to possessions. For whom did she really wear those crêpe de Chine blouses, those accordion-pleated skirts, those doeskin shoes with matching handbags? For herself? Or for one of the shadowy men friends—escorts, lovers, whatever—who populated her conversation? And surely it was an emotional strain leading such an unorthodox existence, however high-principled?

As if in confirmation of this, Dodie had reverted to the subject of husband-hunting in India:

'You see, Ma's fussed because next year I shall be thirty. Thirty! It doesn't seem possible, does it?'

'It does to me, I think,' said Mary, wondering about it. 'I'm thirty next year too, remember.'

'Oh, *you*,' said Dodie yearningly. 'It's different for you. You're properly grown up, you have been for years. People sort of—have faith in you. They don't in me.'

There was a silence, during which Mary thought they were both remembering that morning on the railway bridge at Harrogate years ago when she had lost her temper with Dodie and had told her she exploited people and had no character. Neither had ever mentioned that occasion since, but Mary thought that it was nice of Dodie to speak as she just had. But then Dodie had never borne grudges; it was one of the good things about her. Anything said to her seemed to drop into a deep pool, from which it would not be retrieved and held up as evidence.

Suddenly Dodie said, intensely: 'What I'd really like is to have a baby on purpose, on my own, you know. By a eugenically perfect male. That would be the ideal way, Pete says. No matrimony, no complications. Marvellous.'

'I think you might find being a mother on your own a little hard,' said Mary, feeling stuffy and middle class as she said it. At another level she felt that she understood and sympathised with Dodie's desire. But why have a child by some

119

anonymous eugenically perfect male if you could have one by a man you loved?

On fine summer evenings Mary would sit learning up her 'Path and Bac', seated by her open window to get the last of the daylight. In the evenings the traffic in the Camden Road diminished to a trickle of motor-cars bound for the West End and the occasional lorry off to the Great North Road. You could hear people talking as they idled by over the warm, stained pavements. Young men and girls 'walking out', holding hands and giggling, or pressed close together in a private dream after the early house at the cinemas turned out. Their thin, fervent, Cockney voices sometimes reached her where she sat.

Girls, ordinary shop-girls and copy-typists, she thought, were so much prettier than they had been even ten years earlier. The decade that was just over might not have been a particularly prosperous one for England; there had been unemployment ever since the war and it was apparently rising. But, seeing these girls with their little bobbed heads, their faces made dolly-like with lipsticks and creams, brave and gay in their new, cheap, artificial silk dresses and scarves, you felt that times, for them, were better than they had ever been before.

Of course, for most of them, it all went after marriage. They had too many babies and lost their teeth and let themselves go. You saw a lot of that, in the hospital and 'on the district' round the Pentonville Road, where she had recently had her first close-hand experience of babies being born.

She wished, in a way, that these young girls would not have to go through all that, becoming torn and spoiled, their bodies slack, their energy and enthusiasm bled out of them . . . Yet what better thing did most of these girls who passed before her window have to hope for, if not to marry their tight-suited young men and bear their children? From the bottom of her heart, at a level inaccessible to reason or decision, Mary envied them.

And at this level, too, the warm summer seemed to stir her, provoking imagination and memory. This time last summer, mentally closeted with her sick mother, she had hardly been aware of the profusion of flowers on the street barrows and their tender scent as she hurried to work in the mornings, of the absorbed couples entwined, silent as shadows, in certain doorways as she walked briskly home at night. Now her senses seemed to be perpetually, interminably, alert.

She remembered Eric Evans and Walter Lambourne. She remembered James. Or rather—since James was still at St Jude's and their paths crossed frequently—she remembered certain moments with him and wondered if she could have acted differently and to better effect. Since that disastrous evening at Dodie's he had gradually retreated from her and was now little more than a polite acquaintance.

One day the word got around that he was engaged. Smiling, James neither confirmed nor denied it, and by and by it was known that his fiancée was none other than the daughter of the Professor of Medicine. They were to be married towards the latter part of next year, by which time it was confidently expected that James would have qualified. Meanwhile—he unbent so far as to explain to Mary—his fiancée, who was only nineteen, would be happy doing courses in cookery and flower-arranging.

Mary was surprised and humiliated to find how much she minded.

She could never afterwards remember—and did not much want to remember—whether it was before or after this that she had fallen in love. The experience, though brief in its acute phase, was highly disturbing, mainly (she supposed mistakenly) because there was no excuse for it. The man was the registrar with the 'firm' of a neurologist to which she was then attached. He was, by general consensus, extremely intelligent, personable and good with patients—a promising boy with a bright future. He liked Mary and joked with her—teased her as, long ago, the Boys had done, Roland in particular; and once or twice took her to American Talkies, making her enjoy them by sheer force of his own eclectic enthusiasm.

But he probably liked her no better than he did several other girls. And in any case he was far too professionally ambitious to want to tie himself to anyone or anything at this stage in his career. Knowing these facts, and having always

121

believed that knowledge was a great defence, Mary was shaken by the strength and pain of her unvoiceable yearning for him.

She set herself to 'get over it' as quickly as possible, and thought she had. But long afterwards, even when her life was different and far more satisfying, the sight of his by then well-known name on a committee agenda or at the top of an article in the *Lancet* could still stir and distress her.

At last, towards the end of that aching summer, she and Olive had a short holiday in the Austrian Tyrol, and four days in Vienna during which they stayed in some grandeur with a Shapira aunt. 'This will have fortified us a bit for our final year's grind,' said Olive with determination. Mary assented gratefully, but felt incapable of telling even Olive how much more the holiday had done for her than that. Olive had travelled since childhood, and spoke French and German with ease; Mary teased her sometimes about the exotic-sounding reminiscences she would unthinkingly produce, and quoted at her Eliot's 'When we were children, staying at the Archduke's, my cousin'. But this was Mary's first expedition abroad, and she felt as if it had opened windows for her she had never known were there.

She returned to Kings Cross and to the Camden Road with fresh eyes. How garish London was! It was more prosperous than Vienna and less old-fashioned, but somehow more fragmented and socially divided. The contrast between the rotting Georgian streets east of the hospital and the bright new villas that were pushing London's edge further and further into the mutilated countryside struck her now with unpleasant force. And how smug the British were, even when they were complaining that times were hard! And how little they seemed to know or care about anything that was going on anywhere else in the world. It was as if they really did think that to be born British was the human norm and that all foreigners were an inadequate and faintly laughable fancy-dress interpretation. Long after, Mary was to regard that brief trip abroad, more than anything else, as a turning point in her life.

One Saturday afternoon in early autumn she was returning home from a damp shopping expedition when she saw coming along the road a figure who looked familiar. As it approached with a striding, easy gait, mackintosh flapping open over grey flannel trousers, it resolved itself into Dr Stanhope, the pathologist who had been kind to her when her mother had been ill. They greeted one another uncertainly. He had, of course, forgotten her name; it had been over a year since they had met. 'My memory for names isn't what it was when I was twenty,' he said, with unnecessary apology. Then, feeling self-conscious and daring, she asked him in out of the rain to have a cup of tea.

Dr Stanhope had been visiting an old colleague in Muswell Hill, and was now walking home across London. 'Do you usually go about on foot?' she asked, noticing his efficient-looking boots.

'Not that much in London, as I don't have the time, unfortunately. I'd like to—it's much healthier than tubes. No, most of my walking is done on Sunday, in the Chilterns. Or on the Yorkshire Moors, when I take a bit of leave.'

'I did some good walks in the Tyrol, this summer,' said Mary. 'For the first time really. I did enjoy it. I don't know why I never thought before of hiking in this country. I must.'

She half hoped that he would suggest that she come walking with him some time, and after a while, and a second cup of tea, and a number of direct questions about her present life, he did.

Mary's last year of clinical practice, the last before she took her MRCS and LRCP, was busier than ever. Pressure was put on the final-year students, on the grounds that they would have to withstand this when they were junior doctors or in a busy general practice, and they might as well get used to it. But Mary's crowded routine was penetrated now by a further element, which gave an extra, private definition to the weeks' cycle: she would be going for another walk next Sunday, or had been on one the week before which was still nourishing in retrospect, or was at the least looking forward to a planned one in two or three weeks.

Only about one weekend in three did they meet for any length of time. Dr Stanhope's small boy, Charlie, was living in Sussex, being cared for by his dead wife's parents, and very often he spent part or all of the weekend there.

'It must be a little strange for you, having your son brought up by other people,' she hazarded once, thinking of Oliver and Roland and Nigel and of her own mother. And he answered briskly: 'Yes, it's not ideal. But they wanted to very much—Margery was their only child. And, in the circumstances, it seemed the best solution.'

She gradually came to understand, without him telling her so, that relations between himself and his wife's parents were not easy. They were, he said, 'quite wealthy': they had possibly not been overjoyed at first with their daughter's choice of a husband. For she also understood, from what he told her of his education—a northern grammar school and scholarships—that he had not come from the same social class as Margery.

His name was Lionel. 'The sons of ordinary but aspiring people are often given these imposing names,' he remarked ruefully to her.

After he had kissed her one day, matter-of-factly and nicely, standing with his back against a tree trunk on Ashdown Forest, she thought:

This man is a friend. He means well to me. Whatever happens in the end, we have nothing terrible to fear from each other.

She knew she was not in love with him, this almost middle-aged man, in the way she had been in love with the young registrar. But that other experience had been so painful that she felt she would willingly relinquish its possibilities for ever.

In the summer of 1932 Mary and Olive passed their final exams. They were both now qualified doctors. John Hershey was already a junior partner in a general practice in Kensington, and he and Olive married. Olive had intended to get further experience in midwifery but within two months she was expecting their first child. She described herself wryly as 'a shocking advertisement'. She and John were both keen supporters of the newly formed National Birth Control Council.

A year's registration in hospital was not then compulsory,

but Lionel advised Mary to do at least that. Right away, he said, she could probably get a job in general practice in one of the new suburbs where a woman doctor would be well-received, but there was not much future in that: if she wanted to become a consultant eventually she should go about things the proper way.

She supposed he was right. At any rate she was touched by his faith that she had both the ability and the will to become anything as grand as a consultant. With his help she got herself accepted at a large local hospital in East London—the Mile End General.

Lionel himself worked for the London County Council: his work related to public-health issues rather than to individual pathology. He was far more politically aware than she was and a committed—though not extreme—Socialist. The Labour government's cut in the dole, the year before, had angered him deeply. His family's financial straits in his childhood were not, he admitted, something you ever really put behind you. Under his unaggressive but persistent influence she found her own political ideas taking shape and substance. In particular he directed her attention to what was happening in Germany.

'I don't like it,' he said. 'This National Socialism sounds good—efficient, back-to-the-land and so on—but it's a narrow authoritarian movement. And an anti-Semitic one.'

The very phrase was new to her. But it was not new to the Hersheys, and the four of them spent sober but productive evenings together. Inside herself Mary knew that John and Olive, though they liked and respected Lionel, found him a little too serious and lacking in their own brand of flippant humour. Decent, intelligent, well-informed, original even, thoughtful—she could imagine them reeling the adjectives off together—but not witty. No, not 'amusing', that paramount criterion of the era.

She herself thought Lionel *was* witty sometimes, in his own dry, understated way, when he and she were alone together, but she had to admit that, in a group, he tended to be a little stiffer, very faintly on his guard, however relaxed the rest of the company. Perhaps the social insecurity of having grown up as the scholarship son of a railwayman never quite left you, however professionally successful you were.

The one occasion at that period when Dodie met Lionel neither of them had liked the other at all. Dodie, it seemed, had moved on from throwing riotous parties to giving more carefully concocted dinners (delicatessen food served by a hired maid), at which there was usually at least one face known from the West End stage or one name from the review pages of the more popular newspapers. Mary enjoyed these occasions, though she was aware that she was now invited more often to fill a gap at table: 'my cousin who's a doctor' evidently carried more resonance in Dodie's ears than 'my cousin who's studying medicine'. She was also aware that Dodie, whatever her own declared principles, had still not abandoned the fairy godmotherly idea of 'finding someone' for Mary. It was some time before Mary mentioned Lionel's existence, and when she did Dodie seemed a little put out—perhaps because she had not heard of him before, or perhaps for another reason.

'Well, for heaven's sake! Bring him along then. A morbid pathologist sounds pretty daunting, but I daresay Cedric Harkinshaw and the Broadmains would be tickled to meet one.'

Mary had misgivings. Lionel did not enjoy the kind of drawing-room comedies such people appeared in; like James, he would regard them as frivolous, while they for their part would find him 'dreary'. Not 'amusing' anyway. Nevertheless, since the general effect of Lionel's presence in her life these days was to make her braver and more sure of her own values, she dressed for the evening with resolution and care. Lionel himself tended to look slightly crumpled whatever he wore, and was vague about what tie might go with what suit: he always made a slight face at the prospect of putting on a dinner jacket, though reluctantly agreeing with her that at least that was easy because you couldn't go wrong with it. She had thought for some time that she could have gone out with him herself wearing anything, so long as it was unobtrusive, and that he simply wouldn't register it; but once or twice recently he had seemed to notice what she had on after all, even murmuring with uncertain appreciation that she looked 'elegant'. Thus encouraged, she had bought herself some higher heeled shoes and a dark blue crêpe de Chine dress in the new, longer length. Like that, with her plaits wound into a more elaborate chignon than her everyday one, she studied herself in her landlady's flawed glass and discovered that she looked distinguished and—yes—almost beautiful.

She had recently wondered whether to cut her hair; few women of her age wore theirs long any more, and a permanent wave might be nice and easy. But when she had mentioned the idea to Lionel he had looked so alarmed that she had laughed and said:

'All right, all right, I won't then!'

Later he had said hesitantly: 'Of course, if you *want* to cut it . . . I suppose it would be more convenient short?'

'Oh, not necessarily, I should think. I mean, I'm used to it like this. And once it's up it's up.'

Some conflict seemed to be going on in his mind on this unfamiliar subject. At last he said:

'I do realise it may be annoying when your hairpins fall out as you jump over ditches. But *I* like the way they do.'

'Like the White Queen?' she suggested, amused and touched. She had never realised he noticed such things. But Lionel had not read *Alice*; he had never read most of the children's and semi-adults' books that formed the background to her own mental landscape. The reading matter available in his own childhood home had been largely polemical, he said: his father had been a Methodist lay-preacher and a follower of Keir Hardie. He had been well into adulthood, he told her, before he had understood that one might read a book out of sheer enjoyment and interest, rather than to confirm an attitude of mind; and she noticed that he still tended to regard all books, fiction as well as non-fiction, as repositories of information, to be absorbed with a locust-like enthusiasm and efficiency. He was never without reading matter of some kind.

She need not have worried about Dodie's stage friends. Whatever their limitations, their manners were so extravagantly polite and friendly as to seem un-English by the standards then prevailing, and this helped to bridge the gulf

127

between them and Lionel, who became almost loquacious. The awkwardness of the evening, when it came, occurred between Lionel and a guest she had not expected—Willie.

She had not seen Willie since before her mother had died, though he had written her a warm letter of condolence with sentimental reminiscences of childhood which had surprised and touched her rather, in spite of their quarrel years ago. She knew from Dodie that he occasionally came to London these days, but essentially, it seemed, his life lay abroad.

'Still Paris?' she asked. 'I thought of you last year when I passed through Paris with a friend, but I hadn't got your address.'

But Willie said that he was 'more or less based in Berlin, these days'. Since the slump Paris was 'finished', whereas Berlin was 'quite amusing'. When pressed by Dodie for details he spoke of the theatre of Max Reinhardt, of this and that magazine in which he was 'to some extent involved' and of 'some interesting people and ideas about', but he spoke, as always when asked about his own activities, in a curiously off-hand manner of one concealing rather than revealing the true springs of his nature.

Eager to share her experience with him, Mary talked to him of Vienna: Willie, it turned out, was knowledgeable about baroque architecture (not then fashionable) and finally admitted to having published an article on the subject several months before in the *Illustrated London News* and to be contemplating a book. The Broadmains and Cedric Harkinshaw, fundamentally uninterested in anything but themselves and their friends, were generous enough to be vaguely impressed by such evidence of high culture, and Dodie's dinner party seemed to be going well.

Then by inevitable degrees the conversation moved on to the situation between Austria and Germany and to German politics in general, about which Willie was, as usual, well-informed. Unfortunately so was Lionel and, after having been silent for an ominously long time, he interrupted Willie abruptly to say:

'Why do you keep referring to him as "Herr" Hitler?'

Willie, whose salmon mousse still lay unfinished on his plate—he had always been what Ellie Denvers had called a 'tiresome eater'—removed a cigarette from his case and placed it in his holder before answering. Then he said in a smug, little-boy voice:

'Because it's his name.'

'You know quite well what I mean,' said Lionel, adopting in his turn the tone of a bullying schoolmaster. 'Why "Herr"?'

'Because,' said Willie, inhaling and blowing smoke deliberately through his thin nostrils, 'although of course I have certain reservations about the man, I happen to admire him greatly. He's really doing something for Germany at last—in my opinion. And in any case he's going to be the next Chancellor, you mark my words.'

'I'm afraid I agree with you on that point,' said Lionel vigorously. 'But that is not, for God's sake, a reason for adopting a reverential tone when his name's mentioned.'

'I wasn't aware,' said Willie in a deliberately flat voice, 'of so doing. Surely, whatever the crudities of politics, we need not discard the common civilities of life? And "Down with the Hun" was all very well fifteen years ago, but surely we have moved on a little since then?' He stared at Lionel insolently, with the stare of a young—well, youngish—man taunting an older one. Mary almost expected him to add, 'All that sort of anti-German feeling's a bit *vieux jeu*, isn't it?'

Lionel had indeed been in the war. He had been in the RAMC in Flanders, a time of which he almost never spoke. He was now strongly inclined towards pacifism—not that Willie could have known that. Lionel said sharply:

'Surely you can tell the difference between anti-German feeling as such and being against current trends in Germany. The two are not synonymous, you know.'

They hate each other, thought Mary suddenly. They may not know it yet, but they do. They stand for such diametrically different things, not just in politics and values but in personality too. Lionel so straight, almost brutally clear-sighted, impatient of nuances. Whereas Willie is all deviousness: he's made an art of self-concealment, almost as if that were his principal preoccupation. Oh, what is he hiding, really? Is he homosexual, as Dodie used to say? But I don't feel he really cares about that sort of thing at all, so perhaps it is something quite other . . .

Dodie, sensing that her party was disintegrating, said hastily:

'He seems a ghastly little man to me—Hitler, I mean. Surely nobody takes him seriously . . . I thought it was Communists we were all supposed to worry about.'

'That,' said Lionel evenly, 'is precisely what Hitler does claim to be worrying about. That is the ostensible justification for National Socialism.'

'Oh well, I don't know,' said Dodie airily. 'Socialism—Communism—it's too silly! As if people really lived their lives in terms of these ideas. If you ask me it's all a sort of pretentious game. And I don't see why foreigners shouldn't be left to play what games they want in their own countries, so long as they don't interfere with *us* . . . Darling Willie, you haven't eaten your mousse. Eat up, do, or no crème chantilly!'

As they walked in the cold towards Chalk Farm tube station, Mary said:

'She does have a point, Lionel.'

'A bloody inane one, if I may say so.'

'All right. Yes. But—there *is* something a bit artificial and self-regarding about all these orthodoxies, Lionel, admit it. After all—would we really rather the Soviet Communists took over in Germany than the National Socialists?'

After a pause, Lionel said carefully:

'I agree with you. In a way. But it is, if I may say so, one thing to hold that view from an informed standpoint and another to hold it, as your cousin Dodie does, from a position of vacuous ignorance. Honestly, Mary, you'll say it's naïve of me but I never cease to be shocked when people like that, who've been educated to some extent, who've had all sorts of opportunities—and Dodie's a *writer*, for God's sake—are so totally and wilfully uninformed about the world about them. Can't they read the papers? Don't they listen to the wireless? What do they talk about all the time? Go on, tell me: what was Dodie's last novel about?'

Mary had to think. 'She had one published not long ago, but I haven't read it yet. I did read the reviews, now what . . . ? Oh yes, I know: it's about a woman in love with a man, but he's in love with another woman, and one of the

130

women—I'm not sure which—goes mad and kills herself. That's it, it's called *Oh Willow*—from Ophelia, in *Hamlet*, you know.' She added, with a private amusement, 'I remember us doing *Hamlet* together in the Upper Fourth.'

'Did it get well reviewed?' asked the relentless Lionel.

'Well—not as well as her others have, no. I think she's marking time a bit. I know she wants to write more plays, but of course it's difficult just now to find backers for plays.' It came to Mary in that moment that what she had said of Dodie was true in a more fundamental sense also. Dodie's life, evolving so precipitously a few years earlier when her first two books came out, now seemed to be marking time generally. But perhaps this was a good thing? It could mean that she was maturing, was less avid for experience of any and every kind. Since the early intensity had apparently been a prelude to that mysterious breakdown it was no doubt just as well if Dodie were now content to live her life at a slower rate, to be less wantonly ambitious, more like her old, affectionate self—in a word, to settle down.

But what if Dodie's talent required an inner intensity and tension in order to evolve? Pretentious as Mary had found her first two books, there was no doubt that they had had some arresting and memorable quality, a precocious almost-brilliance about their mixture of reality and romantic fantasy which, in spite of its slightness, impressed and disconcerted. In 'settling down' too comfortably and reassuringly might Dodie in fact lose the very quality in herself on which she had staked so much? The subject of life versus art was not a familiar one to Mary, but she had a generalised idea that creative minds sometimes needed an atmosphere and a life-style that was actually damaging to them as people . . . She relinquished this subject for the moment as too difficult. In any case, Lionel was saying something also:

'Love,' he was saying scathingly. 'The eternal novelist's preoccupation. As if there were nothing else in life. And as if human passions did not have a social context like everything else. What do these lovesick characters in your cousin's latest novel do for a living?'

'I don't think the reviewers said. Perhaps the novel doesn't say.'

'Huh,' said Lionel with satisfaction.

Mary was aware of having played up to this by her own tone and by her deliberately simple description of the novel, and felt that perhaps she ought to be standing up for Dodie more, but she was preoccupied with a private thought of her own which his offhand dismissal of love had set in train. While the people who inhabited Dodie's novels might be obsessed with their own emotions to an unbalanced and unrealistic degree she and Lionel seemed to be avoiding that issue almost too successfully. Sometimes she thought that, between his work, his teaching, his medical committees and his little son in the country (whom she had yet to meet) and the new, exhaustingly long hours of her own job they would never manage to see any more of each other than they did now, or to develop their relationship any further than they had already. What did he want from her, ultimately? What did she want from him? On that subject each had remained elaborately non-committal.

By common consensus neither of them mentioned Willie. Probably, thought Mary, several more years would elapse before she saw him again anyway. After what now seemed to her an unnaturally protracted youth she was moving at last out of the orbit of the family in which she had grown up; she was financially independent, making new friends at the hospital and among Lionel's professional circle. There was, she thought happily, no reason why she should *ever* see Willie again.

She did, however, see him again, and only a few weeks later—at Christmas in Esher. It seemed it might be the final time. When she arrived she found that an atmosphere of 'The Last Day in the Old Home' was pervading the place and the occasion. Uncle George's alarmist remarks a couple of years earlier on times not being what they had been had turned out to have some substance. In 1931 'jute had collapsed'—at least that was how it was expressed in the Denvers' household, creating for Mary an absurd mental image of great piles of sacking lying sprawled and useless on a tropical wharf. A business associate in Dundee had also behaved badly. Uncle George, after all his years of guilty, self-justificatory affluence, was now, it seemed, ruined. Or at least partially ruined: the spacious mock-rural life in the neo-Queen Anne pile at Esher was to end, for ruin was, apparently, to consist of renting a 'service flat' in Holland Park. Would not that, Mary ventured to suggest, be expensive in its own right? Her remark was not well-received. Did she, Uncle George enquired indignantly, expect Aunt May, at her age and after all these years—*and* with her history of nervous weakness—to act as a skivvy? There was no answer to such a question and, not for the first time, Mary reflected how odd it must be to be Uncle George and to live in a world populated largely by phantasmagoria of your own making. Dodie, with her capacity for inventing her life out of scraps and gestures as she went along, had a touch of this too.

The collapse of jute seemed to have left Uncle George with fewer occupations than ever. He was, however, much pre-occupied with something called the Empire Movement, which Mary understood to be a lobby for tariffs giving preferential treatment to imports from the Empire, but which Uncle George appeared to regard as a union of stalwart, true and knowledgeable ex-India and ex-Africa hands against the forces of 'Jewboys', 'the jumped-up left' and the twentieth century in general. The movement had been invented by Lord Beaverbrook, and Uncle George spent much time every morning reading the *Express* and, in the evening, the *Evening Standard*, with the meditative devotion of a loyal subject. He had also been belatedly converted to the wireless, which he now regarded as a force for good.

'He should never have left India,' said Dodie to Mary, with one of her disconcerting fits of perspicuity. 'He'd be much happier there, drinking on some verandah with squads of docile servants kow-towing to him. Being the *burra-sahib*, you know. He's no one here—never has been. He minds.'

'Of course, you can remember all that,' said Mary. Dodie had spent almost all her childhood in India, far longer than the Boys had. It was odd that she so seldom mentioned it. Surely it must mean something to her? But when Mary tried to talk to Dodie about the freedom movement there, or about Gandhi, Dodie just shrugged and said she'd never been able to be interested in such things.

'Anyway,' she said, 'India was so dull.'

'Dodie, how *can* you say that?' Mary was shocked with an emotion that, as she afterwards realised, came from her memory of the Boys' passionate sense of their lost land rather than from any rational ideas she herself might have about the place.

'Oh it was, Mary, you don't realise. So hot, and everyone younger than me or else much older, and never anything much to do that didn't make you hotter . . . It was always afternoon, somehow, and I spent those afternoons—yes, *all* of them, it seems now—reading a book I had called *London, Heart of the Empire.* Full of pictures of Piccadilly Circus and buses and costermongers and things. I longed to live in London—I do still think it's the most glamorous place in the world, actually, and I still get a thrill just going to the theatre or out to dinner, however often I do it. Oh, I envied you all so, because I knew you lived near London and must go there sometimes.'

Mary was silent with amazement. Never for one moment had it occurred to her that Dodie, who was so pretty and towards whom everyone softened, might envy her prosaic self.

Now, of course, it was a little different. On reflection, her present life—just in the last year—did seem to be modestly enviable . . . But of course Dodie, with her own full, slightly mysterious existence, would not have wanted to lead that sort of life at all.

That Christmas afternoon the King broadcast to the nation for the first time, and they were all constrained to listen including Willie, who had come down for Christmas Day. He looked civilly bored, and sat smoothing his hair and surreptitiously fingering the pages of a book, which turned out—Mary looked at the title afterwards—to be *Jew Süss.*

'I see you're reading that great anti-Semitic work,' she said to him in an undertone, as cups of tea and unwanted, heavy fruit cake were being handed round—a scant two hours after Christmas dinner.

'Oh, I wouldn't say that,' he answered, with his usual infuriating possibly-right knowledgeability. 'I realise it has that reputation among certain circles—particularly among people who've not actually read it—but it's a most interesting and complex study. You should try it, Mary.'

Feeling convicted of parochialism and received opinion (for indeed she knew of the book only by hearsay), Mary held her peace. Perhaps fortunately, the long, tedious day of enforced goodwill allowed no obvious opportunity for them to exchange further words together, and Willie certainly did not seek one.

She did not think of him again till the end of January when, as both he and Lionel had predicted, Hitler became Chancellor of Germany. By that time Willie was back in Berlin.

The following summer the Hersheys' baby was born. It was a boy, and they called him David. They had rented a house on the Thames, full of watery lights and shadows; Olive and a nursemaid stayed there for two months, with John coming down at weekends, and Mary for a holiday. Her year in hospital had been taxing; sometimes she had even felt too tired to go out to a meal or a lecture with Lionel when he suggested it, and in any case her long hours on call had made it difficult to plan arrangements. She had given up her room in the Camden Road, put most of her possessions into store, and had been living in the hospital. Long after, her paramount memory of that year (when so much of eventual importance had in fact decided itself) was of regularly answering her telephone in a blurr of sleep, giving instructions to the ward sister or the houseman, struggling into her clothes—and finding as she crossed the courtyard below in the dark or the dawn that she had only at that moment woken up completely, and was uncertain where she was going or what she was doing.

Olive, when this was described to her, was wistful.

'I wish I'd managed a year's registration. I feel I've dropped out of everything. I wonder if I'll ever get back?'

'Oh, I'm sure you will. You loved it so.'

'Yes, but . . . The baby seems to have changed everything. He really does.' She held him closely to her white, veined breast, swollen now with milk, but her face above looked sad. 'And John keeps saying, "Let's have another while the going's good." He's quite right, of course; over thirty one shouldn't

135

wait too long. But I'm afraid that, by the time I ever do get to practise medicine again, I'll just be too *old* to get back into the way of it.'

'Oh, I'm sure you won't,' said Mary at random, distractedly. Her attention had been arrested by what Olive had said before: *over thirty one shouldn't wait too long.*

Thirty-one. If she herself were ever to have a child . . .

But how, amidst her present life and her plans for the future, could a child ever be fitted in? Even if—? She knew herself to be already infinitely changed by this first year of real doctoring, competent and responsible to a level she had never thought to achieve so soon, if at all. Olive's own fears might well be justified. In medicine you had to keep on doing it; you couldn't be half-hearted about it.

She had already arranged that that autumn she would do a further registration at the Mile End in Gynae. and Obstetrics. It was an obvious choice for a woman aiming at an eventual consultancy.

'And next summer,' Lionel said happily, 'you can take your MRCOG.'

'I won't get it in one year. Not with all that going out on deliveries at night.'

'Well, you can try it next summer. It doesn't matter if you have several shots at it. The thing is to get it in the end.'

Towards the end of her fortnight in the house by the green river Lionel came over to fetch her in a car borrowed from a friend. He drove her, slowly and with occasional jerks, down to Sussex, where they had a careful and civilly exhausting lunch with his in-laws, the Elwins, Charlie's grandparents, and she met Charlie at last.

As they drove back again towards the Thames Valley in the late afternoon, Lionel said moodily:

'Oh, they're not bad people really—not bad, no. But they do drive me insane sometimes as I sit listening to their clotted rubbish. The old boy used to be a civil servant, as you gathered, but he knows nothing—nothing. No wonder the country's in the state it is. Anyway, I hope you didn't find it too nerve-racking.'

'No, because it's all familiar to me,' she said; and explained. 'They're exactly like my Uncle George and Aunt May. Well, not exactly, because no one's exactly like anyone else, but right out of the same stable . . . Oh Lionel, *do* watch the road!'

'Sorry. It's when I get interested in what you're saying . . . I'll stare straight ahead, there.' He did so, and fell silent. He disliked dividing his attention. After a while Mary said:

'The funny thing is, of course, that they—the Elwins, I mean—also think that England is in a bad way. But mainly for the opposite reasons from ours.'

'Quite.'

'Except for the countryside being ruined with little villas. At least we managed some agreement on that.'

'Did we?' said Lionel uncertainly, his eyes still dutifully fixed on the road.

'Yes, over that rather delicious apple charlotte, don't you remember.'

'I don't like pudding much, as you know—I never seem to need it . . . Yes, I do remember now, but I went on being annoyed because, on jerry-building and ribbon-development and so forth, people like that are right for the wrong reasons. Behind all their remarks about horrid little houses there isn't a criticism of the architecture or the lack of planning, you see, so much as the horrid little people they think are going to live in them. Basically, people like the Elwins do not want clerks and shop-assistants to have decent homes.'

'Oh Lionel, is that quite fair? I think it's more that they simply don't think about the people who are going to live in all these new houses—they just don't want the countryside ruined in a wasteful, silly way. Any more than we do.'

'Yes, but the difference is,' pursued the implacable Lionel, 'that people like that think they own the countryside by divine right. God knows why, in the case of the Elwins. Their roots are just rich trade, not landed gentry or anything like that, yet to hear them go on you'd think they had feudal rights over that self-conscious little village where they live. Margery was brought up to think of her father as a squire, just because that house of theirs is called the Old Manor House, though they were newcomers then and her father actually caught the eight forty-two or whatever to town each day like anyone else. And they didn't like it that I took

137

Margery to live in London. It's this sickening rural snobbery that has got the English middle classes by the guts. You'd never think, to hear them go on, that the wealth they enjoy is almost entirely created by industry. It's a debilitating mass delusion that they have of being the backbone of Olde Englande, sitting there in their fake-Jacobean home counties so-called manor houses. A fantasy to distract them from what's really going on in the world—'

During his last few sentences the car had slowed almost to a standstill. A Daimler behind them hooted.

'Damn!' said Lionel, and stalled the engine.

'Park for a minute,' said Mary sympathetically, thinking how tired Lionel looked. 'I want to stretch my legs anyway.' She was wondering, as she had done many times before, about Margery. Lionel had never spoken directly of his dead wife to her; her name cropped up only obliquely, in a passive way, in relation to her parents or to phases of Lionel's life. At first Mary had supposed that her death had been a great blow to Lionel and that this was why he preferred to keep off the whole subject of his marriage. Lately, however, she had hoped there might be another explanation. But this seemed no time to ask.

When she got back into the car again she said tentatively:

'Charlie is a dear little chap, Lionel.'

She meant it. The bright-eyed, nervous-looking little boy, who seemed to be locked in a state of permanent conflict with his old and deaf nurse, had touched Mary. He appeared to her a child who, even in that indulgent household, was asking in vain for something—some reassurance, some estimate of his own worth. But she felt awkwardly that whatever she said about him would sound obligatory and insincere.

'He's a bit spoilt,' said Lionel shortly.

'Yes, that episode with the gravy at lunch . . . But, poor little boy, he's not five yet, is he? And I think it must be difficult for grandparents to hit the right balance between expecting too much and expecting too little.'

'Mmm. I'm not sure the Elwins could ever do that. They spoilt Margery too, you see. And Nanny was *her* old nanny, of course . . . I must say, I'd like to send Nanny packing. She muffles him up in far too many clothes, as you saw, and I've

138

a suspicion she fills his head with all sorts of rubbish about Long-Legged Scissormen and Dirty Habits and Christ knows what: he has nightmares, I know . . . But unfortunately the whole situation's out of my control. For the moment.'

Mary felt a little sorry for the Elwins, in prospect, for if the day should come when Lionel would feel able to reclaim Charlie, Lionel, she sensed, could be ruthless in pursuing a course that he conceived as right.

'He's a friendly little boy anyway, Lionel. That's the main thing.'

'Yes, I believe he is,' he said more warmly, giving her an appreciative look. He added: 'You seemed to hit it off with him, anyway.' But she was afraid that he too was just saying it because something of the kind had to be said.

She felt tired from the undercover strain of the day, and a little depressed by Lionel's tough and cerebral attitudes. She was unprepared and at first uncomprehending when he stopped the car again by a well-known view, turned to her and said shyly:

'You don't start again at the Mile End till September, do you? . . . I was wondering if you and I could go away together for a bit before that? To Brittany, perhaps? But maybe you've got other plans for that time.'

'Not really,' she said, unconsciously adopting his own calm and practical tone. 'Dodie's offered to lend me her flat. She's going to Biarritz for the month. That's nice of her, because it's awfully inconvenient being homeless. I've got to be out of my present room at the Mile End on the 28th because young Napier will be needing it—he's doing my job while I'm away—and half my worldly possessions are stacked in the Hersheys' attic as it is.' She laughed nervously: 'Sorry, I'm blathering . . . What did you say about Brittany?' *Perhaps I didn't hear right.*

'Just that I'm planning a holiday there. Walking, looking at those carved crosses they have, getting some swimming in and so on—I wondered if you'd like to come too?'

She sat with her hands in her lap. After a while she said:

'Of course I would love to come, Lionel. But I'm not sure I've got enough money at the moment to pay my way. Although I know France is very cheap—'

He said almost impatiently: 'I wouldn't ask you to pay your way. Well, naturally not.'

She digested this, and at last said with considerable difficulty:

'You mean—you want me to share your room and—and everything . . . *Is* that what you mean, Lionel? Please say at once if it isn't.' *If he says no I've misunderstood, I shall die of misery and embarrassment. One is warned about such offers from girlhood, but never that they might not be clearly made.*

'Yes,' he said. 'Yes, that's what I do mean. I'm sorry; I was trying to put it delicately, but I'm no good at these things and I see I've been genteel to the point of obscurity. Yes, what I had in mind is that we would be together, just quietly away from everybody, and share a room and a bed and, as you nicely put it, everything. I would like that, and value it very much. But if you don't feel this is the sort of offer you can accept from me I shall quite understand.' And he went on sitting there, his own hands on the wheel, not looking at her, though she wished very much he would.

In a small voice she said presently:

'I'm sorry to have been slow on the uptake. But I thought—that you didn't want . . . I mean, I had the feeling you just wanted us to go on being friends.'

'That isn't precluded,' he said swiftly. 'But—oh Mary, surely you realised that sooner or later it had to come to this point between us? I won't insult your intelligence by using the cliché "we're both grown-up people" but that is, after all, the case.'

'It was just that the question never seemed to arise before . . . I mean, you never suggested . . .' *I thought perhaps he wasn't interested.*

'No, because there's a time and a place for these things and you and I seemed to have so little of either commodity! You could hardly take me back to your room at the Mile End for the night—that *would* put paid to your career—and my digs in Bloomsbury are hardly more suitable, what with Mrs T's excessively motherly interest in my diet and habits. And anyway, I know what the pressures of this first year have been like on you, and I haven't wanted to add to them with demands of my own. Mary, believe me, the last thing I want is to be any sort of impediment or problem to you.'

She thought distractedly: 'He doesn't realise—he simply doesn't realise that I would never see him in that light. He thinks my priorities are all the same as his. He thinks I'm different from other women.' But pride prevented her from disillusioning him, and she went on sitting quietly beside him till it belatedly dawned on her that he was still waiting for something.

'You haven't answered my invitation,' he said at last in a neutral tone. 'Does that mean the answer is no?'

'Oh Lionel! I'm sorry, I thought I had. I'm being hopeless, aren't I? No—I mean, no the answer is Yes. Yes, I would love to come to Brittany with you. Thank you for suggesting it.'

Only afterwards, replaying the scene obsessionally and lovingly in her mind, did she reflect—and giggled to herself—that to thank a man for a suggestion of this order could hardly be part of the usual convention. But then she *felt* thankful, so why not be polite anyway?

Over thirty. A grown up. And training to be a gynaecologist, of all things. Soberly she registered the fact that if it hadn't been Lionel it would have had to be somebody, some time soon. But she was glad and relieved that it was going to be Lionel.

Dodie was packing to go to Biarritz. Mary was going to stay in Dodie's flat till she herself went to Brittany—though she had left the details of that plan obscure where Dodie was concerned, saying simply that she would 'probably be spending ten days in France with some hospital friends'. Dodie seemed incurious for once; she was preoccupied with her own imminent journey, whose details were also obscure to Mary. Each mentally absent in some measure, they chatted amicably in Dodie's bedroom, where the yellow chintz curtains were drawn to keep out the stale warmth of the London summer.

Dodie was taking an inordinate number of clothes for the seaside, Mary thought, but then the point of Biarritz was probably not the beach itself but the casino and the big hotels. She herself had nothing with her these days that could not go into a couple of suitcases. As she had said to Lionel, it was inconvenient being homeless, but such was the itinerant life she would probably lead for several more years, moving from one hospital job to another. And in any case she found something satisfying in living without material ties. She felt as if her childhood and youth were finally all packed away and she was free of them. They could sleep undisturbed in crates in Maples store and in the attic of the Hersheys' house in Kensington till she wanted to reclaim them; and perhaps she never would. Even three years ago this prospect would have seemed daunting and bleak, but when the centre of your life was your occupation, having no fixed home and few possessions had a lot to recommend it.

In the same way, what for years she had imagined would be a nerve-racking moral or emotional decision seemed, in Lionel's hands, to have been suddenly transformed into something simple and normal, a friendly private compact for a specific purpose. Beyond this she did not for the moment look.

Nor did she reflect that, for a supposedly simple adult arrangement, the Brittany plan seemed to have a remarkable capacity at the moment to drive all other thoughts and plans from her mind and make everything unconnected with it seem unreal.

'I can't decide,' said Dodie, 'whether to take the blue lace one as well. It *is* my favourite—but then I've worn it a lot already this summer. What do you think, Mary? You're always so organised.'

'Well, Dodie, that lace must be difficult to pack, and you've got four evening dresses already. Surely that will do, even for Biarritz?'

'I suppose so,' said Dodie doubtfully, standing there looking very slim—almost skinny, Mary noticed—in a one-piece black petticoat with butterflies appliquéd to the shoulder straps. She added after a moment, half inaudibly: 'But we might be moving on from Biarritz, you see.'

'Really?' said Mary. 'But I thought you were coming back in September to join Aunt May and Uncle George in Bournemouth. I'm sure Aunt May told me on the phone you were.' She had registered at the time that Dodie was a surprisingly dutiful daughter to her ageing parents. She was completely taken aback when Dodie sat carefully down in an empty space on the bed next to a pile of slippery underthings and burst into tears.

It was—as Mary felt she should have realised before—another of Dodie's mysterious love affairs. Why Dodie had never fallen in love with someone who could, so to speak, have been produced in daylight was a question she could hardly go into at that moment; Mary simply held Dodie's hand and invited confidences from her which presently, in a fragmented way, came.

Married, said Dodie. Yes. And older than herself—quite a bit older. No, she would rather not say his name, if Mary would excuse her: it was quite a well-known one.

In imagination Mary saw an unwieldy lay figure—actor? columnist?—fiftyish, in permanent evening dress (for Biarritz); the personification of the Edwardian seducer with a waxed moustache and opera cloak. She struggled but failed to substitute a more modern and probable phantasm; after all, Dodie was, like herself, over thirty, and presumably must know what she was doing. Or did that make it worse? She asked sympathetically:

'Has this been going on for a long time?'

'Well, I've *known* him,' said Dodie, with nice discrimination, 'for—oh—over a year. But—as I say, now we're going abroad together.'

The distinction Dodie seemed to be making was disconcertingly familiar. Mary wondered in passing why Dodie and her unknown man had to go all the way to Biarritz when Dodie had her own comfortable, private flat? But no doubt the explanation lay in the man's married state. An alarming possibility occurred to her. Dodie was packing so much, and had mentioned 'going on' from Biarritz to some other place—

'Oh Dodie,' she said, shocked. 'Are you and this man running away together—for good, I mean?'

But Dodie, compressing her lips together, drying her tears and shaking her pretty head back and forth, would not commit herself. Perhaps she did not know herself.

143

'Have I met him?' Mary asked, with a sudden, uncomfortable image of Norman Broadmain, the actor, and his pretty, kittenish wife Sybil. Surely Dodie wouldn't do that? But even as she formed the thought instinct told her that love could be so important to people as to overwhelm all considerations of morality, decency, concern for others. How could it *not*? If that registrar had been married but had nevertheless felt for her as she had for him . . . Confused, she pushed the thought away. Why think of him, now of all times?

No, Dodie said firmly, Mary did not know him. She added: 'I can't explain, I can't. But oh, when I met him it was like—like recognising someone I'd been missing all my life till now. I can't *not* go abroad with him, whatever happens. You do see that, don't you?'

Soberly, Mary agreed that she saw. She did believe at any rate that Dodie was telling the truth as she herself saw it. She supposed that Dodie's tears were no sort of appeal for help, or counsel, but simply a despairing recognition of the nature of things, and did not presume to comment further. That Dodie might, in fact, be in a state of distress and fear for a much simpler reason did not for a moment occur to her. Dodie was experienced; that had been taken for granted between them for years.

At any rate, she reflected afterwards, it looked as if her anxiety that Dodie's life might lack the intensity necessary for her as a writer was groundless. She only hoped that Dodie's fragile psyche, subjected to the permanent intensity of existence in some Continental spa (did adulterous couples really exile themselves to such places these days?), would stand the strain.

—And what would poor Uncle George and Aunt May say? That mattered. To pretend, in a modern-minded way, that it did not would be cruel and stupid. Dodie was not cruel . . .

Returning unwillingly but frequently to the matter over the following days, Mary found that the whole episode in Dodie's bedroom had upset her irrationally. A curiously theatrical and stereotyped atmosphere seemed to surround the little of the story that she had heard; the piles of silken clothes, everywhere the concentrated residue of Dodie's expensive scent, the pigskin cases yawning open, the room with

144

its enclosed yellow light—these in retrospect seemed like a pictorial cipher for a relationship that was in itself claustrophobic and damaging. The word is Sin, she said to herself at length. Old-fashioned, undeniable sin, of which the wages are, if not death these days, then something subtly worse. You do not like to think of Dodie going off to live in sin in some foreign city where she will be essentially alone and no one will understand how vulnerable she really is.

But, true as this was, it was not just concern she felt; it was also a more resentful distaste. She found she minded about Dodie's affair in a personal way, as if it was somehow impinging on herself. She hadn't wanted to hear about it then, not one bit. It was like having some ugly distorting mirror (with a heavy, rococo Edwardian frame) held up to her own unique private life. The simple, almost blind pleasure she had felt in looking forward to going to Brittany with Lionel was to some slight extent tainted. Were she and Lionel, too, just fulfilling a squalid Anglo-Saxon convention, sneaking off abroad to gratify their desires because—so conveniently—what happened abroad did not officially count? But of course it *did* count. Would this trespass into new ground blight their relationship in some subtle, horrible way, and change Lionel's own attitude towards her, turning him into a stranger? *There will be no going back*, she warned herself austerely. *If it is a mistake you cannot undo it.*

In Lionel's real and reassuring company she could dismiss this feeling and even smile at herself for being so old-fashioned and romantic. Lionel was not married; still less was he some sort of God of the Underworld figure drawing her away from daylight things and offering her seeds of pomegranate. He was free to do exactly as he liked. So was she. And what, for goodness' sake, could be further from the conventions of furtive sexual passion than their daytime plans for walking and swimming and looking at Breton chapels and wayside crosses?

But in the sleeping compartment in which they at long last found themselves the sense of their private relationship being peopled by ugly and less exclusive shadows returned. *The night-sleeper to Paris*—the very phrase seemed apposite to Dodie's life-style rather than to her own. The cramped,

145

vibrating mahogany-lined space, with its two bunks one above the other, was like a children's playhouse, the sort of thing she and Nigel would have enjoyed together when they were young. And this, absurdly, even indecently, was to be a place of irreversible significance to her. And to how many others before?

'Bunks are not ideal for sharing,' the practical Lionel remarked. 'But I daresay we'll manage.' And he disappeared down the corridor.

After some hesitation, Mary undressed. *Sous le lavabo se trouve un vase.* She would have liked to use it, but was inhibited by the possibility of Lionel's sudden return. Did people, perhaps, get used to these casual intimacies once they were married? For the first time in her life she realised to what extent, being fatherless, she had grown up in ignorance of many things.

She had spent years now in close contact with bodies, conscious and unconscious, living and inert. She had pushed tubes into men in an extremity of pain, soothing and hushing them as she did so; she had with her own hands probed scores of women, bestowing on them an easy smile and reassurance— 'Just relax and breathe out; this won't hurt.' Yet now, as she stood there in her new pyjamas, a sense of ignorance and inadequacy possessed her. This wasn't her sort of thing at all, this rocking, claustrophobic train—she should have known better at her age. She and Lionel had made a ridiculous, embarrassing mistake, too silly even to be called terrible. She would have to apologise and explain, try to get him to see—

When Lionel came back, having apparently been shaving, he found her in tears. He did not, however, seem disconcerted.

Towards the end of that week she woke early one morning. She lay, sensing rather than seeing or hearing a movement which she at first took hazily to be within herself, a kind of pulse, but which she eventually realised to be the light window curtain which moved to and fro, patterning the sunlight. English, they had not drawn the shutters the night before, and the Brittany sea-wind was entering through a chink and stirring about the room.

Everything—wind, sun, Lionel's regular breathing, foot-steps, wheels and the occasional motor in the narrow street below—seemed to be finding its own response within herself, a vibration as if her physical substance had undergone some change, of nature or dimension. Words formed on the surface of her mind: '*All flesh is grass.*' But the phrase did not carry for her its traditional message of austerity, loss and the abneg-ation of the flesh, but one of vague but momentous unity, a consolation for death itself.

'Why did no one ever tell me,' she had said at some point in the night, 'that it was like this? So lovely, I mean.'

He said: 'People who know keep it to themselves. Like we shall.'

'But the women we see in Gynae. and so on . . . They *complain* so about it. Lionel, it's awful. The best they can say for their husbands is "He's very good. He don't bother me often."'

'I can hardly hope for such a recommendation myself, at present,' said Lionel blandly. He added after a moment: 'No, seriously Mary, your experience isn't necessarily general. It isn't only down-trodden working-class wives who find it distasteful to share their bodies with someone else. I have the impression that quite a lot of what pass for reasonably happy, enlightened women never really enjoy it either. I think you're rather exceptional, my love, in having taken to it so readily.'

She thought: *he's speaking out of close personal experience; that's why he's choosing his words so carefully*. She longed to believe this was so. She was invaded by an innocent, yearning desire to be everything to Lionel, to make the present glorious to him and the past, by comparison, a poor thing. She did not at that moment reflect that, to Lionel, the past might simply not matter in the way it did to her.

At another moment, unequal to conveying to him the strength of her own feeling, she asked him: 'What do *you* think about when you're making love?'

He answered after a moment, as if a little surprised:

'Why—I don't believe I think of anything much. We're together, and I like that—and it's a very nice way of spending some of the night. A pleasant pastime, you might say!'

147

'They ought to recommend it then in those magazine columns called *Pastimes and Hobbies*,' said Mary, giggling weakly. Lionel's tactlessly truthful answer, inadequate as it might seem in a lover, did not cast her down, for she was too happy with him then to be touched by disappointment.

Called to the ward telephone, she kept her eyes on the partly screened bed where her houseman had just set up a saline drip. The woman in the bed had been dying when she was brought in; was dying still. If she was, after all, to survive, the next twenty minutes would probably decide it.

'Is that you, Mary dear? It seems *so* difficult to get hold of you.' The voice, breathy and indistinct on the telephone but unmistakable, assailed her ear with a shocking inappropriateness but did not at first penetrate her mind.

'Just a minute,' she said sharply. She laid the receiver on its side and returned to the bed. 'Are you getting any stronger pulse?' she asked the houseman, laying her own fingers on the inert wrist.

'I think so. But she's very floppy, isn't she?' They stared at the face, yellowish against the white pillow, eyes sunken and almost closed, mouth sagging. Only the brown hair pushed back from the forehead seemed to belong to a woman still young enough to bear a child.

'Perforated uterus,' said Mary.

'Do you think so?'

'Mmm. I think so. Too much blood to see anything, really. The usual thing—a bodkin or something, I suppose. I've packed in gauze tight, but . . .'

She returned to the telephone.

'Hallo, Aunt May. What can I do for you?'

'I was saying, dear. I had quite a job to get hold of you. How *are* you, dear?'

'Quite well, thank you.'

'And how was your little holiday in France?'

'It was very nice. Look, Aunt May, I am rather busy just now.'

'Well, this won't take a minute, dear, but I just wondered if you could pop over here to Holland Park this evening and take a look at Dodie.'

'Dodie—I thought she was abroad?'

'No, no, she came back—oh, over a week ago. She's here while her flat's being painted, and she did say she'd come to Bournemouth next week. But dear'—Aunt May lowered her voice to a penetrating whisper—'she is acting a little oddly. Well, not odd exactly, but *strange*—'

'Strange?' said Mary. 'How—tell me?' She craned her neck to look again towards the bed, where the houseman was attempting once more to find the woman's pulse.

'Well, I hardly know how to explain, Mary, but she doesn't seem quite *herself*.' Aunt May's undertone had the nervous embarrassment of one referring to an indecent bodily function. 'You remember that little nervous collapse she had—oh, years ago now? Well, naturally we can't help wondering . . . I expect everything's all right, she seems quite *happy*. But'—more briskly—'we would just like you to check her over, dear.'

The houseman had abandoned the pulse and was now trying, apparently with further difficulty, to locate the heart-beat with his stethoscope.

Mary said rapidly: 'Look, Aunt May, I think you'd better get hold of your own doctor.'

'Oh, but we'd rather keep it in the family, dear. I don't suppose it's anything *much*, so I don't want to bother Dr Cheetham—he's our GP again now we're back in town, did I tell you?—you see, for some reason Dodie's never cared for him. You know what she's like. And after all, dear'—louder, and more firmly—'You are a doctor yourself now. I said to Uncle George, I was sure you would be the person. Just to check her over, you know. I thought she might be anaemic— she looked so pale when she came back from the Riviera— but now she seems quite feverish—'

'Just a minute,' said Mary peremptorily, laying down the phone again with Aunt May's voice still contained like a serpent inside it. She went back to the bed.

'I think she's gone,' said the houseman miserably.

Mary used her own stethoscope, to no avail, lifted an eyelid, tested for breath.

'It's not your fault,' she said to the houseman.

'She just went. Like that. Gave a sort of sigh—then nothing.'

'I know. It does happen. She's lost an awful lot of blood. She was very weak.'

She returned to the phone.

'Aunt May—can I ring you back?'

'Well, dear, I was *hoping*, as I said, that you could come over tonight. I'll just tell Dodie you're coming to dinner. She'll think it's a social visit—'

'I can't come to dinner tonight, Aunt May. I'm on call.'

'Well, after dinner, then?'

'I'm on call all evening. All night, in fact. Look, I'll ring you tonight at about eight—'

'Oh Mary, can't you come over? We've no one else to turn to. You don't understand, I'm so *worried* about Dodie. She doesn't seem to have slept properly for nights, and she just *talks*, on and on—' Aunt May's own voice rose higher and more insistent. 'All about some *man*, and understanding things. I'm sure it's all nonsense, but really your uncle and I don't know *what* to think. We hoped that Dodie would calm down for you, but now you say you won't come over—'

'I'll ring you at eight,' said Mary. 'Or as near to it as I can manage.' She added in a frenzied tone near to Aunt May's: 'I *have* to go now. Goodbye, Aunt May. Try to keep Dodie indoors. And ring your GP.'

That evening, before making her promised return call, she rang Lionel.

'I'm having my supper,' he said. 'It's Mrs T's day for Irish stew.'

'I don't care,' said Mary for once. 'Listen.' She told him what Aunt May had said. He heard her out.

'Sounds a bit manic to me,' he said laconically, as if to deflate mania by his own tone.

'That's what I thought. Not that I know anything much about psychiatry.'

'Mmm. Was she like that before? The previous episode, I mean?'

'I think, I'm not sure. I never actually saw her then. Oh Lionel, what am I to do?'

'Do? Nothing. It'll get sorted out without you. Relatives are the worst people to help in these cases because, whatever they say, the patient doesn't believe them. And you've got enough of your own work to do.'

'Yes. A woman died on me today. And we've just had a breech delivery that didn't go too well.' It was tempting to submit to Lionel's viewpoint, but even as she did so she felt it was biased, too limited. Dodie might be a rich woman with an indulgent family, not a poor one bleeding to death from a self-induced abortion, but that did not mean that her problems were not real too, that she was not in danger of another sort. To make moral distinctions between one kind of human collapse and another was not good doctoring. Or kind.

'I suppose I could go over there in the morning,' she said.

'In the only time you can be sure of a few hours' proper rest? Don't you dare, Mary! God Almighty, doesn't it occur to you that it's only because you're a woman that they think they can call on you in this way? If you were a man they wouldn't.'

'I know.'

'Come to that, they probably wouldn't if you were a married woman. Married women are supposed to have really important things to do. Like cooking their husband's dinner—or entertaining him while the servants cook it, more like. But you, of course, as an unmarried woman can be summoned any old time it suits them.'

There was a silence between them that was weighted, not with dissent, but with a shared uncertainty. The subject of marriage had been aired between them. On their return from Brittany Lionel had made it clear that he was happy for them to marry if that was what Mary wanted. But he had added that, as they both already knew, a public marriage would put an end to further advancement in her career. An alternative—his suggestion—was that they should marry, but keep the fact private and virtually secret. But in that case they could hardly set up house together in a manner adequate to include Charlie. Surely, Mary said, feeling calm and realistic as she believed Lionel wanted her to be, the main purpose of his remarrying would be to have his son with him? Without that, what was the point?

Lionel, for once, had no answer: his feelings seemed divided. She was divided herself, on one level genuinely agreeing with him that it would be ridiculous to compromise everything that she had worked for. On another level, the knowledge that Lionel wanted to marry her gave her joy and obscure relief. But this she kept to herself.

Inconclusively, they had let the matter rest. In any case, while Mary was doing this further registration there was no possibility of their setting up any sort of household together, married or unmarried, even on a weekend basis.

Now Mary said ironically:

'I wonder if Aunt May would still think she could summon me if I was living in open sin with you?'

'If it was so open that your Aunt May knew about it the hospital authorities would get to know too, and then where would you be?'

'I know: out of a job next year. Oh, Lionel. It seems that if we marry I'm penalised for being conventional and if we don't marry I risk being penalised for being immoral. It's a hard life.'

'Did anyone ever promise you, love, that it wasn't?'

In spite of Lionel's advice Mary called at the large block in Holland Park the following morning. She had been summoned to the ward three times in the night and had slept badly in between. She had, however, since breakfast reached that state beyond exhaustion, familiar to junior doctors and to the mothers of young babies, in which she felt that she could, after all, continue indefinitely to walk, talk, listen, react, make judgments—so long as her back did not begin to ache too much.

Dodie herself opened the door of the flat, letting bright, artificial light into the padded, bronze corridor with its Egyptian bas-reliefs. Under the new service-flat regime no servant lived in, and the Denvers appeared to subsist largely on food 'sent up' from the expensive restaurant on the ground floor. Aunt May had seemed childishly entertained by this novel way of life the last time Mary had seen her, but since her existence was now almost occupationless Mary wondered how long it would be before Aunt May's own dormant 'nerves' would surface troublesomely. She had even been turning over in her weary mind, as she made her way over on the underground, the possibility that the agitation about Dodie was in reality a neurotic outburst of Aunt May's own.

Then Dodie opened the door with a sweeping gesture, drew Mary to her in the same movement, embraced her warmly, and said:

'Darling, how lovely to see you! We can have a really good chat. Look, I just want to tell you, before we start, that it's *all right*. I mean, I know Ma's worried but it's simply that she doesn't realise—I was in a bit of a state when I got back from Biarritz, and goodness, anyone would have been, you'll understand when I tell you—but now everything's quite different, and suddenly it's all come clear—and it's all wonderful, Mary, it really is!'

'Oh, I'm so glad, Dodie,' said Mary weakly. Then, feeling that her tone lamentably lacked the warmth of Dodie's own, she added:

'In that case, perhaps I'd better go away again. But it really is nice to see you back—'

'Go away?' said Dodie sharply, her sparkling eyes suddenly afraid. 'Why? Why should you want to leave me?'

'Just a joke,' said Mary uncomfortably. 'Honestly, Dodie, I *am* pleased to see you. You remember, last time we talked, you thought you might stay abroad, and that worried me a bit.'

'Did I?' said Dodie, apparently without memory. 'Oh yes, perhaps I did. But so much has happened since then . . . Darling, come in here and we can talk.' She led Mary into the smaller of the flat's two overcrowded sitting rooms and, to Mary's amazement, turned the key in the door behind them. 'Keeps the servants out,' she explained with a wink.

'But you haven't got any servants here.'

Dodie burst into bright peals of laughter. 'Darling Mary, you are a scream, you really are! I wish I was a wit like you—you're wasted in that grim hospital of yours. And on that dreary young man. Or not-so-young man, I should say, but I expect you like that . . . How is he, by the way?'

'He's very well, thanks,' said Mary stiffly, but Dodie wasn't listening. She had flung herself down on the sofa, and was running her hands through her short, waved hair. Mary noticed then how thin she had got again, and that Dodie was dressed, a little oddly for ten thirty in the morning, in a backless cocktail dress, no stockings, and a pair of sheepskin slippers.

Dodie lit a cigarette and blew smoke at Mary, screwing up her eyes in a new way that seemed to be copied from someone. Dodie had always been prone to acquire the gestures of whoever had been her most recent companion.

'Oh, *so* much to tell,' she said. 'I really don't know where to start. It's very complicated and fascinating, so you'll have to listen hard. Well: in the first place, I'd got that trip to Biarritz all wrong—'

'Had you?' said Mary, trying now not to match Dodie's excited tone but to moderate it by adopting a prosaic manner herself. Dodie continued regardless:

'Yes, of course I had—but I can see why too, and I'll tell you that in a minute as well. You see, I thought Clive wanted me as his mistress. And you thought that too, didn't you?'

'Dodie, I've no opinion. How can I have? I can only go on what you tell me.'

'Oh yes you did, you thought I was going to Biarritz to sleep with him! Well—I won't hold it against you, though I think it was rather low of you, frankly, to think that—shows what *you've* been getting up to recently, Mary darling . . .' Her eyes sparkled again at Mary with a sudden, disconcerting perception, but she continued before Mary could reply:

'But it was all much, *much* more complex than that, as of course I should have realised from the beginning. You see—' She leant forward and laid a thin hand on Mary's arm, then gripped it. 'Clive was *testing* me,' she said in a tone of rapt revelation.

'Oh . . . was he?'

'Yes! Don't you see? He didn't really want us to go to bed together—how could he? What we share is far, *far* too precious and exceptional for that. That would—spoil everything.' She shuddered, in a revulsion that appeared genuine. 'He admitted it himself. But he wanted to be *sure* of me, you see—to know that I'm bound to him, in another way, for ever . . . It's all right now, of course, because I understand! I told him that in the letter I wrote and left in our room in that

154

hotel—oh, what was its name? Oh, I suppose it doesn't matter—I think it was the Hotel de l'Angleterre—no, *that's* the one where we went to dine and ours was nearer to the casino—'

'Dodie,' said Mary, intent less on information than on interrupting the flow. 'Have you heard from him since you got back to London?'

'Who?' said Dodie sharply. She looked frightened again. 'Heard from who.'

'Why, this man, of course. Clive. If that's his name.'

'So you *do* know him,' said Dodie, gazing at her with exaggerated shrewdness, trying to hold her eyes. Mary looked away. In that warm, cluttered room, where Dodie and herself sat surrounded inappropriately with the random carved screens and brass ornaments of the Denvers' years in India, she was beginning to feel trapped again as momentarily on the night train. She was caught—but far worse this time—in Dodie's mental world, a claustrophobic web of Dodie's own concoction. She felt sickish, almost light-headed with tiredness. Dodie had started to her feet again, and was gazing at herself intently in a looking-glass; suddenly the sight of the slight, oddly-dressed figure, with its dangerous fragile beauty, goaded Mary into a desire to be brutal, even sadistic. Oh to break this web, this shell of glass, whatever it was, that was insulating Dodie from real life, real pain, from the demands and rhythms of the flesh, from time made real. '*I am a hall of glass*' indeed . . . More sharply than she wished, Mary said:

'Dodie! Stop looking at yourself and answer me: *have* you heard from this man since you came back to London?'

'Of course I have,' said Dodie confidently. She added, in an entirely matter-of-fact tone:

'That's to say, he *writes* nearly every day. But I don't get the letters because they burn them, you see. They think I don't know, but I do.' She laughed again, her bell-like, impenetrable laugh. I am above petty resentment or fear, the laugh said.

'*Who* burns them?' said Mary in deep foreboding. 'Your parents?'

'Well, they don't do it themselves, but they get it done. The servants burn them, of course.'

155

'What servants?'

'Why, the bearer and the *khitmagar* and all the rest of them,' said Dodie with impatient matter-of-factness, as of one tolerant of others' failures. 'That is, they collect them and give them to the *mali* to put on the bonfire. Just like they've done for years with the Boys' letters. Pa and Ma are jealous, don't you see, of the relationships I have. Especially Ma . . . Honestly, Mary, you are slow sometimes! I'm bored here, let's go out—'

It was Lionel who, summoned by phone at lunchtime, got Dodie committed temporarily to a mental hospital. This was an act for which Dodie never afterwards forgave him but, as Lionel said, he could bear this fact with equanimity.

His argument, brushing aside Aunt May's tearful suggestions regarding 'a nice quiet nursing home', was that on the staff of this particular hospital—the Bethlem Royal—was a distinguished psychiatrist who had had some success in treating what was then still called *dementia praecox*. Certainly, either in consequence of her treatment there or following some natural cycle of her own, Dodie did recover.

Mary believed that Lionel, like herself, had acted in good faith, doing the best he could for Dodie. Yet beneath this rational view there lurked, for her, an unspoken perception of other, less defensible emotions involved in their joint judgment. 'Being cruel to be kind' was an unpleasantly seductive course of action, if you did, really, dislike and disapprove of a person. Of course she herself did not dislike Dodie; rather, she felt something akin to a yearning, maternal love for her. But when had this kind of love ever precluded the obscure desire to get one's own back? Dodie herself knew that.

The feeling that Dodie, however manic and deluded, might have been grasping at some perverse truth about the nature of life which she herself was strenuously denying haunted her mind between sleep and waking. It took some time to fade.

In a newspaper, she saw a picture of a well-known, middle-aged actor, 'ex-matinée idol' as he was spitefully described, called Clive Palumbo, and wondered suddenly if this were

Dodie's Clive. And in what sense had he indeed been hers? Had she known him well, or possibly not even at all? He was getting divorced, it seemed.

Later in the year a small news item on the front page of an evening paper indicated his death 'from an overdose'. His star had evidently declined; he did not rate the larger type. She wondered if Dodie knew about this event, but dared not ask. Dodie was normal again now, slightly aloof and subdued, and was said to be writing another book.

Anything seemed possible.

PART FOUR

In a public lecture in the late 1960s, Mary said:

'. . . These statistics of new clinics, gradually opening through the 1930s and even in the war years, tell a heartening tale of endeavour and achievement. But it must be emphasised that it was not till the 1950s that we could see for ourselves impressive improvements in both the maternal and the neo-natal survival rates, and a general diminution in the pathological conditions that had appeared in our clinics up to that time. This improvement was due directly, of course, to the effects of the 1948 National Health Act, in bringing into the hospital orbit a whole stratum of society which, up to then, had been poorly served if not totally neglected. It was also due, in a more general way, to the overall rise in standards of living in the post-war era—a rise unexpected at the time, I might add, by those of us who were old enough to remember the economic depressions and hardships of the inter-war period. It seems that you have to give people the wherewithal to improve their *expectations* of life before you can hope to improve the quality of that life in more specific ways—a message which the Third World in turn is now having to learn.

In conclusion, and in illustration of this point, I should like to tell a story from my own experience which I have often told—so those of you who have heard it before must bear with me—but which I think is appropriate here. I could tell a worse one, but this conveys its message just as well, I think. It was when I was a young and relatively raw doctor working as obstetric registrar at the Mile End Hospital—in the building that was destroyed in the blitz. The system was that my immediate colleagues and I were each on call three or four nights a week in rotation, either

161

to the wards or to the district. The great majority of births were still home deliveries, of course. I can tell you, we became very familiar with the pathetic interiors of those streets of East End cottages—pathetic because, even when the occupants made great efforts, their stock of bedding, clean sheets, towels etc. was usually so very small, and an emergency like childbirth could find them quite inadequately provisioned. In addition, many of the families had no notion of hygiene or even common cleanliness, and some babies were born into conditions which I can only describe as disgusting. A colleague of mine, Ian Napier, used to keep his hat on in those houses because, he said, of the bedbugs that otherwise dropped into his hair! Though I should add—in case that makes him sound unsympathetic—that he went on to start an East End practice that was a model of its kind, and virtually gave his life to those same patients.

Anyway, late one evening I was just about to get undressed in my room at the hospital when the porter sent a message to say that a man was waiting for me in the front hall to take me to his wife. This was the usual system, you see. There were no private phones to speak of in our district, and not many public ones; people did not then have the phone habit. So if the midwife attending the case needed help—if, for example, she judged that forceps might have to be applied or the patient taken in as an emergency—she would usually send the father or another relative to the hospital in person to fetch one of us.

That evening it was a father waiting for me, apparently patiently, with apologies for disturbing me. I asked him if something was amiss with his wife's labour, but he only said that the midwife thought I 'ought to have a look at things', so I assumed it was just a slow labour: nothing in his manner suggested a real emergency. I had my bicycle with me which I always used on the district, but he didn't have a bicycle, so he pushed mine for me politely, I remember, while I walked beside him. It was a lovely summer night—1934, it must have been— and I believe we even talked about the Test Match which was then on. He was a cricket fan, and so was my—that is, the man who was later to become my husband, so I was able to keep my end up in this conversation.

Then, when we got to the house—I remember it was in Jubilee Street, it's all been demolished round there now—I discovered the midwife almost frantic waiting for us. Her patient was in obstructed labour and great distress, and the baby's heartbeat was weakening. I rushed round knocking up the local

162

publican to get at his phone, calling a hospital ambulance, getting a message through to alert the theatre—when I came running back to that little house, I fully expected to have a dead baby and a dying mother on my hands. But, wonderful to relate, the baby had rotated a little on its own—it was in transverse lie—and the midwife and I between us were able to make use of that small shift to turn it some more, and one way and another we got her properly into second stage at last. But she was at the end of her strength, poor woman—couldn't push—I had to use forceps: she was a very small woman, and how I extracted that infant in one piece I shall never understand. I can tell you, I found myself praying at one point, to a God I had not believed in for many years. But out it came in the end, with nothing worse than bruising, just as the ambulance arrived. The mother coped splendidly in the last few minutes too. I hadn't given her any chloroform, which was what we still used then, because I had been afraid of depressing the foetal heartbeat still further.

When it was over, and I had sent the ambulance away again and stitched the mother and we were having the usual cup of tea with tinned milk prepared by a neighbour, I asked the father why he hadn't told me the true state of affairs earlier.

He said he hadn't wanted to be a nuisance, and you could tell he really meant it. He thought he was behaving as he should. As if he had no right to demand that his wife or baby should be saved. No right to demand anything at all.

The mother also told me something I found instructive. She said that her last labour too had been protracted and difficult—something that should have been in her notes but wasn't—and that after it 'the doctor at the hospital' had warned her not to have another. I understood this to be the consultant for whom I was working, who shall be nameless. I asked what suggestions he had made for achieving this end, and the mother said: 'Oh, he didn't say, and I couldn't ask him, could I?'

Well, this confirmed a feeling I had had for some time about the way our methods were working—or rather, not working. This particular consultant, whose name I am not mentioning, was not a bad man in his way: he wasn't deliberately obstructive, as some were, and I knew that he would occasionally unbend so far as to suggest the use of a sheath if he were asked directly. But the point is that he would not do so unless specifically challenged, and of course the sort of woman confident enough to do that was, in a sense, the one least in need of help. It was the shy, quiet, humble couples like this pair, full of good intentions

163

but of limited intelligence, who most desperately needed more than our help: they needed our understanding and active guidance.

Downstairs in the kitchen I broached the subject of sheaths to the husband, but of course as I was the 'lady doc' the poor man was dreadfully embarrassed. And anyway—as he managed to say to me—sheaths were relatively expensive, and he was only doing casual dock labour. They couldn't afford the three children they had already, quite apart from the question of the mother's health—the mother's life, I should say.

I knew little about birth control then myself, from a professional point of view. I knew there was a women's clinic in West Kensington, the first and most famous one, of which many of you will have heard: two friends of mine were interested in it. But my patient was a typical East End woman, and West Kensington might as well have been Paris for all the chance she had of getting herself there. It was then that I decided there *must* be somewhere for women like this in or near their own district. I said so to Ian Napier when I got back to the hospital that night. He was a blunt person, who came to the point, and he said, in his Lowland Scots accent: 'In that case, we shall just have to start it for ourselves. Or *you* will, because you are a woman and they will trust you.'

And that is how the Dalston Women's Welfare Clinic first began. Ladies and Gentlemen—thank you very much.'

—And the polite clatter of smiling applause came, as always now, in that warm, comfortable hall, where no one disapproved of anything any longer and there was money to spare for every new venture and the much-discussed and lauded past was as remote and flat as a dream recounted by someone else.

And yet it's still there somewhere, thought Mary, as she sat down at last (public speaking seemed more tiring than it used to be) and let her mind wander for a few moments' rest during the Chairman's thanks which would be followed by questions from the floor. It's still *there*—that staircase off the Kingsland Road, the lavatory halfway up with a roaring, faulty flush that we all had to keep an eye on . . . That second-hand couch and the gas-ring on which we sterilised the speculum and trial caps, and Miss Bailey-Smethwick in her broom cupboard of an office on the ground floor, hung with old news photos of suffragette rallies. Dedicated to saving women from Men, she was; I was careful never to get into too intense a discussion with her—she was so useful as a secretary, so devoted to the cause . . .

They're still *there*, the women with their awful underclothes and their terrible, grotesque, matter-of-fact, apathetic tales of squalor, suffering and degradation. Still there, because the past is never really over, whatever all these young people here today think, whatever I thought when I was young. It comes back and back, and each time it has a different face, but it's always the same, the same . . . Ah no, I'm wrong, that's something different, something more personal—the altered people who go on playing the same roles down the years, the friend or child or loved man who comes back again in another guise, as if time really was cyclic after all . . . I'm confusing two things; I must be getting old after all.

'Look,' said Olive. 'This is the Pro-Race pessary that Marie Stopes favours. And this is the Dumas one. And this is the Mesinga Dutch cap which *I* think is better.'

Mary handled the thick, reddish rubber objects with interest, but with a flicker of distaste from somewhere deep inside herself. She knew she should get one for herself; it wasn't fair on Lionel to expect him to go on being the responsible one indefinitely, though it had been his suggestion in the beginning and he had never complained. But something about these neat, essential objects repelled her, in spite of intellectual conviction. No wonder they were stocked by what had come to be known as 'surgical goods stores': they were indeed like the rings for insertion into women suffering from prolapse. In a hospital setting they would have seemed unremarkable, but as adjuncts to private passion they were daunting. She did not doubt their efficiency. But this in itself carried a message she did not entirely like.

She told herself not to be subjective and ridiculous. These objects were being fitted by people like Olive into women who had already had as many children as they wanted, if not more. Their attitude could only be one of grateful, prosaic relief. If wealthy women chose to use these same devices to postpone childbearing indefinitely, thereby storing up trouble

165

for themselves, as opponents of birth control believed, then that was their business and no one else's.

'How many sessions do you do in Kensington?' she asked Olive.

'Just two a week—evenings, that is; we're a strictly after-hours outfit because that's the only time the women can leave their husbands in charge of the children and come along to us. Anyway, they mostly prefer to come after dark, when they think they won't be noticed by the neighbours, poor things! But I'm going to have to give up soon, for a few months . . . Yes, another on the way. Ironic, isn't it? John's awfully pleased, anyway. He's becoming positively patriarchal, it's quite alarming.'

Another year at the Mile End, as senior house officer in Obstetrics; Member (at her second attempt) of the Royal College of Gynaecologists. Then two more years at St Jude's, attached as senior registrar to a rather forbidding woman gynaecologist who was nevertheless a supporter of what was now beginning to be called the Family Planning Movement. Under her prestigious encouragement, the Dalston Women's Welfare Clinic, which Mary and Ian Napier had improvised as a one-evening-a-week service for their own patients, grew, flourished, and began to become well-known in the Movement.

Mary always felt that she would not have got the clinic going without Napier's help and support and, more indirectly, Lionel's. She believed herself to be a good learner and a good executive, but not the stuff of which pioneers are made. She thought the same was true of Olive, who had been encouraged into her work in West Kensington by John and whose deepest creative energies were currently absorbed elsewhere: Michael Hershey had been born in 1935, less than two years after his brother. But there was no denying the fact that outwardly the clinics were very much a female preserve. As in home midwifery, there was an atmosphere there of cosy, almost conspiratorial female makeshift; indeed Mary invited the local midwives to take an interest and to direct patients to them. In return, the Clinic bought a few rubber sheets and other oddments to lend out to women due to be confined. To avert the stigma attached to 'dishing out contraceptives' or even 'experimenting on the poor . . . in a slum' (there were one or two implacably unsympathetic local councillors in the borough of Hackney), the Clinic staff encouraged women to bring to them more general 'women's troubles' in addition to their specific request. Sitting in their petticoats on hard chairs in the tiny waiting room, otherwise shy and inarticulate women would sometimes be overheard swapping commiseration or home-remedies, and occasionally even ribald reminiscences accompanied by gales of laughter; while from the street directly below rose the shouts from the evening vegetable market and the acrid scents of meat and vinegar from the pie shop.

Long after, Mary was to remember these days with nostalgia. But at the time she was sometimes irked by a fetid undercurrent, a hint of feminist solidarity grown sour and rancorous. It wasn't just Miss Bailey-Smethwick with her suffragette photos and her surreptitious nips of gin from the thermos she always brought with her; in some way or other, when you got to know them well, many of the women doctors and nurses who gave their time and skill to the Clinic, and some of the volunteer fund-raisers, turned out to be working off some private unhappiness or grudge. Most were unmarried. One doctor, an enthusiastic and committed young woman from the London Hospital, had to be tactfully eased out when it became apparent that she had been counselling women unofficially about grounds for divorce and the withholding of conjugal rights. 'After all,' said Mary to her, 'we are supposed to be making sex in marriage easier and more enjoyable for our customers, not more difficult.'

'Oh, *enjoyment*,' said the woman scathingly. 'You surely don't imagine that enters into it for most of our clients, do you? That strikes me as a highly romantic bourgeois attitude, if I may say so.'

Mary knew what the girl meant, but thought the remark grossly exaggerated and partial and in any case she much resented it. It occurred to her afterwards that an altruistic desire that other women should discover in sex what she herself found was the most positive reason for her own involvement in the Movement. The presence of other, conflicting

167

reasons was not something which she had either the inclination or the time to examine. Life was full.

Indeed, over-full. The times that she and Lionel could get away together for a couple of days were sparse, too intensely prized for relaxation, too quickly over. Weekends in hotels in the Cotswolds when it rained; a night in a bed-and-breakfast place at Rottingdean where they had quarrelled absurdly about whether or not to visit Charlie the following day (Mary wanted to and Lionel, for some reason, did not). Another night at the Mitre in Oxford where Lionel had told Mary, out of the blue it seemed to her, that when Margery had developed the symptoms of pernicious anaemia he had felt himself blamed by her family for this, as if they really believed he had brought contamination and death to their daughter from the mortuaries where his work took him. Mary refrained from asking if he himself might have harboured the faint shadow of such an irrational guilt within himself; she knew the answer she would get to such a question. But she stored the fragment of information away in the meagre stock that, for her, constituted Lionel's past. For all his frankness in some respects, he could be a dauntingly private person.

It was a life with moments of great intensity and value, but expensive, nerve-racking and ultimately unsatisfying. In 1936, when Mary was back at St Jude's, they decided after all to marry.

'We'll keep it quiet,' said Lionel. 'No competitive married couples' dinner parties.' (Had Margery tried to institute these? Mary inevitably wondered.) 'And of course now you're becoming known you'll keep your own name. But this way we'll be able to get some peace and privacy together, and if anyone does challenge you you'll be able to silence criticism with your marriage lines.'

'And we'll be able to have Charlie to stay sometimes . . . For weekends, I mean? Half terms—' They had found a flat in an ugly but convenient block near Baker Street. Charlie was rising eight, and there was talk of boarding school for him. Mary felt sorry for the immature little boy, and Lionel himself did not come from a background where boarding school at eight was regarded as normal, but in the circumstances they agreed it was a good solution; Lionel said categorically that Charlie must not spend his entire childhood with his grandparents.

'I only wish we could have him for most of the holidays,' said Mary hesitantly.

'If we did we'd have to get a full-time housekeeper, and even then it would hardly be fair. A London flat . . . What would the boy do on his own all day with a housekeeper? You couldn't be there.'

'No. But Lionel—if and when we *do* have a child of our own . . .?'

'Well, that'll change everything, won't it? Let's wait till it happens, Mary. We'd have to publicise our marriage then, I suppose.' His tone was clear, direct as ever, not evasive but—not enthusiastic. Did he really want her to have his child but was concerned, as usual, not to take the lead in any issue that would affect her life and future so radically? Or was he indifferent, refusing to envisage the possibility till it occurred? This was almost the only topic which they did not seem able to discuss easily.

The idea of her aiming at a consultant's post was tacitly dropped between them. She was being approached now for advice on the opening of new clinics: it was beginning to seem that the future for her might lie, not in the conventional mainstream of medicine with its anti-female prejudices, but in this rapidly developing sideline. In any case, as Lionel said, anything could happen in medicine, society and in the country as a whole in the next few years. Including, as seemed increasingly likely, another war.

They were married in a registry office in the small northern town where Lionel's mother still lived. It was the same week that the Spanish Civil War began—a convenient way of recalling both dates, Lionel afterwards remarked with unconscious brutality. A day later they drove south again in the Austin 7 Lionel now owned, picked Charlie up in Sussex and took him for a week's holiday at Studland Bay. It was only half successful. Charlie, at first garrulously excited, grew quiet after a day or two and was inclined to mope and even to weep; he resisted Lionel's attempts to teach him to swim with skinny, shivering obstinacy. He obviously hated the cold, tumbling waves in which Lionel himself took such ascetic delight.

'He's been mollycoddled,' said Lionel crossly. 'That damned old Nanny. Just as well he's off to school in September.'

'Poor little boy, he's homesick,' said Mary, recognising the signs from long ago in the Boys' youth, from Nigel in particular—'We should have realised he might be. He isn't really used to us. It's all strange to him.'

She worried some more about Charlie being despatched to school so young, but what else could they do? And it was such a customary arrangement—

In the night, she said to Lionel:

'I think he's disappointed in me.'

'Surely not. You've put yourself out to please him, bought him that boat . . .'

'I don't mean that. It isn't anything I've done or not done. It's just that—I'm not his mother.'

'But he knows that.'

'Does he? Oh, I know he does in theory, but he's only young. Didn't you notice how pleased he was—quite unnaturally pleased, I thought—that day we went down to Sussex to tell him I was going to be his stepmother? And now he's disappointed and he keeps looking at me sideways. You know, Lionel, I do believe he thought at some level that I was actually going to turn into his mother. Or into someone special anyway. And of course I haven't.'

'Oh surely not,' said Lionel again. But he spoke without conviction.

Charlie was sent to a mildly progressive school where the boys wore corduroy shorts and windcheaters and morning prayers were replaced by discussions, current events and recitals from the school's own renowned orchestra. Mary agreed with Lionel that the atmosphere there was far pleasanter than in most prep schools and that the Head and his wife couldn't have been nicer. Yes. But Charlie was not really happy there, Mary could tell. That hysterical-puppy pleasure when they went down to see him, the shaming and shameless floods of tears each time he had to return after a holiday or a half-term . . . Surely childhood should not be eked out between two such extremes? And

Charlie was not coping well with his work; his reports complained that he was dreamy and a chatterbox, silly and occasionally disruptive. He was not generally popular.

Persistently and for the first time in years, the Boys reappeared in Mary's mind, those other exiles from normally parented childhood. They were there in her like an ache that was unrequitable, like an old wound that had never been healed. But the Boys had had her own mother's almost undivided attention and love—and her own—and, most importantly, they had had each other. Charlie was on his own. His grandparents' holiday spoiling did not extend as far as putting themselves out in any significant way for their restless child visitor. However many efforts she and Lionel made for him, he was not stupid and knew that he did not come first with either of them. Her heart bled for him, not because she loved him but because she could not love him more.

The following year they shared a holiday with the Hersheys and their little boys in an hotel on the Isle of Wight. Long afterwards, one of Mary's most vivid if inappropriate memories of this whole period was of the green lawns leading down to the private beach, and John Hershey revealing a gift for inventing stories and games which managed to include an eight-year-old, a four-year-old and even intermittently a two-year-old. Mary and Olive, knitting boys' jerseys in the shade of a Wellingtonia, were allowed to be what John referred to as 'legless participants': every so often Charlie or David would come panting out of the rhododendrons and hiss at them, 'You're captured pirates now,' or 'Pretend you think I'm dead—' and Olive would say, without pausing in their adult conversation, 'Yes, all right, we're pretending that,' which was apparently all that was required.

True parenthood was a special club, thought Mary, whose members displayed a casual expertise that could not be taught. Under Olive's and John's influence she basked in her temporary, honorary membership, but felt she could not cut a convincing figure in it on her own. Lionel, who became restive in the sheltering garden, was out striding the downs.

'It's marvellous of John to take so much trouble to entertain them,' she said.

'Oh, he enjoys it himself, he wouldn't do it otherwise,' said Olive, with the slight edge of cynicism that maternity seemed to have enhanced in her. 'He's an impresario *manqué*, you know. And it's been awfully nice for David to have an older child to play with; Micky's company isn't exactly mind-stretching for him.'

'No, I suppose not.' Mary viewed the portly toddler, currently turning himself round and round on the lawn till he collapsed in paroxysms of fat chuckles, encouraged by Charlie. She said hesitantly:

'Charlie does seem to like younger ones, I'm glad to say. Perhaps because he's a bit young for his age. And I think he finds their company a relief, after boarding school.'

'I bet he does,' said Olive in a sympathetic tone that indicated what she thought of boarding schools. She added in a neutral voice, counting stitches:

'Perhaps you'll provide him with a little brother or sister. He needs that, I think. Even though the age-gap would be rather large.'

'Yes, he does, I agree.'

'. . . Trying?'

'Mmm.'

'No luck as yet?'

'No.'

'Well, you've only been married a year.'

'I'm thirty-five, Olive.'

Olive said nothing for a bit. Then she asked where Mary was going to be working in September.

'At Queen Caroline's. As SHO. I thought it was time I had a look at the more genteel side of the business. After all, the birth-control movement isn't going to stay in slum clinics for ever—we hope.'

'I envy you,' said Olive drily. 'I'm a bit sick of my slum mothers myself. But what can I do?' Mary could not tell if she were being tactful or if she meant it.

After a minute Olive added: 'Perhaps the work won't be

172

so hard at Queen C's, and that might turn the trick for you . . . You do too much, Mary. You have for years.'

'I feel perfectly well.'

'Even so.'

One autumn evening a woman at the Dalston Clinic said, as Mary leant over her, 'I think there must be something wrong with me.'

Mary briskly reassured her, but added:

'You haven't had any children yet, though, have you, Mrs Cohen?' It was rare, in those days, for the clinics to see a woman who was not already a mother several times over.

'No. That's the point. And I do want a baby. I was hoping you could do something for me.' A quiet, sensible tone of voice. A quiet, resolute little woman with a faint foreign intonation, socially a cut above their usual customers.

Washing her hands, Mary said slowly:

'You know, we're in the business of stopping babies here, Mrs Cohen. Not the other way round. People almost never seem to come here with your problem. I have the impression it's quite rare . . . But do tell me about it. Perhaps I can suggest something.'

She took a case history. But there was nothing in the woman's story to suggest previous damage, no mention of an abortion—though of course one never knew. It seemed to be just one of those things. '*The working class breed like rabbits, my dear*' . . . '*Of course these clinics are doing good work, you know— can't let the lower classes breed unrestrictedly while our sort doesn't. Bad for the nation . . .*' The uncaring public voices clamoured in her head and she suddenly clenched her fists in impatient anger and frustration.

'What does your husband think about you coming here?' she asked. It was the standard question by which the Clinic covered itself against charges of spreading dissension within a marriage.

The woman's face crumpled suddenly. 'He doesn't know I'm here. He doesn't really want a child himself, you see.'

'But he's not doing anything to prevent it?' asked Mary, unpleasant and graphic images rising in her imagination.

'No—oh no. He's not like that. But he doesn't want it, that

173

I know. He's glad I haven't fallen for one. He says the world is in too bad a way these days to bring children into it.'

'Lots of people *say* that,' said Mary thoughtfully. 'But it doesn't seem to stop them having children. I don't think it has much to do with it.' She had been struck by this happy phenomenon.

'He means it,' said the woman, still crying helplessly. 'It's since he was hurt in one of those Blackshirt rallies—it's made him bitter. Two years ago, it was, down Stepney where we were living then.'

'I remember. I used to work near there.'

'We're Jewish, you see,' said the woman superfluously. 'And Party members. At least, my husband is. I've got family in Austria and Poland—it isn't nice for them there now, I'm worried about them, specially my aunt. They've taken away my uncle and she doesn't know where he is. And my husband's brother was killed in Spain last month.'

'I'm so sorry.'

'It seems like everywhere you look there's trouble . . . Oh, do excuse me, I just get so depressed about it all. Perhaps my husband's right, it's no time for a child. Do *you* think the next war's coming, Doctor?'

'I'm afraid I do. And maybe even sooner than we think. But, Mrs Cohen, that's *no* reason why you should not have the baby you want. The last war didn't stop people having babies. On the contrary. So do keep trying. Aim at the middle of your cycle or just before, as I said. I'll prescribe a tonic for you. And try not to work too hard—what is your job, by the way?'

'Machinist.'

'Oh yes, of course. Well, do try to get all the rest you can. And fresh air. And try to see that your husband does as well. It might turn the trick.'

You're still a young woman. Not thirty-five. Not thirty.

Riding her bicycle slowly through the backstreet miles between Dalston and Baker Street, Mary thought: that woman's husband is wrong, but for the right reasons. The world *is* in dissolution. Or rather, it never got put together again in 1918. It was patched up temporarily—just an armistice, as Lionel says, not a treaty, nothing really decided or

174

changed—and now, nearly twenty years later, it's coming to bits again. Hitler, Franco, Mussolini, Mosley ... These awful streets with their sooty, decaying Victorian houses: a whole city, behind the main streets, just gradually falling to bits and no one doing anything about it . . . The endless, squalid poverty of these women's lives, the men in those northern towns who've *never* worked. Jarrow . . . And money spent on by-passes with road-houses on them. Why shouldn't another war come, finally to wipe it all out and precipitate a real change? Lionel says one must still be pacifist on principle, but he knows that it's coming; he even says so.

Just suppose there *were* some mysterious influence at work on politically sensitive people, like Lionel, like Mrs Cohen's husband, inhibiting their fertility at this time because they are too aware of the coming dark . . . Am *I* too aware of it?

Oh, don't talk such rubbish. You, a doctor.

But this is not medicine but the source of life itself. Do we really know what it is, what those bits of rubber are doing? Do *I* know?

I fiddle around in my rational, sensible way, giving good advice and counselling small families, for all the world like a Victorian social reformer handing out soup and tracts—and all the time I, Mary Denvers, cannot achieve the one thing I really want in life, the one thing the stupidest, dirtiest, most hopelessly worn woman can apparently achieve over and over again without even meaning to.

You must admit the irony of the situation. It would even be funny if it wasn't so painful. And did not go on—and on—

During those years before 1939 Mary saw less of Dodie than at any other time in her life. Their ways had diverged too far after she and Lionel had seen Dodie into mental hospital during her baffling collapse in 1933. Mary had the impression that Dodie, understandably, avoided them. In any case, Dodie had now moved from her studio in Primrose Hill to a flat off Kensington High Street, not far from where her parents were living. Like Uncle George, she complained about the cost of everything but seemed, on the rare occasions when Mary saw her, to be living on a fairly extravagant level with a number of wealthy friends. Dressed in London black, with her hair always beautifully done, her face carefully made up and her nails long and red, she now wore the effusive social manner of the upper class and the smart theatre world like a mask: it was as if her one-time youthful enthusiasm and warmth had fossilised into a carapace which no longer expressed her real self but protected it. Mary, at any rate, had no idea where the true streams of Dodie's life now ran.

She was told, however, by a garrulous left-wing friend of Lionel's who made it his business to 'keep an eye' on Mosley, the Mitfords, Wyndham Lewis and various other public figures including the Astors, that Dodie was moving on the fringes of this world. She had apparently visited Germany (where Willie was once again living) in the company of an aristocratic Englishwoman currently celebrated as the lady friend of a prominent Nazi.

'I don't like the sound of your cousin at all,' concluded Lionel's friend, with the gusto of one who feels his rudeness is morally impeccable.

'I hardly think she's a sinister figure,' said Mary drily. 'She was always very innocent, in the days when I knew her well. Even,' she added, suddenly realising that this was true, remembering 'Pete', 'to the extent of having schoolgirlish crushes on other women.'

Willie had apparently got himself some part-time job not in but 'connected with' the new British Council.

'How very suitable,' said Lionel coldly.

'Oh, poor Willie . . . Yes, I'm afraid he is the archetypal dilettante, isn't he?'

'Poor isn't the adjective I should use. Pretty snakelike, I'd say.'

'Really, Lionel, you make him sound like a spy.'

'Well, are you sure he isn't? He's a Fascist sympathiser, anyway.'

'He's a snob, basically,' said Mary wearily. 'And Fascism appeals to snobs, doesn't it? It's dogmatic, and puts people in their places. You don't realise the power of innocent snobbery in the upper-middle class, Lionel, because you don't come from it.'

'Thank God.'

'But it's there and I can see it. People like Willie and Uncle

George and Aunt May—and the Elwins—they're all engaged in trying to protect their superior little patch against the lower middles and Communists and Socialists and Jews and foreigners and all the other bogeys. It's a lifelong obsession with them. Oh dear, Lionel, I never used to think in these terms. It's your fault; you've taught me to.'

'Good. And how does Dodie fit into your scheme? Is she obsessed with her social position too? She seems to have been climbing pretty successfully, by all accounts.'

'Ah, I don't know about Dodie. I'm sure she's obsessed by something—think of her mental history—but I don't know what it is. I have a feeling it might be . . .'

'What?' asked Lionel as she hesitated.

'Emptiness.'

'What do you mean, exactly—emptiness?'

'I don't know.'

Lionel's lecturing commitments had been growing, and he had published a book on his subject which had become a standard text. It made money, and for the first time he and Mary found themselves comfortably off. They bought a good car, a Rover, as a long-term investment. In the summer of 1938, Lionel was offered the Chair of Pathology at Manningham University, the largest medical school in the north of England.

'You must take it,' said Mary.

'But you don't want to come to Manningham?'

Mary considered. It was true, her work and contacts were all expanding in London. She could hope to rebuild them in Manningham, but she had no ties in the north, as Lionel did, and did not find it attractive. And there was Charlie at school in Kent—

'We'll keep our home in London,' said Lionel. 'And I need only spend three or four nights a week in Manningham and mainly in term-time—for half the year, that is. There's a good train service. I'll get a room there.'

'It seems dreary for you—and expensive.'

'Well, we can afford it. One advantage is that I'll be able to see my Ma a bit more often. She never says anything, but I know she'd appreciate that. And I can get a lot of reading done in the train.' He was, Mary saw, half attracted to the idea. Domestic comfort had never meant a great deal to him.

'I could come up to Manningham sometimes to spend the weekends with you,' she added. 'For a change.'

'Yes, you could. Dear me, it'll be quite like old times!' And he kissed her with a warmth unusual for him outside their bedroom, and went away somewhere.

That same year Mary was elevated from a Member to a Fellow of the Royal College of Gynaecologists and was co-founder of a new Family Health Centre in Paddington in which the Hersheys were also involved. For the first time they were doing family-planning work in reasonably spacious premises with paid office staff. There were daytime sessions and, partly as what John called camouflage, baby-clinics and a child-immunisation programme. John, who wanted Mary to give more time to the Centre, told her she should give up hospital work and start a private practice instead.

'You've got the reputation now. You'd do well.'

'I know, but I enjoy the hospital work. It's so varied.'

'You can't be a junior hospital doctor for ever.'

'I know that too. You leave me alone, John! You just want someone to run your Health Centre for you.'

'That's right,' he said, and grinned. He was one of the most popular and successful doctors in west London. All his patients loved Dr Hershey. That was axiomatic.

'Let Olive do it then,' said Mary loyally.

'She's got the boys.' John seemed in no hurry for Olive to extend her work commitments. They entertained a lot as well.

Everything, thought Mary, was going splendidly in her life and Lionel's—except for the one thing. Time was ticking away, carrying her along with it, eroding week by week, month by month, the years that remained in which she might realistically continue to hope. Sometimes, as month succeeded month and all fruitless, her cumulative private disappointment was so acute that she almost felt it would be a relief when eventually she reached forty, the age at which, by general consent, active hope should be abandoned. Yet that still would not be an end of it; women did have babies after forty, sometimes even at forty-five . . . Neither to hope nor to relinquish hope: an impossible assignment.

And public time was ticking away too, with a constant sense of the future already there, fully formed, waiting its moment of birth. The previous spring German troops had occupied Austria; refugees now appeared in Lionel and Mary's social circles, and jobs were found for some of the more distinguished. Most of Olive's Austrian relatives were now in London, occupying the large Shapira house in Eaton Square like deposed royalty. 'They sit *about* so, the poor dears,' said Olive distractedly. In Lionel's first term at Manningham the Munich crisis over Czechoslovakia came and went, followed by an uneasy calm. Lionel resigned formally from the peace pledge league, and seemed to spend much of his time when in London in conference with other pathologists debating topics he either could not or would not share. In April 1939 conscription was brought in for men of twenty and twenty-one. Mary's thoughts turned, as they quite often did these days, after an interval of many years, to the Boys. She remembered how pleased and excited they had been at the prospect of soldiering at an even younger age. One night she woke from dreams crying inconsolably. It took her a while to understand why, and Lionel was in Manningham so she could not tell him.

That summer they had arranged to take Charlie and another little boy from his school on a seaside holiday in Brittany. They hesitated for weeks before going; Germany appeared poised for another advance, but where or when was not clear. In the end they went to Brittany—partly, Mary felt, because the Elwins were apprehensive and disapproving and that made Lionel stubborn. They had a rewarding holiday and got safely back to England, sunburnt and gorse-scratched, the weekend before Germany invaded Poland.

On Sunday, 3 September, after Chamberlain's speech and the instant air-raid warning, Mary was hastily packing Charlie's case for him: Lionel was going to drive him down to the supposed safety of Sussex. At the London mainline stations other children were being massed for evacuation, with labels round their necks. Charlie, excited by the false

179

alarm warning, was being obstreperous and silly. His grand-parents, Mary felt, were welcome to him at the moment. She herself, like every other doctor in London, had been alerted to expect mass slaughter and injuries; all normal clinics had been cancelled. Her mind was on that, not on the missing pyjama bottom for which Charlie had refused to look. (But had he possibly wet them in his sleep and hidden them? That had happened several times before—)

The doorbell rang.

Charlie skittered off to answer it, and returned to report loudly that it was a man who wouldn't say what he wanted. Mary went distractedly out into the hall. On the doormat, looking pasty as he had done in childhood and clutching a suitcase, was Willie.

'Mary, my dear . . . Can you take in a poor refugee? I was evacuated from Germany yesterday. I've had a ghastly journey—they took the sleeping cars off at Metz. And all one's friends seem to be away.'

There was something in the atmosphere of that weekend that made Mary welcome him kindly, and made even Lionel tolerate his presence. Willie, as Mary said, looked so pathetic and conciliatory; he could hardly fail to know now that he'd been backing the wrong horse these last few years. And at such a moment, with total war and the end of civilisation confidently promised, there was something about a face from childhood that evoked a feeling transcending prejudices. She installed him in Charlie's just-vacated room (the sheets *were* dry; good) and went to organise lunch for them all.

It turned out that Willie had attempted to stay with Dodie—who, predictably, had been out of London that sunny weekend, at one of those country house parties which were to symbolise so much to a future generation and enter into the mythology of the outbreak of war. Willie had found her flat deserted and had come on to Mary and Lionel. Dodie returned halfway through the following week; she had stayed away under the impression, very generally shared, that London was about to be reduced to rubble. Mary overheard Willie having long *sotto voce* anxious telephone conversations with her, about other people whose names were vaguely familiar. It seemed as if, in the world both Dodie and Willie frequented, the war was treated as a personal disaster for individuals, an appallingly thoughtless blunder on the part of yet other people who, 'one had hoped', would have known better.

Willie at any rate, it seemed to Mary, was salving his own embarrassment and humiliation by a sudden yearning concern for others and for their valuable collections of pictures and porcelain, now much at risk in the houses of Kensington and Belgravia. 'It makes one quite tremble,' he repeated a number of times, to Mary and to unseen telephoners. Mary had never heard the cold Willie so solicitous before: it was as if the emotion that the outbreak of war had stirred in *him* was an unwonted tenderness. Perhaps he really did have a heart after all. Nor had she ever known him so eager to run errands or to set tables. ('As well he might!' Lionel remarked with grim amusement. But he refrained from any comment to Willie's face, and fortunately was out himself most of that week.)

As soon as he decently could Willie removed himself, with profuse thanks, to Dodie's flat in Kensington. And there, all the autumn and into the winter, he stayed—till it became apparent that, whatever the official situation, the war proper had not yet come. No bombs fell on London, and the ARP drank tea and knitted and were resented. Evacuees played noisy games in their gas-masks on village greens till, tiring of the gas-masks and becoming more and more homesick for the streets that were their native landscape, they trickled back to the cities. By Christmas they had almost all returned. The forces of the Reich occupied Poland but not as yet the Netherlands, and the possibility that France might fall was not seriously considered. It was a subtly nerve-racking, de-moralising time of anti-climax, silly jokes naggingly repeated, and insistent popular tunes. London was, the newspapers continually declared, 'gay' and 'fuller than ever' as, with an air of bravado, men went out to theatres and restaurants in the suits they had worn all day. Uniforms appeared, both familiar and strange, and new foreign terms ran easily off people's tongues.

One day in January Mary ran into Dodie in Oxford Street; they had a hurried and unsatisfactory cup of tea together in

Lyons—Mary, late for a Paddington clinic, regretting that she had said yes. Dodie looked radiant: in her smart-woman's black she seemed that day almost like a little girl in borrowed clothes, chattering excitedly about places and people unknown to Mary, showing off about someone she airily referred to as 'my Free Pole'. No doubt, thought Mary, he followed in the tradition of unsuitability established by Dodie's previous men. And how well the present limbo of false life and false war suited with Dodie's footling existence. She forebore to make any censorious remarks, but not for the first time when she left Dodie she felt both resentful and drab, as if she herself were illogically at fault and Dodie were dancing to music drabber people could not hear.

'I hate this time,' she said to Lionel. 'We got so keyed up—now it all seems unreal.'

'This will pass too,' said Lionel. 'The real thing is still coming.'

'You think?'

'I do think.'

'Willie evidently doesn't. Dodie told me that he's off to France next week.'

'For God's sake, why?'

'Dodie was a bit vague, she didn't say much. Something about the British Council in Paris having a job for him. I should have thought Paris would be crawling with people like him at the moment from other council offices in Europe—but you know Willie; he's happier abroad, always has been.'

'I know Willie,' said Lionel unpleasantly. 'And I should imagine he's off now because he wants to avoid being conscripted when it does all get going.'

'Oh really, Lionel, you are uncharitable sometimes. Willie's pushing forty—must be, he's nearly two years older than me—*and* he was turned down in the last war because he had asthma.'

'Did he indeed? Well, he may find that this time hopping off across the Channel isn't such a clever move after all.'

Mary could see that Willie, particularly when abroad, was too useful a repository for many things Lionel disliked about British society for Lionel to moderate his views.

About the future, Lionel was, as usual, right. In April 1940, when the 'phoney war' was so well established that everyone was used to it and business was continuing as usual, Germany invaded Norway and Denmark. In May she overran Holland and Belgium, then proceeded almost unimpeded into France. By mid-June France had fallen. At the end of the month the remains of the British forces were picked off the beaches at Dunkirk.

Like many other people of their education and tastes, Lionel and Mary grieved for Europe. Going about her daily work (though London had emptied again in a new wave of panic evacuation) Mary felt an obscure, continual ache within herself for Vienna and Paris where she had been happy, for the beaches of Normandy and Brittany that this time last year had been so near and which now were as inaccessible as Eden—or India. She ached too for those cities she and Lionel had planned to visit and now perhaps never would, for Rome and Florence and Siena. When, in the unthinkably distant future, the war was over for good or ill, would these places even be there still to see?

She had little time to brood. In May, when the possibility of England being invaded had begun to seem serious and near, an American pathologist in Baltimore, with whom Lionel had been in correspondence, wrote offering to take Charlie into his family home for the duration of the war. Other medical couples whom Lionel and Mary knew were considering similar offers; several small boys at Charlie's school had already been sent to the States or were about to be, and, with the school itself planning a hasty retreat to Aberystwyth, there was an atmosphere of dissolution in the air. Lionel was in favour of letting Charlie go.

'It seems a bit drastic, Lionel . . . And it isn't as if the poor little boy had had an entirely secure childhood as it is.'

'My dear, he isn't a baby. He'll be twelve at the end of this year. As well as the safety question I think this could be a good opportunity for him. The Hannakers have boys about that age themselves and America's probably a better country to be adolescent in than Britain, all in all. Don't forget that otherwise we'll have the public school problem looming— with the distinct chance, as far as I can see, of not getting him

183

into anywhere educationally good, even if we swallow our scruples and decide that's what we want. (And that's assuming that England isn't invaded and the schools taken over.) I don't know why he's so hopeless academically, but there it is; no point in hounding him to pass exams if he just hasn't got what it takes.'

Lionel's matter-of-fact tone hid, Mary knew, a deep disappointment in his son. It occurred to her that, concerned parent though Lionel was, he might in a way be wanting to send Charlie to America to get rid of him. She suppressed the thought, and its implications, as too painful.

In early June, a few days after Dunkirk—the week when Lionel was to abandon Manningham in exam-time, fetch Charlie from Kent, take him to say goodbye to his grandparents, and escort him to Liverpool to join a party of children due to leave on a liner for New York—Mary had a call from Dodie. The previous month, Uncle George and Aunt May, shaken at the curtailment of service facilities in their block and frightened by the increasingly strict rationing, had joined the new exodus from London. They were now, with many complaints, staying in a private hotel in Ross-on-Wye. Dodie had joined them there. On the phone she sounded subdued and self-excusing:

'Poor old things, they're getting on, you see, and they *worried* so about me being in London. It's aged Pa, this war business, I think.'

'I suppose it is hard on their generation seeing it starting all over again,' said Mary. Her private opinion was that both the elder Denvers had aged in the last two or three years, their querulous, ineffectual selfishness becoming more pronounced and their grasp on reality slighter than ever. She thought it was just as well they were out of the way, safe in Wales—if one could be said to be safe anywhere at the moment—and was struck, not for the first time, by Dodie's dutifulness in bowing to their wishes. Or was Dodie frightened of bombs too and glad of an excuse to leave London? In all honesty, it seemed unlikely. Bombs were not the sort of thing that scared Dodie. A thought struck her.

'By the way, Dodie, have you heard at all from Willie?'

'Willie . . . No, why?' Dodie sounded vague. This was evidently not what she had rung up about.

'Well, because of what's been happening in France, of course. I mean, when last heard of he was there, wasn't he? Have you any idea if he's got out?'

'Oh . . . no, I haven't heard from him for ages.'

'Some British people who've been caught out there have been getting away from Cannes, I believe—on colliers and fishing ships, that sort of thing. So he may well turn up here again. If not, I imagine he'll be interned, poor old Willie. I hope he's all right.'

'Oh, Willie will be all right,' said Dodie dismissively. She added: 'Willie always lands on his feet.'

A little surprised at Dodie's coolness, but thinking that she was probably right, Mary let the subject drop. She said:

'Did you want to ask me about something?'

'Yes . . . Actually, my dear, I wondered if I could come up to town and consult you? Professionally, I mean. Something up your street.' Dodie's voice was social, and a little hard and awkward.

'Well, you know, Dodie, I don't actually see private patients. You *could* come to the Paddington Centre, I suppose.' She made her voice discouraging, hoping Dodie would reject the idea. But to her surprise the offer was accepted.

Three days later she appeared in Mary's room at the Centre halfway through an afternoon session. She looked, Mary saw with concern, much less well than she had done in the winter, and much older. She seemed to have put on weight, the face framed by the collar of her smart linen coat-frock was puffy and her hair had been set in hard, unbecoming ridges, presumably by a Ross-on-Wye hairdresser. All the same, sitting in the waiting room among the Centre's more usual clients, she must have looked amazingly out of place. Mary wished, the moment she saw her, that she had been firm and recommended another doctor. But she could hardly have done so without finding out what was on Dodie's mind.

'I'm sorry to be a nuisance,' said Dodie dully. She added, with what might have been a touch of maliciousness, 'I expect you're frightfully busy as usual.'

185

'Not really. The hospital's pretty hectic, but here half our patients are evacuated or off with husbands on compassionate leave or trying to get married in a hurry. As a result we've had some desperate ladies come panting in for our help, but none of us knows quite where we are. Half our staff aren't here either . . . Anyway, you're here: what can I do for you, my dear?'

With hesitation, as if this were not what she had really come to say, Dodie produced a list of imprecise symptoms: insomnia, indigestion, 'nervousness', tiredness, backache, occasional crying fits. Mary looked carefully into her face as she spoke, searching for signs of that hysteria, mania, *dementia praecox* or whatever it was that she had seen in Dodie seven years before. But Dodie did not seem at all elated, let alone irrational. Rather, there was an air about her of slight clinical depression and flaccidity. She also sounded, for the first time, like her own mother: such a list of carefully nursed complaints was the sort of thing Aunt May was intermittently inclined to produce.

'—I was wondering,' Dodie concluded irresolutely, yet with an air of one producing a more optimistic suggestion, 'if it could be the change of life?'

'I hardly think so. You're not forty yet. Not even nearly.'

'I'm thirty-nine at the end of the year,' said Dodie, with a childish air of 'so there!'

'I know that, Dodie; I'm thirty-nine next year too. But it's rare for the menopause to come so early, you know.' Mary had often met this illusion before, though mainly among tired working-class mothers. Some of them, from their mid-thirties on, seemed to yearn for the 'change' as if it would indeed be at one and the same time a real change in their circumstances, a reassuring excuse for any and every physical problem, and an end to an ever-present worry. But there seemed no discernible reason why Dodie should wish to join the dreary female club of the self-consciously menopausal.

'Mother had awful trouble with the change,' Dodie remarked. 'I remember her in Switzerland when I was seventeen.'

'Yes, I daresay. But Dodie, you aren't your mother. Everyone has their own physiology, and history does not

186

have to repeat itself. And anyway, as I say, I very much doubt if you've got there yet. If you were going to be *forty-nine*, now . . . But nothing you tell me sounds specific to the change of life. Have your periods become irregular, for instance?'

'Oh,' said Dodie self-consciously. 'Didn't I mention that? I meant to . . . No, I haven't had the curse lately.'

Mary laid down her pen: 'Dodie, just what do you mean?'

'Oh, it's often frightfully irregular with me.'

'Yes, but when was the last time?'

'Oh—December, I think. Or January. I'm not sure. Moving to Ross in a hurry, I've mislaid my diary. So irritating. Mary, you can't think—'

'But it's now *June*. Have you ever missed so long before?'

'I—no, I don't think so.'

'What do you mean, you don't think so? Come on, Dodie, you must know. Women always do.'

But Dodie seemed genuinely confused. 'I did think it seemed a bit long. That'—triumphantly—'was why I thought it might be the change of life.'

'But my dear old thing, there is a more usual explanation. Much more usual. Come on, let's be frank about what's really worrying you.'

But Mary saw, as she scanned Dodie's pale, only vaguely anxious face, that her cousin really did not seem to know what they were talking about. Could hysteria produce such a refusal of common knowledge? Yes, of course, one knew that. It did not, for the moment, occur to Mary that Dodie's ignorance might be of a genuine and deeper order.

She wished again that she had not agreed to this appointment. But Dodie's behaviour seemed, in its subdued way, so strange that she dared not risk sending her away to see someone else.

'I'd better take a look at you. Just get undressed, will you? You can keep your petticoat on.' Unlike many of the Movement doctors, she disliked examining friends or indeed anyone she knew socially. She and Olive had kept away from each other in that respect. She felt that a degree of formality was helpful to both doctor and patient at such moments. But

187

Dodie seemed unconcerned, getting up on to the couch like an obedient child.

So that when, a few moments later, she suddenly began to scream and push her away, Mary was almost as shocked as Dodie.

'For heaven's sake—what's the matter?'

'Don't do that, I can't bear it! It's horrible—'

'But Dodie, I must, if I'm to find out—what's the matter with you. You said I could examine you.'

'I didn't realise this was what you meant.' Dodie seemed frantic, trembling and resisting, making herself rigid like an angry cat. She was not, either emotionally or physically, the experienced woman Mary had for so long supposed her to be. It was with considerable difficulty, and terrified tears from Dodie, that Mary established what she needed to know.

Although she often had to deal with frightened or pathologically shy women she felt shattered herself by this confrontation; in it, her whole relationship with Dodie stretching back through the years, with its nerve-racking mixture of intimacy and constraint, seemed to have come to a crisis. And how on earth am I going to tell her? she thought, running water slowly over her hands. She returned to her desk to make notes, giving Dodie, behind the screen, time to reassemble herself and dry her eyes. But when Dodie finally emerged, and Mary quietly announced her finding, bracing herself for more tears, Dodie just stared at her and said in apparently genuine disbelief:

'Oh, I *can't* be.'

'Well, you are. About five months, I would say. Dodie, didn't you even notice yourself getting fatter?'

'Oh . . . I don't know. My weight's always varied a lot. But I don't understand, how *can* I be pregnant?'

'My dear . . . By the usual method, I imagine! Come on, Dodie, you have *had* intercourse with someone; even if it was only once or twice, you'd much better tell me about it. Was it your Free Pole?' Hearing her own voice, artificially matey and prying, Mary loathed herself, and the situation. But she was trying to jolt Dodie into some recognition of reality, and was also anxious on her own account because she was afraid, from experience, that the next request would be for an abortion. That had to be refused, of course—no question about it, and in this case it was too late anyway—but it always made her wretched to do so. She knew that a desperate woman, in any social class, usually did not take no for an answer, and that her refusal would often just drive the woman to a less scrupulous practitioner with the attendant risk of damage or death. It was a moral dilemma she had often discussed with colleagues but to which she had never found a satisfactory answer, even on the theoretical level.

But Dodie, once she had incredulously accepted the idea that she might, after all, be expecting a baby, did not mention abortion. She looked thoughtful and still glum, but not nearly as shocked as Mary had feared. It was as if the true implications of the situation had not yet got through to her.

'When will it be born?' she asked, after a silence.

You tell me, thought Mary. You know what you've been doing better than I do. Out loud she said:

'About mid-October, I should think, if my diagnosis is right.'

Dodie made a face. 'What a bore! I was hoping to go to friends of mine in Scotland in the autumn. If we're not invaded by then, I mean. Or even if we are . . .'

'Well, you won't be going anywhere for a few months,' said Mary shortly. 'Except to a good nursing home in some safe area. I can recommend one, I think . . . Dodie, are you—that is, are you in touch with the father? He ought to know, you know. Even if'—painfully, thinking of Dodie's previous attachments, 'he's not in a position to marry you.' Trust Dodie to pick some Free Pole of all elusive, romantic, unsatisfactory liaisons. 'Free', indeed. I bet he is. I wonder if poor Dodie is much in love with him.

'Oh, I couldn't possibly tell him,' said Dodie at once with a shudder. 'I mean—I'd be awfully embarrassed. I needn't really, need I?'

'Well, you don't *have* to, no, it's up to you. Particularly if you feel you don't need his financial help.' The extraordinary inadequacy of Dodie's response, when she was not actually being asked to stand physical probing, defeated Mary. She was used to women who were desperate, women who saw the child growing in their bodies as some monster, a cancer even,

189

to be rooted out at any price. With tears, rage, threats of suicide, she would at least have felt on familiar ground. But Dodie's near-casualness baffled her. *La belle indifférence* . . . Would Dodie get through pregnancy and childbirth without another descent into insanity? The signs hardly looked good. Mary was deeply concerned for her, and for the child. She said hesitantly:

'Dodie, I don't approve of unmarried mothers trying to get everything too cut and dried till the baby's actually there, and they see what they've got, so to speak. But I do think you should make some tentative plan. Are you—that is—I suppose you would think of getting it adopted? . . . But you needn't answer now. Come and see me at the flat one evening and we'll have a proper talk.'

She felt nervously exhausted by the last twenty minutes, and by all the other things of which she ought to be thinking: the hospital (to which she must return this evening); the problems in the immediate future of the Centre—they had lost half their nurses and most of their volunteers; whether Lionel and Charlie had got to Liverpool safely. What a moment for Dodie to pick! But of course she hadn't picked it. And even as she tried to tell herself that Dodie's problem, however momentous, must take its turn along with others, a new, revolutionary idea invaded her mind. If Dodie did not—as seemed probable and even desirable—want to keep her baby, should she and Lionel offer to adopt it?

For the next few days she carried the question round with her like a physical object she could not put down. She rode back and forth across London's unnaturally empty streets with it on her bike, ate her abstracted hasty meals with it beside her, listened to the news on the wireless with it, lay down with it at night. Lionel had returned to Manningham; although she spoke to him twice on the phone she did not feel she could announce her idea to him in such a way. She did not even tell him she had seen Dodie. Time enough for that, she told herself, when Britain wasn't facing its worst danger since Napoleon, time enough when Dodie—who was supposed to come and spend a night at the end of the following week—had taken some sort of decision herself.

But again and again, as she framed this delaying thought,

her common sense and conscience prodded her into the recognition that Dodie's decision would almost inevitably be influenced by her own. If she expressed herself willing—even eager—to adopt this baby? If she were to intimate (and it was, after all, one aspect of the truth) that she and Lionel *needed* a child to bring up together properly, and that this baby offered probably the last and only chance, for Lionel as much as for herself—?

Yes, all true. But there were other truths as well. Such as that Lionel might now regard himself as too old to start fatherhood all over again, and had never liked Dodie anyway. She knew how fair and reasonable he was—consciously fair, consciously reasonable, that was part of the difficulty—and knew that if she were to say that she wanted above all things to keep and bring up this child of Dodie's, this one descendant of the Boys, he would accept her decision and her wish. But was this attitude in a father sufficient?

And in any case, *did* she want a baby herself above all else, now of all times? Lionel's baby she would still have welcomed with rapture, whatever the practical difficulties, whatever the future of Britain—but who knew what this baby's father might be like, what undesirable traits it might inherit from him, let alone its mother's instability? Yet again, the thought of it going for adoption among strangers was acutely, almost unbearably painful. She could give up her hospital work, as John had anyway suggested, become a part-timer like Olive . . . But then at this moment Olive and her little boys were in Dorset, evacuated, and Olive's own career had disintegrated into a question mark.

No, there was no right answer to the question, only two different flawed alternatives. The question continued to burden her.

She did not seriously consider, during that week, that Dodie might keep the baby herself. That was almost unheard of, for a woman of Dodie's class. And Dodie, she now realised, was far more convention-bound and timid than she had ever appeared.

Yet that, in the end, was what Dodie decided to do. Not that she told Mary in so many words. She wrote evasively from Ross-on-Wye, thanking Mary but cancelling her planned visit to London. The next news Mary received was a letter in July, in Aunt May's elaborately loopy hand, couched in terms of the blandest prospective grandmotherhood. From its tone Dodie might have had a solid husband respectably absent in the army. Dodie, she wrote, was 'taking things easy', had bought 'some pretty smocks' and was 'getting down to knitting'. It was *so* nice that she should be able to join forces with them in Ross; the local GP was a nice little man and had booked Dodie into a quite splendid nursing home in Hay. When the baby was born Dodie was going to find some nice cottage and some nice Welsh girl as a nanny. 'Now he's got over the first surprise, yr Uncle G is quite thrilled!' wrote Aunt May—and all the rest of the letter was about the shortcomings of the hotel, the ingratitude of staff these days, the prospects of soap-rationing and the uncouthness of the 'slum evacuees'.

This uninformative communication annoyed and upset Mary a good deal, for reasons she was too honest not to recognise. She tried not to grieve for her half-formed, unshared dream, but did not entirely succeed.

How typical, she thought, of Dodie not to bother to write herself. But then what more could she have said? The decision she had apparently taken was so momentous and far-reaching that any justification of it would have been superfluous. But did Dodie understand this herself? One could not tell, with her; her ignorance on many subjects was shot through with sudden, bleak, acute perceptions. Had she, in those unreal, nerve-racking weeks after Dunkirk, discovered in herself a new wartime courage, a capacity after all to break with the past and with convention, becoming for once the independent female spirit which figured in her novels and in her fantasies about herself? '*What I'd really like is to have a baby on purpose, on my own, you know.*' Dodie, ten years back, in the house at Esher. Mary would have liked to think that thus, albeit by accident, Dodie was fulfilling an old and deep-seated ambition. The idea had an intellectual appeal as well as a human one. But when she tried it out on Lionel, after telling him what had passed and showing him Aunt May's letter, he said at once:

'Dodie doesn't sound to me as if she's breaking with the

192

past or being independent. I mean, she's gone home to Mum, hasn't she? It's more as if she's taking refuge in being a child again herself. I doubt if she's considered at all what bringing up a child will mean.'

'Oh dear, yes, you may be right. Come to that, there seems to be a general myopia all round, doesn't there? I suppose it's just Victorian upbringing, but you would think from Aunt May's letter that she and Uncle George had forgotten the facts of life. He's not shocked at Dodie's baby, you note. Just "surprised".'

'Oh well, they're getting a bit gaga, aren't they? It's interesting the way people, when they feel themselves getting old, often start just ignoring things they don't like. It's as if they're afraid to go round disapproving any more of the younger generation because they are the ones now in power. It's a bit degrading in a way—that abandonment of a lifetime's principle—but it's often just as well, like now . . . I notice the same thing in my old Ma. You know what a fervent Methodist she's been all her life? But now, when I go over to see her, she'll not only let me bring beer into the house for myself, she's actually learnt to enjoy a glass of stout herself. "For her nerves", you understand.'

' "It's the wor wot's done it." '

'Quite.'

Mary tried to tell herself that for Dodie to keep the baby and bring it up was the best of all possible solutions for everyone, even in these times. If only Dodie's mental stability were equal to it.

Several times she caught herself indulging in a daydream in which, once the baby had reached some reasonable age like four or five, Dodie collapsed again dramatically and definitely and she and Lionel stepped into the breach . . . She was ashamed of this fantasy, yet it persisted and elaborated itself.

For the second time in her life she was bitterly, secretly jealous of her cousin. Dodie—of all people. The acute pain, however, was of brief duration: she had many other things on her mind. The nature of life, like the news from the war's shifting fronts, seemed to change from week to week. It was as if time were rolling faster than usual. Perhaps for others, languishing in the static frustration and anxiety of safe areas, with time in the long, dark, country nights to yearn and miss, it was otherwise. But for her, as for so many people, personal hopes and ambitions were swept away in the dissolution of normal life. In her present state of mind she welcomed the change.

The Family Centre in Paddington was requisitioned as a casualty station and rest centre after the first big air-raid of September: temporary accommodation was found the following week, but it became obvious that the further plans Mary and the Hersheys had for it must be shelved 'for the duration'. With the raids, Olive inevitably remained in Dorset; John, his junior partner called up and his senior one incapacitated with a heart attack, was inundated with calls, even though most of his wealthier patients had left town. Mary herself decided that the time had at last come for her to break with hospital work, though not in the way John had suggested. Ian Napier was struggling single-handed with his East End practice, his work grotesquely augmented by the flow of casualties; every night that fine and moonlit autumn, between 7 September and 2 November, the German bombers returned. In October, Mary joined Napier in his lock-up surgery off Commercial Road, Stepney. She was to spend much of her time there till 1945.

That same month Dodie, in Wales, gave birth to a daughter, but it was to be a number of months before Mary even saw the child. She hoped the birth had gone smoothly, in spite of Dodie's age and attitude, but she had no details; the idea that she had once, briefly, dreamed of having this child as her own, seemed quaintly out of date. How could she seriously have contemplated such a thing? She was far too busy. However, between despatching a hasty telegram of congratulation and the belated purchase of a teddy in Selfridges—how low on stocks all the shops were—she did spare the odd thought for the child's shadowy father. Was Dodie in touch with him at all? Did he even know he was a father? Probably not, but was that right? Even freebooting Polish military officers, wrested by war from country and background, might be supposed to have paternal feelings. Oh, probably he had just disappeared, posted abroad . . . he might even be dead by now, or had a wife and children in Poland anyway. These things happened in war. For the first time in many years she remembered Susan, and Dodie's disgusted and incredulous reaction.

That month too she and Lionel, who had conscientiously made some enquiries, received Red Cross notification that Cousin Willie was alive and unhurt but had been interned after the fall of France in a camp near Dijon. 'All his own fault, the silly sod,' said Lionel.

'How grim for the poor old thing all the same. Him with his taste for Earl Grey and Bath Olivers.' She remembered Dodie saying, 'Oh, Willie always lands on his feet,' but this time she could not imagine that he had.

'No grimmer than for all those Viennese intellectuals we've interned on the Isle of Man, all neatly gathered together for the Nazis to come and find.' This was a current preoccupation of Lionel's.

'No, I know that really. It's just that Willie has always seemed so helpless. In some ways.'

'Oh, he'll be giving little lectures to the other camp inmates on porcelain or baroque architecture—or on how Mosley's a jolly good chap and the British will come to their senses soon and sue for peace, I shouldn't wonder. Willie'll bob up again, you'll see.'

She and Lionel were apart a great deal. It was inevitable and unremarkable; everyone, or almost everyone they knew, was in the same boat, and they were lucky in that at least they were both in England, if not in the same city. There was no petrol for long journeys, even for doctors; travel by rail was too laborious and hazardous for Lionel to come up to London regularly, and from the beginning of 1941 Manningham itself was heavily bombed. Rising fifty, Lionel was too old for any form of military service, but he devoted his energies and experience to Manningham's wartime public-health problems, and Mary sensed that the centre of his interest had shifted there. It was no doubt right, in his position, that this should be so. Both of them were often up at nights, fire-watching or on emergency call in their respective cities; when possible, they used to ring each other up wearily at seven in the morning to compare notes. Even in the brief periods for

195

which Lionel did come to London a domestic life together was for the moment more or less shelved; they were both too busy to spend time shopping and cooking and, with the increasing rationing, these activities were in any case becoming more and more taxing.

Mary told herself that she was lucky not to have the burden of trying to feed a family at the moment. In a time like this it was surely only logical for two healthy people in middle life such as Lionel and herself to live as separate individuals rather than as a couple? Other yearnings seemed swept away by the pressures of each succeeding day. It was as if the bombs that had devastated the City and the East End and made gaps in terraces all over London had destroyed far more than bricks and stone.

Every few weeks a short airmail letter would arrive from Charlie, ill-spelt, uninformative, concluding with a row of childish crosses. By and by he began to use more American phrases, and the little he did tell them about his life in Baltimore became more allusive and unintelligible. By and by, too, the row of crosses ceased; after all, he was growing up.

When, occasionally, she thought of him Mary's heart bled obscurely for this boy towards whom she had been so well-intentioned, whose needs she felt she had not met—this boy who was the only son she was ever likely to have, whom she had failed to protect against his father and who was now growing away from her towards adulthood in the care of strangers in an unknowable land. But this, too, she thrust aside; it was just one of the unassuageable private griefs and regrets of the war and many people, she told herself, lived with far worse ones.

In any case, apart from certain specific, repetitive worries—how had Manningham fared in last night's raid? Would the surgery in Stepney be standing when she arrived on her bicycle in the morning?—she enjoyed her present life, makeshift and scrappy as it was. After years in one speciality she felt stimulated by the variety that general practice brought. She did not mind snatched meals in canteens and British Restaurants, or broken nights, or bicycle rides through a London where the only light came from burning buildings and where she had to keep dismounting to pick her way over patches of splintered glass, glinting white and red on the deserted roadway. Even the destruction around her, though it shocked, was not necessarily depressing; hadn't she and Lionel always said that half these dreadful, crumbling, Victorian terraces ought to go? Something good might come out of the ashes of this after all.

She also enjoyed the one night every week that she fire-watched, in Paddington at the Centre, usually with John Hershey or with another colleague. It was their one chance to sit down quietly and talk and laugh together and discuss cases and reminisce, and plan for the hypothetical and distant future. She brought soup, in a thermos, to sustain them, and they used to sit wrapped in blankets: the winter of '40–'41 was, unkindly, one of the coldest of the century. John usually brought a bottle with him. 'Grateful patient whisky,' he would explain airily, pouring the now-rare liquid into the centre's tea-cups. He seemed to be able to drink large amounts of it himself without showing any effect, but it made Mary sleepy; the night when a stick of incendiary bombs finally came sailing across the mainline station and the canal and down on to their block she was curled up oblivious on one of the examination couches. Fortunately, however, John had taken a stroll, as he called it, up on to the roof a little while before, and kicked the bomb that landed there into the street. It burst into a blaze in the empty greengrocer's on the opposite corner, and filled every window in the cold street with spectral flames.

As the worst winter, and the worst time of the war, eased at last into spring the raids became fewer. Often now one was able to sleep through undisturbed. One evening, though, as Mary walked from Baker Street over to the Centre in the soft, shabby dusk, she found that the block next door to the centre had received a direct hit. It had been a short run of Georgian houses converted to a private hotel. Now most of it was a great mound of bricks, charred timbers, plaster, ashes and projecting oddments of rag, wood or metal which she did not like to scrutinise too closely. Over all hung a dusty miasma, the familiar smell of a bombed house: chalky, acrid with a hint of cordite, yet with a sickly, almost sweetish tang as well.

The site was roughly cordoned off, and an ARP team were rooting about with picks and shovels, but with the leisurely, dispirited air of men who know there is no urgency. Watching them was John Hershey, hands in pockets, whistling an operatic aria under his breath.

'I didn't know about this,' she said, hurrying up to him.

'I knew this morning. I tried to ring you but you weren't in the surgery.'

'No. I was out most of the day. We've got a measles epidemic, on top of everything else. And of course as they all spend every night down the shelters in Stepney, anything like that goes round like wildfire—young babies, the lot.'

'Measles is a better fate than this.' John jerked his head at the heaps of rubble. 'The people in that lot should have been down the shelter.'

'Do they think there are many under there?' The place had been a dingy residential establishment, mainly occupied by the elderly and rootless. Mary remembered particularly a bearded man with a wing-collar and pince-nez who had often stood by a ground-floor window looking out; the centre staff had nicknamed him 'Freud'. He had once, in the street, engaged her in a polite Middle European conversation about the performance of the RAF, whom he referred to as 'our boys'.

'They brought nine out early today, a workman told me, but only two of them were alive and he said one of those was very poorly. The hotel register's been destroyed, of course, and they don't know exactly how many people were living in the place.'

'Aren't the police supposed to have a record?'

'Apparently they haven't. The owner and his wife and child are still down there somewhere. They were in the basement—but that, in the circumstances, didn't do them any good.' John normally remained indecently cheerful in the face of illness, injury and death. Mary had seldom heard him sound so grim.

'I think I can hear a cat mewing,' she said suddenly. She listened, and it came again, a tiny, distinct noise like tearing silk in the silent, traffic-less street, where the only other sound was the intermittent scrunch of the workers' tools.

'Yes. They've been hearing it for hours, one of the men told me. They can't locate it. Poor little blighter's probably unreachable anyway.'

Mary felt cold and very tired. Sometimes, in the midst of destruction, one small, specific thing abruptly seemed unbearable. Into her mind came the image of a man, an elderly patient of hers in Stepney, whom she had last seen standing still before a bombed house watching men at work, as John had been. The difference, however, was that it had been his own house. On her way to another call she had spoken to him, got no answer, hesitated for a few minutes, and had finally delivered him, thankfully, into the care of a WVS lady and had hurried on. He had gone out of her mind till now; she ought to check up on him, visit him—but where was he living? She ought to do something; impossible to do everything. Impossible to do a tenth of it . . . She felt her chest swell physically with what she took to be resentment and frustration, but suddenly realised, as her throat tightened, was actually grief, pushing upwards from some deep, obscure source. She swallowed hard. This would not do—

'John, I can't stand this. Let's go next door.'

'Want to?' John looked right at her for the first time that evening. 'I warn you,' he said, 'I've been in there already and it isn't that cheering a sight. So if you're not feeling strong—'

'Oh, I'm strong,' she said lightly.

The house the Centre currently occupied was also part of a converted terrace. It had not been hit by the bomb, but had taken the force of the blast. Every window was out, but the blackout screens had deflected the glass into the street and most of it had been shovelled up. Because the screens were still up, the rooms to the right and left of the hall were dark as they peered into them, even though it was still daylight; but the hall and stairway, which were normally murky since the skylight had been covered with blackout paint, were unnaturally light. The last rays of the sun streamed down the flights, turning the plaster dust in the air to a milky haze.

'Skylight's gone,' said John. 'And a bit of the roof alongside.

199

I spoke to the council's man about that: they're going to try to get a tarpaulin across it tomorrow. Hope it doesn't rain tonight.'

'So do I. John, is this house *safe?*'

'Think so.'

'It feels sort of—insubstantial. Light and dark in the wrong places. Suppose the rest of the roof falls in?'

'The main timbers seem all right. I got one of the chaps on the site next door to take a look. Oh, the ceiling's down in one of the top rooms—that's where all this plaster comes from, it's like giant bird-droppings on the landing—but the other ceilings seem okay. For the moment. The real trouble is, those glass-fronted instrument cabinets in the main surgery have caught it and everything's in a mess. I never did like those bloody things.'

'Who was here last night?' Mary wondered that she had not thought to ask before.

'Young Lawrence and one of the volunteers . . . they're fine. They were in the Morrison shelter under the stairs when the bomb landed. Must have been a big one.'

'Wonder who was on top,' said Mary with a weak giggle. Young Lawrence was an enormously fat, asthmatic final-year medical student, whose main and shining virtue was a passionate interest in obstetrics.

They spent several hours trying to reduce the dislocated surgeries to some kind of order. The blast had had odd effects, devastating one corner, stripping paper from the wall or leather from a couch, shattering a row of bottles, yet leaving other items of furniture or equipment intact. In the windless evening the house was nevertheless full of odd, small noises; specks of plaster dropping from the ceilings, soot suddenly tumbling inside the flues into the old, covered fireplaces. Boards and banisters creaked, bricks settled. Mary did not feel as sure as John did that the shaken building was safe at all.

Late at night they stopped for a rest. She produced a flask of soup. 'It needs warming up, I'm afraid. I left home in rather a hurry.'

'Oh damn, because the gas is off. Yes, I forgot to tell you. The main is cut, further up the street. I'll have to bring a primus over tomorrow for the sterilising. Luckily the water's still on.'

'Well, that's that; no soup, I'm afraid,' said Mary heavily. She wanted soup. She felt exhausted.

'Nonsense. We'll build a fire.'

'Where? Oh John, *not* on the floor.' (He was quite capable of it.) 'You'll set the place on fire, and that really would be ironic.'

'No, of course not on the floor, in the grate. Watch me!' And, with a surgical spatula, he proceeded to wrench off the plasterboard covering the fireplace and break it into bits. He built a fire with this, and with patients' records selected by him from the filing cabinets—'Busby! Let's burn Mrs Busby. I happen to know she's moved to Somerset, two years ago. I'm sure she won't be back . . . And poor Mrs Hanrahan died of *post partum* haemorrhage six months ago. She should never have stayed in London, I told her that but she wouldn't listen to me, of course—why should she? We'll burn her too—'

The soup was warmed. John had no whisky with him that night, but he produced a bottle of claret.

'Our reward. I've been saving it for just such an occasion. Come on, Mary darling, it's full of iron and vitamins. Just the thing for you. You look done-in.'

As they sat and drank together Mary was disconcerted to find herself suddenly crying a little. She could not think where the tears came from. John noticed, took out his handkerchief, and wiped her face for her. As he did so she remembered that evening, so long ago, when he and she and Olive had been to *Journey's End*, and afterwards in the restaurant she had cried inconsolably. Now, as then, he seemed blessedly unsurprised at her behaviour.

'Don't upset yourself, lovey. I know it's disappointing seeing everything here in such a state, but it'll all come right in the end.'

'It's not that, John, not that really. Oh, I suppose I *am* tired and upset . . . But actually I was feeling sad about quite other things. An old man down in Stepney I ought to look up. And a kid I saw today with measles and very sore eyes, and the father's just been killed in North Africa . . . And that poor little cat buried alive next door . . . And other things too, that aren't really sad at all . . . A man I used to know years ago in the very early days of the Movement called Eric Evans. He seems to have disappeared now; I haven't heard of him for years and I suddenly wondered where he was. He was such a good person . . . And all the people who used to live in this house too. When it was a family house, I mean, and Paddington was a nice place to live. You suddenly think of them, running up and down those stairs in long dresses, getting ready to go out to a party, falling in love, having children—and they're all gone, just *gone*, all that life and hope and busy-ness, and soon this house'll be gone too. They'll surely pull it down after the war. If it survives that long.'

'You need a little break,' said John, with a cynical expression. 'Such profound thoughts! You're overstrained.'

'We're *all* overstrained, John, don't be silly. Look at the life you lead yourself.'

'Oh me, I'm indestructible.' He thumped his chest in a parody of a prize-fighter's stance. 'But I thrive on it. You seem unhappy—'

'No, I'm not! That's where you're wrong. That's the odd, indecent thing. Really, in spite of all the awful things that are happening all round us, I'm not a bit unhappy. If you want to know, John, in an odd way this is one of the happiest times of my life. I can't explain it. It's as if one is—freed. Of all sorts of things. Moving on the frontier of time. It's strange.'

After a pause John said: 'Has anything happened to you recently? A family tragedy or anything?'

'No—oh no.' She thought of Dodie's baby, far away in Herefordshire and as yet unseen, and wanted, suddenly, to tell John about that whole episode, but he was saying:

'You and Lionel all right?'

'Yes—oh yes, I think so. I mean, he's away such a lot. But we do manage the odd weekend in the country. And then you and Olive are apart too. I'm in no position to grumble.'

'You ought to go down and see Olive again, she'd love to have you any time. It's hellish boring for her down there, stuck with the boys and country neighbours and other evacuated wives. She enjoyed your last visit a lot. I can't get down there much.'

'Yes, I must. I'd love to see her again. It's just—time.'
It had been strange going to Dorset, seeing Olive, who
had always seemed destined for a career, turning herself
assiduously into a rural housewife, growing vegetables,
making jam, chopping wood, talking of keeping a goat; while
Mary, who had always privately felt herself to be more
ineffectual and palely female than Olive, was here in a blitzed
house at night, responsible for no one but herself.

'She's doing some baby and post-natal clinics for the local
practice, isn't she? She told me she was going to.'

'Yes, she is, but it's uphill work, I think. They're a sticky
lot in Dorset'—he put on a mock-rural accent—'They've
only just about heard of contraception, and they think it's an
invention of the Devil to allow the village girls to be immoral
in peace. Which, of course, it is.' He laughed loudly in the
echoing house, and poured more claret into both their glasses.

Some time later, as she lay dreamily back on her chair with
her head against its hard back, she heard a new, strange noise
in the stairwell. An irregular, dispersed ticking.

'John . . . What is it?'

'That, my girl, is rain falling through the hole in the roof.'

'Oh—damn.'

'Quite. Oh well. Nothing we can do about it. At least we
seem to be having a quiet night . . . Mary?'

'Yes?'

'Why don't you come and lie beside me on this blanket?
It's warmer here, by what's left of the fire.'

Obediently, she did so. He settled a couple of the hard
examination-couch pillows under her head. The rain inten-
sified, pattering on the upper flight of stairs, on the delicate
mahogany banister-rail, occasional big drops penetrating
down on to the plaster dust in the hall near at hand. Lying
there listening to it was like being inside and outside at the
same time, as if the house itself had undergone some fundamental change in nature and everything else was altered too.
When he put his arms round her and kissed her for a long
time she did not resist.

'Mary darling . . . I think it would be nice if you took off
those dusty clothes you're wearing and came under this
blanket with me and let me love you.'

'Oh John—but I've got my period.'

'I don't mind that,' he said equably.

'But I do.'

As soon as she had said it, she was no longer sure. Did she mind? In truth, it had never occurred to her that at such a time one might—that civilised people would . . .

Lionel never . . . But from the thought of Lionel at that moment her mind side-stepped. No, she would not think about Lionel now. He had nothing to do with this. Nor had Olive. She put her arms round John, and held his compact, weighty body close to her.

But, evidently taking her at her word, or sleepy too, he contented himself with kissing her face for a while, then drifted off into insensibility, his head pillowed heavily on one of her breasts, his hand holding the other as David or Michael might clutch a stuffed toy.

PART FIVE

In September 1943, during the Salerno landings that were like the turning tide of the war, Mary went down to Herefordshire to stay with Dodie, Aunt May, and Dodie's little daughter Joanna.

The 'nice cottage' envisaged by Aunt May had not materialised, or only in a flimsy, make-believe form. The grandmother, mother and child (Uncle George had died after a stroke the previous year) lived in a clapboard construction in the grounds of the hotel, which was called the Cottage but was more a garden annexe. With an Indian-style verandah, it was pleasant in the fine, autumn weather in which Mary saw it, but she thought it must be cheerless in winter: the walls seemed paper-thin. There was a bathroom, with its own geyser, and a colony of spiders which were objects of grave interest to the almost-three-year-old Joanna, but there was no proper kitchen, only an electric kettle and a paralytically slow hot-plate. Lunch, the main meal, was regularly taken in the hotel dining room; the evening meal consisted of sandwiches sent over on a tray from the hotel kitchen and consumed in front of the one-bar electric fire. Dodie's sole culinary activity seemed to consist of making junkets and purées for Joanna, who did not appear to appreciate them much, preferring the hotel's Woolton Pie and ketchup.

To Mary, accustomed to the frenetic activity of wartime London, it seemed a curiously passive life. Of course it was, in its reduced way, all of a piece with Aunt May's preference for the service flat in Kensington; but one might perhaps have expected that Dodie would regard running a proper house as part of the motherhood role into which she had so wholeheartedly thrown herself? But, recalling Dodie's 'studio' and her pre-war dinner parties of delicatessen food, Mary realised that Dodie had never truly cooked or kept house, and anyway regarded the care and nurture of Joanna as a full-time occupation in itself.

She played with Joanna constantly, inventing games for her, telling her long serial stories, explaining things and admonishing her. Mary had to admit that, either in consequence or by a happy chance, Joanna was a rewarding child. Although a chubby doll in her smocked dress and matching hair-ribbon, she seemed much older than three; it almost came as a surprise to find she could not yet read. At first sight she was a miniature version of her mother at the age when Mary had known her—the same dark eyes and lustrous, curling hair, the same social precocity. But on more careful scrutiny the personality looking out from those eyes was different: she was more beetle-browed than Dodie, her mouth was fuller and different, her chin more determined. Mary was wary of seeing another family likeness by mere wishful thinking, but in fact there was no mistake about it: Joanna strongly resembled her dead Uncle Roland. Eventually, with hesitation—the name was so long unspoken—Mary mentioned this fact to Aunt May and Dodie. They agreed enthusiastically, and Aunt May added:

'She draws beautifully too, Mary, just like poor Roland . . . I sometimes do think, you know,' she added comfortably, 'that there *is* something in reincarnation. I know no one thinks much of Mrs Besant these days, but when I was a girl she was a *great* figure.'

The next hour or so was spent admiring Joanna's drawings, which, though infantile in conception, did indeed seem to have a flair for colour and form unusual in a small child. At no time was there any mention of Joanna's unknown father. It would have been unthinkable for Mary to wonder aloud if Joanna's talent, like her dark looks, could also be derived from him. She wondered if Joanna knew anything at all as yet about her father or even that children *had* fathers.

Most of the time Joanna behaved, in nursery parlance, 'beautifully', meaning that she chattered away to Mary about her huge family of teddies (which she seemed to prefer to dolls), said 'Please' and 'Thank you' and climbed into Mary's lap to show her a book. Then, at lunch in the hotel dining room where the one elderly waiter shuffled forgetfully among the resigned tables, Joanna threw a tantrum because she was not allowed to stir the mustard, and had to be removed, screaming, and trying to bite her grandmother's arm.

'I suppose now you'll think I've spoilt her,' said Dodie resentfully, flinging herself into a deckchair when Joanna had retired balefully for her afternoon 'rest', which seemed to consist of bouncing on her bed.

'No, I won't,' lied Mary. (She sympathised with Dodie. She had suffered the same thing herself sometimes with Charlie.) 'She's such a bright little thing and—of course you're marvellous with her, but she must get bored with no one to play with . . . Haven't you got a nice nursery school somewhere near?'

'Oh—not really.' Dodie wrinkled her nose. 'There's a convent that takes them in the mornings at four, but I'm not keen on that—all that Catholicism and so forth, and the nuns are said to be awfully strict and old-fashioned. Otherwise there's only the elementary school, and that's out of the question.'

'Oh? What a pity. Some of the country ones are quite nice, I believe. And when the war's over you could think again. How wonderful to be able to say that at last!'

'Oh, the village school's impossible, my dear, believe me. Full of the most ghastly slum evacuees. You wouldn't believe the trouble we've had—'

'Yes, I would,' said Mary firmly. 'You forget, Dodie, I work in an East End practice.' But it had already become clear that Mary's life in London, and indeed London itself, was without any interest or reality to Dodie these days. It was as if there had been some profound mental shift in her, paralleling the physical change that was more immediately apparent. One would never think, meeting her now, that she had spent years lunching at the Savoy, dancing at Quaglino's, dropping casually into Harrods as her local shop. It was not just that she had put on weight and let her once sleek black hair go untidily grey. The slightly gushing, stagey social manner of recent years had gone too—and that was a relief—but the grace, conscious or unconscious, that had always characterised the old Dodie had been abandoned as well. The woman who had once adopted, in succession, the gestures of the people to whom she had been attached, like a pretty child dressing up, now tramped around in flat brogues, sat with her legs apart and her skirt riding up, blew her nose copiously and then stared into her handkerchief. Her cotton frocks were almost aggressively crumpled, and bore the marks of Joanna's little shoes in her lap.

It was as if she had abdicated her role as desirable female in favour of her small daughter. It was a phenomenon Mary had often seen in working-class wives, who changed so quickly from bouncy girls into blowsy, tired drabs—but then they had good reasons. Dodie didn't. And in any case Dodie's attitude seemed, in a curious way, not to suggest the middle-aged woman she had physically become but a schoolgirl besotted with some hobby or passion. Coming down to Herefordshire, Mary had feared to find that Aunt May would be the one really in charge, with Dodie an irresponsible absentee mother, a prey to her old moods and instability. She had not been prepared for the possibility that Joanna would now be the sole topic on which Dodie would discourse with animation, not just the centre of her existence but the whole of it, its one point of reference. A tentative question as to whether she were writing anything these days had produced only a dismissive headshake, as if the very idea was inapposite.

Now Dodie was leaning forward to say earnestly, on the subject of schools:

'Mary, have you heard of the PNEU system?'

'Vaguely, yes. It's some sort of home tuition, isn't it?'

'Yes, and anyone can do it. I mean, you don't need to be a qualified teacher. They supply all the books and lesson-plans and test-papers and everything, from nursery age right up to School Cert. That's what I think I'm going to start Joanna with, next year.'

'But I thought that was meant for people living right out in the wilds with no school near—people on colonial stations and so forth?'

'I've told you, the schools round here aren't right for

Joanna. She's very highly strung, Mary. She may seem cheerful enough, but she has nightmares. Asthma too, sometimes, in winter. I don't want her picking up colds all the time . . . And I think I can teach her better than either the nuns or elementary school can. She and I do have a rather special relationship—as you must have noticed. Quite often, you see, we know what one another is thinking without having to say it.'

The intensity in Dodie's manner worried Mary slightly. She did not know what to think. She had always disapproved of the coldness and lack of interest in their small children among the British upper class, what she and Olive stigmatised as the 'Nanny-is-marvellous' syndrome: certainly one could not accuse Dodie of that. She said carefully:

'I don't doubt you could teach her very well, for the time being. She's obviously benefiting from all your lovely stories and games. But surely, Dodie, one sends a child to school not just for the lessons but for it to be with other children?' As she spoke a small shadow of personal guilt—Charlie—hovered in her mind. Such, such were the facile things she and Lionel had said to one another.

'Oh—she doesn't care for other children much,' said Dodie dismissively. 'They seem babyish to her, I think. *I* never did at her age either . . . Oh, Mary! I know all mothers dote on their children—well, nearly all—but Joanna *is* special. You can see that, can't you?'

The journey back to London on Sunday evening took many hours. At first Mary enjoyed the leisurely ride through the countryside just touched with autumn, where the corn was stooked in the fields and cows were being driven home for milking along lanes that no war had ever touched. This was a better moment than the same week four years ago—better than they had dared to hope. England was not, after all, in the hands of a German Gauleiter; London had not been destroyed. She and Lionel and nearly all their close friends were alive and working; the news from Italy was exciting. For the last month there had even been rumours about a Second Front being opened sometime soon in France. Putting Dodie out of her mind for the moment, she felt happy. When an American

211

soldier fell over her suitcase as they were changing trains at Swindon and knocked it over, she smiled forgivingly at him. He apologised as if he had done a real injury to some valued friend. But then Americans were often like that. She dismissed him, too, from her mind. Lionel, who had spent August studying the special problems of Belfast, was going to be in London this week: they might even manage to invite a few friends round for an informal meal as in the old days. The nights had been quiet recently. Vegetables were good and plentiful at the moment . . . She began to plan, and dozed off, waking with a jump to the sound of the loudspeaker at Reading where, unexpectedly, they had to change again.

The third train trundled slowly through the gathering dusk with its blackout drawn: Mary's carriage was uncomfortably crowded and stuffy. She went out into the corridor but that, as usual, was full of young sleeping soldiers, gross yet innocent-looking in the postures of death, sprawled over their kit-bags. She was about to return when an American voice spoke to her:

'Can I offer you my seat, ma'am?'

It was the young officer who had fallen over her case earlier. Or not so young, she now realised, looking at him. He was somewhere in his thirties, a beaky, dark face. He said insistently:

'I just came out to stretch my legs. I've got a seat in the next car. I'd like you to have it.'

'Well, it's awfully kind of you, but I've got a seat in there. I just came out myself to get away from the cigarette smoke.'

'Ah, mine's not a smoker. Follow me.' He set off purposefully down the corridor, so she followed. He installed her, disappeared to fetch her case—'I'll recognise it, after my mishap with it'—and determinedly made room for it on the rack. He then stood inside the carriage with his back against the door and settled down to talk to her, which she had not expected but realised that she should have. 'Oh damn,' she thought, torn between irritation and amusement, between a hint of a headache on the one hand and an inevitable sense of gratification on the other. 'He's trying to pick me up. Goodness. At my age.'

In fact, as she knew, she had changed little in the last

dozen years, and now looked younger than she was. In Dodie's thickened, unexercised company she had felt like a young girl.

His name was Laurie Brown, but when she tried a mild query about this solidly English surname he revealed that his father had assumed it because the family's real name was full of Js and Ks and Ws. He had, she observed, those odd, light eyes that dark-complexioned Russian Jews sometimes have, the legacy of some violating, non-Semitic ancestor, or a whole succession of them. He was from Philadelphia, a city that was nothing to her but a name. In peacetime he had been theatre and music critic on a Philadelphia evening paper, but he had also worked as a journalist in New York and in various other places. He spoke with great enthusiasm of cities, and asked Mary hopefully if she had read any Damon Runyon, but she had not. He was an amateur clarinettist, and had played at the Cotton Club in Harlem. He had also played at Preservation Hall in New Orleans. All this was strange to Mary. Her life and Lionel's had never contained much music, though neither of them was tone-deaf. Nor had she ever been to America. She could offer no opinions on most of what Laurie Brown said, but she listened, at first resignedly, then with mild pleasure; he had a warm, ingenuous manner that touched her—it was almost as if he believed he knew her already, but that of course was impossible—and his un-British desire to share interesting facts was one with which she sympathised. In between, he politely but insistently extracted from her full information about her work, about Lionel and his work, about her stay in Hereford, and finally about Charlie.

'Oh, Baltimore's not far from Philadelphia,' he said. 'If I get back there before the war's over maybe I could call on your stepson for you—take him a gift or something?'

'It's awfully kind of you . . .' How inadequate this sort of American made one feel. 'Are you—are you likely to go back there yet?'

'Well, I'm here till the New Year on a job, supposedly. But you never know.'

At Paddington, he offered to get her a taxi. It was notorious that taxi drivers favoured prospective customers wearing

213

American uniform. She explained that she lived near, and then of course he insisted on carrying her suitcase to Baker Street for her, through the warm wartime dark where the torches of pedestrians bobbed like fireflies. When they reached the block she said—a shade too firmly, as she realised afterwards, but she had been anxious about it as they walked along:

'I can't ask you up, I'm afraid.'

She left him to divine whether this was because Lionel was or was not at home (she did not in fact expect him till the next day), but Laurie Brown laughed and said at once, as if he were more aware than she in spite of his ingenuous air:

'I didn't expect you to. You've probably got a lot to do. I'll give you a call towards the end of the week, if I may?'

She did not refuse. He had shaken hands with her, and was briskly stepping away, when she said: 'But you don't know my name.'

'Yes, I do,' he said over his shoulder. 'Your professional name's stencilled on your briefcase—isn't it?—and what I take to be your married name is on the label of that valise of yours I had a good opportunity to examine. I'll be in touch, Dr Denvers.' And he saluted and departed, leaving her wordless. After a few paces his tall, leggy figure was covered by the dark, and yet she went on standing there, believing she could still see him striding away from her down Baker Street, a ghost of twenty-five years ago, unencumbered, happy, young.

Much later in their acquaintance, she had said to him:

'I thought—right at first—you were behaving as if you had a special purpose. As if you somehow knew, from the time we met—'

'—That we would be able to offer something to each other?' he suggested gently as she hesitated, inhibited by clichés.

'Yes. Yes, that's what I mean. But then I told myself that this was ridiculous. That nobody falls just like that for middle-aged lady doctors on station platforms—even in films it only happens to young girls—so I decided instead that you were simply behaving like Americans *do* behave when they're on

214

their own in a strange country and meet someone . . . mildly congenial. But I must say I was awfully impressed by your persistence.'

'I meant you to be. In fact, I don't usually behave like that.'

'I know that now.'

'I worried quite a lot that week,' he said. 'About whether, by the time I did ring you up, you would have thought better—or worse—of being friends with me. *I* knew I'd been pushy, and I had to be, but I didn't want you to think so . . . I was also afraid, because of the reputation GIs inevitably have over here, that you'd think I was just aiming to get into bed with you.'

She said, with difficulty: 'Laurie—I'm sorry I can't go to bed with you. It's just—Oh, the way things are. Or the way *I* am.'

'Okay, okay,' he said easily, though it was the first time the subject had been directly broached between them. 'I know, you're married, and I wouldn't want to upset that. We have a great time together, these evenings. I really enjoy your company, and if you want to leave it at that, it's fine by me.'

'It's not exactly that I *want* to leave it like that,' she said, struggling with two incompatible emotions in a way that was new to her. But he changed the conversation.

Afterwards, she felt displeased with her last remark. It was good of him not to press her, when it was so obvious that he, as a youngish and single man in a foreign country, would have liked to share one thing more with her than conversation, meals, drinks and walks around the evening streets. The least she could do, she decided, was to keep any conflict on the matter in her own mind and out of his sight.

She believed, in her fundamental innocence, that she herself thought of this man from another world just as a good—no, a dear—friend whose temporary company was enhancing her otherwise rather austere life. This, she said to herself, was one of the great bonuses of the war; not only had it jerked everyone out of their usual routine and given them other things to think about, it had brought together all sorts of people who would otherwise never have met. Laurie, with special American Forces access to tickets, took her to plays,

215

concerts and films to which she would not have thought of going; in return, she walked him round the battered City and East End on Sundays, showed him Spitalfields and Covent Garden market and the pubs by the river. They both enjoyed themselves a great deal, and Mary at any rate did not speculate on the intensity with which she experienced these officially innocent pleasures. Everything, with Laurie, was such fun. Nor did she ask herself why she had not introduced him to any of her friends—to John Hershey, for instance, or to the other woman doctor at the centre, or, come to that, to Lionel. Ian Napier had met him, but that was only because, when he could lay his hands on a Staff car, Laurie had sometimes come all the way down to Stepney to pick her up after the early-evening surgery. Ian lived in his own world of work; he would not gossip.

Laurie took her to restaurants which seemed lavish to her, though not to him on his large American salary, and in return she began cooking him supper sometimes in the Baker Street flat. For almost the first time since before the beginning of the war she found herself carefully planning menus, making quick dashes down to Soho on her bicycle in quest of some hard-to-obtain, mildly exotic commodity such as mushrooms or tomato paste. It was fun to do this for someone as appreciative and interested in food as Laurie. (Lionel never noticed much what he ate and had few dislikes or preferences, except for a taste for strong cheese acquired in France and an uncharacteristically sentimental attachment to tripe and onions, derived from his childhood.)

She did not reflect that she was behaving in every way like a woman in love, or dwell on the implications of the fact that she and Laurie were now seeing each other, or telephoning, almost everyday. After all, he was not in London for long, he would be off in the New Year, they must make the most of each other while they had the chance . . . She was, simply, happy.

So, as a more experienced woman than herself would have told her, eventually the evening came in the Baker Street flat when her finely balanced equilibrium between wanting and not wanting tipped suddenly, almost undramatically, as if this had already long been a foregone, though hidden, conclusion. All at once, it was too late for Mary to turn back from the course on which she and Laurie were set.

A memory that had bothered her intermittently for eighteen months chimed again in her head:

'*I've got my period.*'

'*I don't mind that.*'

'*But I do—*'

Cowardice, to seize on such an excuse, with such a person as John Hershey. Timidity and prudishness, anyway. A failure in giving, in understanding, at a moment when it had perhaps been important that she should give, should understand. Since then she had often felt ashamed, had regretted her ostensibly moral, decent refusal.

This time there was no such excuse, no false decencies, and there would be no regretting. Gladly and knowingly, she pulled off her clothes in the bathroom and went to join Laurie, who was lying on the divan in the spare room that had once been Charlie's.

'Did you know we would in the end?' she asked him a few days later. Laurie was a person curiously (to her) without prejudices or preconceptions; this accounted for both his innocent, heart-warming interest in everything about him and for a certain lack of direction she occasionally perceived in him. He had fallen into his music-and-theatre-critic post by accident and natural aptitude, after a string of other jobs in journalism all over North and South America. The war, his call-up and his eventual transfer to England had not come as a disruption but as yet another quirk of fate, another and potentially interesting new departure. When they had met on the train from the West Country he had been visiting Dorset to 'see where Hardy's people came from': since leaving school at sixteen he had read a great deal of English and European literature, much more than she had herself. Yet for a man of education, even self-acquired education, he seemed to her curiously without ambition; had he been drafted to North Africa or Italy he might never, he said, have bestirred himself to come to England at all. Living among colleagues with very clearly formulated goals, with life-structures and long-term plans, she found Laurie's lack of fundamental

217

attachments disconcerting. He had returned to Philadelphia, he said, after his mother was widowed, but she too was now dead. In his mid-thirties, he had acquired no wife, no child, and this she found strange too, having experience of how loving and cherishing he could be, how much pleasure he seemed to get from doing things together with her. So—

'Did you know we would sleep together in the end?' she asked, almost wistfully, trying to plumb such convictions as might exist in a life that was, by comparison with her own, so makeshift. He laughed, but said, apparently truthfully:

'Oh honestly, Mary, I don't know. Now of course it seems as if we were all the time travelling that way, from the first moment we met, but then that's the way life makes things look . . . Of course I won't deny that I hoped we would, from the start, because that's the way a man thinks—or I do. But I was *not* going to hustle you into it. Things have to be right, and if you'd never felt the moment had come, well then—it wouldn't have come. And that would still have been okay by me. I'm easy about these things. You may not believe that, because we haven't known each other that long, but believe me, it's true.'

'. . . *There's a time and place for these things, and you and I seemed to have so little of either . . . The last thing I want is to be any sort of impediment or problem to you*—' Words from another voice (yet not less dear) and another life. Without guilt, but with an anguished sense of the long-term truth of Lionel's words, she held Laurie to her.

The days and weeks passed for her in a new landscape. She, who had believed herself middle-aged, sensible, prosaic and almost tediously responsible and right-thinking, was a woman in love, a woman having an affair, and furthermore a woman capable of giving herself to more than one man at a time. How horrifying, even physically disgusting, she would have imagined this only a few months earlier—would have dismissed it as something, for her, unthinkable. Yet it was easy—easy if you loved them both. For the huge, unspoken presence of Laurie in her life did not make her value and appreciate Lionel any the less. Far from wanting to turn from him (as adulterous persons in novels traditionally did), she found to her surprise and relief that, on the rare occasions when he came to London, she felt, if not particularly close to him, at any rate gentle and loving towards him. Desire, and the desire to make another person happy, were not, it seemed, rationed. On the contrary.

The discovery appalled her a little, yet it released in her a strength on which she gratefully drew to help her in this new country of the emotions that she was inhabiting. For the first time she was experiencing the poignancy and intensity of a love without a prospect, and discovering that, contrary to a popular prejudice, love is not necessarily diminished by being denied a future. It may on the contrary, she thought, be the stronger, because it must exist on its own volition without any supporting structures. To what could she and Laurie look forward? Nothing—any alternative answer was still more intolerable to contemplate. So they lived consciously in the present, like people under threat of execution, savouring each day, each meal together, each expedition fitted in, each gift to one another, tangible or emotional.

'You give me so much,' he said to her, a number of times. She answered him in kind. One day it occurred to her how odd it was, considering that loving and giving were basic tenets of Christianity ('To give, and not to count the cost; to fight, and not to heed the wounds—') that conventional sexual morality was so heavily biased in favour of an unloving, ungenerous, self-protective stance. In her particular occupation, she thought, she should have given more and tougher-minded consideration to the subject before now; instead, she had just accepted the traditional moral package, watered down with a bit of mildly progressive charity. No longer, she told herself. She would have to rethink her assumptions.

Of course the basis of the traditional morality was the risk of pregnancy for the woman and the natural desire of men not to find themselves supporting other men's children. But then she and her colleagues were setting out assiduously to change that, weren't they? The overt policy of the Family Planning Movement was to earn respectability by catering strictly for the married, but if a woman came along to the centre claiming to be married Mary herself asked few questions, and she was sure many of the workers acted

219

likewise. She and her colleagues had always repudiated with genuine indignation the charge that the Movement was inciting immorality, or would 'destroy the sanctity of marriage'. Now she found herself wondering, with wry amusement and a dawning enlightenment, whether these critics were not actually right, if not in their moral indignation at any rate in their perceptions. Perhaps the presence of contraception as a fact of life was slowly but surely going to change not just people's life-style but their most basic assumptions about sexual behaviour? Would the generation of babies now being born look back one day with amused disgust on a society which prized coldness, ungenerousness and the refusal of experience and called that 'being good'? It was a disturbing but invigorating thought.

She communicated these ideas to Laurie, who smiled and did not disagree: his own open, unpossessive approach to these matters could hardly have co-existed with conventional morality. 'My main concern,' he said, 'has always been not to get anyone into trouble, or hurt them.' But, as if realising that this sounded glib, he added quickly, 'But that's a kind of cowardice too, I guess.'

She thought he was right, but was interested that he apparently knew it too, and lay for a while beside him in silence, thinking of its implications. His mind, however, was moving in a more practical channel, for after a while he said:

'For instance, I have always made sure, before, that a woman's got herself fixed up—you know—and if not then I take care for her . . . No, I know I didn't ask you, but in your job I reckoned I didn't need to.' There was an edge of question in his voice.

After a substantial pause she said, in as neutral a tone as she could manage:

'But you know I don't use a cap or anything. You're an experienced man, you must have realised.'

'Yes. It's puzzled me a little.' His tone too was neutral, restrained, as if he didn't want to trespass on her territory. 'It's also puzzled me a little,' he said after a while, 'that you don't have a kid of your own. We've never talked about that, so I figured you didn't want to . . . But perhaps now you do?' He was peculiarly sensitive to her mood, and to what she did

220

not say as much as to what she did. In his own uncommitted, undemanding way he accompanied her very closely. She sometimes felt that she had, privately and undramatically, been alone all her adult life till Laurie had come.

She told him about her failure to have a child—hers and Lionel's. He said at once, a simple central fact that she had known herself for years and had never wanted to face:

'But it may not be you at all. It may be him.'

'He fathered Charlie,' she said, prevaricating.

'Well, he was a younger man then, wasn't he? Things change.'

'They do. And I'm not a young woman any more, Laurie. Whatever the situation once, I think it's probably too late for me now anyway.' Another simple fact, which she had known since she had turned forty. But, again, actually to say it was amazingly painful.

After a while he said, not accusingly but with a wondering interest: 'You haven't yet come to the age at which it's out of the question—you don't need me to tell you that. And your body's still young . . . You're taking a risk with me, you know that, don't you?'

'Yes,' she said guiltily. 'Yes, I know, I'm sorry, it was wrong of me, but—oh, Laurie! I can't start using a contraceptive. Not now, after so many years of hoping. I *can't*—'

'Hey, I'm not asking you to. Far from it. Look at me, Mary, look—' She did so, and he said, holding her by both wrists:

'I said I'd always been afraid of getting someone into trouble, and that in some ways I'm a coward about these things—about relationships . . . But all I can say is, if you want a baby enough to risk one from me, and if by some chance it works and I give you one—no one would be prouder or more thrilled than me, even if it wasn't something I could ever tell to another soul . . . So there, ma'am, there's an offer for you I've never made to anyone before.'

They did not talk about it any more that night. But several times, over the weeks left to them, he reverted briefly to the matter, not with anxiety but as if the possibility, however remote, made him feel happy.

Once, however, he asked, calmly, as if he'd thought the

221

whole thing through: 'Would he accept it? . . . Or would it cost you your marriage?'

'I don't know,' she said with difficulty, disliking his ready-made phrase, trying to be honest: 'I think he might. He—he's a very good sort of person. But of course I couldn't necessarily expect him to.'

'I don't look anything like him, do I?'

'Not a bit—but how do you know?' She and Lionel had never kept photographs of each other around the flat; Lionel disliked such things.

'You showed me that snap of Charlie the people in Baltimore sent,' he said promptly. 'I could see he couldn't have anyone like me for a father. It would probably be equally obvious that my child wouldn't be your husband's. But I guess that's a bridge to be crossed if and when . . .'

She was a woman with her lover in the middle of a war, she was a woman who might—just might—still hope for a child. The implication for the future was enormous. Yet in other ways for her, as for so many people then secretly, similarly placed, the future did not, for the time being, exist. Contrary to the whole tendency of her life up till that time, she lived in the present, and was happy.

Laurie had once confessed to her a 'dread of scenes—a fear of people making demands on me I can't fulfil'. She had resolved never to make a scene: what right, indeed, she thought, had she to demand anything from him beyond what they now freely shared? None. Only once, as the year neared its end, did she let her resolve slip so far as to let him know how much she dreaded his departure.

'I'll be back,' he said.

'Really?' She had not known this. Perhaps he was just saying it.

'Almost certainly. In the spring, I should think . . . The Second Front is coming, you know.'

'We seem to have been hearing about it for so long I've rather lost faith in it.'

'It is coming, all the same.' He was a captain, with a liaison job; she knew that he probably had access to more information than she. She still dreaded the approaching moment when they must part. Everything seemed so uncertain.

But as Christmas came near a flu epidemic invaded London. She was ill for several days, and so rushed at work, once she had recovered, that even Laurie was a little displaced from her thoughts. The nagging, unproductive worry that Laurie's last few days in London would coincide with Lionel's return for a brief holiday was in the end solved with brutal completeness. Lionel's mother was ill, not with flu but with something with a more daunting name to speak: Lionel telephoned to say that he could not leave her, so two days before Christmas Mary travelled northwards on a train full of exuberant troops going on leave. They spent a sober Christmas and New Year in the small terrace house in the town where Lionel had passed his boyhood; and early in January they followed his mother's coffin to the big municipal cemetery nearby, accompanied by a sprinkling of old men with blue suits and flat caps who called Lionel 'lad'.

'I'm sorry you've been so mucked around the last fortnight,' said Lionel to her, as they walked back to the house they would now have to clear. 'I hope Ian's been able to cope without you and that you don't find too many crises piled up for you when you get back.'

'So do I. Ian's a great coper, as you know, but he had flu himself and wasn't looking a bit well when I left . . . Oh well, I'll find out on Monday.'

'Mary—it was good of you to come up here for all this. Ma did appreciate it, you know. Thanks.'

'Oh, Lionel,' she said, moved, and a little shocked. 'I couldn't *not* have come.' She meant, for his sake, rather than her mother-in-law's. How could she have left him to go through his mother's death and funeral on his own? The idea had not even occurred to her.

When she got back to London she found a loving but brief letter from Laurie, saying that he had been posted back to Washington 'for the time being' at forty-eight hours' notice.

She also found Ian Napier, in his surgery but shivering with fever, and even ready to admit himself that he ought not to be on his feet. She diagnosed pneumonia and had him admitted to their old hospital. The next two weeks were, for her, so exhausting that when at last she had a brief space in which to contemplate her own feelings she found that the moment of anguish had somehow passed. She was able to settle down with hopes for the spring, with only an ache of missing Laurie rather than a sharp pain.

Once she dreamed of him. At least, she thought it was him, but by the end of the dream it seemed to be someone else, instead or as well: the young registrar from St Jude's she had not seen for years. How odd, she thought, confusedly, that she had never noticed before that they were alike . . . But of course they were not, really.

At the end of January bombs began to fall spasmodically on London again. One of them destroyed a wing of the Mile End Hospital which was Mary and Ian Napier's 'local', and from which he himself had only recently emerged. There were innumerable practical problems, nothing to buy in the shops, and less goodwill than there had once been: after four years of war people were tired, tempers were short. For the first time Mary found herself hating and resenting the war, in spite of what it had brought her. And still the rumoured Allied invasion of Europe did not come.

Letters came from Laurie, not frequent but affectionate. She tried not to wait for them too longingly, not to build on them too much—for what, indeed, was there to build? There could, she told herself, be no castle in Spain, nor in Philadelphia nor anywhere. She read some Damon Runyon, and wrote to him about that.

She had not, of course, become pregnant. She felt both a deep-seated disappointment and a great relief.

In early April, when the weather had been unusually fine and dry, so that reservoir water was as short as every other commodity, Mary travelled down to Dorset to spend a weekend with Olive and the little boys. She had done this a number of times before and always found there refreshment and rest; the meandering journey on the branch-line train, during which she would begin to shed her London tenseness, the long ride in the station taxi, dropping other passengers off on the way, the final joyous arrival down the dark, unmade lane with Olive silhouetted in the lighted doorway to greet her. It was a thatched cottage, lit by paraffin lamps, with a wood-burning kitchen range. Much of the wood came from the forested slopes immediately behind the garden, where David and Michael spent their time, when not in school, playing elaborate games and building camps among the bracken. They at least, thought Mary, would have a wonderful childhood on which to look back. They were eleven and nine now. She was impressed by the way Olive, in spite of her yearning to be back at work in London, had resisted the temptation to send them to boarding school. Instead they went to a local prep school as day boys, departing with a farm milk lorry before eight in the morning.

'I don't approve of boarding school at this age,' Olive had said categorically. She added this time, as they sat before the kitchen fire, nursing bowls of her home-grown onion soup, 'John says it's the low, mollycoddling Continental influences in my background. I'm sure he's right. But.'

'Well, of course he'd like you in London with him,' said Mary, thinking, remembering.

'Yes, but . . . one's children do come first you know, Mary. They have to, biologically. David's been giving himself independent airs recently, which I daresay is good, but he's still a little boy needing maternal care, and Micky's a baby as yet—wanting to be cuddled at bedtime and so on. Oh, they'd cope without me, I daresay, like those poor little boarders at the school have to, but it would be bad for them and why should they? There'll be plenty of time when they don't need me so much any more and this war, please God, is over, for John and I to have fun together on our own. How is the poor old boy, by the way? You see a lot more of him than I do at the moment, and his letters are always so scatty that I can never tell *what* he's up to. He will write to me on prescription pads, and the other day I got someone's script for M and B, all muddled up with stuff about the centre and about a patient asking him to come and deliver her cat's kittens.'

'Oh yes, I heard about that. I told him he should do it and then send in his usual bill.' Mary paused, momentarily wondering what to say. Her private opinion of John was that, like many people in London these days, he got through his excessive workload by smoking and drinking more than was good for him. As a doctor with many well-placed patients he was more able to indulge in tobacco and alcohol than were people who had to depend on rationed supplies. And, as her own experience had broadened her view of other people's probable private lives, she had concluded that John was not very likely to be spending all his nights alone. She did not feel like saying any of this to Olive, and perhaps after all there was nothing to worry about that would not come right when times were different anyway. She said:

'Well, he misses you of course. We all do. But then a lot of people miss a lot of others these days. It just has to be borne . . . I think you have the harder time, Olive, all in all.'

Olive was thinner these days. Her once-delicate white skin was a little weather-beaten, but she looked fit and well. Though her hands were roughened by gardening, chopping wood and milking goats on chilly mornings, her dark eyes and hair were those of a still pretty and desirable woman. But now, as each time Mary had come, she sensed a deep-seated frustration in her friend, not a resentment but a chronic, long-term impatience for this self-imposed exile to be over. The physical tasks with which she filled her days were not, Mary had come to understand, just a courageous response to wartime shortages or a way of providing herself with more challenges; they were also a means by which Olive got rid of the insatiable, unfulfilled physical energy that burned away somewhere inside her.

'How are you getting on with the Mafia?' Mary asked. 'The Mafia' was Olive's name for the local medical practice, whom she was grudgingly allowed to assist.

'Oh—a bit better, I think. I've got District Nurse very much on my side these days, which helps because they daren't offend *her*, and even that old fool Carey tolerates me more amiably now that I help him over the rape cases.'

'Rape? Here?' Mary thought of the tiny station where she had arrived, and of the village with one shop and pub a mile distant, of the taxi driver who knew everyone and of the deep, deep quiet of the fields and hills under the veil of night. She said with a small giggle:

'I wouldn't have thought rape was a great feature of life in Little Trenthyde.'

'Well, no, not an outstanding activity,' agreed Olive drily. 'But we've got this GI camp, so-called, up beyond the forest—actually they're Canadians, but the village people don't make the distinction—and the men come down to the pub and to dances in the church hall. They've got transport, of course, and money, and they *are* glamorous, many of them, I must admit. The local girls get swept off their feet, literally. They allow themselves to be taken up into the woods for what they think is just going to be a bit of a cuddle, but the men have other ideas and won't stop there, and I must say I don't entirely blame them. They're only young themselves, most of them, and they probably think it's what the girl expects, whatever she says. Then, a day or two later when the girl has thought about it, and sometimes told her Mum or a friend, she comes along to us all upset with a tale of rape. Naturally, by that time it's rather hard to substantiate—which in itself shows you that it's not out-and-out assaults that we're dealing with. So my role is to receive them sympathetically but to discourage them from pressing a charge. I tell them just to pray they're not pregnant. Carey, of course, wants me to give them moral lectures, but I tell him I'm a doctor, not a preacher; it isn't my job to encourage that sort of false-morality-after-the-event. Which is what most of these rape charges really amount to.'

'London's packed with Americans and Canadians too, these days,' said Mary self-consciously. 'But of course it's harder to rape someone in Hyde Park, and anyway I suppose London girls are more sophisticated.'

'They're not all virgins here,' said Olive, 'but they're hopelessly innocent, most of them. The men talk about love, and promise to marry them quite often, and the poor little saps believe them. Of course once a man gets posted away the girl doesn't usually hear from him again. It's the old thing—that what happens in a foreign country doesn't count, from his point of view. He's seen his chance and taken it and that's all there is to it, for him.'

Mary looked across to her leather shoulder bag (a present from Laurie) which was lying on the kitchen table. In it were Laurie's last two letters, in one of which he referred to the likely possibility of his returning soon to England. Travelling down in the train she had felt an uncertain desire to tell Olive—something—if not everything, about Laurie. She so longed to speak of him to someone, and who else but Olive, so dear, so separate from London, so absolutely discreet? She might even tentatively suggest bringing Laurie down here for a weekend . . . But she saw now that it was out of the question.

'*Olive . . . I slept with an American myself during the autumn.*'

'*Olive, I'm helplessly in love with him . . .*'

—No, no, unthinkable. She felt chilled and obscurely deflated. Her own private, magic joy and suffering was abruptly presented back to her in commonplace guise. Why should Olive speak of what might, after all, be momentous human relationships of lasting import, with such casual cynicism? Because that was just the traditional tone everyone did adopt when talking about local girls and Yanks? Or for some reason more personal to herself, some disappointment, some frustration. ('They *are* glamorous, many of them, I must admit.') On an impulse, she said:

'Do you have anything to do with the Canadians yourself, Olive? With the officers, I mean?'

Olive stared at her sharply, then laughed, as if deciding to treat the question as a joke.

'Mary, if you knew village life you wouldn't ask that! My dear, one can't sneeze here without the milkman telling the postman and the postman telling the Garage and the Garage telling Mrs Garage and then the whole WI knows, and next thing Mrs Randolph at the big house is ringing me up to ask impertinent questions. I'm inevitably well-known here, from the practice, and if I took to hobnobbing with Canadian officers—even respectably in the pub—village gossip would have one or more staying here at night with me before I'd time to say "Have this round on me"! No, I just have to be Caesar's wife. No option. Hey ho! John can sleep quiet at nights . . . Which I suspect he does *not*, entirely, knowing Johnny, but let's not go into that.' And she sprang up restlessly—a thin, even elegant figure in her old blue slacks, to shift a saucepan of vegetable peelings that was simmering on the stove for the chickens.

The dangerous moment passed. Neither of them said anything further on the subject.

On the Sunday they took a picnic lunch up into the sunlit

228

woods, where pale primroses were bunched in the clearings and the bare branches of the larches and birches were already developing a fuss of green. It was amazingly warm. The boys refurbished last autumn's camp, then ranged the woods seeking birds' nests, real or imaginary. The two women spoke of Charlie, and Olive said warmly:

'When this bleeding war is over, you and Lionel and John and I must take all three boys off on a holiday together again—like the Isle of Wight that time, remember?'

'It would be lovely.' Mary hesitated. 'But by the time he comes home Charlie may be grown up, you know. They seem to grow up so fast in the States. And he's fifteen now.'

'God, is he? I hadn't realised. Yes, he must be, I suppose . . . Well, at least it looks now as if the war will be over before he's call-up age. That must be a comfort to you and Lionel.'

'Yes,' said Mary quietly. 'It is.'

If Charlie had to go to war I would find it unbearable. Why, when he is absent anyway? I don't know. But I would.

Because he would get killed—Charlie, so vulnerable, so foolish, so insufficiently cherished?

Yes. Because he would get killed. Another one.

With a lump in her throat, she said: 'I usually write to him on Sunday evenings. I'll probably do it on the train. I'll send him your love, shall I?'

'Of course. And the boys', if he remembers them.'

Love . . . such an ambiguous word. Such a frail and ultimately ineffectual thing to send on thin paper across the Atlantic. For years on end.

As Mary was collecting together the few things she had brought with her and putting them into her case Olive came to the door of the small, oak-beamed spare room.

'Mary . . . I've been meaning all the weekend to ask you . . . What do you think of this little lump?'

She was standing with her blouse undone. As Mary, instantly alert, approached her, she looked away.

'I don't think, myself, it's anything much,' she said in a casual tone. 'Look—left side . . . Yes, there . . . I just thought I'd get another opinion, and who better than yours.'

Mary carefully palpated Olive's rather large, still beautiful white breast. The lump in question was not, as Olive said, obviously alarming to the touch. 'It feels more like a nodule to me,' Mary said uncertainly.

'Yes, that's what I thought.' Olive's tone was over-eager, emphatic.

'But one can never be sure. And I don't like diagnosing friends—I find it difficult for some reason. Have you got anyone local you can consult whose opinion you trust?'

'Huh, I'm not showing it to Carey,' said Olive, buttoning her blouse. 'He's the sort of old fool who'd recommend radical mastectomy "to be on the safe side". Honestly, Mary, he's the limit; he's always telling patients they ought to have their teeth out as a cure for constipation or something, and he sends people off to the cottage hospital to have their perfectly healthy appendixes removed.'

'No, *not* old Carey.' Olive seemed, not surprisingly, a bit obsessional about him. 'Haven't you anyone good in Dorchester—or Bournemouth? Oh, I forgot; the coast's forbidden to civilians now, isn't it?'

'Yes. I think I'd rather see someone in London anyway, being a London girl. Oh well, I shall just have to organise myself up there again for a day and a night, won't I? What an effort. It's not the boys that are the problem, it's the chickens and the goats.'

'You do that,' said Mary firmly, but not convinced that Olive would. She had had experience before of doctors who would not themselves follow the good advice they would give to a patient. She decided that she would mention the matter to John and so get him to put pressure on Olive, even if it worried him and even if Olive were annoyed with her afterwards for breaking a confidence.

But Olive did not come up to London just then because, later in the month, civilian rail travel was at first restricted, then virtually banned. The Allied invasion of France was imminent, everyone knew it; it hovered in every conversation as an unspoken fact, a momentous reality that had as yet no date, locale or even a name.

Mary thought sometimes of Olive, and worried about her a little. But not as much as she might have done. Because

230

Laurie had suddenly returned to London, and nothing else now, compared with his presence, seemed quite real.

The Normandy landings began in the first week of June. Day and night, army convoys rumbled towards the coast. But London was still full of American and Canadian forces who were not scheduled to go 'over there' just yet, and Laurie was among them.

Later that month a new kind of bomb began falling on London. They were flying-bombs, V1s technically, pilotless rockets that appeared without warning and were as likely to come by day as by night. Londoners soon learnt that if the machinery was still roaring the bomb would pass harmlessly overhead: 'When the engine cuts, it's time to duck' was the sporty slogan bandied about. Most of the bombs landed south of the river; those that got as far as central London were very likely to cut out overhead, by which time, Mary and her neighbours wearily concluded, it was rather late to take effective cover. There was little rhythm in these attacks; you could not, if you were busy, spend your life running down into the shelters. Like many other people, Mary ignored the flying-bombs and hoped for the best. She particularly disliked the nights, however, when suddenly the peace would be broken by an approaching chugging noise which grew louder and louder like an express train in the sky; many of these nights Laurie now kept her company.

'Oh dear,' she said, gradually releasing her grip on him as another train roared 'safely' off into the skies above Swiss Cottage or Hampstead, 'I'm glad you're here, but I do hope our mangled bodies won't be found inextricably entwined when this building receives a direct hit.'

'Oh, I don't know,' said Laurie placidly. 'Not a bad way to die, if one must—in fact, I can't think of a better way than in your arms. Anyway,' he added, 'I expect someone would tactfully separate us before calling up our relatives . . . Such situations must happen a bit these days, you know.'

'You really aren't afraid of death, are you?' she said, envying this man who gave no hostages to fortune. He said at once:

'No, I've no problem there—but I'm afraid of being old. I

231

told you I'm a coward really. Being old and decrepit—not being able to run any more, or do this . . . I just can't imagine how I'm going to face it.'

'Perhaps you won't ever have to,' she said, an instant fear igniting within her. Fairly soon he too would be going over to France.

But neither Mary nor Laurie was killed by a flying-bomb.

In early July, Olive at last got up to London to see her chosen specialist; she telephoned Mary in Stepney. She and John were going to dine out with his parents that night, she said. Her appointment was for the following morning, and since it would be Mary's afternoon for the Centre they agreed to have lunch together near Baker Street. 'I'll ring again in the morning to find out what time you look like being through with surgery,' said Olive happily. 'I must say, it's lovely to be here.'

But at eleven the next morning, when Mary was busy inspecting tonsils, pregnancies and minor injuries caused by flying glass, it was not Olive who rang but John Hershey. And it was not to say that Olive was looking forward to her lunch with Mary, but to tell her that their Kensington house had been hit the previous night while he himself had been out on a call. Olive and the elderly housekeeper had both been killed outright.

Later that afternoon it was Mary who set out with John in his car on the long journey down to Dorset, to break the news to his children, his and Olive's. Olive had arranged for them to stay in the boarding house at their school during her two days' absence.

'I suppose you'll leave them there for the time being?' Mary asked, as they drove through Dorchester. John just nodded miserably.

'. . . Oh, they'd cope without me, I daresay . . . But it would be bad for them, and why should they? . . . Micky's a baby as yet, wanting to be cuddled at bedtime . . .'

'. . . There'll be plenty of time when the war's over for John and I to have fun together . . .'

She set her jaw, but tears rolled down her face.

John had to return to London the following morning. Mary, at the pressing invitation of the headmaster and his wife, who seemed out of their depth in tragedy, stayed on another two days. Ever afterwards, her main memory of that time was of walking dusty field paths beside tall wheat, with David going on ahead swishing a stick and Michael clinging wordlessly to her hand. Once again, she was a substitute mother; once again she knew the inadequacy of the role.

From the headmaster's study she telephoned Laurie to tell him when she would be back in London. He was in an office, so she did not expect an intimate conversation with him, but something particularly monosyllabic and strangulated in his speech made her suddenly ask:

'Laurie—has it come? Your order to go?'

'Yes. It has.'

'When?'

'Tonight. I was just going to write you a letter.'

'Please do that anyway, Laurie,' she said, after a pause. He said he would.

She was conscious of trying to handle her distress almost physically, as if it were some great beam laid across her that she could barely support.

She wondered afterwards if he had known for some time his likely date of departure, had known it anyway by their last night together, and had not told her because he could not face her distress. But then he, too, could not have foreseen it would turn out to be their last.

So, in the weeks that followed, Mary grieved for both her friend and her lover, and each grief seemed to impinge on the other, complicating it and yet not displacing it, leaving no place of refuge. To the one absence she had, incredulously, to give the name 'death', to the other simply 'away in France', yet in terms of life as it is actually lived both absences were, and were not, death: both were unassuageable. She grieved alone.

Finally, at the end of August, just after the news had come that Paris was liberated, when John was with his boys in Dorset, she and Lionel went on a brief holiday to the Lake District. Lionel was, she realised, looking horribly tired. He was a little remote from her, as so often these days, but kind and considerate, and the holiday seemed to do him good. For the first time in years they began making tentative plans for 'after the war'.

In the next twelve months people began to come home.

Willie appeared from France just before Christmas 1944. Earlier in the war Mary and Lionel had received notification that he had been released from his internment camp under licence, but had heard nothing further. Now they learnt that he had been living in the South of France among a group of other British exiles, who had settled on the Riviera years before for the good of their health.

'Which can't have done the poor old things any good at all,' said Mary. 'I wonder if Willie will be very thin. I believe food's been very short in the south . . . I wonder, come to that, what he's been living on.'

She rang Dodie in Herefordshire, who said testily:

'Mother and Joanna and I are Willie's only real relatives, so far as I know, but he always seems to put your name down as next of kin. I suppose he thinks of you and Lionel as *responsible people*. No, I haven't heard anything about him arriving, and frankly, my dear, you're welcome to him. I'm up to my eyes: Joanna's got whooping cough—it's been quite an ordeal.'

Mary commiserated, suppressing the reflection that this wasn't a *very* serious illness in an otherwise healthy child past babyhood, and rang off. It was apparent to her that she and Lionel would probably have to have Willie for Christmas. She nerved herself to show kindness to a physically broken and emotionally cowed refugee.

But neither broken nor cowed did Willie turn out to be. Physically he had changed a good deal, but if anything he was a little plumper than he had been before. Balding in 1939, he had lost most of his hair and seemed older than forty-four, but this was not so much due to his looks as to his manner. His war experiences had changed him, but far from making him 'more human' (a hope warily expressed by Lionel) they seemed to have turned him from an offhand twentieth-century intellectual into a pompous and slightly arch old gentleman of the previous century. Mary and Lionel, discussing him with weak humour in the privacy of their

234

bedroom (he lay in Charlie's old room at the end of the hall), could only conclude that he had adopted this pose as a protective colouring during his internment and that it had stuck.

It was also true—Mary remarked that one was always hearing it but that she had not fully realised the fact till this moment—that the social changes wrought by the war in England had been profound. The term 'pre-war' was now being used, in a wistful or condemnatory tone according to the speaker's views, to indicate not just an historical epoch but a whole way of life and assumptions that had gone and probably would not return. Willie, having spent his war isolated from all this accelerated change, in the bosom of an elderly expatriate community who still thought of London in terms of top-hats, muffin-men and 'pea-soupers', was as fossilised in his views as a Rip Van Winkle returning to the world, not five, but twenty-five years later. On every side things shocked him: the queues, the regulations and the way neither money nor an upper-class accent could assure extra privilege, the lack of servants in people's homes and 'all these women running about the streets in trousers', whom he seemed to regard as personally taunting him. He had developed a bad cold, and could not seem to understand why no one was more interested in it. He left electric fires burning, used soap lavishly, and helped himself to food in the kitchen while Mary was out without apparently realising that almost nothing was unrationed. When Mary pointed this out to him he said mournfully:

'My dear, you must forgive me. I'm simply *not* used to all this. Socialism, as you know, has never been my thing, and I quite thought we were fighting for freedom, not for Lord Woolton and Messrs Strachey and Shinwell.'

'Don't be silly, Willie, it's nothing to do with Socialism,' said Mary crossly, conscious of a half-lie. 'I know it's all strange to you, but you really must try to be a bit more aware of the situation.'

'You mean I must "muck in" and "do my bit",' said Willie with heavy irony. His eyes glinted behind his glasses. Mary thought: he's enjoying this. At some level he's playing a game. Why?

'Willie,' she said boldly, 'Lionel and I have been wondering: what did you use for money in the South of France? I mean, it must have been very difficult for you—'

'Oh my dear—' He waved a hand in his old cigarette-holder gesture, as if dismissing yet another wartime sordidness. 'One has one's resources. As you know, I've always been interested in pictures and china, and when I was in Paris that winter and spring before the Germans arrived I did quite a bit of useful buying. A lot of people were wanting to sell stuff then, you see . . . And then, when the commandant kindly got me released from that boring camp—a most cultured fellow, my dear, quite the best sort of German, I must tell you about him—I managed to continue the good work.'

'Buying and selling?' asked Mary, puzzled. Surely this was difficult for a foreigner in an occupied land.

'Well, *advising* really. Putting people in touch with people . . . People are always glad to have a knowledgeable person to help them. And you'd be surprised at how much taste and interest in nice things some of the German officers had. Most cheering.'

'In other words,' said Lionel furiously when this was retailed to him, 'your cousin Willie has been buying Limoges dinner services cheap from French Jews selling up because they were on the run and selling dear to gullible German Gauleiters. Who, no doubt, wined and dined him. No wonder he was eager to get out of France quickly when he was offered a convoy! I should think he got out just in time. And if he's not careful he'll get prosecuted here under the Trading with the Enemy Act.'

'He's not actually my cousin,' Mary pointed out irrelevantly after a pause.

'Then all the more reason to shift him from this flat as quickly as possible,' said Lionel with ruthless logic.

'Oh dear, yes. I'm inclined to agree with you. But I think you may be wrong about him, all the same. Willie isn't Machiavellian or evil. He can even be quite kind. He wouldn't do someone down deliberately. It's more that he's amoral, and very ignorant really, for all his worldly ways. He *is* human, in the most ignoble way. He's silly, basically. He always was.'

'Silly or not, the less you and I see of him the better . . . Can't he go off to Dodie again? They always seemed two of a kind.'

'Well, I'll suggest it, but I don't think Dodie will want him. Not till that awful cold he's got is better anyway . . . Still, Aunt May probably has a soft spot for him, so I expect they'll take him in.'

She asked Willie his plans the following day, but added that of course Dodie was rather wrapped up in Joanna these days. Willie looked puzzled.

'Joanna? Joanna? I'm not quite familiar, as you know, with the cast of all these domestic dramas that have been enacted in my absence. Who is "Joanna"? Another of our Dodie's bosom friends, I suppose?'

Mary stared at him in amazement. Then it dawned on her. Of course, Joanna's birth, indeed Dodie's pregnancy, had not been manifest till after Willie was back in France. There was no reason why he should have known anything about Joanna if no one had happened to mention the child to him since his return, and apparently no one had. She hastened to explain.

An expression of what appeared to be genuine disgust and distaste spread across Willie's face. He looked like a man confronting a decomposing dog, or the evidence of an uncontrolled attack of vomiting. 'What a perfectly ghastly story,' he repeated several times in an undertone, looking round as if Joanna's existence were a secret and a stranger might be lurking on the landing. Mary felt extremely irritated; she herself had been shocked at the somnambulistic way Dodie had gone about the business, but she could hardly say so if Willie were going to adopt this old-maidish attitude at the mere thought of an illegitimate child. Instead, she said, conscious of a slightly fatuous briskness in her tone which belied her real thoughts:

'Thousands of people have to bring up children without fathers, Willie. Dodie's got money of her own and is otherwise just in the position of any war widow now. Presumably she passes herself off as one. It's the obvious thing to do, in the circumstances.'

'My dear . . . Of course you're right, you're so sensible, you

237

always were, but—*really*. What a sordid little tragedy . . .
And you mean to say that poor Aunt May has taken it all
on the chin? I can hardly believe it. Of course one knew
that standards have slipped appallingly during the war, but
still—'

Mary lost her temper.

'Willie, how *dare* you refer to a four-year-old child as a
"sordid little tragedy". Have you no perception of what
actually matters in life and what doesn't?' A confused consciousness of her own unfulfilled hopes with Laurie seethed
within her. She knew that buried emotions were fuelling her
anger, and that she was to some extent being unfair to Willie,
but she snapped:

'Lionel is right; you really are a defective human being.'

After that, there was nothing left for Willie but to remove
himself from the flat which, to do him justice, he attempted.
She heard him telephoning friends and acquaintances in a
subdued tone, and blowing his nose in between. But London
was full to overflowing; he evidently failed to billet himself
anywhere, and by evening in any case his cold was so bad
that Mary felt she must be kinder to him and assure him he
could stay. That evening he had an alarming asthma attack.
It seemed that the ailment which Lionel had never believed
of Willie was real after all.

Mary slipped out herself to get him some ephedrine at the
all-night chemist in Wigmore Street. When she returned she
found him still wheezing, but calmer. His face was clammy
and there were dark rings round his eyes. 'He really isn't at
all well,' she said to Lionel in their bedroom.

'I know. I did what I could for him. Asthma's an odd
thing . . . Did he tell you, Mary, about his being beaten?'

'God, no—when?'

'In the internment camp, I gather. Or on the way there.
He wasn't entirely clear. He was very distressed when he
decided to tell me, but it's true all right—he's got the marks
of it, all this time after.'

They looked at one another. Mary felt a sickened distaste
as at something obscene—a reaction not so very different,
she later reflected, from Willie's reaction at the thought of
Joanna's birth. Of course, beating was always obscene. But it

seemed to have an extra edge of horror to it when the victim was someone as squeamishly over-civilised as Willie. How had it come about, had it gone on for long, had he cried out—? She did not like him any better for the information, but she felt a shocked, embarrassed pity for him. She also felt that she must have failed him in some way, if he had been forced in the end to confide in Lionel, whom he feared, rather than in herself.

'I think he's near some sort of breaking point,' said Lionel suddenly. 'We'd better keep an eye on him.'

But the next day Willie was much better, and three days later, with his cold reduced to a self-pitying cough, he was almost his dapper self again. Not long after that he managed to acquire the loan of a two-roomed flat in Bloomsbury from a friend who had fled from the V2s, the newer and nastier form of flying-bomb.

'Oh, that'll be convenient for you,' said Mary, genuinely glad for him.

'Well, of course it's madly convenient for the BM, and I hope to get some reading done there. But, my dear, North Gower Street—!'

'Lionel lived near there for years, before we were married,' said Mary coldly, forgetting her good resolutions. It was clear to her that for some reason Willie regarded the very name 'North Gower Street' as a joke, like 'Barker's Bargain Basement' or 'Potters Bar': she heard him telling people on the phone—

'My dear, I've found a little nest for myself in *North Gower Street* . . . A governess I had once hailed from there. It makes me feel quite sentimental.'

When he left their flat he gave her and Lionel a beautiful small picture by a French Post-Impressionist that he claimed to have 'picked up the other day for very little, my dears'. He was an enigma. She tried to dismiss him from her mind; not entirely successfully.

In the summer, after the bonfires and the illuminations of VE Day, the children began to return from America. Among them was Charlie.

'Children' a lot of them no longer were. Like many other

parents who had waved goodbye to small boys in shorts or to little girls in neat cotton frocks and hair-ribbons, Lionel and Mary found themselves receiving back a near-adult with an American accent and outlook. Charlie turned up at Victoria Station wearing a crew-cut, Trilby hat and plus-fours, which were evidently the Hannakers' misguided conception of what a sixteen-year-old British boy might wear. He was as tall as Lionel and rather more stooped. Mary, who went to meet him, failed to recognise him at first, and he, more woundingly, failed to recognise her. It was clear that his British childhood seemed to him dim and unreal.

He also made it clear, almost as soon as they had returned 'home', that he was not a kid and was not going to be treated like one; the matter seemed to be on his mind. Tales had filtered back to America of British 'teenagers' (as they were apparently called) being a deprived and oppressed section of the community, condemned to school uniforms, caning and early bedtimes; Charlie lost no time in explaining to Mary that he and the Hannaker boys had been used to doing 'pretty much as we liked', that he had held a driving licence, that he smoked, that 'dating girls' had been a regular part of his life, and that trips with 'the gang' to the glittering casinos of Atlantic City were a routine matter to him.

It would have been easier, thought Mary distractedly, to cope with his determined bid for adult status if he had been mature for his age, but she presently realised that his gangling limbs concealed a boy not very different from the cocky, nervous eight-year-old she remembered so well. His would-be sophistication did not extend as far as attempting to conceal his boredom and loneliness. He lounged interminably about the flat, great feet on chairs, infuriating Lionel by chewing gum and by belittling the British contribution to the war as opposed to the American. Nor did he hide his contempt for the dull, stodgy meals which were all that could be produced, most of the time, on 1945 rations. His yearning for steaks and hamburgers, big glasses of milk, Coca-Cola and orange juice was obviously real and almost physically painful to him. He seemed to have no ambitions, beyond going back to America again as soon as possible; he did not noticeably read, and had no interest in medicine or science. He and

Lionel had nothing in common—except a degree of obstinacy and contentiousness. Though Lionel, in London on holiday, escorted him to museums and films and tried to interest him in the Labour victory in the General Election, it was clear to Mary that their lack of sympathy for one another was turning into something near to dislike.

For her, irritation with the awkward, argumentative boy was shot through with love, sometimes at unexpected moments. There was something in Charlie's would-be fierceness, and in his way of moving, that was like Lionel— but it wasn't just that; presently she realised who else he was evoking for her, by his accent and the very words he used. The Hannakers had done their duty by him, according to their lights, and sometimes he could be almost ceremoniously polite in a way that contrasted touchingly with his gaucheness at other times. He carried parcels, opened doors, called his elders 'Sir' and 'Ma'am' with an unselfconscious flourish. When, once or twice in a brief moment of joke and relaxation, he called Mary 'Ma'am', her heart moved, and she knew from what other source the love she felt for him was springing.

One day she asked him:

'Didn't an American friend of mine—of ours—once call on you in Baltimore?' She knew that Laurie had done so, between his first and second time in England. She longed, simply, to speak of him, and to hear Charlie do so. But Charlie just said in a bored voice:

'Oh—yeah. He was in the Army, wasn't he? He didn't stop long. I had to go out anyway. I had a date.' As if struck with homesickness at the very thought, he looked miserably out of the window at the wet, Sunday expanses of Marylebone Road, then picked up from the sofa a comic she had seen him looking at on and off half the morning.

He must, said Lionel categorically, continue with some sort of education, however much he protested; dammit, the boy seemed barely literate. In the end, as the autumn term arrived, they sent him off to the mildly progressive co-educational boarding school in the north which John Hershey was considering for his own boys when they reached thirteen. 'I'll get him in for you,' said John, and did. He'd been at school himself with the headmaster. John could usually arrange things.

It was little more than a year since Olive's death, but the Hershey family had, at any rate on the surface, recovered. Perhaps they had been helped by the acceleration of time that war brings, piling new events up as a barrier against the old. David and Michael were boarding in Dorset, and in the holidays were shared around between Hershey and Shapira relatives. Mary would have liked to do more for them, but was not really in a position to, and felt that perhaps she was not needed anyway. For some months John had drunk and smoked more heavily than ever, and on one never-after-wards-mentioned evening he spoke of guilt and regret, and wept in Mary's arms. But now he seemed cheerful enough again, even ebullient. He had begun to mention a 'friend' called Myriam, so it did not come as a surprise to Lionel and Mary when they were invited out to dinner to meet her.

The restaurant was expensive, and crowded with vaguely well-known faces; the meal was excellent in spite of the nominal price restriction in force. Myriam herself was elaborately dressed and made-up and enthusiastic about everything. She was a nurse in a private nursing home, it seemed, a war widow with no children. John, sweating and beaming, exerted himself to the utmost to make sure these guests, about whom he cared so much, all enjoyed themselves, and more or less succeeded.

Walking home afterwards through the streets of the West End where now, at last, the buildings shone with lights again, Lionel said:

'Well, I suppose she's quite suitable really.'

'That's called damning with faint praise,' said Mary drily. The good wine they had drunk tasted sour in her throat. She realised that she felt very depressed.

'What would you rather I said? . . . I've never been attracted to gushing, over-dressed ladies of a certain age myself, but that's beside the point. John's always had slightly flamboyant tastes.'

'Olive wasn't in the least flamboyant,' said Mary painfully. Having said it, she realised what it was that had lent such a peculiar colour to the evening; although Myriam's style was quite different from Olive's, physically they did resemble one another. Markedly, in fact.

'No, but their house was pretty opulent, and so were a lot of their social circle . . . Remember their wedding? That's his background, and Myriam fits in, I suppose.'

After a pause, Mary said hesitantly: 'She's not *nasty* or anything, of course.'

'Quite.'

'And I suppose we must make up our minds to like her for John's sake. And the boys'.'

'Quite.'

Early in 1946, Mary left Ian Napier in Stepney. A new young man, fresh from the RAMC and married to a nurse, had joined the practice; Mary felt she should go now before she became involved in Ian's visionary post-war plans for a Health Centre that would be part of the rebuilt East End which was supposed to rise triumphantly from the ashes of the old. She was tired of general practice—and, after six years, just tired. The expansion that the war had interrupted was planned at the Paddington Centre, now back in the original premises. She decided to concentrate her energies there, and otherwise to do something she had been promising John Hershey for years that she would do, and start a private practice. As he said, now was the moment, with old specialists who had hung on 'for the duration' retiring, wives returning to London and husbands coming back from abroad. She rented a consulting room in Wimpole Street two afternoons a week, and presently extended this to three.

At the beginning of 1946, too, John had married Myriam. 'I wish he hadn't rushed into it so,' said Mary to Lionel.

'It's eighteen months since Olive was killed. He has those boys on his hands, being spoilt by competing grandmothers. You can't blame him for wanting to establish a proper home for them again. Most men in his position would.' For once Lionel seemed to be more tolerant than she was herself.

'*You* didn't,' she pointed out, 'when you were left with a child. It took you years to get round to marrying me!'

'Ah,' he said with a faint smile, 'but I'm fussy.'

243

He didn't, Mary could see, really care who John married: he didn't mind visiting the new Hershey house, half a mile from the old one and in the same kind of Kensington square. Why should he? He had liked and valued Olive, but she had not been his special friend. He did not wince, as Mary did, to see the handsome, polished furniture acquired by Olive now covered in a litter of china ornaments, some valuable, some of no quality whatsoever and all at odds with John's print collection. He did not mind the fact that the vases were now filled with artificial flowers of the sort found in a ladies' hairdresser.

'Were they? I didn't notice,' he said when Mary remarked on this after a visit.

'They were. *And* in their bedroom. Which, by the way, has a vast bed with an apricot satin and lace quilt and curtains to match. Must be pre-war stuff. Or else export-only. Probably that, come to think of it. Rag-trade connections of Myriam's, I imagine.'

'Oh well . . . They seem happy enough.'

'Very *consciously* happy, yes. Showing off about it. You feel all the time that Myriam's playing "Look at us, aren't we the ideal family—aren't I a lovely, sweet mother to these two poor motherless boys." I tell you, by the end of the evening I feel quite exhausted at all the admiration that's being demanded of me.'

Lionel turned and looked hard at Mary, for the first time in this conversation giving her his full attention.

'Mary. This isn't a bit like you. What's the matter with you?'

'Nothing's the matter with me. It just makes me curl up inside to see John with someone so—so—' She found that the word that expressed much of her meaning was 'common'. She baulked at this (Lionel would despise her for it, and quite right too) and instead substituted weakly 'so very ordinary'.

'You don't find an exceptional person like Olive everywhere,' said Lionel carefully, having digested Mary's remark with more attention than she had meant him to. He looked at her again, and said thoughtfully: 'You sound almost as if Myriam had done something to you. Yet I'd say she's a well-meaning woman in her way . . . It's not your way, of course.'

'No, it isn't. Oh, I know you think I'm being catty, Lionel. But I just hate this awful, uxorious, self-admiration society she and John have set up. The way they can't keep their hands off each other too, even when we're there . . . You'd think John, at any rate, would know better.'

'You sound almost jealous,' said Lionel bleakly. He added: 'I admit that my ability to keep my hands off you in public has always been total, and that perhaps our own divided life-style is not the best advertisement for marital unity. Still; we manage.'

'I'm not jealous, you fool, how could I be?' said Mary furiously—and immediately began to wonder if it were true.

They said no more. But two weeks later, when Lionel had returned from Manningham again, he said:

'I've been thinking about the Hershey ménage . . . Would you like to know what I've been thinking?'

'Of course,' she said dutifully, though the whole subject was painful to her.

'Well, as you remarked earlier, Myriam looks something like Olive, and there is anyway a superficial resemblance of race, occupation *et cetera* . . . But only superficial. At a deeper level there's no similarity at all, I'd say.'

'You mean, Myriam's a sort of ersatz version of Olive. A botched attempt at replacement?'

'Ersatz if you like, yes, but I wouldn't say botched. I'd say that, at the very deep level where these things operate, old John knows what he's doing. I think that perhaps, at that level, he's deliberately picked, second time round, a woman who will be no sort of real rival to Olive. Someone he won't get passionately involved with, you see. Just a cosy wife-figure. Someone who won't really influence his life.'

'I see . . . And hence all this playing Look-at-us-we're married?'

'Exactly.'

'Lionel . . . You really are quite clever sometimes.'

'Thank you, my dear. I'm paid to be clever. I have a Chair, remember,' he said annoyingly.

245

Now that the war was over, even though the austerity life of rationing and shortages seemed to have become a permanence, their own life returned to a more ordered sequence, with Lionel coming to London regularly at weekends and vacations and Mary making brief trips to Manningham in between. Charlie came to London in the holidays. There were several other American or would-be American children at his school, with whom he seemed to have formed a defensive alliance against the rest of the world, but at least a sympathetic master had managed to interest him in traditional jazz, and he now played the clarinet, badly.

'That American who came to see you in Baltimore played—plays—that,' said Mary, pleased.

'Oh, yeah—' he said vaguely. 'But I wasn't interested in it then.'

Fortunately too (for he was malleable, they discovered, not to say easily led, behind his façade of obstinacy) the school had now imbued him with a mild form of left-wing orthodoxy. This seemed largely unthinking, and did not relate to his emotional attachment to the USA, but at least it provided some common ground for him and Lionel. The post-war Labour government was doing its best to live up to its promises. Mary approved of much of what they were doing; she herself had been advocating some of it for years. She wished, though, she could feel more personally excited and exhilarated by it, as Lionel apparently did. Was this partly because it had been with Olive that she had shared her strongest commitment to a cause in the past, and Olive was gone?

Yes, partly. But the war seemed to have obliterated other things for her, besides Olive.

The war was over and yet, as after the previous war, 'over' did not seem the word for something whose effects were so long-lasting, something whose packed momentous events, both social and personal, could only be sifted and digested slowly in the years that lay ahead. So many years, perhaps. Perhaps even as long as she had lived already. The thought daunted her. In her thirties, and through the war, she had felt time fleeting from her, with herself perpetually in pursuit of it. Now, all at once, there seemed to be so much time ahead. Too much: she could not quite think what she was going to do with it.

Mary saw Dodie and Joanna during these years, but only intermittently. Dodie and Aunt May had decided not to return to London ('no place for a child') but to move back to their 'old haunts' near Esher. They moved, as it turned out, in the middle of a worse winter and fuel crisis than any of the war, and two months later Aunt May died of pneumonia in the local hospital. After the funeral, Dodie was very bitter about the Labour government. Willie, who was there too, took her part. Mary refused to argue.

'It's just so appalling,' said Willie provocatively, 'to see everything people thought they were fighting for filched from them . . . Look at the rate of income tax. Simply punitive. And this nationalisation's just a form of legalised robbery. Look what it's done to the mines. And the railways are going to be next, we hear.'

'Ghastly,' echoed Dodie. Mary said nothing. Lionel had always been in favour of nationalisation. She herself was not so sure.

'It's the illogic of the whole thing,' said Willie, lighting up one of the cigarettes he now had so much trouble buying, and returning to what had become one of his favourite themes. 'One's friends on the Continent say things are booming there—controls coming off, shops full of food, life getting back to normal just as it should. And what do we have here as a reward for winning the war? Rationed tinned whale, and a lot of whining Socialists telling us we're so lucky to have them in power.'

'Snoek isn't rationed, that's the thing about it,' said Mary tartly. He brushed this aside.

'I tell you, most people in this country don't realise it but we're becoming the laughing stock of Europe. It's tragic. And now it seems we're simply planning to hand India away on a plate.'

'Then why don't you go and live abroad again, Willie?'

'What annoys me,' said Dodie energetically, 'is that in spite of all those Germans who are supposed to be starving in Berlin and places one still can't get a servant at a reasonable

247

price. I mean, it was understandable not to be able to during the war, but I did think that when peace came we'd be able to have Germans as cooks and maids and gardeners and things. After all, who won the war?'

'Dodie, you didn't really think that, did you?' said Mary, shocked but also entertained.

'Yes, I honestly did. So did Mother. We all did, down in Wye.'

'But you can't really have expected the British government to pressgang Germans as domestic slave labour? That's one of the things the Nazis did.'

'I do think Dodie has a point, you know—' began Willie, with a playful, slightly malicious glint in his eye. Obviously he was entertained too and, not for the first time, Mary wondered if he really believed in the stances he adopted or just enjoyed annoying people like herself. But Dodie broke in quickly:

'No, of course not *slave* labour, Mary. I'd be prepared to pay wages, and of course treat a person decently. But I can't afford pounds and pounds a week, the way things are now. Mother didn't leave much, you know . . . Joanna and I will just have to manage on our own.' Pathetically.

'With a daily woman,' put in Mary firmly. A scrap lunch had been served to them by a capable-looking person referred to as 'Mrs B'.

'Yes, of course with a daily woman. Good heavens, that's the *minimum*—Mary, why are you laughing? Willie, you are too—stop it! At Mother's funeral, too—'

'I don't know why Willie is laughing,' said Mary truthfully, 'but I'm laughing because, if I didn't, I'd cry—like you are now.' (For Dodie was in tears.) 'Come on, Dodie dear, I'm sorry I laughed. It is, as you say, a funeral lunch, and we're all a bit overwrought. Let's have some tea, or coffee if you can spare it, and talk about something pleasanter . . . Where's Joanna? I had hoped to see her before I have to go.'

'Oh, she's round at the house of one of her little friends. I didn't think a funeral was any place for a child . . . She's *so* enjoying this nice little school I've found for her, Mary, she's really blossomed. She did need school—I remember you saying so once.' That was a flash of the old Dodie, ready to praise and admire, bearing no grudges. Mary said warmly:

'I'm longing to see her again. I did so enjoy taking her to *Peter Pan* at Christmas.' It was true. Joanna had been a rewarding companion and an enthusiastic, if innocent, dramatic critic ('Peter's bottom's a bit big, wouldn't you say, Auntie Mary? . . . But Captain Hook's just right, he makes my tummy go funny.') 'Perhaps,' Mary continued, 'you'll bring her up to London again soon, and she and I will have another treat?'

But Dodie, for a one-time ardent Londoner, was oddly averse to going near the place these days. It was as if, Mary thought, she were frightened of the past in some way and wished to keep away from its territory. How much had the episode with that mysterious Pole, which had apparently produced Joanna, marked Dodie? Mary could not begin to guess: Dodie had literally never referred to him again.

Mary said: 'If you don't want to come up yourself, couldn't you put Joanna on the train and let me meet her at Waterloo? . . . No, I suppose she's a bit too young for that still.'

'Good heavens, yes, she's not yet seven,' said Dodie, looking shocked at the thought.

As she travelled back to London Mary thought vaguely that Dodie's present life seemed a very reduced one for someone who had once appeared so determined to seize whatever the world had to offer. It was a phenomenon she had noticed in one or two other wives who had spent the war in safe areas with their children: their experiences had been so different and so much less formative than the experiences of those who had worked in towns or been in the Forces that they seemed to have lost touch with what was happening and to have little perception of how they might or might not re-make their lives now, in the maelstrom of peace. Marriages were breaking up because of it, one heard.

Wouldn't Dodie be isolated in that ugly little brick house she had bought (referred to as a 'cottage' but really a semi-bungalow in a row with others)? Perhaps, by moving back into the district where she had been a wealthy young girl, she had thought to create for herself, and eventually for Joanna, the social life of that period, but no one entertained much these days. (Would they ever again?) Mary found Dodie's evident devotion to Joanna touching and, since Joanna obviously thrived on it, she was not inclined to criticise; but she herself had had the experience of growing up as the only daughter of a mother on her own, and was aware that the life could be solitary and restricted. In her case, everything had been transformed and immeasurably enhanced by the presence of the Boys in the holidays, but there were no boys in this generation to come and irradiate Joanna's childhood. It seemed a pity, thought Mary, that if Dodie were going to have one fatherless child she should not have done the thing in style and had two. What *would* Willie have said? At any rate he seemed to have swallowed his distaste sufficiently to resume relations with Dodie, but there could be little in the charmless brick 'cottage' and in Dodie's absorption in motherhood to draw Willie there often. As far as Mary knew, he had reconstructed for himself in London his old, secretive life on the fringes of art, scholarship and moneyed society. He was doing research, he had told them, for a book on oriental porcelain—'My contribution, my dears, to getting back to pre-war standards. A wistful gesture in the direction of gracious living in these horribly plebeian times.'

Dodie had mentioned writing again. That would at any rate give her something to do.

'Dodie, how lovely! Another novel?'

'Oh no—no, a children's book this time.' Dodie looked faintly surprised that Mary should have supposed otherwise. She said: 'Those stories I've been telling Joanna for years have become quite a saga, and I thought I might as well publish them.'

'Oh yes. I remember hearing some of them that time I came down to Wye. About the maid called Nancy who got everything mixed up? They sounded marvellous. What a good idea.'

'It's for Joanna, really,' said Dodie deprecatingly. 'I'm thinking of calling it *Joanna's Book*. She's awfully thrilled at the idea.'

But *Joanna's Book* was never published. When—tactlessly, as she afterwards realised—Mary asked about it, Dodie said offhandedly that of course publishers were frightfully short of paper these days and were having to make cuts all round. On another, later occasion she said bitterly:

'You know, Mary, publishers simply aren't interested in good, original work for children these days. All they seem to want is more stupid pony books. It's all part of this horrible new world we're living in.'

It could, thought Mary, be true. In its way.

In 1948, to an enormous chorus of acclaim and dissent, the National Health Service was launched. Doctors like Mary and Ian Napier and John Hershey found themselves in a minority among their colleagues in being in favour of it and, even then, John cast doubts on the principle of treatment being totally free: people did not value what came absolutely free, he said, and he had the strongest objection to being rung up by bumptious patients wanting free prescriptions for aspirin and liver salts. Mary was not at all surprised to see that, like most practitioners in his situation, he continued after the Act to maintain a thriving private list. However, he had put in a great deal of work at the centre over the years, and she did not begrudge him the part-time consultancy he was presently offered in a new Obstetric and Gynae. department in a large teaching hospital. The out-patient section, in a one-storey building in the hospital grounds, was his special province and pride; he called in a famous architect (a patient of his) on the internal design, and managed to get the place opened, with maximum publicity, by Princess Elizabeth, who had had her first child not long before.

A few days before the official opening he invited Mary to lunch and showed her round. Light, bright, airy, well-equipped, and supplied with the kind of furnishings and murals that were to become celebrated as 'Festival of Britain' style within two years, it looked, in 1949, amazingly modern and impressive, auguring great things for the future of socialised medicine. By comparison the serviceable, well-used Paddington Centre looked drab and conservative. The Dalston Women's Clinic, up its two flights of rickety stairs over the pie shop, seemed a memory from another era.

'What a pity you can't do FPA work here too,' said Mary, looking round her, pleased and cheered by what she saw.

'Sshh, we shall. At post-natals. And other times, once we get going.'

251

'You be careful, John. You know how wary the hospitals have always been of this, and they'll be more so now it's all public money. Mind you don't end up with another of those "sex on the rates" rows on your hands.'

'Pooh,' said John. 'Who's to stop me? I can do what I like here. I've made sure the people on the team all see eye to eye on this. And anyway, Mary, it's going to come one day, you know—a properly integrated Family Planning service, I mean. It can't not.'

John was right. But it took a few more years than he perhaps imagined in those hopefully exhilarating days as the 1940s neared their end and, by the time it came, John himself was no longer there.

Now he said meditatively, standing in the middle of his new kingdom, where the painters and electricians were still at work:

'I'm wondering whether to have David and Mike out of school for the day when HRH comes over to snip the tape.' The boys had not after all been sent to the co-educational school in the north which Charlie had attended. (Charlie was now doing his national service.) Mary had felt faintly let down when John had opted for a conventional education at St Paul's for his boys. She suspected that Myriam had wanted St Paul's because she thought it smart. She said, laughing:

'Well, I don't know, John. The opening of a Gynae. department's hardly the occasion for adolescent boys, is it?'

In answer John gestured, almost awkwardly for him, at the wall over the main reception desk. There, a decorator had just finished nailing up the separate, polished wooden letters of an inscription. It read:

'*The Olive Hershey Unit*'.

That same year exchange controls were relaxed and it at last became possible to travel abroad again. Mary was invited to an international convention on birth control in Philadelphia.

'Why me?' she said to John Hershey, pleased but surprised. 'You've fixed this, haven't you?'

'Well, I told them I'd encourage you to go, but Dobermann would've asked you anyway.'

'But why?'

'Because, Mary, you're one of the best-known people in Family Planning circles in this country, that's why.'

'Don't be silly,' she said at once. 'If I were well-known I would know it—wouldn't I?' She was genuinely disconcerted when John, and two volunteers from the centre who were with them, burst out laughing. She had never thought of herself as well-known. Could it be true?

'You must go,' said Lionel later. 'You'll make useful contacts. John's right: the whole picture of Family Planning is changing; it's getting very big. And anyway . . . you might enjoy America, however ghastly it is. It'll be a new experience for you.'

'Yes, I expect I should.' Lionel had been anti-American ever since Charlie had come back from there, and the developing cold war, with its attendant anti-Communist phobia, was not improving his opinion of the place. She did not ask him if he wanted to come with her and he did not suggest it. When he came to London the following weekend he said:

'Did you accept that invitation to the Philadelphia thing?'

'Yes.'

'Good. You might look up the Hannakers in Baltimore while you're there. It's not far from Philadelphia, I think. I haven't been in touch with Jim Hannaker for some time, but I feel we owe them a lot. I tell Charlie he ought to write to them now and then, in sheer decency. I don't suppose he does.'

'Of course I'll look them up,' she said. 'I'd intended to, anyway.' She added suddenly, before she lost her courage and failed to say it: 'There're several people I want to look up. Including that GI I told you about—the one I met in the last year of the war, and used to go to concerts with.'

'Oh yes,' he said carefully. 'The one who writes to you sometimes. Why not?'

She nodded, not trusting herself to speak. She and Lionel received a lot of letters, between them. She had not thought he had noticed.

When Mary was old the moments of her life which stood out for her most clearly—rendered small and other by distance but still *there*, like the tree'd hillocks on Ashdown Forest over

253

which she no longer had the strength or inclination to walk—
she found these moments were not times of achievement but
simply instants of greatest happiness. Their point was that
there was no point: they were sufficient unto themselves;
their value was absolute, whatever came after. That, perhaps,
was why they lasted.

Playing cricket with the Boys on the green in Tunbridge
Wells, sheltered from any future knowledge. Buying vegetables one spring morning in Kilburn High Road where it
had come to her that, in spite of everything, life was all
right—that one could enjoy it after all. An early visit to the
opera, one extravagantly wet night, with John and Olive,
when they were students. Being with Olive in pre-war Paris
and Vienna. Some walks with Lionel in the first year they
had known each other (here her mental image of time as a
landscape and the remembered reality fused). Brittany, that
first time. Bicycling across London in the dawn with the
all-clear sounding, knowing that another night had been
survived. Being with Laurie in London in 1944. And that
other moment—though for many years, fearful of its brightness, she avoided looking back at it, till it was a long way
behind her and all the landscape had changed—the moment
when her ship docked in New York in 1949, and she saw
Laurie waiting for her.

He had written to ask if he should meet her ship, and she,
not knowing what to expect and afraid of expecting too
much, had written back, 'No, don't bother. I'll come straight
to Philadelphia by train and see you there.' Yet here he was
magically on the quay, unchanged except that he wore a suit
and a soft Trilby hat; he was waving at her, his face trans-
figured with happiness.

The long, shuffling wait in the queue for the Immigration
desks, clutching forms and a lung X-ray picture, was one of
the longest hours of her life. She discovered, with a distant,
clinical interest, that she was trembling, and could not stop.
She hoped the officials would not notice. At last, on the far
side of the customs shed, in what had suddenly revealed itself
as a dirty harbour-side street in the shadow of an expressway,
she found him again—or rather he found her, and gathered
her to him in an enduring embrace. Visualising it afterwards,

it was, she supposed, rather a private embrace to be conducted in such a public place, but what else could it be after five years? Anyway, porters and taxi-touts were probably used to witnessing such moments, at Cunard Pier.

'Oh, I didn't expect you here,' she said, weak with the only-now-remembered scent of his skin, his hair. His hair was greying and was a little thinner. Otherwise he seemed exactly the same.

'Of course I had to come,' he said, as if this were indeed a matter of course. 'Anyway, I thought I'd like to show you New York. You can stop the weekend here, can't you?'

'Yes—oh yes. The conference doesn't start till Monday.'

'I know that. And I called the Madison and told them not to expect you till Sunday night.' He peered anxiously down at her. 'I hope that was all right?'

'Of course it was. It was very thoughtful of you . . . But how did you know about when my conference starts?'

He laughed, the excited laugh of the man who has won something. 'It wasn't hard to discover. I wasn't sure which hospital was organising it—you didn't say, and we've got a lot of hospitals in Philadelphia—but I called around till I found out. Simple.'

The last few hours on the ship she had been bracing herself to negotiate unknown and formidable New York, where everything was said to 'move so fast'. A taxi to 'Penn Central Station, please' had been, for the moment, the extent of her plans for the city. She felt dazed now by the competence with which Laurie had suddenly removed responsibility from her, telephoning 'her' hospital and 'her' hotel in mythical Philadelphia. But of course it was his world here. As he said, it was simple. Here, the relationship they had known in London was neatly reversed, with him as the inhabitant and herself as the visitor to be shown around, younger because a stranger.

Younger? Laurie must be forty-one now; she herself was almost six years older than him. Lying awake at night on the Cunarder, feeling the engine's throb as if within herself, in the two-berth cabin she had shared with a talkative widow from Washington, she had inevitably wondered if Laurie would find her much changed. She, in her job, was in a

255

position to know that she had not aged as many women aged. She had escaped the physical pressures of child-bearing; she had always taken a lot of exercise; her brown hair, though now palely streaked, was still thick and soft. But she was aware of being at a time in her life when the pretence of youth should be over, while Laurie, as a man, was at an age at which he should surely be turning at last to the idea of a more settled existence, a family, some younger woman? The un-named shadow of a possible wife for Laurie had lurked for the last five years, unacknowledged, on the rim of her conscious-ness . . . A woman not entirely unlike herself, perhaps. But American, and ten—fifteen—years younger. And free to love him. He had said nothing in his letters to suggest such a presence in his life. But then she hardly mentioned Lionel in her letters either.

Yet now, at so long last, riding in a cab with him across afternoon New York, she felt young, almost childlike in her excitement at this place, this moment, and knew that it was all right and she need not have worried.

'A friend has lent me his apartment,' Laurie said suddenly. 'Guy I once worked with here. He's away every weekend in the fall at a cabin he has in upstate New York. I thought it'd be nicer for us than an hotel . . . I hope that's okay by you?'

'Of course,' she said at random, thinking how he sounded more American than he had in London, marvelling that he should even imagine she might criticise any of his arrange-ments, question anything, here.

'It's at Tenth Street and Third Avenue,' he said, incom-prehensibly. 'Lower East side really, though it gets called the East Village these days and people have started converting lofts into studios . . . I think you'll like it.'

Again she looked at him in wonder. She would have been perfectly content if he had told her they were about to stay on top of the Empire State Building, or in a tent in Central Park. In any case, she had no perception, then or for most of the weekend, where she was. She went where Laurie led her, and it was only in the long afterwards that she studied plans of New York City and Philadelphia, learnt by heart their street patterns.

The canyon-street under the expressway through which they had left the dock carried them uphill past high, ancient tenements with fire escapes twisting down their flanks, as battered as those of a European city. People of various colours sat about in the soiled sunshine on steps, rubbish blew in the streets paved with old granite setts. Where were the glass towers, the fabulously wealthy citizens, of everyone's dream New York? She was surprised, though relieved, not to be immediately confronted by them. And during the rest of the journey she ceased to register what went by beyond the window, because Laurie took her hand and began to tell her his plans for the weekend.

When they had got there, he said cautiously: 'It's nothing special, as an apartment, as you can see. But I thought it'd suit us? It's stuffy—I'll put on the fan.'

She was standing by the window in the main room, and gestured outwards. 'Oh Laurie—the view!'

They were on the tenth floor, and below them New York stretched away to the end of the island.

He said—and she realised then that he must have been nervous too, anxious as well that five years might have changed things: 'You don't mind my bringing you straight here?'

'How could I mind? It's so lovely.'

'I was afraid that perhaps I was taking too much on myself. That you might have other ideas—want to go on to Philadelphia to meet the other conference people. Or want an hotel room to yourself, maybe.'

'I don't. Oh, I don't.'

'No, no,' he said, laughing, confused, irradiated, 'I see that now. Oh Mary! However often you think of a person who is not there, and look at photographs of them and read their letters, actually *having* them there is something quite different. You are just the same—exactly the same. And yet there are all sorts of things about you that I had lost sight of and only now remember . . . How did we not see each other for a whole five years? It doesn't seem possible, now.'

The same thought had come to Mary. It recurred at intervals that afternoon, as the daylight declined pinkly over the city, and then a glow of artificial light began to come in through the square of window, where they had not yet got up to draw the curtains. *How could I have borne to be away from this loved person for five years?*

—And how will I bear it in two and a half weeks' time when I have to leave him again, with no promise of return?

Hush, don't think like that, it is useless—remember? In 1944 you lived in the present and were happy: this, you have to do again. Your love with Laurie has always had to exist for its own sake, unsupported by your world or his—remember? If you love enough, you can manage it.

Some time later, as if his mind were working antiphonally to hers, he said:

'I was just thinking . . . We've never been together before, I think, for more than one night at a time. And now we've got the whole weekend ahead of us, all to ourselves. And then Philadelphia . . . I can hardly believe it.'

When it was very late they got up and dressed and went out into the night streets. Laurie told a taxi-driver to take them to Times Square. He showed her the illuminated ribbon of news running round the tall building, and then took her to a bar where they had beer and chicken sandwiches that seemed to her enormous. She realised it was after one in the morning.

'Goodness—you can't get anything to eat in London at this hour. Well, I suppose you could in an expensive night-club, but no ordinary place is open.'

'Still like that? I know it used to be, but I thought maybe that was because of the war.'

'Oh no, it's just England . . .' She realised she didn't want to talk about England at all. She said: 'The people in here don't look grand or anything either. Just ordinary people enjoying themselves.' Her own happiness was so present to her that it seemed like a gift of which she was perpetually conscious.

'They're waiters and people from the mid-town restaurants that shut earlier,' he said. 'And porters from the meat markets of Lower West side. And a sprinkling of newspapermen too. I used to come here in the days when I worked on the *Herald*— that's where Gerry, whose apartment we're in, still works . . . Hey, I ought to have got some food in for breakfast, and I didn't. Gerry never has anything in but coffee and juice, and

258

you drink tea in the morning, I remember. I forgot all about it—I'm sorry.'

'I'm not worried about tea,' she said, laughing. 'We can buy some things tomorrow, can't we, and I'll cook you a meal.'

'Fine. No, wait a minute, you're only in New York for two days; you don't want to spend your time cooking. Why don't we save that for Philadelphia? . . . You will be able to spend some evenings there with me, won't you?'

'Of course. Every evening, I should think—unless you're busy, that is,' she added hastily, not knowing his life, his world. 'I should think I'll see enough of the other conference people during the day.'

'That's great, that's what I figured . . . Mary, look: I know you're booked into the Madison—they usually put big conferences there—but do you really have to stay there? I mean, it might be more convenient and peaceful for you to stay at my place. A lot cheaper, too.'

Mary hesitated. At the moment, the thought of spending her nights in Philadelphia anywhere but with Laurie seemed a waste of precious hours. But she was aware that, on Monday, she would have to become efficient, mildly well-known Dr Denvers again ('famous' even, if she could believe John). How might it look to other people at the conference if she disappeared from the hotel? She attempted to convey this to Laurie, who began to laugh:

'Look, sweetheart. You don't say to all those distinguished consultants you're conferring with, "I'm away every night, you see, because I've got this lover who lives in part of a row-house in South Philadelphia with the Italians and the Poles." You just say, "I'm staying with friends." You'll probably find quite a few delegates are; all the best people have friends in Philadelphia. In fact, unless you disillusion them, everyone will assume that you're staying with some fancy medical acquaintance out on Main Line. You don't want to be self-conscious about it.' In a neutral tone he added quickly, 'You can always give directions to the hotel desk to pass any messages on to you without delay.'

'Oh, I expect you're right,' she said as quickly, grateful for his understanding. 'What's Main Line?'

'Main Line is what you would call posh suburbia. What developed along the route of the main-line railroad, you see. There's a lot of money out there, and a lot of Philadelphia good family connections too. We have families like hell in Philadelphia, just like in England—in fact, Philadelphia is a bit of a joke because of it—oh Mary! I've got so much to show you—'

Afterwards, back in England, proffering the presents she had bought—books and shirts for Lionel, dresses for Joanna, a Metropolitan opera house poster for John Hershey, nylon stockings for women friends—Mary found herself becoming inevitably eloquent on the luxury of America. The shops packed with good things, the lavish platefuls of delicious food on offer at even the smallest coffee-shops, the enormous martinis and equally enormous ice-creams, the sparkling urban beauty of mid-town New York under a high autumn sky, the futuristic fountains of the Rockefeller Plaza . . . it was what people wanted to hear, and of course it was all true, as far as it went. Indeed, long afterwards she was to realise with slight surprise that America in 1949 had created for her too a standard of how life could be, not just for the rich but for a broad section of the population, which influenced subtly but permanently her expectations for Britain also. Lionel, unusually acerbic, told her once that she had 'succumbed'— had been 'had' by America. She thought that *he* had succumbed, untypically for him, to a political sclerosis of the imagination, rheumatoid left-wingitis. But she did not say so.

Yet what struck her at the time in America even more forcibly was something running counter to this image of modernity, so that she had difficulty in conveying it: New York was in some ways a surprisingly old-fashioned city. She had visualised skyscrapers as airy, almost insubstantial structures, or at any rate skeletal, like the Eiffel Tower. Long afterwards, looking at recent photographs of the city when she was old and everything had changed, she did in fact discover the cloud-capp'd towers of her imaginings, but in 1949 these had yet to be created; then New York was still a place of high but solid blocks, rather dirty for the most part, with the fanciful turrets of the Empire State and the Chrysler buildings the highest peaks there were. And many things—the wrought-iron elevated railway along Third Avenue with small shops beneath it, the animated garment-trade streets of the Lower East side, the crammed tenements of Harlem where Laurie took her walking on Sunday—these seemed not so much like images from the future as from an archetypal city past. The East End and Hackney had been like this, in the days of the Dalston Clinic: Kilburn had had this cohesive, concentrated feeling when she had first come there as a girl. But no longer. There was something broken and dispersed about London these days. It was, of course, as everyone said, the war that had done it. Yet it was not just that. A few months ago she had happened to go down Kilburn High Road on a bus and had glimpsed the Nonconformist church that had been such a focal point for the district and where Eric Evans had been a preacher. It had become a furniture warehouse.

Philadelphia, when they got there, struck her even more forcibly as a city like those of the last century rather than of any hypothetical future. True, the hospital where the conference was taking place was a modern building, splendidly equipped by British standards. But the centre of Philadelphia reminded her of a French or Italian city, and much of the rest was even more familiar: row after row of three- and four-storey brick terrace houses, recognisably Georgian or early Victorian to her eyes. This was where Laurie lived. She could not conceal her surprise.

'In England, all Americans are believed to live in flats—sorry, apartments. Or in luxurious suburban houses.'

'Yes, but Philadelphia's a very old town. *And* built by the British. Anyway, I only have these three rooms on the top floor, you know. Mrs Kandinsky has the rest of the house—and rents out another room at the back to an old guy who works in the market.'

'Three rooms is plenty for you. And you've made them very nice.' Having trained herself to regard him as someone who travelled deliberately light through life, she had been surprised at the evidence of care and taste his rooms conveyed.

'It's cheap in South Philadelphia. And it suits me. I grew up round here. It's gone down a bit since then, but I still like it.'

261

'Laurie, you don't understand,' she said, for his tone was faintly defensive. 'I really *do* like it too. It's just that I'm surprised, because it's more—more like Europe than I ever expected. I feel quite at home.'

'So you could settle down here?' he asked quickly, in such a tone that she could not tell if he were asking a hypothetical question or making her a proposition. She did not answer, then.

She moved in, using the shower he had fixed up in a closet off the kitchen, sleeping in his arms each night under a striped Mexican blanket; on the wall above the bed was a painting of the Quai du Louvre he had acquired in Paris at the end of the war. On several evenings he collected her at the hospital and they went to performances for which he had tickets from his paper. On the other evenings she cooked him supper, buying food in the Italian market round the corner as if she were in Berwick Street. Her days at the conference passed in a dream. She went to other people's talks and seminars, took notes, gave a carefully prepared talk of her own, discussed diaphragms and rings and wishbones and hormonal levels and 'changing social needs' over enormous, colourful salads in the hospital dining room, expressed herself pleased to meet at last names she already knew from the print of specialised journals—yet all the time she was conscious of playing a part, competently but abstractedly, as if on automatic pilot: her real life was being lived elsewhere, in the intimate streets of South Philadelphia, in Laurie's rooms.

She reminded herself that it was *not* real; a brief and disconnected venture into another existence only made possible because of its brevity, its separation from everything that, for twenty years, she had called normality. All her instincts rejected the information.

The conference lasted for five days, till the following weekend. She had already, in England, planned to take the subsequent week to 'see America'—or some fraction of it. Her passage home was booked early in the week after that. There could be no question of altering it, for places on ships were hard to get and were booked months in advance.

'You might stay a night or two with the Hannakers in

Baltimore,' Lionel had suggested, and she had said, 'Yes, I might.' But she had made no arrangements to do so.

'Do you want to?' said Laurie at once when she mentioned it.

'Not really, no, but—' She was accustomed to being conscientious in such matters.

He began rapidly to sketch out a plan of what they might do together: 'It's just a suggestion,' he said twice, but she realised he had it all worked out. He had warned his editor he would probably be taking the week off, he told her: there was no problem. They could hire a car—there was no problem about that in America either, it seemed—and drive down into Virginia. They could stop in Washington for half a day, just so that she could say she'd seen it. Then they could drive on south, maybe down to the Shenandoah Valley. The countryside would be looking great, he said, with the leaves just turning; the fall was the best time for such a trip, and the weather was still warm down south.

Mary was captivated with the word 'fall', a term which had not impinged on her before. It was a perfectly logical one, the neat antithesis of 'spring', but it also carried exotic overtones which she took a few minutes to identify: the Fall of Man, Eve's fall, fallen women . . . Into her mind came Dodie's first novel, *The Fruits of Experience*, and the heroine's journeying. A preposterous book, of course, and utterly dated now: she hadn't looked at it for years and probably no one else had either. And yet, and yet . . . Her memory of it fused with something from the present moment, as if life were in some small measure imitating art. Or as if it were taking hackneyed, outworn art and breathing a personal life into it in a way she had never dared hope or expect. Yes, she had been unjust to Dodie: that novel had had a message, however much overlaid by fashion and affectation.

How far could they go? she asked Laurie, trying to visualise the South. She thought of the Civil War, of white-pillared mansions and coloured servants and slaves and *Gone with the Wind*, and 'Oh Jimmy, farewell, your brothers fell—way down in Alabama', and of the extraordinary, evocative alienness of other people's history.

A good long way—if they turned the car in at some point

and took the train. 'In fact,' he said—and she could hear the hope and hesitation in his voice, almost like a boy's voice proffering an idea he was afraid might be scorned—'I was wondering if we might go down as far as New Orleans? I haven't been there for several years myself, and you really should see it. If we got there on Thursday, say, we could stay till Sunday evening, and you'd still have time to get the train back to New York for your ship on Tuesday . . . Is it an idea, Mary?'

She said that it was. She said, and meant it, that she would like that better than anything in the whole world.

'You talked about New Orleans on that train where we met!' she said.

'I expect I did,' he said. 'It was the place I sometimes felt really homesick for, more than New York or even Philadelphia.' But she did not think he actually remembered. She thought that, like Lionel, he lived in the present—any present—more than she did.

As they set out from Philadelphia he said, in the carefully non-committal tone he employed when speaking of her life apart from him:

'Baltimore's on the way to Washington. We could stop off there if you want to see these people. I even think I remember where they live. I could leave you for an hour or two.'

'No,' she said. 'No, it's all right. I won't bother.'

It would get in the way. They might want me to stay with them . . . Anyway, I'm not going to.

She did not see the Hannakers. Nor did she telephone an acquaintance of Lionel's in Washington whose number she had in her bag.

She did not leave in Philadelphia an address by which she might be contacted, for there was none to leave. For the first time in uncounted years of work, of responsibility, of marriage, of step-parenthood, she left a place free, untraceable, alone. Except, that is, that Laurie was with her. They were together all the time, day and night, for the next eight days, and she did not even register this fact till it was over. Had she asked herself beforehand she would have supposed, objectively, that they ought to separate for an hour or so from time to time, just to give each other a rest and a little privacy. But, at the time, she did not think of it, nor apparently did he.

They walked on the sunny lawns of Washington. He showed her the White House and the Capitol, and she thought how strange these things looked in colour rather than in the familiar black-and-white of Newsreel pictures. They spent that night in a motel outside the city: wooden cabins round a courtyard, above which the unfamiliar stars were large and bright. Cicadas poured their sound from the trees, and she thought how like Paradise this huge, beautiful, fertile country must have seemed to the first settlers from England, coming with all their troubles, their hopes and fears, and how like Paradise it still was, in spite of the turnpikes and the bars.

By the following night, their eyes stretched by the blue distances of the Shenandoah Valley beyond the red grasses, and by the yellow oaks and maples of Monticello, they were in Charlottesville, in an ornate hotel near the centre of the town. In the dark southern night rain fell in torrents, drumming on the wooden balcony outside their window. To herself, she said: whatever happens in the rest of my life—whatever unhappiness of age, decline, sickness, failure, loss, loneliness—I shall still have had this. Whatever happens afterwards nothing can take this away from me. But she did not say it aloud.

When, on Tuesday, they left the car at an agency in Lynchburg in preparation for getting the train to New Orleans that evening, she said, with the first touch of anxiety she had felt since they had left Philadelphia:

'Laurie, isn't this all being awfully expensive?' The small dollar-allocation that the Bank of England had made to enable her to attend the conference was not enough for her to pay her share on their travels, as she would have preferred. He looked at her almost indignantly.

'You don't need to worry, you know. I've got plenty with me.'

'I know, but . . .' She had grasped that his job, though it was pleasant and gave him much freedom, was not particularly well paid. His life-style in Philadelphia was modest; unlike every other American she met, he had no car of his own.

265

'We've plenty,' he said firmly, altering the pronoun. 'I've been saving up for this trip for years.'

'But it was only last May that I wrote and told you I was coming,' she said stupidly.

'But I've been saving up for it for years all the same,' he said. 'For this—or something comparable. At one time, when British people couldn't get any currency to travel, I planned to come back to Europe. I thought of suggesting you meet me in some city, Paris or Amsterdam or somewhere . . . But then I didn't. I wasn't sure if you would want to.'

'I would have met you,' she said, after a pause. 'I don't know exactly how, but I would have done.'

'But what I really wanted to do was show you my own country, like this,' he said more cheerfully. 'So I saved up, and hoped you would come. And you did.'

Could he really mean it, literally? Had he really been thinking of this, this moment, all these moments, when he paid money into a savings account, money that he was not spending on a wife, a child, a house of his own? He sounded as if he meant it. But perhaps, she told herself, he was just expressing romantic hindsight. Perhaps he really just meant: I saved up for some contingency only vaguely imagined, and how pleased I am that it has turned out to be this.

She knew, for he had told her once, that he regarded money as freedom, nothing more. There must, surely, have been other possible uses for his spare money in the last five years? She did not let her mind dwell on the fact, but she knew that he must have brought other women to his rooms. Other voices must have spoken his name in the night; others besides herself must have enjoyed his warmth and gentleness. It was not possible that he had spent the last five years alone. Yet he spoke as if he had—or felt that he had.

The train shook and roared all night. In her confused dreams she was journeying to India. Other times, other journeys both past and potential, fused together, drawn into one in the locomotive's shivering, lingering whistle over the unknown land. A sense of suffocating excitement possessed her.

The next morning they ate a large, greedy breakfast in the restaurant car amid southern accents, the red earth of Georgia slipping past the windows. The country became gradually more wooded, with small enclaves of weather-boarded houses set down among mown grass and trees. Sometimes there was a toy, porticoed church as well. Further south, the houses were fewer and more ramshackle with peeling paint; their porches held old car seats and bicycles, and small, black children played near the tracks. Creepers began to clothe the sides of the embankments and cuttings, and in Louisiana the swamps began; the trees of the forest stood with their feet in green water, as if this were a primeval land that no white man had yet colonised.

Laurie, to whom none of this was new, read *Billy Budd* for much of the day. 'I always read Melville on train rides,' he explained. Occasionally he read her paragraphs aloud, trying to infect her with his feeling for Melville, but she listened abstractedly, drawn out beyond the glass into this strange country, which was to her all the stranger for having some of the appurtenances of the European landscape she knew —but oddly altered, transformed, as if the train window were a subtle distorting glass. Even the names of the cities by which they passed—Montgomery, Salisbury, Bay Minette, Athens—gave the impression that the map of the Old World had been picked up like a completed jig-saw and dropped from a great height, so that its component pieces were jumbled and scattered. By the late afternoon, when at last the train neared New Orleans, an unexpected depression and dread had settled on to her. Afterwards, she wondered if she had, temporarily, been a little homesick . . . Philadelphia had seemed almost part of her own world, even if an unfamiliar part. This was infinitely more alien.

It had rained again, as they skirted the Gulf coast; the streets were wet and shining, the sky streaked with purple, yet the air, when they opened the window, was as warm and muggy as a steam-bath. A fleeting whiff of her night's dreams returned to her, and she said:

'It must be like this in India. The weather, I mean.'

'Yeah. It's warm. It doesn't really cool down here till November . . . I hope you've got something light to wear, Mary? We should have thought of that before.'

'Yes, I've got a thin blouse. And some slacks,' she said

vaguely. She was thinking: I'll be glad when November comes. All this heat is sick, like over-sweet food. I shall like it best in winter. Then she thought: what's the matter with me? What am I thinking of? We're only here till Sunday.

She had just experienced the odd, transitory feeling of inhabiting the life of someone other than herself, as if a shadow had passed through her. She was aware that the usual explanation for this is that one side of the brain is working fractionally ahead of the other. But she felt, for a disorientating moment, as if she were some other woman in some other period, coming here not just for three days but to take up an irrevocable new life—to marry into it, perhaps.

There must have been such women, she thought, long ago. French women, perhaps travelling to the other side of the world for ever to a city with a French name, supposedly a European city but in reality one mysteriously distorted and changed, a looking-glass city, a place of exile.

'Look,' said Laurie suddenly, coming behind her where she stood by the window. 'There's the Metairie Cemetery.'

Ornate, Italianate gravestones, shining with wet, stretched as far as she could see. A whole city for the dead.

'But the Basin Street one is better!' he said happily. 'There's a voodoo grave there, Marie Vaneau; we'll go and pay our respects to her.'

Suddenly she turned round and clung to him, burying her face in his shoulder.

'Hey, what is it?' he said.

'I don't know. I don't know, Laurie. I really don't.' She wanted to say, 'I feel this is a place of fate for me and I'm frightened.' But she did not say it, partly because it sounded so foolishly melodramatic and unlike herself. And partly because to utter such a feeling might turn into a self-fulfilling prophecy.

The sense of vulnerability and unfocused dread lingered faintly with her that evening, as they dodged about between thunder showers and ate Creole food in a crowded restaurant. But the next morning she was her usual self again and made light of her fears to Laurie.

'Oh, New Orleans is very strong,' he said thoughtfully. 'It

takes people odd ways . . . Some don't like it at all. I was taking a risk, bringing you here.'

'But I *do* like it,' she said fervently. 'I love it.' And that day it was true. They were staying in the French Quarter in a hotel that Laurie had stayed in years before. It was ramshackle, but their room had a wrought-iron balcony overlooking the street, and the whole place seemed to Mary like a setting for light opera. In the cool evenings jazz wafted up from the saloon on the corner.

Laurie took her to visit some old friends of his, a professor of music and his Creole wife, living out near Audubon Park. She admired their luxuriant, overgrown garden, their cats, their black-eyed small children, but none of it seemed entirely real. As they were coming back to the centre of town on the street-car she said tentatively, 'Laurie . . . I didn't meet any of your friends in Philadelphia. I know we were happy just to be together. But now I rather wish I had.'

He said uneasily, as if the same thing had been running through his mind too: 'I know. I did think of it, but—oh, Philadelphia's such a gossipy place. For a big city, it's really provincial. Everyone knows everyone else's business. And though I hardly come of an old Main Line family I know the people you were meeting at that conference of yours. And people love to talk. Well, you're a name in your own world, and I just didn't want you to take the slightest risk of embarrassment—I mean, of anything being reported back in professional quarters about whose company you'd been in. I hope I did right?'

With a slight, background sense of pain that she did not want to analyse, she said:

'Yes, I expect that was wise. Thank you, Laurie.' After all, she hadn't introduced him to any of her friends in London.

It was not that she needed any company but his; it was rather that an obscure female instinct to integrate herself into his life, to be like a wife to him (however temporarily), was at work in her. Much as she was loving this journey southwards, and the variety and pleasure that stretched each day to the full, she regretted that she did not have the chance here, as she had in Philadelphia, to cook for Laurie. And Laurie himself had a talent for intimacy, for creating a private world that felt secure and real. 'Let's go back home now,' he had said unselfconsciously in Philadelphia when it was time for them to return to his flat from a walk or a concert. And one morning he had shoved his mail at her and said, 'Open these for me, will you, sweetheart, while I take a shower.' She had been touched by this gesture, but also disconcerted. She and Lionel had never, ever, opened each other's post, on principle, even obvious circulars.

She told herself that such gestures and words of intimacy might be a game for Laurie, a comforting make-believe which must be seen against the solitary and uncommitted nature of the rest of his existence. Perhaps, indeed, he could create an instant world for two, and appear to inhabit it wholeheartedly, precisely because he was a man with few real ties or hostages to fortune. If he had really been a man to whom relationships were central then he would not have been free now, at this stage in his life, to give himself to her in this way. She told herself that must, logically, be so.

So she was utterly unprepared when on the last day in New Orleans he asked her if she would return to America and make her life with him. They were not in each other's arms at the time, but sitting on the terrace of the Café du Monde by the riverside market, and she knew he meant it because he spoke tentatively, almost coolly, as he did whenever he referred to her life apart from him.

The moment for which she had instinctively longed, and done nothing to avert, had come, and she was appalled. She clutched at her profession to defend herself.

'Laurie, how could I? All my work—which is much the greatest part of my life—is in London.'

'But medicine is international,' he said instantly. 'After all, that's the reason you're here now. It isn't as if you were a lawyer, or even a journalist, who'd have to start again from scratch. British medical qualifications and experience are highly acceptable here; a lot of British doctors have come to the States since the end of the war, because the money and research facilities are so much better. You must know that.'

'But I'm not known here. I wouldn't necessarily be offered the sort of job I'd want.' She suppressed the memory of an exuberant consultant from Washington coming up to her at the conference after she had given her paper and asking leading questions to discover if she were thinking of emigrating.

'There are five teaching hospitals in Philadelphia,' said Laurie implacably. 'Five. It's the medical centre of the USA—that's why your conference was held there. Not counting other possibilities in Baltimore and Washington and New York and Pittsburgh, which are all only a train ride away. Mary, in your position you could get a good, interesting job, believe me—if you wanted to.'

She said desperately, feeling she was cast to play Devil's Advocate against a cause with which she was at heart profoundly in sympathy: 'But Laurie, it's not just work, as such—it's the whole life that goes with it. The people . . . The being at the centre of things . . . I'm middle-aged now; I have to recognise that. I couldn't expect to construct for myself all at once on this side of the Atlantic—and perhaps not ever— the kind of associations that I've built up for myself in London over twenty years.'

His face shut. He said stiffly, after a moment:

'Well, I know I don't come of old Philadelphia stock. My great-grandparents weren't married in the Gloria Dei church, and my grandfather wasn't a member of the Athenaeum. In fact most of my ancestors died of pogroms or starvation in some Baltic ghetto before my own father and my mother's father had the wit to come here. But I don't attend first nights in a zoot suit or drink beer from the can and, when I get invited to a reception, I manage to pass as a cultured fellow. I think I could offer you some sort of life, Mary.'

Infuriated by his sudden, untypical lack of perception— for in spite of his ironic tone she could tell that he meant what he had said—she cried:

'How could you think that was what was worrying me? I'm not the sort of person who cares tuppence for your stuffy Main Liners, or whatever they are. I'm English, thanks. I don't *need* to. We have people exactly like that in England, only much more so, and I've never had anything to do with them either.'

She would have added, 'Do you imagine that, if I'd been a snob, I would ever have married Lionel?' But of course

271

Laurie had never met Lionel, and knew nothing of his background.

It was her own fault. By keeping the reality of Lionel tactfully out of Laurie's sight, feeling that this was the only decent way of conducting this other relationship, she must inevitably have given Laurie the impression that Lionel was a shadowy figure, someone who no longer mattered very much to her. Of course, the truth was that, when she was with Laurie, Lionel did not matter. No one but Laurie mattered.

She said, more humbly: 'I wouldn't expect you to "offer me a life", Laurie. Oh, I'm sure we'd have a lot of happiness together. But I'm used to making my own life, you see.'

'Yes, I know you're unusually independent for a woman,' he said. 'You're quiet about it, of course, but it's still one of the first things I noticed about you. That,' he added swiftly, getting in a clever thrust, 'is why I think you could stand transplanting yourself. I agree that many women couldn't do it, or wouldn't . . . But you could.'

Confronted now with basic facts she thought: it's not true. I'm not really independent at all. I never have been. Rather, I am hopelessly in thrall to other people, to their ideas and needs. I do not act, I just react. There's a paradox here. Living with Lionel (when he's there), being Lionel's wife, I have learnt to be 'independent' because that is what he has always wanted, has praised me for . . . Long ago, I developed a separate career to please him. My life has been shaped by his image of me, far more, I think, than he has ever realised.

It would be a fine irony—or a piece of poetic justice—if, after all these years, Lionel's settled insistence that I have a life of my own apart from him should culminate in my leaving him to set up a new life with Laurie. A second man who likes to be unencumbered, who likes 'independent' women, and for whom, in turn, I would shape and change myself to fit his life and preoccupations . . .

Well? Every individual can only go where his life takes him: Lionel himself believes that. Laurie is offering me the chance of a brand-new life, at an age when so many women are stepping on to the long, long downhill slope to old age, decay, loss, extinction. They appear in my consulting room

272

and parade their irremediable grief to my attentive ears; grief that goes by many names, like 'backache' and 'insomnia' and 'migraine' and 'my memory these days, doctor', but is really grief for the long tunnel of decline. They refer to it with pseudo-briskness as the change of life, but for them it isn't a change, not at all; it's merely the inexorable, piecemeal loss of all the things—status, comeliness, energy, love—that have made life worth living. I don't tell them so, of course. But I know it.

She had an insane desire to accede to Laurie's request. To throw prudence, caution, loyalty, even what she had known as self-respect, to the winds, and go with him. To escape from the slow, wearing accretions of habit and time, and swing out into a new cycle. If she had enough courage—

An image that was years out of date crossed her mind: Dodie as a young woman, ruthless and gay. Yes, the Dodie of that era would have enthusiastically commended her for such an action. Perhaps even the Dodie of today would jealously admire it.

It was (of course) out of the question. All the time she envisaged it she knew that. It wasn't so much a matter of choosing between the 'right' course and the 'wrong' one but of trying to weigh two different versions of right which simply were not comparable. Courage was real but so was callousness. 'Being true to oneself' had genuine worth, no doubt, but so did keeping faith with one's past self. No, she could not do it, however much she might long to, and that was perhaps a failure in her—not the moral victory it might seem, but a secret defeat. The reason she could not jettison her old life for the chance of a new and perhaps even more worthwhile one was the same as the reason she would never be an outstanding doctor, an innovator, only a good one, following sympathetically where others lead—Lionel, Napier, Hershey, long ago Olive . . .

She said at last, in a small, apologetic voice: 'It isn't just my work. I really could not leave Lionel. We've been together a long time. He—he's not young any more. In another two years he'll be sixty . . . I just can't, Laurie. It isn't that I don't want to. But to do so would go against—so much.'

After some time Laurie said glumly:

'Well, I guess I knew that would be the answer, really. If you were prepared to leave your husband for me you wouldn't be the person you are.'

It was a flattering and simple way of putting it, and she left it at that. But, for the first time in the course of their relationship, she felt consumed with guilt. She had believed too readily what he had said of himself years ago. 'I'm easy about these things,' he had said; and, 'I'm a coward about relationships': on these words, remembered out of context, she had built an image and relied on it to protect them both. Yet all the time, over the years, something had been growing between them, something rare and of incalculable value, and now she had hacked it down—or so stunted its growth that it could never flower. She stared wretchedly at the empty coffee-cups on the café table.

Later she said humbly, trying to make amends where, fundamentally, none could be made:

'This—just being together—has been wonderful for me for its own sake . . . I do hope it's been worth it for you too.'

'You know it has.'

She feared it must inevitably have been devalued for him by her refusal to transform it into something more. But he said after a moment, with a look on his face as if he had bitten on a tooth-stopping:

'You pay for everything; I've always known that. "Take what you want," said God. "Take what you want—and pay for it." These two weeks have been some of the best of my life. I'll pay for it, afterwards, in missing you . . . You too, perhaps?'

'Oh yes,' she said fervently, quailing in advance at the thought of the return to New York alone, the embarkation on the ship, alone. Across thirty years the memory of another loss pricked her. Nigel. They had planned to set up house in India together.

'I'll come back here,' she said. 'I don't know when, but I will. Travel is getting easier. There are planes now. I *must* come.'

'I certainly hope so,' he said. But he did not sound very certain.

274

'Could you come to England?' she asked, recalling what he had said before. But he said, politely but firmly:

'No. I don't think I could do that. In the circumstances. Do you?'

He is punishing me, she thought. He is punishing me for killing off the future we might have had together, and he is right to do so.

On the Sunday evening they took the train north. It had been agreed between them, in the long ago security of the beginning of the week, that he would get off the train in Philadelphia and she would go on to New York. They still had more than twenty-four hours together in their two-berth compartment, but once the train journey had begun she thought, there was no escape, the end had begun too; they were in the tunnel.

'I could come on to New York with you,' he said suddenly. 'See you on to the ship—'

'But you've got to be back at work tomorrow evening.'

'You're right. I have. *The Magic Flute.* Shit. It's the only Mozart opera I've never liked, and now I know why . . . I could scrub it.'

'No, no,' she said, almost shocked. 'You said you would be there; you must be.'

'Ah, what a good wife you are,' he said heavily, and kissed her before she could protest at this sickly joke.

As the train went through the unknowable suburbs of New Orleans, passing again by the Metairie Cemetery and the road signs to Mobile and Baton Rouge, she thought: this *was* the place of fate for me. I wasn't imagining it. But not of fate seized—of fate refused. I shall never come back.

I suppose this last week has been the crossroads of my life. An 'agonising choice' people call it, don't they? But it hasn't been that, no, not at all. Much more of an inevitable confirmation of something I always really knew about myself; about the way things are.

PART SIX

As THE 1950s GOT UNDER WAY THE WORLD OF ENLIGHTENED Socialism that people like Lionel and Mary had confidently welcomed in the years immediately following the war became oddly overlaid and altered by something that had not been predicted but was everywhere apparent; a growing prosperity. For the first time in Mary's adult life there was full employment; for the first time the young working-class wives who came to her at the Centre were as physically fit as the middle-class patients she saw in Wimpole Street, and often almost as well dressed. It seemed to her that they got more out of their marriages too than the wives of the '30s had. They spoke, not infrequently, of pleasure and happiness, while their mothers had spoken in terms of 'putting up with it' and 'letting him have his way'. The children playing in the streets no longer looked fragile or pasty, but seemed bursting with free milk and orange juice. The Welfare State, even its grudging opponents admitted, did seem to be working. Mary, not inclined by nature to stringent political analysis, accepted this apparent fact at its face value, and was thankful and a little triumphant—for hadn't she and like-minded others always maintained that working-class families would readily adopt middle-class standards if only they were given the chance? The fact that the mounting wave of Western prosperity, in which Britain was simply a participant, was nothing to do with Socialist ideals and might in the long run work against them, was not a truth that presented itself to her, any more than it did to others who were more politically conscious than she.

In her case, too, there was an extra dimension bestowed on her by her American journey. In America she had seen poverty, but she had also seen large numbers of ordinary people living good lives, with a freedom and comfort that many in Britain could not even imagine. It wasn't just the war, she thought: there was something fusty and ill organised and dreary about traditional British life that transcended class and income. She understood far better now Charlie's craving for the sheer smells and taste and feel of America when he had returned to England in 1945, and told him so. If Britain was changing, as people nervously said, quite apart from the effects of the Welfare State, then thank God, it was time.

She had dreaded, coming back from America, that she too would suffer hopeless pangs of disorientation and longing as Charlie had, if for a different reason. But once the accumulation of days and weeks had deadened the acute pain of wanting Laurie she found she was actually stronger and happier than she had been before. She was puzzled by this, at first, but then, in her own terms, her time in America could not be regarded as anything but a success—a nourishing, sustaining, fulfilling experience. She valued beyond price what it had given her, and knew from his letters that Laurie valued it too—that he had got over his disappointment (if the phrase was not too inadequate) and did not hold it against her. He was not, after all, the 'marrying type'. She felt an enormous, tender gratitude towards him.

She also felt that their brief two and a half weeks had taught her something about valuing things for their own sake and letting the future take care of itself. Surely this was something to understand for the later decades of life? So, in the 1950s, she lived determinedly in the present, and was simply glad to see a number of her old professional wishes and ambitions fulfilled. The impetus of that time of change and progress carried her and many others away from the past, away from the griefs and losses of war, in a way that the economically stagnant 1920s had never done. She was grateful for that too.

From time to time, though, she registered that this decade was not a good one for those of her contemporaries who now thought of themselves as the older generation. Those who had, for whatever reason, missed the formative experience of the war, were ill-equipped for the post-war world too. The very social changes which caused people like Mary to feel in control of the present and expectant for the future appeared to others as an assault and a reason for further retreat into pre-war ways of thought and behaviour. People like Willie, perpetually talking about 'getting back to pre-war standards' and about 'pigging it on one's own in these democratic days', determinedly putting on a dinner jacket for the theatre and in general adopting the stance of an ageing Roman in the face of the barbarian invasion, were of course a joke. But when Mary noticed the same tendencies in Dodie it seemed less funny. Odd, too, as she said to Lionel, when one remembered how Dodie in the old days had been up with the latest fashion, from clothes to literary styles. 'It's as if the mechanism's stuck.'

'It always was a bit erratic, though, wasn't it?' he said. 'I seem to remember her quite clueless about anything beyond her own immediate interests.'

'Yes, I suppose you're right. But she seems a bit clueless now about things that one *would* think she'd be on the spot about. Look at all this business over Joanna's school . . .'

'I'd rather not,' said the pitiless Lionel.

This had been a protracted saga. Since Joanna was the focus of her mother's life it was perhaps natural that Joanna's education should be a particular cause for discussion and concern, but, in this case, it seemed a pity that Dodie could not decide what she wanted. In her young life, Joanna had been sent to a bewildering number of schools (at least, Mary found the profusion and variety bewildering; what could Joanna have found it?). These included a Rudolph Steiner school that Dodie had thought would 'bring out her artistic potential', an even more eccentric progressive school that had started up near Esher and about which Dodie had been volubly enthusiastic for a term and a half till Joanna began coming out with four-letter words and 'peculiar stories'—and now, currently, an old-fashioned girls' boarding school of what struck Mary as a particularly limited and footling sort. As a corrective to the progressive school it might, she supposed, have its points; but why couldn't Dodie see that its academic standards were low, its self-consciously 'attractive' country-house building ramshackle, its facilities minimal, its headmistress a gushing snob? (Mary had accompanied Dodie to several Parents' Days.) But apparently Dodie could not see any of these things. The chief virtues of the school in her eyes, as far as Mary could tell, were the negative ones that it was small, that Joanna would not be 'pushed' or 'regimented', and that she was allowed home for the day every Sunday. Joanna, it appeared, was too 'original' and 'highly strung' to be given a conventional, thorough education, much less trained for Oxford or Cambridge.

'Really, in some ways,' said Mary ruefully, 'Dodie reminds me of Uncle George! I mean, the way he got all enthusiastic about Bessemer and sent Dodie there—and paid for me to go to keep her company—then all at once changed his mind and said he "didn't want her to become a blue-stocking" and sent her somewhere quite different. Oh, isn't it depressing when people in middle age turn into their own parents?'

'Well, I imagine that your Uncle George was trying deviously to hang on to his little daughter and cramp her chances of developing a life of her own,' said Lionel austerely. 'Just like Dodie is doing with Joanna now.'

'Do you really think so?' said Mary anxiously. Perhaps because Dodie talked so much about Joanna's creative talents this had not struck her.

'I do, yes. It's not uncommon after all. Is it?'

Charlie was working for an engineering firm in Dundee now. They seldom saw him. Mary wrote regularly, and got an occasional brief, awkwardly affectionate note back.

She said warily: 'But Dodie identifies with Joanna tremendously. Too much, in a way. I wouldn't think she'd want to do anything to cramp Joanna's chances. I mean, she always seems so ambitious for her. All that special art and drama coaching, for instance.'

' "Art", "Drama",' said Lionel. 'That's just what I mean. Not School Certificate, Mary, you notice, or a proper grounding in a foreign language.'

'Mmm. Or science, come to that. Do you know, that ghastly little ladies' seminary she's at doesn't even have science on the curriculum? And when one thinks that

Bessemer started teaching Chemistry to the whole school in the year I was born . . . No, you're right in practice, I do see. But I don't think it's deliberate policy on Dodie's part, if you see what I mean. Just—ignorance. Dodie was so badly educated herself, as a girl. So badly loved, come to that. For all their fussing, her parents never really seemed to want the best for her. Oh, poor Dodie, her life hasn't really been all that fortunate, though when we were young she seemed to have everything, and all that success of her first book . . . And now she's all on her own. She does adore Joanna. I do hope there aren't big disappointments for her there too.'

Mary tried to see Joanna regularly, having her to stay for a weekend each holidays, taking her to the theatre and buying her carefully chosen presents. She did this partly because she was conscientious, and knew that, if anything were to happen to Dodie, she herself would be almost Joanna's only relation, and partly because she was genuinely interested in the precocious, skittish little girl. Little? Well, perhaps not. Joanna was in her teens now, and would soon be taller than either Mary or her own mother. Although she still appeared in childish frocks and white socks, her little-girl chatter had recently given way to silences and an intermittent expression of brooding intensity. She drew and painted well, with a slapdash but impressive command of material. She played the piano too, in an equally impressionistic manner—but that might have been partly the style encouraged by the school music teacher. Certainly the embarrassing 'recitations', replete with expression and gesture, that she was encouraged to give on Parents' Days could be laid at the door of the school, who presumably chose the material: not Shakespeare but Henry Newbolt, nor Chekhov but L. du Gard Peach. Joanna's intense, full-lipped face above her white-collared school dress extracted every ounce of drama from this poor-quality material; there was, thought Mary once or twice, something intellectually or emotionally famished about the child. She tried herself to insert a little mental nourishment, and good advice, on Joanna's brief holiday visits, but it wasn't easy; on her last visit, in particular, the once-confident Joanna seemed to have withdrawn into a fastness of obscure adolescent preoccupation. What did she

283

think about? Impossible to probe too far. On Joanna's last night in London Mary heard her sobbing loudly, almost luxuriantly. After hesitation, she went in.

'My dear child—what *is* it?' She strongly suspected it was nothing much, but the sight of Joanna's flowerlike face on the pillow, red and swollen now between the billows of her dark hair, touched and moved her beyond her better judgment.

Joanna was not particularly coherent. Something about no one liking her at school and she not liking anyone much, except one girl—'and she's ill now, and isn't coming back next term and might *die*'. Something about a boy pen-friend she hadn't been allowed to have. Something about not being able to help minding things awfully—'Mummy says she's always been just the same, and that people like us can't help it. Oh, I *do* wish we could help the way we are—'

'We can,' said Mary firmly. She was not going to have the impressionable Joanna poisoned with this fatalistic nonsense, not if she could help it. Honesty compelled her to qualify: 'At least, we perhaps can't help the tendencies we've been born with, but we *can* control our behaviour and lead the sort of life we want to live and think we ought to live and make ourselves happy that way, even if other—things—still remain problems.'

That, she supposed, had been the guiding principle of her own life, on reflection. If, indeed, she had had a guiding principle, which was open to doubt. What apparently seemed to outsiders an energetic, competent career with planned goals sometimes seemed to her, as she looked back on it, a life lived much of the time with the uncertainty of a dream, an existence perpetually in hostage to time and chance, scored by irrelevant strokes of good fortune and bad. Yet she reiterated firmly to Joanna:

'People *can* run their own lives. They don't have to be just—blown about on winds of emotion, being hurt by things. You'll see that more clearly once you're a little older. Things will get better. You'll have more choices. You'll see.'

'Mummy says not.'

Mary refrained from retorting: 'That indeed is what has been the matter with your mother's life.' There would be time enough to indulge in criticism of Dodie in a year or two more, when Joanna needed that to help her to break free of her mother's stifling influence. Oh, poor Dodie—

'Mummy says I've got a double dose of sensitivity. Inherited from her and from my father, you see.' As if encouraged by the thought of this mythical parent, she blew her nose on a handkerchief proffered by Mary, and added more cheerfully:

'He was a Polish cavalry officer, you see.'

'I know he was Polish,' said Mary carefully, wondering what special lien on sensitivity the Polish cavalry had in Dodie's erratic imagination. She asked quickly, guilty at trying to pump the child for information in this way:

'Joanna—do you ever hear from him? Does your mother, that is . . .'

Joanna looked puzzled. 'No, he died before I was born. Didn't you know that? It was because he died that Mummy and he didn't have time to get married. He was awfully brave and got posthumously decorated—for the battle he died in, you know. Oh, I *wish* I'd known him.'

It was a harmless enough fairy story, in the circumstances. And at least poor old Dodie seemed to have negotiated Joanna's childhood without another major breakdown, contrary to Mary's and Lionel's forebodings.

She kissed Joanna good night, and said that they'd talk about her father more, some time, if Joanna ever wanted to.

Dodie herself Mary rarely saw. The decline in personal ambition and sociability that had been apparent in Dodie when Joanna was a young child absorbing all her energies had not been reversed by time but seemed to have settled down on Dodie's life as a deadening habit. Mary had long ago noticed that some women seemed to be chemically affected by childbirth at a profound level of energy and initiative; she was forced to conclude that Dodie was one of a small number who were in some way permanently depleted by the processes of gestation and birth. And in Dodie's case there was an extra element to this picture: it was as if Dodie's final capitulation to the imperative of sex, so long and so hysterically delayed for two full decades before Joanna's appearance, had both cured her instability and killed off something in her also. One should never, thought Mary

285

soberly, underestimate the power of sex. (Though Lionel had always maintained that how a person chose to spend twenty minutes once in a while had been, ever since Freud, ridiculously over-stressed. 'Chose'—that was his word.)

Visiting Dodie now, it was hard to believe that she had ever been stirred by sexual passion, much less that she had radiated the nervous physical consciousness of one who knows she is desired. Sometimes Mary wondered if, after Joanna's birth, Dodie had come to fear another mental breakdown so much that she had almost wilfully excluded from her life and memory everything that could stimulate, retreating from the fear of madness into a soporific, deliberate boredom. Yet Mary had been in Dodie's bedroom and knew that the wardrobes were still crammed with obsolete evening dresses, high-heeled shoes and fox furs; perhaps it had been easier for her just to ignore them and what they represented than to take the decision to throw them away.

In this cluttered house, Dodie spent her days with little apparent occupation during term-time beyond writing Joanna letters at school and taking Joanna's cocker spaniel for walks. On the rare occasions when Mary nerved herself to ring up and suggest a visit Dodie would never come to London and was hardly pressing in her invitation to Mary to come down to Esher instead; she always claimed to have an 'urgent letter' to write, or to be about to 'wash the blankets' or some other household ritual. Yet her house, when Mary actually penetrated it, never bore any particular signs of care and attention: Mary got the impression that Dodie spent much of her time alone, playing Patience, listening to radio serials, and—well, what? Not even drinking, apparently. John Hershey, when the situation was described to him, suggested this possibility at once, as by far the most likely explanation for Dodie's withdrawal, but Mary had never seen any signs of it. No, what Dodie seemed addicted to these days was not alcohol but a series of what Mary thought of, with slight squeamishness, as 'dotty cults': Rudolph Steinerism, food reform, Christian Science, something called Scientology . . . It reminded her of Aunt May (again, that depressing repetition from one generation to another) but Mary could see, on reflection, that this was where Dodie's aptitude for latching on to new ideas, that had been such a feature of her youth, was now being directed. Such social contacts as she had seemed to be mainly confined to short-term friendships with fellow believers in whatever was her current cult. Garrulous middle-aged women with obscure 'unhappy experiences' behind them . . . Once an obviously homosexual man who appeared to be living at the cottage for several months and who (Dodie later recounted indignantly) left suddenly, owing her money. She seemed, Mary noted, to have no sense that this could in any way be her own fault.

It was for these reasons, as well as for a number of others, that Mary tried hard to maintain contact with Joanna and to make her feel that she had a second home in London, if she ever needed one. But Joanna was still bound up emotionally with her mother. It wasn't easy to strike the right line. Once again, the desolating problem of the child that was not one's own . . .

Yet when Mary answered the doorbell early one summer morning in 1955 she found Joanna on the doormat. Joanna was wearing regulation school shoes and white socks, what was no doubt her 'best' home dress—a highly patterned, drape-skirted cotton affair that Mary recognised as an old one of Dodie's—and some heavily applied lipstick. Her face was otherwise slightly dirty. Her lovely hair which, six months before, had been permed by Dodie's 'little man' in Esher, was now a frizzy mess. She looked frightened and tired but triumphant. She had run away from school, she said.

It must, thought Mary, have taken courage and determination, in the over-protected Joanna, for her to have crept out of the school and grounds at night, walked the best part of ten miles to a station where she would be inconspicuous, waited on a bench till the first train in the morning, and then made her way to London and across it to Baker Street. She recounted all this to Mary with gusto, munching cornflakes and toast and marmalade as she did so, but added:

'I was terrified you'd be away or something. The underground took the last of my money, except for threepence.'

Why had she run away? Was she in some sort of trouble at school?

Yes, *awful* trouble. Melodramatically. She had been going for walks out of the school grounds in the evenings after Prep.

'Well, that doesn't sound too terrible. In fact, why shouldn't you go for walks?'

'We're not allowed to go outside the gates on our own at all. No, not ever. Miss P was simply livid . . . Oh, Auntie Mary, I get so *bored* at school.'

'Yes, I should think you would. Good heavens. Even in my day, at Bessemer, we were at least allowed to go for walks . . . Was that really all you did?'

'Well, not really. Actually Miss P thought I was meeting a—a boy, you see.' There was an edge of triumph in her voice as she brought out the emotion-laden word.

'And were you?'

Joanna looked troubled. At length, as if guessing Mary was sceptical, she said:

'No, as a matter of fact I wasn't. I mean, I don't know any boys to meet—not round there. Nor at home, worse luck. But I let Miss P think I was. I mean, she was livid anyway . . . She jumped to the conclusion it was one of the boys from the council school in East Grinstead. She's got the council school on the brain. When we meet any of them, when we're out in crocodile, we're made to turn round and go the other way. It's so *embarrassing* . . . And then Miss P really screamed at me. She was going to get the doctor and everything to look at me today—that's partly why I ran away to you. They'd put me in the sick-room, as if I was infectious or something, and it's easy to climb down from the flat roof outside. Oh, I wish I was dead. Or grown up, anyway.'

'They aren't alternatives, fortunately! Oh, Joanna darling, I'm sorry to laugh, but what a ridiculous mess. So unnecessary. I'm sure we can sort it out somehow and pacify your Miss P.'

'I don't see how,' said Joanna darkly, near to tears. 'Actually she's a bit potty, I think.'

'Well . . . would you like me to ring her up?'

'Could you?'

'Of course I could.'

'But wouldn't you be scared to? Mummy always says—'

'No, indeed I wouldn't. One of the great things about

being a middle-aged lady like me, you know, Joanna, is that one isn't remotely scared by people like Miss P. On the contrary, I shall be fierce Dr Denvers giving my professional opinion, you see. I shall say that in my estimation it's all been a silly misunderstanding, and that I shall only send you back to school if I'm assured there will be no more fuss about it. Something like that, anyway.'

Mary spoke with deliberately cool briskness, wanting to deflate Joanna's over-developed sense of drama as much as to reassure her. She half expected that Joanna would refuse to be sent back anyway. But Joanna did not seem to have thought that far. Instead she went pink, and said furiously:

'I will go back. I know I have to, I know I have to stay till I'm sixteen anyway, Mummy says. And Miss P never actually expels anyone, whatever they do. She pretends it's Christian forgiveness, but really I think it's because she doesn't want to lose the fees. But I won't, I simply won't go back, if you let on I was fibbing to them. Oh don't, Auntie Mary. I can't bear it. Let them think I was meeting a boy—I don't care, I don't care about anything—'

'Well—all right, but I warn you in that case there may be more trouble. And what are you going to tell your mother? We'll have to ring her up in a few minutes. The school have probably got on to her already, and she must be terribly worried about you.'

'Oh, don't tell her either!' said Joanna frantically. 'Don't! You're not to, Auntie Mary. I wish I hadn't told you now. I'll never speak to you again if you do.'

'Joanna dear, what *is* all this? Why on earth . . .' But Mary's voice trailed off inconclusively. She felt that she knew very well why Joanna had staged this drama, this token rebellion with a make-believe boyfriend at its centre. Imprisoned for two-thirds of the year in an institution apparently run by a neurotic spinster and for the rest of the time in the small house at Esher with Dodie's aborted, sexless life as both a model and a warning, was it any wonder that this child (this physically adult creature of nearly fifteen, rather) needed to invent such a drama?

But this common-sense explanation was not, she realised

on further thought, adequate. Memories nagged at her uncomfortably: Dodie herself at Bessemer, and the wounded Tommies episode. Dodie at—what? Eighteen perhaps?— during that year in Switzerland after the War, and the Italian singing-master episode. (Had *he*, on reflection, ever existed?) Dodie's other shadowy men, those non-lovers who had peopled her youth. That man Clive she had made gestures about running away with, before her second major breakdown. Joanna's own father, come to think of it: had he been real? Self-evidently, as there was Joanna. But there was something improbable in it, something about this stereotyped wartime-affaire-with-a-foreigner that fitted too neatly into a fictional pattern . . .

Oh God, don't let Joanna go the way Dodie has. Don't let her waste her life too. Let me be able to offer her a lifeline— another model—

She drew a breath: 'Joanna, let us be clear about this. If you really insist, I will keep your secret this time and let your mother and your headmistress go on believing whatever wild story you've told them. But please understand *I will only do it this once*. There's to be no more wild stories, and no more running away. You're not refusing to go back, so what was the point of it all? No, don't tell me, I think I know and I *do* sympathise; I'm sure that school is very boring. But, my dear girl, we have to live in the real world, not in a dream. Just concentrate, for the moment, on getting some O-levels, or whatever they're called these days, and then when you're sixteen, if not before, I'll try to get your mother to send you somewhere better to finish your education.'

'Are you going to ring her now?' said Joanna after a pause, in a small voice. Her tale told, and the bravado of her journey spent, she seemed suddenly much younger and rather cowed.

'I think I must, don't you? Oh dear. In the circumstances, after what I've promised you, it's not going to be an easy conversation.'

It wasn't. Dodie had indeed been contacted by the school. But, to Mary's great surprise, she did not seem so much anxious for Joanna as angry and disgusted.

'How *could* she?' she kept saying. 'Sneaking out to meet a boy, of all things . . . I just don't understand.'

'Well, really,' said Mary weakly, struggling with her own unaccustomed duplicitous role. 'It surely isn't that uncommon, Dodie, at Joanna's age. Girls mature earlier, you know, than they did when we were young. I mean, I wouldn't read too much into it. Just a natural escapade. I'd have thought . . .'

' "Natural", you say. I'd use another word. I think it's plain nasty, Mary. And as for being not uncommon, as you put it—yes, it *is* common, horribly so. Like so many things in this beastly world today.'

'Oh well, Dodie, girls' schools . . . I expect they all giggled about it together and someone dared her.' (Joanna isn't that sort of schoolgirl, she's a loner, but perhaps Dodie won't know that.) 'I wouldn't take it seriously, you know. Schools get these things out of proportion. Think of Bessemer, and that absurd wounded Tommies' business.'

'What wounded Tommies? I don't remember anything about that,' said Dodie sharply. 'And how can I *not* take it seriously,' she continued, her voice breaking with emotion. 'How my Joanna, who's always been so sensitive and fastidious, could do a thing like that . . . I feel quite sick at the thought.'

'Dodie, nothing's *happened* to Joanna, I promise you. I'm sure you needn't worry so.'

'Oh *you*,' said Dodie angrily. 'Always the calm, self-righteous lady doctor, aren't you? What do you understand about what I feel? For all your wonderful know-how you've never had a child.'

After the episode was over Mary worried not so much about Joanna (who had returned to school quite calmly and was now no doubt enjoying the enhanced respect of her contemporaries) but about Dodie. What did her attitude bode for the years ahead? How could Joanna hope to try her wings and develop teenage relationships if Dodie was hovering over her all the time accusing her of being common and nasty? Alas for the shadow woman who had been 'a hall of glass' and who 'had to be free to live'. Perhaps the contrast between the bright, if illusory past and the drab present was so painful that Dodie could not bear to look back on that brightness and acknowledge it.

291

'She seemed almost hysterical,' she said thoughtfully to Lionel at the weekend, when she had recounted what had happened. 'And so vindictive.'

'I should imagine,' said Lionel drily, 'that now that Joanna is growing up Dodie is building up a pretty lethal jealousy. I suspect that, by the time Joanna's seventeen or eighteen, she's going to need rescuing from her mother, literally and physically, if Dodie isn't to destroy her . . . Dodie's not sane, you know, Mary. You realise that, don't you?'

'I used to think she was more or less sane these days, in a dreary sort of way,' said Mary slowly. 'I used to think that she'd somehow traded all her old dottiness for that—for dreariness, and being a devoted mother. That she was what's called a burnt-out case. But—oh, Lionel. Yes. I *do* see what you mean.'

John Hershey took a less sinister view. Old Lionel took things too seriously, he said—'You and he have too high standards in human relations, you know. It's admirable, but unrealistic.' As far as he was concerned, he said, half the middle-aged women he knew were potty, by any objective analysis. 'I've numerous examples among my assorted in-laws from both marriages. And among my patients. That's one of the unnerving things about general practice that no one ever warns you about. You have cosy Dickensian fantasies of delivering the babies of babies you've delivered, and growing old along with your favourite hypochondriacs. But in practice what it often means is that women you've known as pretty young things, full of life and spunk, gradually transform themselves into overweight, whining disasters, swilling gin and phenobarbitone, a burden to their long-suffering husbands and a menace to their children . . . And no advice one can offer seems to make any difference. Of course it doesn't.'

'You're overweight yourself!' said Mary, laughing in spite of her disapproval of his cynicism.

'Yes, I know I am, thanks. But I'm still basically the *same*, aren't I, as I always was?'

'Yes. Oh yes.'

'You see what I mean? Nothing happens to men in the way it does to so many women. Life goes on, and assorted bits of ill-luck—or tragedy—assail us, but most of us still remain, for better or worse, as we always were. Nothing really changes us. Whereas women *rot*, Mary. You must have seen that for yourself.' He gazed at her with mock threat from under his bushy eyebrows.

Deeply discomforted, mainly by her recognition of some truth in what he was saying, Mary said primly:

'I hope you're not including me in your general condemnation.'

'No, darling Mary, you know I'm not, so don't look at me in that pained way. Like all my favourite women the point about you is that you don't change. You always seem marvellously the same, physically and in other ways too. But that's not the most usual pattern, believe me. Not today, at any rate.'

'I wonder,' said Mary thoughtfully, 'if this century has been a particularly difficult one for women? I won't have the word "rot", it's vicious. But I do know what you mean, John . . . Emancipation hasn't been entirely a blessing.'

'Emancipation—*what* emancipation? Look around you, my dear girl, not at your own particular friends and colleagues but at the average bourgeois wife and mother, and ask yourself how emancipated she really is. Not a bit, most of them. And pig-ignorant with it. Oh, they *think* they work hard because they can't get proper maids any more. But they really do bugger-all. A bit of shopping, a bit of bridge. Golf, if they're unusually energetic. They aren't even particularly active sexually, most of them, as far as I can make out.' He grinned at Mary sardonically. 'I happen to think there's a sexual revolution on the way, in fact. It's all these vitamins we give the kids, and very soon now we'll have a simple contraceptive pill worked out—as I don't need to tell *you*. But these ladies I'm thinking of don't know that. Heads in the sand, the lot of 'em. I sent one woman's daughter off for a termination recently—the girl was barely sixteen, best thing for all concerned—and you should have heard the mother's carry-on. Said I "must have been mistaken in my diagnosis" and how could her little girl possibly get involved in anything so sordid? Silly cow.'

Mary was silent for a moment. She was wondering how

John's pejorative view of women (which surely he hadn't held in the old days?) fitted with his marriage to Myriam. Better not speculate. She and Lionel were rarely invited to the Hershey house as a couple these days. An outsider could never, in any case, judge a marriage. She said after a while:

'So you think I shouldn't worry too much about Joanna?'

'No—why the hell? Kids are tough. Look at my two. And, from what you tell me, Joanna's fighting back. She'll be okay once she gets a real boyfriend, won't she?'

'Yes. I believe she will.'

'Well, then! Have her stay again next winter—bring her round to our place at the New Year. The boys'll both be home, then, and so will friends of theirs. Joanna'll have a good time. She pretty?'

'Yes—potentially very, I'd say, once she's learnt how to dress. But John, she'll only be fifteen still and David and Mike are—what? Twenty and twenty-two? I mean, I'm sure she'd be thrilled, but would they?'

'I'll fix 'em. Do 'em good to think of someone besides themselves for a change,' said John moodily.

Mike was doing his national service, which in his case (for he was very bright) consisted of learning Russian at Cambridge. David was reading Law at London. Well-mannered, personable, self-confident even to the point of arrogance, they seemed indeed a vindication of John's aphorism that 'kids are tough'—and of Myriam's adequacy as a stepmother. If Olive had lived would they have turned out different? More reflective, perhaps; less nakedly eager to demonstrate their own success . . .

Even now, after more than ten years, to envisage that alternative loop of time in which Olive did not die was painful to Mary. She sheered away from it.

As from that other loop, in which Lionel was painlessly absent and she and Laurie lived together in Philadelphia. She still heard from him at intervals. Long, friendly letters, with an affectionate superscription, about books read, films seen, odd people encountered in the street or on his travels. He seemed to travel a lot, roaming North and South America, but he had not (as far as she knew) returned to Europe. He had never married, though she had taught herself to expect that he would, now.

Only once, when she rashly went to see the film of *A Streetcar Named Desire* and discovered it was set in New Orleans, did she, for a few weeks, suffer from the intense, anguished longing for him that she had felt years before. It subsided again, leaving her shaken and reflective. Perhaps, even yet, the future might hold something more for both of them?

Lionel was due to retire from Manningham at the end of the year. It was an odd and slightly daunting prospect, having him in London all the time after all these years. Not that he had ever been irritating or difficult to live with. He would still be doing some lecturing; he had a book to write and was on numerous committees. She had no worries about him occupying himself. But neither of them was used to the sort of continuous married life that other couples seemed to take for granted.

When Joanna was rising seventeen Dodie acceded to her pleas to leave school by sending her to a finishing school in Paris. Telling Mary this on the phone, she sounded for once quite animated.

'I had such a marvellous time myself, that year I went to school in Lucerne. And in Paris too, though then of course I was rather older . . . I do feel it will improve her *chances*, Mary. After all, I must do what I can for her.'

'Chances of marriage', Dodie could only mean. Resolved not to contradict (but what an old-fashioned idea: good heavens, one didn't marry girls off like that these days), Mary confined herself to asking if it wasn't rather expensive.

'Horribly, my dear. I shan't have a stitch to wear for years—not that I ever do have new clothes these days, as you know—but I feel, well, one might just as well spend the money. It all just goes in taxes otherwise to this filthy government.'

The Conservatives had been in power again since 1951, but Dodie did not seem to have noticed. Like Willie, she habitually spoke as if the country were still in the immediate aftermath of war and that revolution was imminent—if not indeed in process. 'Of course, I know you and Lionel have always been Red, but after all most people aren't,' was her way of expressing the matter.

So Joanna was sent off to Paris; Mary gave her supper before putting her on the boat-train. She was wearing a full-skirted, flowered cotton frock over rattling starched petticoats. She had a stole, high-heeled shoes, white gloves, and a small white hat composed of daisies perched over the hair she now wore in a pony-tail. She carried the sort of band-box supposedly used by models. Mary thought the effect charming, but very English. Still, as she was going to an establishment reputedly full of English debutantes . . . It seemed unlikely, in the circumstances, that this expensive venture would even do much towards ensuring that Joanna spoke fluent French.

In the autumn, Joanna returned. Unexpectedly, once again, she was there on Mary's doorstep. This time it was Lionel who opened the door to her. Mary returned from Wimpole Street to find them drinking tea together. Lionel's manner was kindly and non-committal, but Mary could tell from small gestures, or perhaps from his stance, that he was bothered by something. Could it be Joanna's new appearance? Admittedly she looked very different, but Lionel rarely noticed what clothes people wore.

Joanna was dressed entirely in black—a huge roll-necked sweater in which her slim frame disappeared like that of a waif, and a longish dusty skirt. Her hair hung loose about a face that was sunburnt and bare of make-up, except for some heavy black lines round her eyes. She looked extremely tired. Round her neck was a medallion on a chain. She wore flat, strap sandals on dirty feet, and all her possessions appeared to be in a tattered straw basket covered with a cloth. She was a picturesque figure but, to Mary's eyes, bizarre: like a Greek or Mexican peasant escaped from its natural habitat. On reflection, however, Mary recalled seeing girls similarly attired in one of those new coffee-houses in Baker Street. She wondered with amusement and fore-boding, what Dodie would say to this image bearing so little resemblance to the docilely marriageable daughter of her futile aspirations!

'Joanna's been wondering,' said Lionel heavily, 'whether we've heard from her mother recently. Have we?'

'Not recently, no.' (So that was it.) 'Not since shortly after you left in June, Joanna, come to think of it.'

'Nor has Joanna,' said Lionel.

'Really?' Mary sat down to accommodate this new piece of information. Was it true? If she had thought about it at all, she would have supposed that Dodie was probably bombarding Joanna with letters encouraging her to 'make the most of her chances'.

'When, exactly, did you last hear from her?'

Joanna looked uncertain. She thought it was before 14 July. 'Because after that we went to Madame Pûchard's house at St Malo. But letters were all forwarded. And I sent Mummy the address there, anyway. I sent her lots of postcards. But she just didn't write.'

'And it's now—good Lord, almost October. Joanna dear, this is a bit worrying . . . Is this why you've come back to England? I thought you were supposed to stay there till Christmas.'

Again Joanna looked uncertain. She was avoiding glances, Mary noticed, but not as if she were deliberately trying to hide something. It was perhaps that the past few months—a short period to an adult but momentously long, no doubt, for an adolescent, and long indeed for a mother not to write— had opened a great gulf of new experience for her, across which communication with figures from her discarded childhood was difficult. After a while, she said:

'Yes—partly I suppose. But it was also that we all went back to Paris and, after being in St Malo, I didn't like it much there any more. And there was a bit of a row going on. One of the *surveillantes* left . . . Anyway, I didn't think there was much point in my staying. And—' She hesitated.

'Go on.'

'Well, it's my birthday next week. And I did think Mummy might want to see me then and might be cross if I didn't come home. That's what I told Madame Pûchard, anyway.'

Mary found it touching that Joanna, in spite of her transformed appearance, evidently still thought in childish terms of grown-ups being cross with her rather than of the

297

grown-ups themselves possibly being remiss. Mary and Lionel looked at one another.

'I feel guilty that I haven't been in touch with your mother before now,' said Mary. 'We've been reorganising the Centre, I've been so busy ... But I should have tried to ring her up to see how she was getting on.'

'Have *you* tried to ring her?' Lionel asked Joanna.

'Yes. There was no answer. I thought perhaps she was away.' Joanna sounded puzzled, mildly perturbed, not deeply upset. But then, as Lionel remarked later to Mary, no sane seventeen-year-old could feel anything but relief and gratitude at the prospect of being abandoned by Dodie.

'Oh, *Lionel*,' said Mary, exasperated and worried. Really, his civilised cynicism where individuals were concerned did sometimes border on the callous. It also seemed, in what she supposed one must now call his old age, to be growing on him. Admirably logical in theory, perhaps, this Stoic tradition of withdrawal from earthly attachments as life entered its final phase. But in practice she found it a little chilling. Lionel even seemed dispassionate about Charlie these days, amiably disposed toward him but hardly interested.

They tried Dodie's number several times that evening. Still no answer.

'You'd better stay with us till the weekend,' said Mary. 'Then we'll drive down together on Saturday and try to find out what's going on. I'm sure everything's all right really.' She felt more and more sure it wasn't, but did not want to air her fears to Joanna. Under a newly acquired veneer of adult know-how Joanna seemed in an odd state. She was nervous as a cat. Her intermittent, self-conscious chatter about cafés and nightclubs in Paris and St Malo (had this finishing school been all that it was supposed to be?) seemed to cover, like a fine membrane, depths of panic at which Mary could only guess. Mary longed to do more for the desperate-seeming girl, to let her know that she need not pretend so hard to be happy and in control of her own life; but she feared that puncturing Joanna's fragile courage might only make matters worse.

They drove down to Surrey on a resplendent autumn day. Joanna looked unwell, and got out of the car once to be sick.

'Nerves,' said Lionel, and bought Joanna some barley sugar at a village shop.

From the outside Dodie's house appeared much as usual, except that the grass of the small lawn was rank and unmown. The Virginia creeper that covered the front was turning red, and also discarding its leaves on to the verandah. (Since Joanna's birth Dodie's chosen houses had borne a ghostly resemblance to the Indian bungalows of her childhood. The impression was increased, in the present house, by the pieces of Indian carved furniture and brasswork that encumbered the small rooms, a legacy from Uncle George and Aunt May.)

'It looks as if she's away,' said Mary uncertainly, scanning the unswept verandah.

'But there're two windows open,' Joanna remarked in a choked voice. 'And Mummy always locks up carefully when she goes out for the day.' She looked white; glancing at her anxiously, Mary wondered if she were going to be sick again. She said, filled with ill-defined foreboding:

'Look, lovey, you stay in the car for the moment. Lionel and I will have a look round.'

The doorbell was not answered. They went round to the back where there was a greenhouse. Dodie had never grown plants there; Joanna had had it as a playhouse when she was a child, and there was still a jumble of superannuated dolls in a dolls' pram under one of the shelves. How typical of Dodie not to have got rid of these relics. Mary remembered that the warped door of the greenhouse was permanently open, and that it led through French windows into what Dodie called the drawing room, to which it imparted a slightly dismal, aquarian air. Sure enough, the French windows were not latched.

They entered.

At once they were aware, among the carved furniture and the knick-knacks, of a sickeningly and inescapably awful smell. It permeated the whole room, making it unliveable, but seemed, Mary registered after a moment's disgusted recoil, to be coming from behind the sofa. She and Lionel looked at each other in appalled recognition.

They could both diagnose that smell. No one who was a

299

pathologist or who had been in blitzed buildings could fail to do so. It was the unmistakable, nauseating stench of advanced bodily corruption.

They stared at each other and read the same thought in each other's eyes. After all, one saw such cases in local papers . . . It was, however unthinkable, all too possible.

It was Lionel who at last went forward to look behind the sofa.

'My God,' he said after a pause. But not in tones of horror confirmed, more in those of disgusted anti-climax.

It was not Dodie who lay behind the sofa. It was the old cocker spaniel—or what remained of him—curled up in his basket, extremely dead and a mass of white movement.

Mary could only say: 'Thank *heavens* we left Joanna in the car.'

'She might follow us round, though,' said Lionel promptly. 'Better latch those French windows.' He did so. Then, firmly taking Mary's hand, he led her, reluctant and sickened, on a tour of the house.

Little-used dining room empty, tidy, dusty, with Aunt May in the pastels of the 1890s gazing from the chimney-breast. Hall cluttered with newspapers, many of them apparently unread, with a bicycle Joanna must have grown out of several years ago and with a number of empty milk bottles.

The cramped kitchenette was a shambles; sink stacked with unwashed plates and cups, stove thick with grease and embedded, spent matches, table covered in opened tins, a hacked loaf of bread, pots of jam, a withering lettuce and a lump of mouldy cheese. The smell in there, while nothing like as bad as that in the drawing room, spoke of sourness and decaying food.

'Oh Lionel, she *must* have gone away,' said Mary helplessly. 'I'm not so sure.'

The bathroom too was on the ground floor, and a small spare room. Neither of these revealed anything beyond the general evidence of neglect. Lionel made purposefully for the stairs: the house was a semi-bungalow, and only two small rooms, Dodie's bedroom and Joanna's, were perched among the eaves, their dormer windows too high for anyone to look out. Or in.

Halfway up the stairs Mary stopped and clung to the banister rail. She was convinced that there, stretched out on one of those single beds, they would find Dodie. Asleep, or—she could not face it.

'You go, Lionel. Please.'

'Right-o.' His walking boots clumped upwards. It took more than death to frighten Lionel.

With some idea of making amends for her failure of courage, Mary returned to the fetid sitting room. She kept well away from the sofa, but began opening the windows, both the one that looked on to the side-fence of the garden and the one that looked into the greenhouse.

It was thus that, with a startled cry of recoil, she came face to face, almost nose to nose, with Dodie. Dodie was standing in the greenhouse with her face against the French windows, peering in, as if baffled to find it shut against her.

She had, presumably, come in from the garden. She claimed afterwards, with offhand irritability, to have been 'gardening', and was certainly wearing awful old trousers as if to prove it. But in that instant, seeing that apparently disembodied face, framed in straggling grey hair, looming against the dirty pane, Mary had momentarily believed that she was seeing some hallucination that encapsulated Dodie's whole life, some evil manifestation of a decay and corruption of the mind as powerful as that of the body; Dodie imprisoned for ever in her own hall of glass—a small, derelict conservatory where nothing grew and where nothing was kept but Joanna's discarded dolls, piled grubbily in postures of death and rejection.

Lionel was in favour of getting Dodie into the Maudsley in south London—the successor to the old Bethlem Royal— where they both knew people on the staff. But Dodie's GP, summoned with some difficulty from a round of golf, was disposed to send her to a local nursing home whose proprietor, according to him, had 'done wonders' with one or two similar cases.

'He's probably got shares in the place,' remarked Lionel. Neither he nor Mary had been impressed by the doctor, a lethargic and bullying country practitioner who had not

bothered to conceal his contempt for what he called 'head
cases' and had waffled dismissively about the menopause.
Nor were they impressed by the poky nursing home, which
appeared to them to be the local genteel dumping ground,
not only for psychiatric cases but for the senile and demented.
But the man who ran it, one Bonaway, seemed harmless
enough—'If,' said Lionel sardonically, 'any psychoanalyst
can be said to be entirely harmless'—and the place had the
great advantage that Dodie was prepared to go there voluntarily. After some tears, and a good deal of irrelevant prevari-
cation, she had accepted from Mary and Lionel, from the
doctor and from a neighbour who had materialised to offer
gratuitous advice and warnings, the idea that she was 'in a
state of nervous collapse' and needed 'a good rest'.

'Oh, you never know,' said Mary wearily to Lionel. 'I've
never regarded the analytic approach as particularly useful
myself, as you know. But we might as well give it a try. And
that nosy woman who came round—Mrs Beesom, or whatever her name was—she said that poor Dodie had been
having great bonfires in the garden, burning books and
clothes and things. I noticed a lot of charred stuff out there
myself. One doesn't have to be a convinced Freudian to think
that a person who behaves like that is trying to destroy her
past, and that therefore a little poking around in that past
might do no harm.'

Joanna had been kept out of the house which, fortunately,
she seemed to have no desire to enter. When Mary had asked
her apprehensively if there were nothing she wanted to collect
from there (Lionel had smuggled the dog-basket down to
the bottom of the garden and was furtively digging a pit; but
still, the smell—) she shook her head and turned her face
away. It was evident that she wished to abandon the past
and all its material accessories: the house—prison of her
childhood—held nothing more for her, her manner seemed
to say. But it had not been possible (or, probably, desirable)
to keep her away from Dodie altogether. The two had come
face to face in the next-door neighbour's house, the neutral
territory to which the doctor had been called to examine his
patient.

'Oh, *there* you are,' said Dodie moodily, looking at Joanna with vague disapproval as if they had been apart for four days rather than four months. 'I thought you'd left me too.' But she sounded pettish rather than tragic.

Joanna, who had moved forward as if to kiss her mother, now backed away again. Her face went bright red. She looked momentarily like a small child who is about to cry. 'But I wrote to you, Mummy,' she said in a strangulated voice. '. . . And it was your idea that I should go to France, you know.'

Dodie cast a 'humorous', long-suffering, we-know-what-the-ungrateful-young-are-like-don't-we? glance around the assembled company. 'Oh, suit yourself,' she said. 'I don't care; I don't matter any more, I suppose. You never told me anything of what you were doing, did you? I can guess what you've been up to, you dirty little thing.'

Joanna went white, then red again. Perhaps she, like Mary, could read behind Dodie's viciously unfair reproaches the shadow of an undeniable truth. Yes, Joanna had grown up, did not need her mother—much—any more, and was trying to make her own way. Hers was only (only?) the ultimate betrayal that most children must commit against their parents and their own childhood. But Dodie's fragile equilibrium had not been able to stand it. Joanna, who for seventeen years had saved her—more or less—by providing her with a reason for living, was now destroying her.

Mary took the now-speechless Joanna out to walk round the common.

'She is ill, she can't help herself, it's happened before— long before you were born. It's not your fault. Try not to mind too much,' she said, filled with compassion.

'I don't mind,' said Joanna obdurately. 'I hate her, you see. I've hated her for a long time. I just didn't say so.' But a few minutes later she was sick again, at the foot of an elm tree.

Mary was in a quandary: common sense and family duty, let alone love, dictated that they should offer Joanna a home for the moment, but the following week she and Lionel were due to go on holiday, a long-planned trip to Sicily. Had she had only herself to consider, Mary would have abandoned the

303

holiday, even though no further opportunity for it could arise till the following year. But she did not want to ask Lionel to do that, and he did not propose it.

'Perhaps you could stay with the Hersheys,' she suggested to Joanna. 'Would you like me to ask them?' Joanna, who had been to more than one party at the Hersheys since she was fifteen, brightened at this idea. Evidently, thought Mary wistfully, the Hersheys' big, over-heated, luxurious Kensington house, filled with a lively Christmas crowd of assorted relations, represented to Joanna an ideal of family life with which she and Lionel could not hope to compete.

'You know David's getting married soon,' she said.

'I know,' said Joanna jealously. 'You told me. I can't imagine him married! He's so—such fun. What's his fiancée like?'

'Nice, I'm told. I've barely seen her. They met at university. She isn't Jewish, which I believe Myriam minds rather, but John says her family's got "old money", which must make up for a lot.' (Why do I habitually make these snide remarks about Myriam? Really, I must be more careful. It's a bad example to Joanna, apart from anything else.) 'Anyway, they're buying a house in—what's that funny bit of Islington, of all places, that's got so smart now? Canonbury, that's it—and having it decorated with William Morris papers and Victorian furniture, which I must say sounds rather inconvenient to me, but I daresay they know what they're doing.' Actually, she thought, it sounded sickly. Like the way David's set apparently put on dinner jackets to go and see each other in the evening, the way David officiously called men of Lionel's age 'sir', their revival of Anglo-Catholic churchgoing, their neo-right-wing views to match. Was it for this younger generation, she asked herself, that she and Lionel had campaigned for the Health Service, for state education, for the abolition of power and privilege conveyed by money? When David Hershey's son was born, would he be 'put down', if not for Eton then for Marlborough or Charterhouse? David played roulette and drank port, had recently become a member of the Reform Club, and for some reason was proud of these facts . . . Olive would have taught him better than that.

Really, as I get older, Mary reflected, I must beware of turning into a censorious old lady. One thinks, because one does not believe in the Fear of God and the birch and capital punishment, that one will automatically escape the pitfalls of fossilised morality. But in fact, of course, sclerotic progressive views are just as unattractive as petrified Fascist ones. Well—almost.

Every two days Mary or Lionel rang Dodie's nursing home to see how she was getting on. She was going to have a course of insulin therapy, a kind of sleep therapy.

'A bit old fashioned,' said Lionel disapprovingly.

'But it sometimes works, doesn't it? Anything to change the mixture—'

'Anything works, sometimes. Witch-doctoring, loading the person with chains, beating them, casting out devils . . . We really don't have much clue how the mind works, Mary. Historically speaking, where psychiatry's concerned we're still in the Dark Ages.'

'Oh dear. I wonder if Bonaway would agree with you. He seems such a self-confident man. In his own slightly barmy way. I can quite see that he might inspire helpful confidence in his patients.'

'Bonaway,' said Lionel scathingly. 'He's probably too ignorant to know what we *don't* know about the mind. He isn't even a medical doctor, did you know that? I looked him up.'

'He must be, Lionel, if he does ECT and insulin treatment.'

'He isn't. He's got a qualified doctor as a side-kick. I had him on the phone yesterday. Some sort of Central European. I do wish we'd got Dodie into somewhere more reputable, less marginal.'

'Considering,' said Mary with amusement, 'that you don't like Dodie one bit and think she's a lost cause anyway, you're admirably concerned about her welfare.'

'Professional integrity,' said Lionel ironically. 'I can't seem to get out of the habit . . . I must say, I'm longing, after all this, to be off to Sicily.'

The evening before they were due to leave Joanna was despatched to the Hersheys.

305

'I rather wish you'd told her to wear something other than those black clothes,' said Lionel. 'I just noticed the other day that she never seems to wear anything else.'

'My dear, you can't *tell* a girl of Joanna's age what to wear these days. Don't worry, John and the boys will tease her out of it, saying she looks like a Greek Tragedy or something, and Myriam will offer to lend her some dangling earrings ... It's only three weeks before this famous wedding comes off. Mike's at home too, she'll have a lovely time.' At the thought of Joanna, so suitably billeted for the time being, Mary already felt better.

Early the following morning, when they were closing their suitcases and drinking a cup of tea, the telephone rang.

'*Not* patient trouble,' said Mary. 'I can't bear it. You go, Lionel.'

He did, and came back saying: 'Hershey.'

'John? What does he want?'

'Dunno. He wants you.'

With great and unaccustomed unwillingness, Mary picked up the phone: 'What can I do for you, John?'

'Mary—sorry to bother you. I just thought you ought to know something—or rather, to find out if you knew already. Perhaps you do?'

'Do what? . . . Sorry, John, I'm not making much sense of this. What is it?'

'Joanna,' he said impatiently. 'Didn't you realise?'

'Realise what?' she said—and suddenly, as she said it, knew, a fraction before he answered.

'She's pregnant,' he said.

'Oh God . . . John, I *am* sorry. Of course I should have realised, I see that now. She's been sick on and off. We thought it was just nerves . . . distress about her mother. How—that is, how did you discover?' (So quickly, too. What a fool I've been.)

'Asked her,' said John promptly. 'I've a good eye for these things, you know. One gets that, in my sort of practice.'

'How far pregnant?'

'Only six to seven weeks, as far as I can make out.'

'Oh—damn. Blast her. But poor little thing. Poor you,

too . . . John, I'm so sorry. I would never have wished her on to you if I'd realised this.'

'I know that, dear. Anyway, I thought you ought to know, but don't worry—we'll cope.'

Foreboding seized her. She thought quickly: seven weeks plus the fortnight we'll be away, that's still only nine: 'Look, John: if you just look after her for the next two weeks I'll be eternally grateful. Don't let her do anything silly—you know, she just might. Give her my love, and tell her that we'll talk about it all and take a decision the moment I get back. Will you tell her that, please?'

'Of course I will, dear,' he said. 'Enjoy yourselves, have a proper holiday—and don't think too much about this. I wouldn't have bothered you with it myself, just as you're off. But Myriam felt that as you're sort of *in loco parentis* you ought to know.'

'Oh, you were right to ring us—' said Mary, a little shocked at his nonchalance. But he had already rung off.

They enjoyed Sicily, Mary with the guilty pleasure of one escaped from real life, real duties, Lionel with his customary, business-like interest in whatever was on offer. He was reading Carlo Levi. The summer-bleached, heart-rending landscapes contained far more Greek remains than Roman: the whole place did not feel Italian, they agreed, but like a throwback to something older, and not so much European as near-Eastern. Squat, dark-complexioned women carried water jars on their heads; on the outskirts of Palermo families lived in tiny cloth-hung shanties in a crowd of goats, chickens and children.

'This is how I imagine India,' said Mary. 'And an equally old and complex history.'

'You want to go there, don't you?' said Lionel suddenly.

'Always. Since I was a small child and the Boys—my cousins—used to talk about it. When I was young, and they were dead, I still wanted so much to go there that I assumed automatically that I would—that anything I wanted so much *must* be going to happen, some time. You know how it is, when you're young and the time ahead seems infinite?' (Lionel smiled, but did not answer: perhaps, after all, he had

307

never had the luxury of that feeling himself.) 'But life went on, and by and by there never was any time to spare—not enough time, anyway. Yes, I still would like to go there very much. But I don't suppose I shall now. Oh dear,' she added, 'I never thought I'd hear myself say that. Isn't getting older odd?' Lionel was ten years older than she was, though they seldom alluded to the fact: he was still active and healthy.

'I don't see why we shouldn't,' said Lionel. 'All it takes is time and money. We've enough money—we can go on one of the smaller boats, and it can't be that expensive once one is there—and in another five years when you retire from the Centre we'll both have enough time too. So let's.'

'Oh Lionel! But are you sure you'd want to? You've never been that interested in Asia.'

'Oh, me,' he said equably. 'You know I'll find something to interest me. And I expect that between us we can rustle up enough professional contacts there to keep us occupied. Seriously, Mary, you ought to think of doing some gospel-spreading. Birth control is becoming a very big issue there, I hear.'

It was strange, disconcerting, to hear India reduced by Lionel's casual tone to just another place. To Mary it had remained a magic country, another dimension of existence. Of course she had read the newspapers, followed the progress of India's independence ten years earlier, seen photographs of riots, of poverty, listened to ex-Indian 'hands' and their commonplace yet haunting nostalgia; it didn't make any difference. Still, to the child she had once been, India was the mythic, momentous Happy Land sung about in hymns. At the level on which dreams operate, and where reason is powerless, India was the strange country into which the Boys had finally gone.

She did not try to convey this to Lionel: she hardly knew it herself. But she said warmly that, yes, she would love to go to India in 1962 or '63, and that they should work on that plan. She felt disproportionately cheered by the prospect. It was good, at their age, to feel that some definite chunk of future was still there and waiting.

Intermittently, the autumn landscapes of Sicily were pierced for her by another, more poignant image of the nearer future: Joanna with a baby in her arms. One night she dreamed about it. The baby was a boy, and Joanna was going to call it Nigel.

Could it really be? At moments it seemed a preposterous idea. And yet . . . If Joanna wanted to go ahead with this pregnancy she should be given every encouragement to do so, whatever the difficulties. She could stay in Baker Street for a bit; there was Charlie's old room, a cot could be fitted in there too . . . Obsessional, long-suppressed images returned.

She wanted to write to Joanna to say these things. But she held back. She would say them to Joanna's face as soon as she got home, when she was better placed to judge the response. She was reluctant to leave these ochre vistas of hills and valleys that soothed the mind and the eye. But at moments, also, she burned with impatience to return to England.

She telephoned John Hershey the evening they were back.

'How is she?'

'Fine. Up and about again. She'll be okay. How was Sicily?'

'All right. Lovely, in fact—John, what do you mean, up and about?' But, once again, she already knew.

'I mean,' said John, in the impatient tone of one induced to open a subject he had hoped was closed, 'that she's had a termination, of course . . . When? Oh—last Tuesday, I think it was. She was only in for one night. No one here knew, except me and Myriam. The boys thought she'd gone in to have a wisdom tooth out. As I said, she's okay.'

After a long pause, Mary said: 'John, I'm very taken aback by this news. I think I'd better come and see you. In your surgery, if you don't mind, not at home.'

'How could you—just like that? You might have waited a few days longer to consult me. *I* wasn't aware that we'd taken any decision on the matter.'

'Oh, come off it, Mary, what "decision" was there to take? The poor kid needed a termination and was lucky enough to be with people who could get her one quickly and easily. Most youngsters like her aren't. It had to be done, and the quicker the better from every point of view.'

309

'Did you do it yourself?' said Mary suddenly and hostilely. She had been aware for some years, without scrutinising the facts too hard, that John was one of a discreet but growing band of doctors who were prepared to do abortions covertly if they judged that circumstances warranted it. No doubt their motives were excellent. Yet looking now at John's heavy body, his coarse, craggy, middle-aged face, his large hairy hands, she felt a sudden, confused physical revulsion at the idea as well as anger. 'I can do what I like here,' he had once said to her, standing like a king in his new hospital clinic. Arrogance, sickening arrogance—

'Of course I didn't do it myself,' he said irritably. 'That would have been—most unwise. Particularly as she's a guest in my house. I got Warley-Cohen to do it. I've sent several people to him.'

'I see. And who's going to pay his bill?'

'Never mind about that. I doubt if he'll send one, any-way.'

'I see. Done favours for him too, have you? How cosy.'

'Dammit, Mary, what's all this about? I've done a timely favour for your niece, it seems to me, and much thanks I get.'

'Because you had no *right* to act in this high-handed way, John! She's barely seventeen—legally, she shouldn't have had so much as an anaesthetic without a parent or guardian's permission being sought.'

'Oh yes? Well, since her mum's in a bin and you were in Sicily I took that on myself, didn't I? After all, you'd left her with us. And any old way, Mary, you keep intimating that you should have been in on this, but really it was her decision, wasn't it, and no one else's?'

'Oh yes, John, oh yes! I can just imagine how you handled that one—Telling her breezily that it was her decision, but giving her no real choice, no opportunity to refuse. Jollying her along, belittling the situation, taking away its meaning for her. "Nothing at all to worry about, just a little scrape, you won't know a thing about it, there's a good girl, get you fit in time for David's wedding"—Oh yes, no one can refuse lovely Dr Hershey when he's made up his mind, can they?'

After a long pause, John said evenly, 'I never expected you to treat me like this, Mary. You of all people.'

'Well, John, I never expected you to behave like this. So—so without regard for essentials. As if convenience were everything, and the sources of life could just be manipulated at will—at your will at that, not even Joanna's.' In fact she had known for many years that John, her oldest friend, who in many ways she respected and even loved, was like this; she just had not chosen to contemplate the fact.

'You keep suggesting that I forced her into it,' he said angrily, playing with a gold paperknife on his desk.

'I didn't say that. I said that you didn't give her a chance to think whether she might rather have gone through with it and kept the baby. It might have meant an awful lot to her. The man concerned might, too. She wouldn't necessarily have told you, if you didn't ask. You just didn't want to know, did you? "Termination the only sensible solution, too young for motherhood, put it behind you and forget about it"—oh, I know the usual patronising litany. And I also know how inadequate it is and what a lot it ignores. I've had women come to see me at the Centre or in Wimpole Street, still in a state of distress about an abortion ten, fifteen or even twenty years later—yes, even when they've had other children, even when their life seems flourishing . . . No, I'm *not* saying abortion is always wrong' (for John was jeering at her). 'I'm saying that you just don't seem to know what you're doing—'

'And *you* don't know,' shouted John, 'what you're bloody talking about. I'll tell you what you don't know and I do because Joanna told me: she doesn't even know the name of the boy who got her pregnant, or which one of several he was. Do you know what was going on in that so-called finishing school she was at? . . . No, I thought not. Well, when they all went to Deauville or Dinard or wherever it was on the coast, one of the young women supposed to be in charge of them— in *charge*, mind—used to take them down on the beach and encourage them to pick up the local lads. Then they'd all pair off and go off into the bushes or behind the dunes or wherever it was. Would you really expect me to encourage Joanna

311

to go through with a pregnancy started by these schoolgirl fun-and-games? Have a heart!'

After a silence, Mary said: 'Yes, I see . . . I didn't realise Joanna was like that.'

'Like that? What do you mean, "like that"? You're as bad as Myriam. Joanna's too young and too ignorant to be "like" anything. I wouldn't think she's promiscuous by nature, if that's what you mean. I'd say she's a loving creature when she gets the chance. She sounded a bit dazed by the whole thing. Weepy and worried, you know—afraid you and Lionel would be cross, but not really understanding the implications—just wanting to get back on to dry land again. I think she acted as naturally as a little female cat in season, and with about as much foresight. I told her she should just put it behind her and not brood. I suppose you're going to tell me again that this was wrong of me?'

'No,' said Mary at length. 'No, in the circumstances, I can see there's something to be said for that approach. But—oh John, surely you can see, from what you know of Joanna's family situation, that her getting into trouble like that was a cry for help?'

'I know that's one of the favourite theories in FPA circles,' said John loudly and rudely. 'It's the great excuse, isn't it? "We won't actually assist the unmarried and promiscuous, i.e. those that most need practical advice, because they're not *really* needing a diaphragm, you see, they're crying for help" . . . You know what I think? I think it's bollocks. Sex is simply an instinct—that's why it's so hard to resist. To satisfy it *feels* right, like eating when you're hungry or drinking when you're thirsty. There's no need to pretend it's the key to everything, and to make a great psychoanalytical meal of it. I say the satisfaction of desire is just a natural phenomenon, and we'd do best to accept it and plan accordingly. *Your* lot seems to be saying that satisfied desire is in itself a neurotic symptom. Huh. Well, I know who I think are neurotic. And it isn't the likes of Joanna. She'll be all right. You'll see.'

Mary said: ' "Sex is simply an instinct"—you sound like Lionel, saying that,' but she did not argue with him. Her anger was ebbing; she already felt a little ashamed of it,

bruised, sore, uncertain of everything. She added, still trying
to hold her own:

'I'm not sure Lionel will agree with your conclusion,
though.'

He didn't.

'John shouldn't have made it so easy for Joanna. Now
she'll think there's nothing to it, and we'll have the same
problem all over again in a few months' time.'

'Oh, I do hope not,' said Mary with dread.

'Well, for God's sake have a practical word with her,' said
Lionel. 'Instruct her. Get her fitted up.'

'That seems—so cynical, somehow. And like encouraging
her to behave in the same way.'

'Well, what's the alternative? Come on, Mary, you ought
to be familiar with this dilemma.'

'I am,' said Mary crossly. 'You don't understand. It's an
irreconcilable one. We're always arguing about it at Centre
meetings. Ought we/ought we not to extend our services to
unmarried girls? It goes round and round in circles. I'm
absolutely sick of the subject.' She added, with an untypical
morbidness, 'And no one seems entirely rational or really to
be acting in good faith one way or the other. I daresay I'm not
myself.'

She was aware that her anger at John had not been fuelled
only by his high-handed action.

Again, one night, she dreamed of babies, fugitively,
confusedly. Would this obsession never be quite extinct? She
was fifty-five. The menopause had come and gone, without
inconveniencing her. It was long ago, well over a decade, that
she had abandoned all realistic hope of bearing a child
herself. Yet dreams, it seemed, knew no chronology. Past
and present co-existed in a timeless, implacable reality,
unassuaged by reason or experience. Susan's abandoned
baby . . . Dodie's now-abandoned Joanna . . . Joanna's own
aborted infant . . . The child she and Lionel, she and Laurie,
had never had . . . the children the Boys had never lived to
beget . . . These memories, that she had thought laid to rest at
last under the weight of years, awoke and stirred painfully
within her.

313

It was in this state of raw sensitivity that she travelled down to visit Dodie.

She would have gone down before, but 'Dr' Bonaway had asked her not to. His patient had had six sessions of electro-convulsive therapy and also insulin: Mary would understand that patients took a while to recover normal co-ordination, memory and so forth, after such intensive treatment. It was sometimes upsetting for relatives to see them.

Mary did understand. She drove down to Esher (Lionel was away at a conference in the north) preparing herself apprehensively for finding Dodie an inert lump, vague, incontinent, hopelessly damaged in the cause of a return to sanity. Lionel was right: no one knew much about the brain, and both ECT and insulin were potentially dangerous.

But the first impression was encouraging. Dodie was dressed and waiting for her in the nursing home's dim front hall. It was evident that she expected to be taken out to tea, like a child from a boarding school, and her whole manner seemed one of childish pleasure at Mary's arrival. She was dressed—not suitably or becomingly, but without obvious eccentricity—in a mustard-yellow coat and skirt that Mary remembered her wearing years before at one of Joanna's Parents' Days, and a flowery hat of the kind that had been considered 'smart' in the years just after the war, but which now looked both too girlish and over-dressed for everyday wear. The mustard yellow did not suit her now-grey hair, and the skirt, Mary noticed after a while, strained open at the waist; Dodie had been thin when they had taken her six weeks ago from that house full of the stench of death, but she had now put her usual weight back on, and quite a bit more.

Yet once again, as so often long ago, when confronted by Dodie's 'absurd' hat and her enthusiastic welcome Mary found herself feeling somehow at fault: dowdy, rigid, wanting in tenderness. She hastened to embrace Dodie, and to tell her what a relief it was to see her so much transformed for the better.

Only as their conversation developed, first in the car and

314

then in the Oak Tree tea-rooms, did Mary's relief give way to a new unease. Dodie, though not obviously delusional any longer, talked incessantly in a way that precluded communication with the other person. She also had not mentioned Joanna at all.

'. . . Yes, I'm *much* better, Mary. Much. I can see now that I haven't been entirely well for some time.' She paused to bite hugely into a scone from the cream tea she had enthusiastically ordered: a blob of cream remained on her upper lip, but she did not seem to feel it. 'Isn't this lovely?' she said, with vague and touching pleasure, looking round at the horse brasses and obtrusive oak beams, and then continued without pause, talking with her mouth full:

'Dr Bonaway—a marvellous man, Mary, you must have a talk with him—he's giving me regular psychotherapy. *That's* what I've been needing all these years, you see. Dr Bonaway said I needed ECT and insulin just to get me over the immediate crisis, but that now I'm better what we need to do is look into my childhood and find out what caused it all. Simple as that, and I never realised.' She fixed Mary with a slightly accusing look, and said:

'Of course, I was frightfully badly treated as a child.'

'Were you?' said Mary uncertainly. She felt that this was in a way true, but that Dodie probably did not mean it in that sense.

'Oh yes. Frightfully. Mother was awfully jealous of me, you see. And of course Daddy adored me, which didn't help.'

For a moment Mary did not reply. Aunt May had had a number of shortcomings as a parent but Mary did not think that pathological jealousy of her daughter had been one of them. She remembered Lionel's remark about Dodie's attitude to Joanna, and wondered if Dodie were actually talking about herself in code—whether Bonaway was perhaps using this fantasy about her parents as a way into her own problem with Joanna.

'Of course,' repeated Dodie confidently through another mouthful of scone, 'at some level all mothers are jealous of their daughters. Like all women are jealous of men . . . I wish someone had told me that before,' she added plaintively.

315

Mary did not feel like disputing Freudian theory with Dodie. No doubt such theories, foolishly generalised as they seemed to her, had their uses. She said instead:

'Joanna sends her love, by the way.' Joanna hadn't, in fact; when told that Mary was going to visit Dodie she had just said nervously, 'Don't tell her about—you know—will you?' But in the circumstances Mary thought love the only suitable message.

'Oh yes—Joanna,' said Dodie with vague affection. 'Yes, she's getting on quite well . . . You must come to the school Christmas play, Mary.'

'But Dodie—Joanna's left school. She's been away in France. Don't you remember?'

Dodie flushed. 'My memory!' she said, in the flirtatious tone of one excusing a minor lapse. A little anxiously she added, 'It's the insulin, you know, Mary. Or the shock treatment. So they tell me. I don't know which. You must think me a fool . . . But then,' she added ominously, 'you always did, didn't you?'

'No, no, Dodie—don't apologise, it's not your fault, it's quite usual after ECT. I'm sorry I sounded surprised for a moment. I should have realised.'

'Joanna in France, you say . . .' said Dodie meditatively, not listening. 'No, that had quite slipped my memory. I suppose someone invited her? I've always thought it would be nice to send her to a finishing school in Paris, when she's older, you know . . . If I'm back on my feet by then and can afford it, with this awful government taking everything away.' She stared at Mary with eyes that seemed oddly opaque, brown and shiny, like those of a teddy-bear. It occurred to Mary that Dodie was even less on the spot than she seemed, and was putting on an act.

'It's been hard bringing up a child on my own,' she said challengingly, as if she expected Mary to disagree with her. 'Very hard. People don't realise. That's why I've broken down now, Dr Bonaway says. The strain of it.'

'I'm sure it's been hard,' said Mary sincerely, preparing herself to discuss this possibly fruitful topic further. But Dodie had distracted herself again:

'My dear—look at that cake trolley. *Could* we? I do so love

316

éclairs. I must say, this is a jolly good tea, isn't it? I think it's wonderful what these little places manage these days. When you think of rationing . . .' she added vaguely, her mind slipping back again. 'I suppose they get extra points or something.'

In the last few weeks Mary had been preparing herself for tragedy, but the figure in front of her seemed nearer to farce. Feeling that her own grip on reality would become insecure any minute, she ordered cakes. 'Continental pastries,' the waitress corrected censoriously. 'All right then, Continental pastries,' said Mary crossly. Something in her tone must have conveyed itself across the barrier of Dodie's self-absorption, for Dodie suddenly said, with that unnerving sporadic perception one remembered of old:

'You think I shouldn't have them, don't you? You're going to tell me I've put on weight.'

'Well, Dodie, as you say yourself, you have. I imagine that's an effect of the insulin treatment . . . I was just wondering, actually, if for the same reason it's a good idea for you to have quite so much sweet stuff. Did Dr Bonaway warn you about that at all?'

'Dr Bonaway says that I needed insulin and ECT to get me over the immediate crisis,' said Dodie truculently. 'He's a wonderful person, Mary. You really ought to talk to him yourself.'

'Yes, you said.' Mary gazed with concealed anxiety at Dodie's pudgy, double-chinned face, beneath the flowery hat of a younger, prettier woman of another time. Where, inside this sweaty, oddly expressionless mask, where grains of face-powder were stuck in the folds of ageing skin, was the luminously bright, receptive girl who had written books and been admired on all sides? Gone for ever. But nothing was ever really gone for ever—

'Tell me more about what Dr Bonaway says about your childhood,' she said. Clearly they were not going to be able to get on to any other topic but Dodie's state of health. The photographs that Mary had hopefully brought with her, of their holiday in Sicily, of Joanna and the Hersheys at David's wedding, would stay in her handbag.

'Oh, my childhood . . . Dr Bonaway says it will take quite a

317

long time for it all to come out. The damage was done then, you see.'

'Yes. Yes, I believe analysis does take some time. Is he thinking of a full analysis, Dodie, or just psychotherapy?'

Dodie brushed this aside. She leant forward, spluttering crumbs of cream-filled brandy-snap across her own plate and Mary's, and said:

'Willie treated me particularly badly, you know, Mary.'

'Willie—how?'

'Oh well, I was awfully jealous of him, you see—him being a boy. I would have liked to have been a boy myself, of course. All girls do, you know.'

'I never did,' Mary could not resist saying.

'Oh, I'm sure you did. I expect you just repressed it. And Willie knew I felt like this and exploited it. Particularly after the others were killed.'

Trying, for her own sake as much as Dodie's, to inject some real-life observations into Dodie's potpourri of received analytical notions, Mary said thoughtfully: 'Yes, the boys being killed did put Willie in a special position, didn't it, for all of us? I don't suppose it was particularly easy for him, being a survivor and resented because of it . . . Oh, by the way, I meant to say, Willie sends his love and says he'll come down to see you himself some time soon.' *That's what he said and I've dutifully repeated it, but fat chance, I should think: Willie is even more squeamish about mental illness than he is about the physical sort.*

'I never want to see him again,' said Dodie dogmatically, setting down the tea-cup from which she had been noisily drinking.

'Good heavens, why? I'm not a great fan of Willie myself, and we disagree on most subjects, but he's surely harmless enough, particularly these days? I even catch myself feeling quite fond of him sometimes.'

'He exploited me,' said Dodie obdurately.

'What exactly can you mean?'

Dodie's face was suffused with red. She seemed to be in the grip of some suffocating emotion, which it took Mary several minutes to analyse as extreme embarrassment. At last she managed to say, almost inaudibly:

'He seduced me.'

'*Really*, Dodie? . . . Oh. I'd no idea.' Memories tumbled about in her mind. Dodie at nineteen with Willie as an approved escort and dancing partner; Dodie in her twenties, being offhand about him in Paris, saying, 'I think he's One of Those'; Willie's lank hair and pince-nez, his offhand, cold-fish manner—could this almost incestuous seduction be another figment of Dodie's imagination? She was not sure.

'When, Dodie?' she asked. 'When we were very young?' That could explain a lot, on reflection.

'Oh no—no. Much later.' She stared hostilely at Mary. 'But you know really, don't you?' she said. 'You're pretending to be surprised, but you knew all the time.'

'No, I didn't. Really I didn't, Dodie. Somehow I've never associated that—sort of thing—with Willie.' The image was preposterous, embarrassing to contemplate even in imagination, especially when she thought of Willie's own old-maidish prudery on sexual matters. No wonder Dodie was upset. Mary realised that she herself had for years assumed that Willie was impotent, with a flesh-and-blood woman at any rate. Lank, limp . . .

'Of course you know,' said Dodie angrily. 'It was you who told me I was preggers, wasn't it? So how could you not have known? As you said to me then yourself, there's only one way of getting pregnant.' She added in surly triumph: 'I know my memory's bad at the moment, but I remember that all right.'

The images in Mary's mind tumbled like acrobats—then settled into a new and startling picture. The Polish cavalry officer dwindled to vanishing point, then went for good. Well, he had always been an unlikely figure. But Willie— *Willie* . . . Why him, finally, and no one else? Mary was still half-inclined not to believe it. But even as she was busy mentally rejecting Willie as a father for Joanna she recalled Joanna's childhood asthma and Willie's also . . . and their common talent for drawing. Looks were no guide, as Joanna looked like her mother, and her uncle Roland. Children often took after one side of the family rather than the other; the fact that her personality too seemed markedly different from Willie's proved nothing—you could not prove a negative.

319

This did not have the feel of one of Dodie's fantasies. She sensed a real distress and shame. After a long pause she said, as calmly as she could:

'Willie had gone abroad again by the time you came to see me, hadn't he? . . . Does he know he's Joanna's father?'

Dodie, looking down at her plate now, shook her head. She kept it bent, her hat slipping slightly over her seedy grey hair, staring down at the mess of cake crumbs and half-eaten scones before her. Eventually she said in a whisper:

'I never told him. I thought he'd be so shocked. So disgusted to be reminded. I mean—it *is* disgusting, isn't it, Mary? Whatever everyone pretends. All that hair and wetness . . . Oh, I can't bear to think of it, even now. I never meant—I didn't realise. It was only once—well, twice . . .' Her voice faltered into aghast silence.

Driving back to London in thickening traffic, through a gusty, late-autumn rain that flung yellowed leaves at the windscreen, Mary thought wearily that her first impression that afternoon had been right after all. In the dark hall of the nursing home, with Dodie's enthusiastic welcome, she had momentarily seen again the bright, vulnerable, ingenuous child of her earliest meetings with Dodie. For the rest of the painful afternoon that impression had been effaced by the presence of the bloated, damaged, middle-aged woman. Yet, in the final analysis, Dodie was still a prisoner of childhood, and all the rest, through the decades, had been just a shadow-play. Bonaway's analytical approach was not so naïve or so unsuited to Dodie's age after all. As a young girl in Harrogate she had confided to Mary that she thought it would be nicer if people 'didn't grow hair on themselves' and, as now appeared, nothing had ever changed. And the one person who had managed to trick or bully her into submitting to the adult ordeal of sex had been the one she trusted: soft, devious, funny old Willie, that semi-brother and accomplice in juvenile intrigues.

Yet not, apparently, so soft and funny when it came to the point. For if Dodie had momentarily thought to find a refuge in Willie, what, ah what, could Willie have sought in her? Not an adult woman, certainly. Some androgynous figure?

Some fellow adolescent whom he could dominate and humiliate in a mock teasing it's-only-a-game, dear, way . . . someone in his power to hurt?

Yes, it did fit, after all.

Late the following evening Lionel returned, looking tired and old and disinclined to describe the conference. Mary gave him a brief account of Dodie, but said nothing about Willie. That piece of information was as yet too new and unassimilated for her to impart it to anyone, even Lionel.

Joanna was still staying with the Hersheys, ostensibly helping Myriam with the house and the telephone. Myriam, said John, liked company, missed the boys. Mary felt weakly relieved by Joanna's absence that evening. The problem of reconciling Joanna to her mother—and Dodie to her more-or-less-adult daughter—was one that seemed for the moment insuperable.

She slept badly that night, but was woken eventually by the telephone. It was Dr Bonaway in Esher, apologetic and defensive: Dodie had disappeared from the nursing home the previous evening. She had not returned to her own house. Did Mary think he should inform the police?

'Bloody hell,' said Lionel when this was retailed to him. 'Of course he should, the fool. Honestly, Mary, I wish we'd got Dodie in somewhere where she was under proper observation instead of all this genteel rubbish about nervous strain.'

'Oh, for God's sake, Lionel,' snapped Mary. 'Don't be such an Establishment prig. Anyone would think from the way you go on that places like the Maudsley had a methodologically sound cure for people like Dodie. They haven't, and you know it.'

They quarrelled again when Mary returned briefly to the flat at lunch-time, and when she came back in the evening she found a note from Lionel saying he was working late in the RSM Library and that she should not wait supper for him. All evening she stayed in alone, on edge, unable to settle to anything, waiting for the ring on the doorbell. For Dodie would surely eventually come, just as Joanna had come. How could Dodie, of all people, manage on her own? Bonaway had said she had taken her handbag with her, but not her suitcase. A light rain was falling, and in her mind's eye Mary kept seeing Dodie walking the streets between the shut shops, head bent, flowered hat drenched, her mustard-coloured suit crumpled and stained. Not a clown, but a tragic figure after all. Surely the police would pick her up soon?

But it was not till two days later that the doorbell rang, and then it was not Dodie but the police themselves. A person answering to Dodie's description had been found dead in Harrogate on the rails of the Leeds branch-line railway where it runs across the green.

There were two policemen. Mary asked them in to have a cup of tea, which was accepted. She was distractedly aware, as she made the tea, that this was part of the ritual the police were taught for such occasions: when you have broken the news do not leave at once; our police have a social service to perform.

'Relative of yours, I suppose, Doctor?' said the older man with measured sympathy.

'Cousin. But like a sister to me—in some ways . . .'

'Ah. Funny thing is, she gave your name at the hotel, it seems.'

'My name?'

'Yes. She stayed a night at the Hydro—that's one of the big hotels in Harrogate, I understand; never been there myself. The Harrogate police had trouble in identifying her—no personal papers on the body, you see. The Hydro had a Dr Mary Denvers of this address on their register who'd stayed a night and then disappeared. Matter of fact, we received a call from the Harrogate police yesterday asking us to check if *you* were missing from home. But then the Missing Persons Bureau came up with this other name, a Mrs Dorothy Denvers reported missing from a nursing home somewhere in Surrey, so we knew there must be some mix-up. The nursing home had your name as next of kin.'

'Yes. I see. What about identification?'

'The doctor in charge of the nursing home's on his way up to Harrogate now, Doctor. But afraid it'll just be a formality. The description of the clothes tallies, it seems. Doesn't seem much doubt really, does there?' The realist and family man, no believer in raising false hopes, used to these cases in the Force, you understand.

'I see.'

'Funny she should give your name, Doctor. Glad we didn't get as far as bothering you yesterday. Might have been even more upsetting for you.'

'Yes.'

'*You've no character*', I said, as we stood on that same bridge. '*You're transparent. You get your colour from picking up things around you . . . You make use of people.*'

Thirty-odd years ago? Something like that. I've always remembered it, because I've always felt guilty about it. So pointlessly cruel. And Dodie, it seems, must have remembered it too.

'Nervous depression, was it, she was in the nursing home for?'

'You could call it that,' said Mary. 'Yes, I suppose you could. But really I don't know.' She thought: but Dodie wasn't *miserable*; it wasn't that. I don't believe that she actually wanted to die. It was more that she wanted to be different, to make a complete change. 'I really don't know,' she repeated.

'I daresay it'll come out at the inquest . . . There'll have to be an inquest, I'm afraid, Ma'am.'

'Yes. Of course.'

'Just a formality.'

Oddly it was not Mary but Lionel who remembered, the next day, that the heroine of Dodie's first and most successful novel had also died under the wheels of a train. Mary cried then.

'And I always thought she borrowed that from *Anna Karenina*,' she said helplessly.

Later in the night she woke and thought of Dodie's complete aloneness, and cried again. Lionel woke too, and comforted her.

'I should have paid more attention years ago—done more . . . I saw the way she was going . . .'

'You did more than anyone else.'

323

'That isn't saying much. It wasn't enough, not nearly. I didn't care *enough*, didn't take her seriously any more . . . I patronised her.'

'I never thought you did.'

'No, nor did I. But I did, Lionel, I did. That was the way I rejected her. And she knew it—she wasn't nearly such a fool as she seemed. She went and killed herself after seeing me. I was the last person she talked to. Oh, I wish I'd tried harder. I wish I'd *been* harder on her. Not to care enough about someone to get angry with them any more, that's a pretty thorough form of rejection, after all—'

Lionel stirred uneasily. He said: 'Hang on a minute. You know, I've never thought much of this widespread idea that suicides are the rejected of society.'

'Haven't you? . . . No, I didn't know that.'

'Well, nor did I till just now. But the more I think about it the more sentimental it seems to me. Just plain not true.'

They lay quiet for a while. Mary could hear the regular intake of Lionel's breath, feel his heart beating faintly somewhere under her fingers. He said presently:

'We are each of us separate and responsible for ourselves and none of us can save the other. Each of us only develops a reasonable life, with good relationships in it, by our own efforts—you know that as well as I do. When one has done so there may be moments when another person can offer a bit of help or support. But that's almost incidental; the basic functioning has to be our own.'

'For you, Lionel, I do see . . . And perhaps for me too.' She had many reservations about that for herself, but did not feel like going into them. Not then—not ever perhaps, now. She said after a while: 'I don't think what you say is true for everyone.'

'For everyone,' he said emphatically. 'It only seems otherwise.' His body was warm beside hers, his arm tightened slightly round her. He even stroked her hair, where it was damp with sweat or tears. And yet he was speaking alone, and by what he said he left her implacably alone also.

'All this about people making each other happy,' he said, almost testily. 'It's well-intentioned, I daresay, but it's rubbish, actually. I didn't marry you to "make you happy",

324

and I've certainly never laid the burden on "making me happy" on you. It's a most offensive approach to another individual, when you come to think of it.'

(*'I wouldn't expect you to "offer me a life", Laurie'* . . . But he had expected to.)

She lay quiet, saying nothing, and presently Lionel returned to the subject of Dodie. 'No one could have done anything for her,' he said. 'Not you, not anyone.'

'But perhaps—if she had found someone to marry? Someone who really cared about her and saw through all those games she used to play? . . .'

'Then she wouldn't have wanted him. No doubt there *were* people, when she was young, and she didn't want them. She only liked people who would go along with whatever fantasy she was currently playing and throw back a flattering image of herself . . . That bunch of actors, years ago . . . Those ghastly people who went in for naturopathy, or whatever it was . . . That's why you were never close to her, my love. You couldn't be.'

Mary thought: I know what he means, but he's wrong too. We *were* close, once, in a secret, competitive, wordless way— Oh Dodie! She's gone, and I shall grow old now. A sensible, cheerful old woman . . . She hid her face against Lionel's pyjamas.

'Far from being rejected by society,' he continued remorselessly, 'people like Dodie are the rejectors. Look at the way she rejected even Joanna, once Joanna wasn't her creature any longer but showed signs of turning into an adult with her own needs. Doesn't it occur to you that killing yourself is the ultimate form of rejection, a slap in the face for everyone— particularly Joanna? A pretty bloody thing for a parent to do, I'd say.'

Mary lay beside him and heard his vigorous words, felt the quiet beat of his blood, that beat that one day, too, would cease. No, Lionel would never kill himself while he still had his health, while he could still work. But Lionel sick, Lionel seeing his life effectively over, would take his own decision alone, quietly and ruthlessly, just as he took all others. She shuddered, and for once his physical warmth gave her no comfort. 'A body's just slosh,' he had said several times. The temple of the soul, that was all. Intricate vaults of muscles, nerves, veins; an ark of the flesh, a Holy Place, the only one we have. The seat of creation, the only fragile, imperfect medium through which we can express all feeling, all longing, all commitment. Just slosh.

After some time she said: 'But I don't think that Dodie actually wanted to die. I think that this—this suicide—was a desperate attempt to struggle through into some new sort of life. I'm not at all sure, you see, that she really understood that death was there.'

Perhaps this remark made no sense to Lionel, for he did not reply. Presently he said, pursuing his own train of thought:

'We must do things about Joanna, though, Mary.'

'Yes, of course.'

'Will she want to go to the funeral?'

'She said no, yesterday, but I will ask her again, to be sure . . . She seems to be taking it too well, Lionel, it's almost alarming.'

'Mmm. I suppose after this she'd better come and live here for a bit? I mean, she can't stay at the Hersheys for good, and she'll need a home base for several years yet.'

'Yes, I was thinking that myself. And in fact I suppose I'll be her guardian. Would you mind if she lived here?'

'Of course not,' he said equably. 'You know I don't mind things like that. Perhaps,' he added with more enthusiasm, 'we can send her to a Polytechnic or somewhere, to get a bit more education. I'm sure she could do with it.' He was always cheered by the thought of someone getting more education.

Joanna, however, had other ideas.

With her recent experience, the desperate, secretive girl seemed to have disappeared just as, two or three years earlier, the confiding child had done. In its place was a calm, only slightly uncommunicative, apparently organised young woman. She had even got rid of her dusty, voluminous black clothes and bought herself a couple of brief dresses in the new shift style. She looked smart, in a slightly disconcerting, un-English way.

326

She said, politely but firmly, that she did not want to go to a Polytechnic, thank you. Her French was not bad now; she would like to improve it. On her own, she enrolled at an *au pair* agency and got herself a job in Toulouse—a long way, Mary was relieved to note, from Paris or St Malo. There was, she said confidently, a course in History of Art she could follow there at the university, but Mary felt this was mainly a pretext for leaving behind every place and person connected with her childhood.

Joanna had not, Mary reflected wryly, read the bit in current Family Planning literature about an abortion leading to depression and a sense of failure. On the contrary, it seemed that in outwitting her own body and facing the implications of life and destruction within herself, she had won a victory. By this crude act she had vanquished Dodie: both the dead, alienated failure and the once-adored mother. It was a little appalling, perhaps, but admirable in its way; Mary, though disappointed and vaguely hurt (for she would have enjoyed having Joanna in Baker Street), admired Joanna's courage.

She felt, however, that sheer common sense demanded that she say a few words to Joanna before she launched herself decisively on adult life. Not about Willie. Not yet. She was entirely undecided about what if anything she should ever say to Joanna on that matter. Willie was in any case now joint trustee, with herself, of the small capital Dodie had left, so he and Joanna would have a relationship of a sort. It was not the past that preoccupied her for the moment, but Joanna's immediate future.

Did she now understand precisely the facts of life—the risks she ran?

Yes, thank you. John Hershey had explained, been awfully kind . . . He was so nice. The nicest man Joanna had ever known.

'Yes, very nice.' Feeling that she sounded insufficiently enthusiastic, Mary hurried on:

'But Joanna, did no one ever give you advice about this sort of thing before?'

'Oh well . . . they used to talk about eggs and things in fifth form Nature Study. And Miss P used to carry on sometimes in

Assembly about Not Making Ourselves Cheap. But that was after the juniors had been whistling at the choirboys out of the top windows—just her usual hysteria.'

'I see. Not very useful guidance. And no one else ever in the holidays—?' But no, Mary reflected, thinking of Dodie and the fetid little house in Esher she herself had just finished clearing, they probably hadn't. Incredible as it seemed Joanna had been allowed to reach the age of seventeen without this most elementary information for adult life in mid-twentieth century England.

Joanna bit her lip. 'Well, of course we used to read magazines a lot at school. The letter pages, you know. The letters mostly say, "Should I let my boyfriend make love to me?" And the answer's always "No, if you do you will feel bad and guilty." But it isn't *true*, is it? There's nothing in sex itself to make a person feel bad. On the contrary.' She faced Mary challengingly.

'No. No, I agree, it's not true . . . You found that out?'

'Mmm. And another thing: the magazines never explain that sex is nice. No one explained that. I mean, I couldn't think why anyone would want to—till it happened to me, and then I knew all right. But by then it was a bit late.'

'I see,' said Mary, feeling inadequate in the face of Joanna's bizarre clarity. 'Dear, dear, what a misunderstanding. Well, at least you won't be taken by surprise again.'

'No,' said Joanna confidently. 'I won't.' She added after a moment, eyeing Mary to see how she would take this:

'All this magazine stuff about "being immoral" and "doing wrong"—Myriam tried that on with me the other day, but it's all pretend really, isn't it? I mean, something like sex can't be wrong in itself, only in the effect it has. (I worked that out just recently.) I couldn't get Myriam to see it, though; she got all upset and huffy. She's pretty stupid, Myriam, isn't she?'

'Yes, she is—but I think it ungrateful of you to say so, Joanna. It's been very kind of Myriam to have you, considering that, as you say, she is as she is.'

'I know,' said Joanna crossly. 'But one can't just go round being grateful and not saying what one thinks. That's another

thing . . . "Ashamed", "grateful"—they're all Miss P words
. . . Anyway, do you see what I mean?'

With some wariness Mary said that she did. She did not
retail Joanna's remarks to Lionel. She was afraid that, in
spite of his matter-of-fact words, he would not approve. She
did not entirely approve herself. But she saw that Joanna, far
from being cowed by her experiences, had been pushed to
grapple with the nature of things, and that surely could not
be bad?

The more she thought about it the more she was inclined
to see emerging in Joanna a new kind of woman, a sort which
the old-fashioned progressive orthodoxy of Family Planning
circles had as yet hardly glimpsed. Why, the clinics were still
inviting such unmarried girls as approached them to 'bring
your fiancé or your mother with you' and regarding the more
temporarily attached as pathological 'cases' in need of
'counselling'. John was right after all, damn him. It *was*
rubbish.

Once again, as a dozen years earlier, she found herself
having to question and modify her own long-held views.
It was harder, in one's fifties. She worried a good deal,
in an unfocused way, and found herself arguing with
colleagues. One accused her quite violently of losing her
integrity and 'selling out to the forces of moral degradation—
creeping Americanism and so forth'. Afterwards Mary came
to laugh at this accusation, but at the time it caught her
on a sensitive place, and she heard herself reply, no less
pompously:

'No, I'm not. I'm trying to stick to my own integrity—to
the truth as I see it.'

'Well, *I* feel you're letting us all down,' said her colleague
angrily. 'You never used to think like this.'

'I daresay not. But what is a mind for, if not to change?' It
was an aphorism of Lionel's that had always irritated her.
Now she took refuge in it, thankfully.

At the end of that painful and dislocating autumn, when
Dodie's possessions had been dispersed, her house had been
sold and Joanna had gone determinedly to Toulouse, Charlie
appeared in London. He had with him a short, red-haired

329

girl with a pronounced Glaswegian accent; her name was Maureen, and he announced that they were to be married in a fortnight's time.

'She's so dumpy!' said Mary helplessly to Lionel. She meant not only that Charlie's great, stooping height looked ill-assorted beside Maureen, but several other things as well. As Maureen was only twenty-two she hardly qualified yet for the description 'homely little body' yet that, clearly, was what she was destined to become.

Lionel laughed, and said: 'Well, fortunately there's no rule that a wife has to be tall and elegant and attractive to her father-in-law!' But Mary knew that he too was disconcerted.

Maureen was a typist in the office of the Dundee firm where Charlie was employed. She came from a Roman Catholic family and had many little brothers and sisters. Mary told herself that it was logical and predictable, when one came to think about it. Charlie had never shown many signs of seeking out for himself the kind of society that Lionel and Mary kept. On the contrary, his most pronounced natural attribute was chameleonism. Sent to America, he had turned himself into a regular American boy; dragged back to England and sent to a co-educational boarding school, he had doggedly remade himself in a mildly unconventional, anti-Establishment mould. Cast by the vagaries of life, first into national service without a commission and then into the far north of Britain, into a world of large, oily machines and five o'clock teas, he had simply conformed once again to the ethic of those around him. For Lionel or Mary even to hint that he had not aimed very high in picking Maureen would have been sheer unkindness. And, knowing Charlie's obstinacy, it would have been pointless anyway.

'It's lucky,' said Mary, 'that the Elwins are dead.' (Both Charlie's maternal grandparents had died soon after the war.) 'They'd have had a fit.'

'Yes, they would.' Lionel looked not entirely displeased at the idea. 'My Ma would have approved of Maureen, though,' he added nostalgically a moment later. 'They'd have talked about baking together.'

But Mary, after an animated dinner party at the young Hersheys' house in Canonbury, could not help feeling a little sad at the contrast with Charlie's probable life-style. Though Lionel said nothing, and was generous at the time of the wedding, she rather thought he felt the same.

She was glad when the year ended.

PART SEVEN

Mary said:

'... Looking back, I would say that the time of greatest development for the birth-control movement was not the establishment of the principle of socialised medicine after the war, important as that was, nor yet the final incorporation of family planning services into the health service in 1968. It was, rather, the increasing *respectability* of the whole subject from about 1960 onwards. Far-reaching social changes were going on at the time. It had traditionally been the policy of the Association to follow public opinion rather than risk alienating support by setting out to change it. If, in retrospect, the Association's methods and ways of publicising itself seem to have become considerably more aggressive in the early 1960s, this in itself was largely a response to the rapidly changing climate of public opinion.

Perhaps the best way of illustrating the speed and scope of this change is by a concrete example. In the mid-1950s an unmarried client attending our clinic would be asked the date of her forthcoming wedding; and the normal practice was not to give the girl her diaphragm cap or whatever at once but to take her address and send it to her, carefully timing its arrival for the week in which she was due to be married, if not for the wedding morning itself!'

She paused there, knowing from experience that at this point in her lecture a gasp of surprise, followed by a murmur of increasingly mocking laughter, would rise from her medical-student audience. As this died away, she continued:

'—And yet less than ten years later not only were we prescribing the contraceptive pill on a mass scale, and encouraging general practitioners to do so; we were also setting up new clinics specifically for the young and unmarried. The very thing which, years ago, we had had to keep promising everyone we would never dream of doing! Moreover, making things easier for the immature, the promiscuous and the inadequate, from being regarded as a betrayal of our aims, came to be considered in many quarters the most important contribution the movement could make. It is, let me tell you, a curious and salutary experience to work for so long in a crusade that not only do you see all its original aims fulfilled but, almost as a response to this, you see some of them overturned. Mind you [she added quickly—students tended to be a prosaic lot and a bit simplistic in their reactions]. Mind you, I very much applauded the changes, on the whole. The extension of our services to all those in need, regardless of the so-called moral issue, did not seem to me as out of keeping with the basic tenets of the movement as some of our more conservative members felt.'

A girl student in the front row asked a question about psycho-sexual counselling. Hadn't that, she asked knowingly, been a very important development too in the 1960s?

'Ah, you'll have to ask Dr Lawford about that. She's coming to give you your next week's lecture, and that's really her subject, not mine. She's had a great deal of experience in that field, in fact she was one of the key people in the setting up of the special-problem clinics. She's more or less retired now, like me, but I'm sure you'll find her very interesting.'

She's an obsessional, prurient old bore in my view, but it's right you should hear her; you can judge for yourselves. I never did like her dry, technological, veterinary approach in the days when we worked together at the Paddington Centre—or the slow, ironic gusto with which she would recount to us her patients' problems in every detail—and now that I hear she's lecturing to these new women's groups on 'creative masturbation', God help us all, I feel all my instinctive suspicion of her confirmed.

Well, none of us moves quite as fast in old age as we did in youth, or yet in middle-age, and I daresay I have—finally—become a slow old woman, not up with the latest thinking. But I still think I'm right about her. And about all this sex-counselling in general. Oh, it all sounds quite plausible and friendly, and I expect it does help some couples—let me, as ever, be consciously fair—but there's something naïve about it all the same. Something unreal.

—Ah, what is reality in the country called sex? In your peaceably exiled seventies do you know—did you ever know? Does the mystery at the heart of all that intense, ephemeral sensation lie, as you thought for so long, in the knowledge of its terrible potency, the constant background awareness that this is the source of life, the perpetual half-promise that this transitory passion of the flesh and blood may create a permanent creature of flesh and blood? . . . Or does it, rather, lie in waking up in the arms of someone you love, and knowing, even at that moment, that there can never be a child of this union—that your being together can never ever be more than this, this moment—and yet feeling that this is enough, that nothing on earth matters, or ever will matter, as much as this?

She dragged her attention back to the front row. The knowledgeable girl was asking another question. Was she some colleague's daughter—or granddaughter? One ought to remember these things.

'—Yes,' she said, trying to collect her thoughts. 'Yes, you are right. In the last few years of my full-time working life I turned my own attention more to sub-fertility, which was another new aspect of our work which we were also developing in the 1960s. In fact I found it such an interesting and encouraging field—one we'd never dreamed of in the old days, when our whole concern was to stop babies!—that I did not begin to retire at sixty, as I had planned, but went on full-time till sixty-five. The developments in that field, in fact, keep me occupied even now. They will be the subject of my last lecture in this series.'

It was in 1962 that Mary turned sixty. The Paddington Centre was flourishing and had moved to new premises. (The old building was due for demolition under a comprehensive scheme for the Harrow Road; a motorway was going to be built, it seemed.) When Mary's colleagues wanted her to stay on she agreed readily, feeling that her mental and physical energies were undiminished. But she warned them that within the next two years she would like to take substantial leave to go on the journey to India she and Lionel had long planned. He, at any rate, could not postpone this for many years more. There was an extra reason for her continuing at the Centre. Although everything was as it had always been in one sense nothing was exactly the same, for John Hershey was dead now. 'Oh me—I'm indestructible,' he had said to her once, in the bomb-blasted house that was now empty air above a car park. But he had not been. A massive heart-attack, without warning, at fifty-nine. To the weeping and obscurely accusatory Myriam, Mary had said that of course he had been overweight (he'd known that himself), he had worked compulsively, he had been a smoker, but that it was still statistically an arbitrary and cruel blow from fate: one simply could not predict these things . . . She thought to herself that Myriam, who had been a nurse, should have known this, and should not have demanded so frantically to be told 'why' this had happened. But then grief took people in strange ways. She was surprised herself at the strength of her own sense of loss and regret for him. Unlike Olive, whose loved shade had been elusive, John returned to her many times in dreams. He had been such a solid part of her life over so many years.

Because of the abruptness of his death he had left his affairs in some disorder, and Myriam would not apparently be as well off as she had expected to be. John must have earned a good deal, Mary and Lionel speculated, but he had spent a good deal too, these last few years; and any capital had come from Olive's family and would pass now to the boys. Myriam would have to sell the big house in Kensington and move somewhere much more modest.

'But surely,' Mary tried to comfort her, 'you wouldn't have wanted to keep it on anyway, a house like that? Even if you let the surgery and waiting room, it would still be awfully big and expensive to run.'

'You don't understand—it has such memories for me. Every room. Oh, how can I bear to let it go?'

'How can you bear not to, you mean? My dear, you can't live in a museum. Look what it did to Queen Victoria. Wherever you live, no one can take the past—what you shared with John—away from you. That's yours forever.

Why don't you get a flat somewhere in Islington near David and Penny? Some of those Georgian squares off Upper Street have got quite smart now.'

'Oh . . .' Myriam's painted mouth drooped sadly. Her painted eyes reddened again, suffusing with tears. She said self-pityingly: 'I don't want to be a nuisance to them.'

'Well, why should you be? On the contrary, it's much more convenient, I'd have thought, being round the corner from each other—well, round several corners, perhaps—rather than on the other side of London. You could baby-sit for them—I should think they'd be very grateful. They go out a lot, don't they? And paying anyone to do anything costs such a lot these days.'

David Hershey and his wife had two children now. Penny, a confident young woman, had announced more than once in Mary's hearing that they were 'planning four' and that she meant to have them close together so that, within ten years, she would be able to return to her career in a publisher's office.

'So amusing to hear you younger ones talking like this,' said Mary on one occasion. 'Because, you see, in my youth planning your family meant *spacing* it. Before the war we were all stuck on the idea that having children very close together was bad for them and bad for the mother. That concept seems to have been quietly dropped now.' She had spoken not censoriously but affectionately, admiring the pretty, healthy children, moved by clinical interest in the phenomenon. But Penny had become defensive, as if she thought she were being criticised, so Mary had not referred to the subject again. Perhaps Penny was less self-confident than she seemed.

Mary's suggestion of a grandmotherly role for Myriam was not well received either. Myriam drooped still further. She remarked presently that she wasn't quite in her dotage *yet*, thanks, and that surely one need not, even in one's late fifties, give up all hope? It dawned on Mary that Myriam, inconsolable as she seemed over the loss of John as a person, was also, in a more general way, desperate at the thought of widowhood and wondering if she could evade it. Well, it was an understandable reaction: Myriam had been a widow before, when John had married her. But Mary couldn't help being a little shocked that a third husband was apparently the only consolation and solution to life that Myriam could envisage—for what else could that remark, about not giving up all hope yet, mean?

'Mike wants me to come to New York for Christmas,' said Myriam drearily. 'I don't know if I'll go, though.'

'What a good idea. Why don't you?' Mike Hershey was flourishing there as a director of television commercials, on a reported salary which Mary, when told it, had laughingly declined to believe. It was surely ludicrous that any human being who was not a president, a High Court judge nor a brain surgeon should be paid so much, still less at twenty-seven? Not that youth seemed to have anything to do with earning power these days, or only in inverse ratio to the traditional one: on all sides one read or heard of the young enjoying enormous prosperity. It wasn't that Mary grudged Mike his fairy gold: she had always been fondest of him, since that long-ago, intolerably sad day in 1944 when he had clutched her hand all the afternoon as they walked through cornfields. It was just that it seemed so extraordinary, when she thought of how things had been in the 1930s, and how they had all had to save and plan.

'You go,' she said to Myriam. 'It'll do you good. You'll enjoy it.'

'Yes. I suppose I might.' Myriam spoke as though through a layer of grey wool. 'I've got my cousin there too. She lives in Brooklyn, though.'

'You've been before, haven't you?' Myriam, she recalled, had accompanied John on a working trip. Because of this, Mary had not asked John to look up Laurie, as she might have done if John had been alone. The two men would have enjoyed talking opera together. Or at any rate she would have got a keen pleasure from the thought of them doing so. That she and Laurie had no friends in common was one of the small, long-term sadnesses of the situation.

'Yes. Actually,' said Myriam, showing more animation as she recalled the glowing past, 'that was a bit awkward, because my cousin had wanted us to stay with her and was rather miffed when we didn't. But I mean—how could we have? We were booked at the Waldorf Astoria. John had all

sorts of people to see. We were out literally every night . . .
Oh, *such* fun, Mary.' Her eyes threatened to fill again. Quickly
Mary said:

'You go, my dear. It won't be the same, of course, but I'm
sure Mike'll give you a good time. He's a sweet-natured
fellow.' *If only she has the sense not to stay too long.* 'He lives in
Manhattan itself, doesn't he?'

'Oh yes. East fifty-seventh street.'

'Upper East side. Very nice too.'

'I'd forgotten you knew New York,' said Myriam, as if
New York were her own property and she was not sure if
Mary had a right to it. 'When were you there?'

'Oh—more than ten years ago now.' Possessed by a
sudden, mischievous desire to shock Myriam and give her
something to think about besides herself, Mary said:

'I went partly for work reasons. And partly to see someone
I was very fond of.'

'Oh—a man?' said Myriam doubtfully.

'Of course.'

As soon as she had said it Mary knew that she had been
wanting, needing, to say that to someone for years. And
ironically it turned out to be Myriam, whom she neither liked
much nor trusted, who was the eventual recipient of this
homeless confidence. Of course the circumstances—Myriam's
bereavement, an atmosphere of temporary intimacy—had
provided the moment. She was vaguely aware of wanting
sincerely to offer Myriam something, some admission of her
own, some admonition also: see, other people too have their
problems and griefs—

Myriam was turning the matter round and round in her
ruminative mind. Eventually she said:

'But you decided not to stay in America.'

'I decided not to stay. There wasn't—any question—really.'

'Who was he? Were you awfully unhappy about it?'
asked Myriam romantically, evidently hoping to hear much
more.

'Not awfully, no. Rather unhappy, yes. But,' she added
lightly, 'one gets over things. One really does.' She felt light,
as she said it. Unlike poor Myriam, she herself was happy
these days. To change the topic of conversation as quickly

341

as possible, feeling that she had been fatally indiscreet, she said:

'We were talking of grandchildren a moment ago—step-grandchildren, rather, but you and I are both in the same boat there. I must show you the photo Charlie has just sent us of Maureen and the new baby. He's become a wonderful photographer, he really has.'

'New baby . . .' said Myriam vaguely, still preoccupied. 'How many does that make?'

'Three. They got married the same year as David and Penny, but you see they've been even more productive! Of course I don't think Maureen has any other ambitions than having babies, so I suspect they'll just keep on having them, for a bit anyway. I must say, Charlie's awfully sweet and proud as a father. I'd never have guessed he'd be so interested . . . Isn't it funny that they're all so keen on getting down to babies these days, when you think how old fashioned that used to be considered?'

But Myriam did not seem to have any views on this. She just said pathetically: 'Well, *I* always liked babies. I only wish . . . By the way, how's Joanna?'

'Joanna is fine too, thank you.' *I know what made you think of her, but you might have disguised the connection.* 'It looks as if she and Tom are going to get married, which we're pleased about.'

'Tom?'

'Oh, you know, Myriam, you and John met him in our flat in the winter. Tom Webber, the boy—young man, rather—she's been living with for the last year.'

Myriam looked disapproving, and said complacently: 'Well, of course I'm old fashioned about these things . . . Has he at least got a job?'

'Of course he has,' said Mary, rather fiercely. She greatly appreciated Tom, whose competent manner and ironed-out northern accent reminded her fugitively of Lionel when young. 'He's got a very good job on *The Economist*, and so he should; he got a First at university.' It was a source of surprised relief to Lionel and herself that Joanna, after running through various off-stage attachments in France, Italy and Israel, should have settled down at twenty-two with someone of

Tom's quality. Lionel rudely described it as a miracle, but Mary herself took a different view; she thought it showed the persistence of basic personality despite the pressure of environment. It was not a currently fashionable view, but it was one to which she found herself more and more drawn. Joanna, in spite of her peculiar upbringing and its disastrous culmination, was her own person. It had been obvious when she was a small child that she was 'bright'; this had been overlaid in her teens, but now that she had the right sort of companionship and encouragement it was surfacing again. Tom had not been foolish when he had picked her out. And, beyond intelligence, Mary felt there was something solid in Joanna. It seemed to her that Joanna, whatever her faults and her apparently unplanned life, had an independence and toughness of thought she herself lacked, and she both admired and envied her.

Of course it could be said that Willie too had a courage and an eccentric integrity of his own, even though his was mainly devoted to shutting his eyes to everything around him that did not fit his prejudices. As to the real level of his intellect Mary had long reserved judgment. He had, for many years, apparently been at work on his definitive study of oriental porcelain of the tenth to the fifteenth centuries; a subject which, as Lionel once remarked, might have been deliberately chosen by Willie as a cover for inactivity, if for nothing more sinister. It had certainly been chosen, Mary thought, as a conscious, almost baroque snub to the twentieth century. She had the impression that he published articles from time to time in learned journals, but that the book itself would never actually see the light of day. Willie was in his sixties now, and his asthma was bad every winter. Feeling sorry for him, she would visit him in the over-filled and over-heated little house he had bought at Kew, for no apparent reason, when his North Gower Street eyrie had been demolished for redevelopment. He would read her snippets of his work in progress in his breathy, period voice that was like someone playing Noel Coward.

'Oh, poor Uncle Willie,' she said once to Joanna. 'He loves the *idea* of scholarship, you know. He really is like Mr Casaubon!'

Joanna looked blank at this reference but, when it was explained to her, she said she would read *Middlemarch*. And apparently she did.

Mary had never told anyone (except Lionel, of course) that Willie was probably Joanna's father. She sometimes worried whether she was right to keep such a fact to herself— whether Joanna did not have the right to know. But Joanna was still very young and unsettled: there would be time enough to tell her when she and Tom were married. Or, better still, when she had children of her own, to protect her against the sick, decomposing past.

Willie himself never showed any special interest in Joanna, now that she was of age. There was nothing to indicate that he suspected he was her father. He was always so secretive, however. Could he know, after all?

Could he, in fact, *not* know, when one considered the matter carefully?

Yes, being Willie, probably he could.

The winter of 1963 was the coldest of the century. Dirty snow lay piled in the streets, water-pipes froze, then burst, electric power was cut down because the power-stations could not keep pace with the demand. It seemed like the winters of the war and the immediate post-war austerity all over again, and, like millions of others, Mary went about her usual occupations as if under siege. Thus it was March before she realised that it was an unusually long time, months indeed, since she had had a letter from Laurie. He had not even written at Christmas, though of course she had written to him then.

Her first thought was the instinctive 'He's got married'. But this was immediately followed by the more rational reflection that, after all their years of shared news and ideas, Laurie would not have funked writing to tell her so. He had never been that sort of coward.

She thought of ringing him up. After all, it was easy these days, and not even particularly expensive. Yet something held her back: they had never once telephoned one another. What right, she thought, had she to do so—to intrude on him in that way? He was probably on his travels again: he would write when he wanted. Or he had written, from Guatemala or somewhere, and the letter had got lost—

In the end she wrote again herself, a carefully unworried letter, describing their awful winter in light-hearted terms and saying she would like news of him.

One Saturday morning when she was alone in the flat (Lionel, who did all the shopping since his retirement with scientific efficiency, had gone to Sainsburys) an airmail letter that looked familiar dropped through the door. She picked it up eagerly—and then gazed stupidly at the writing on the envelope. She recognised it, but it was her own, and it was crossed out.

The envelope was franked 'Addressee deceased—Return to sender'.

After a while she went out and walked unseeingly in Regents Park. It was a blustery day in a cold, nasty, late spring, and gulls were crying above the lake, snatching food from the regular waterbirds.

The letter was crunched in her hand inside her coat pocket. On a sudden confused impulse she took it out and tore it open, as if it might after all contain some word from him, some message in code. But of course all it contained were her own bright, calm, ignorant words, written months before. Words penned to a ghost who, even as they were written, had perhaps been beyond contact for ever.

It was the letter she had sent at Christmas. It had taken all this while to come back to her—lying in a box in some neglected hallway, in some bureaucratic morgue? It would probably be weeks, or even months, before her more recent letter returned, like a ghost itself. Or like the body of a drowned man cast up on an irrelevant shore.

His strong, serviceable male body—his fine hands—that lived so in her heart and memory, now lived nowhere else. He had gone, and she had not even known it, and this had been a fact for months already. And he had died so far from her, in every sense, that there had been no one to write and tell her. No one, it seemed, to write letters at all. He, who had made her feel more companioned, more lovingly accompanied than anyone else since she had been a child, had died as he had

345

lived, essentially alone. Sitting on a park bench, she crossed her arms over her stomach and moaned audibly to herself.

'*But he was younger than me*—' she kept saying, and realised eventually from the looks a passer-by gave her that she was muttering aloud. Whatever she had envisaged happening 'in the end', whatever vague fear or hope she had harboured, it had never been this.

She knew no one to ask how he had met his end. A few years earlier he had moved to a different address in Philadelphia, and she had no idea about his landlord or landlady.

Eventually it occurred to her that the newspaper for which he had written theatre notices should know. After all, there might even be some mistake, some other Laurie Brown . . . No, she dared not hope that, but she wrote to the paper's editor and, after a long delay, a polite letter came back: Laurie Brown had not worked for that particular paper for several years, but enquiries had been made with another local paper known to have employed him. The writer regretted that, according to his information, Laurie had been one of several journalists and personnel from an international agency who had been killed in a light plane that had crashed over Mexico on a charter flight the previous November. His next of kin was stated to be a Mrs Norah Orbach, of such-and-such an address in Chicago. Perhaps she would be able to provide further details.

It was a kind and efficient letter, and Mary meant to write a note to thank the unknown editor for his trouble. But she never did. She never wrote to Mrs Norah Orbach either.

For the very first time in her life, she found herself unable to do things she thought she ought to do, unable to work properly or read or even think. She cancelled some appointments, failed to turn up at a couple of Centre meetings. After a fortnight or so she got back sufficient grip on herself to perform mechanically, but she felt like the victim of some hidden plague, secretly set apart from the world of living ordinariness, the world where all sorts of different things mattered.

'One gets over things. One really does,' she had said to Myriam the previous year, airily and arrogantly. How wrong she had been. How could she have imagined that time, mere time and the distractions of living, had made her invulnerable where Laurie was concerned? The news of his death had blotted out time and had shown the distractions for what they were. Nothing was ever really abolished or changed, and hadn't she always known that? Oliver and Roland and Nigel were dead, and now Laurie was dead too. That state of hopeless mourning, which had been a fundamental condition of life from the time she began to emerge from childhood, was something she had sought energetically to flee, combat with the accumulation of the decades, had dared to believe was obsolete, something that had happened to another person—what vanity. After a whole lifetime it had caught up with her again, agonising and irremediable. And this time, she thought, it would not let her escape again. She had not the strength, or the time.

She tried telling herself, 'It was what he always wanted,' remembering him telling her, here in this flat nearly twenty years ago, that what he feared was not death but being old. But it was no good, no good, a piece of sophistry: he need not have died thus, in his fifties in a pointless accident; he could reasonably have hoped for another twenty years of active life. And in any case, her mind clamoured, it wasn't what *I* wanted. *I* needed him, if not in the flesh (that unthinkable luxury) then at least in some sense *there*, communicating at intervals, writing, 'I am sending you the book about Wagner that I mentioned'; writing, 'I wish we'd seen *The Entertainer* together, it made me remember those wonderfully awful British coffee-shops.' Writing 'love, dearest Mary, look after yourself, ever, Laurie.'

Keeping him thus in a separate compartment of my life, I never realised what a crucial component of it he had become. I hadn't 'got over' him at all. I'd just made a secret place for him, a place where my dreams, however unformed, could go. And they did. I never realised—never honestly acknowledged to myself—the extent to which Laurie and a life together with him remained for me a perpetual possibility. I did think, yes I really did, that some day when Lionel is gone I would spend my last years making a home for Laurie, who might by then need one. And now he has gone, and he'll never know how much I loved him and valued him, because I never felt it

347

was right to tell him. And all that enduring potential between us—that unspoken promise, that other loop of time—is nothing and nowhere and there will never be anyone like Laurie for me again.

The days dragged on into a wet and uncertain summer. She went about her accustomed tasks, but for once she found it hard to listen when Lionel told her about an article he was writing or when patients told her of their hopes and fears. She was listening, but elsewhere: to what, to whom? Each night she went to sleep, exhausted by the effort of getting through the day, but woke again before dawn, tensely alert. Food tasted odd, unappetising. She wondered vaguely if she were physically ill—liver? gall bladder?—but did nothing about it. She half-hoped she might be. A mortal sickness held no terrors for her. She would almost welcome it.

On the days it did not rain she drove up to Hampstead Heath after work to swim in the secluded ladies' pool behind the chestnut and willow trees. She had taken to doing this in recent summers as a means of preserving health and figure a few years longer. Now she persisted in it blindly, partly as a piece of routine to fill the days, partly because the resulting physical tiredness might help her to sleep for longer. She no longer felt any pride in her body as she lowered it into the deep, green, receiving water, but rather that she was blotting it mercifully out, resigning it—a stale, tired thing—to the forgiving elements. She thought she was, must be, at the end of her life as a woman: in a very few more years her durable frame would collapse into the shrunken, wrinkled cadaver of age, as irrelevant to physical passion as that *other* body, broken on a Mexican mountain top. It did not matter, now. Lionel was old, and had withdrawn from her.

One evening, however, when she arrived at the pool, plodding along the Heath path, something occurred which jolted her out of her lethargy. The gate was locked, with a police van drawn up near it, and through the trees she could see men in waterproofs dragging the pool. A notice chalked on a board said that a 'person' was thought to have drowned there the night before.

She hung about for a few minutes, while other would-be

348

swimmers came and went and collected in concerned clusters. Presently she was told that the person who was supposed to have drowned herself was a woman known to her by sight and also by reputation, an elderly member of the Fabian Society well-known for her busy, distinguished career, her balanced views.

She came home and told Lionel about it, and found that she could, after all, care. When she had finished he took her hand in an awkward, unfamiliar gesture, and said, 'We haven't talked recently about going to India.'

'No. We haven't.' A flicker of interest awoke in her. 'Would you like to talk about it now?'

'Well, I've been meaning to. I've been putting it off . . . Mary, I think you ought to make definite plans to go next winter. Winter's the time to go, I'm told, and it would do you good.'

'But we were going to go together, I thought,' she said.

He began to speak again, carefully, logically: he had obviously worked out beforehand what to say. At first, the words dropped like pebbles into the water of her mind, making no sense to her. Then, as they settled into her consciousness, they did.

'But why didn't you *tell* me?' she said at last. 'Why didn't you tell me you were having chest pains—and why didn't you tell me when you went to see Barford about them? When did you go, anyway?'

'About ten days ago. I was going to tell you.'

'I should hope you were,' she said indignantly, preparing to be annoyed with him and his hermetic independence. Then the true impact of what he was saying came home to her. No, she must not get angry at Lionel, not now, not ever again.

Avoid stress, Barford had said. Maintain as quiet and regular a life as possible. Take gentle exercise—but no long walks, no running upstairs, no tiring journeys. No reason, that way, why you shouldn't live for a good few years more . . .

But angina will kill him in the end. It is a sentence of death. I know that, and so does he.

She asked him what he would like for supper. He said he

349

would like spaghetti. He said he had bought some today, and that there were tomatoes and onions and a tin of mince in the larder.

Later, as they ate spaghetti bolognese, she said, trying to keep the reproach out of her voice: 'I do wish you'd told me right away.'

'When I first got worried I thought I might be fussing unnecessarily. Old gents are always suffering from imaginary pains in the chest, you know. It's a well-established complaint.'

'But these weren't imaginary. And once you'd seen Barford . . . I don't like to think of your keeping something so important to yourself. That must be stressful in itself.'

He said neutrally: 'Well, my dear, you've been keeping things to yourself too in the last few months, I have the impression. And I didn't want to intrude my problems on you as well.'

'I wish you had,' she said. How could I not have noticed when he had a spasm of pain? I *have* been slipping.

'Well, now I have. But while we're still on the subject, Mary, you're not looking a bit well yourself. You haven't for some time. And all this early waking. I do sincerely mean it when I say I wish you'd make that trip to India. It would do you a world of good—a complete break, a new interest . . . There are quite a few people there who would be glad to see you and would look after you. I had a letter from Chowdhury the other day. He tells me his sisters are running the Family Planning outfit in Amritsar. I'm sure he'd have you to stay.'

She said, in a tone as cautious as his own: 'Thank you, Lionel. I will think about it, I promise. But I'm not quite sure that I'll go.'

'But you've always wanted to.'

'Yes. But, you know, sometimes "always wanting" to do something solidifies, then sort of atrophies . . . I expect I'll always think about India, and like reading about it. But I'm no longer sure I still want to go there. It might turn out to be—too late. Some sort of mistake. They say the reality of India can be hard to take. Perhaps it's better to keep it as a dream.'

350

'It's just as you like, of course,' he said with courteous incomprehension. 'But I think you may be making a mistake.'

'One makes a lot of mistakes. The only choice is which one to make.' *And I don't, I don't want to make the mistake of going off to India and enjoying myself and putting Lionel out of my mind and then suddenly getting a letter or a cable saying that he is ill, is in hospital, or—Oh, I don't want him too to die alone.*

After a few minutes she said: 'I know I always said I wanted to go to India. That was an idea I'd had right from when I was a child. My family roots lie there, as you know. I was conceived there—Isn't that an odd thought? But, really, I think that America has been my India, if you see what I mean. That trip I made there, when I saw so much, fulfilled the basic yearning I'd always had to discover somewhere on the other side of the world. An alternative country—' As Lionel remained silent, she added after a minute, feeling inadequate to convey what she wanted: 'It's as if my imagination is a bit vague on geography, like people used to be when Columbus discovered the place, and it's got the two sorts of Indians confused! Anyway, I'm no longer yearning to set off eastwards. To see what I wanted to see—what my cousins used to talk about when we were young—I should have gone years ago, when India was still part of the Empire. Not now.'

He said carefully: 'Well, you could go to America again instead. If you liked.'

'No,' she said. 'No. Perhaps I should have gone again before . . . But not now.'

He said, and she could see it cost him something to say it, a breach against his own principles, his own sense of privacy:

'That American who writes to you sometimes—that music critic—?'

She told him then.

Presently he said, with a kind of dispassionate pity in which there was also a note of apology: 'I'm sorry you felt you had to keep all this to yourself—his dying, I mean. Of course, I see why. But I'm sorry, it must have been hard for you. I can see that in some sort of way he was important to you . . . I think these things are worse for women than they are for men. In fact I think that women have hard lives.'

'*Do* you, Lionel?' she said, very much surprised. He had never intimated this to her before. She had always supposed that his lifelong, decent feminism was motivated not by pity or any other emotion but simply by his highly developed sense of natural justice.

'I've come to think so, yes, these last few years, looking round at our contemporaries. Take poor Myriam Hershey, for example. How utterly redundant she is now. All because she's done what nature and society both asked of her and no more. She's lived through her husbands, and much good it's done her. Women are programmed by nature far more heavily than men are, and then nature has no more use for them. I've come to see that more clearly as I've grown old, and have had more time to think . . .

'Remember my mother, and how pleased she was to have me there when she was dying because I was all she had—*all* to show for her whole life—and she hadn't had me there for years. Not really. Oh, I'd visited her regularly of course, but I wasn't *there* with her and she knew it, poor old Ma. That's the great unwritten tragedy of the son or daughter who "does well", you know, Mary. By their very success they inevitably leave behind the mother who nurtured them in the beginning. It's hard, very hard . . . Did you know that orthodox Jews, in their prayers, thank God for not making them women? And they have a point, they really do.'

Mary said passionately, stirred beyond all her expectations by hearing Lionel speak in this way:

'I have never wanted to be anything but a woman myself. I've been glad and happy to be one, and have had a good life because of it. So there.'

'Yes,' he said, ruthless in pursuing his point. 'Yes, I know, you've managed very well. But it hasn't always been easy for you, I do know. And some of the ways in which you've done well have been at the expense of other, more specifically female things that you perhaps wanted and needed very much. I have known that, Mary.' He added, more shyly, as if disliking the stilted phrase but unable to find a better one: 'You haven't always been able to fulfil yourself as a woman. I—I'm sorry about that.'

'That's all past and over now,' she said quickly, terrified of

352

what ghosts he would revive. He seemed as if he wanted to continue, but then looked at her and desisted.

Much later that night, when she had thought he was going to sleep, his hand stole across the wastes of double bed that separated them. He found her hand and held it.

'I'm glad . . .' he said after a while, and added something she could not hear.

'What was that, dear?'

'I'm glad,' he said very low, 'that you didn't leave me. I know I haven't been the right husband for you, in some ways . . . But I'm glad you didn't go. At one time I thought you might.'

Aghast to hear him say this, now, she said: 'I never seriously considered it for a moment. Oh Lionel! How could I have?' She wanted to add something like: 'Most of the life I have had has been given to me by you.' But she did not, for he had never liked her to speak in that way.

'You could have,' he pursued inexorably, his hand still in hers. 'I would have let you go. But—I would not have liked it.' His voice trembled. 'Selfish, I know, but there it is. It's true what they say. Men are selfish . . . I'm glad you didn't go.'

Barely two years later, when he was the one to go, slipping imperceptibly away from her into coma, from coma into death, leaving her alone to hold his cool, dry, old man's hand beside the hospital bed, she remembered his words with loving irony, and tried not to feel bitter about them.

In death, his thin face and his hair, still more brown than grey, looked young and vulnerable as she herself had never known him. He looked like Charlie.

When Charlie came south for the crowded memorial service—there had been no funeral, Lionel leaving his body to the hospital—it occurred to Mary for the first time that Charlie's present life-style was not so unsuited to Lionel's son after all. From living in Dundee with Maureen and his workmates Charlie had abandoned both the public-school and the American intonations that had characterised his earlier speech, and sounded more or less what he now was: a highly skilled northern blue-collar worker in a time when

353

such people were enjoying a prosperity undreamed of in their ancestors' day. Yet apart from his money (which he paraded with innocent pride, buying Mary an unnecessarily large lunch in a steak house) his ancestors on Lionel's side would have recognised him at once, she thought; he was one of them, far more than the isolated scholarship boy, Lionel, had been. Charlie had returned to the family's roots.

He apologised over lunch that Maureen had not come down as well. 'She's still nursing Patrick,' he explained.

When was Maureen ever not nursing? 'You must let me recommend you a nice book on the rhythm method,' said Mary naughtily. Maureen, of course, was a Roman Catholic, and the newspapers were currently full of the Pope's disappointing refusal to sanction the contraceptive pill. 'How Lionel would have enjoyed the opportunity to be caustic about the Pope,' Mary thought.

Joanna and Tom had been at the memorial service too, Joanna enormously pregnant. She, to Mary's surprise, looked bathed in tears afterwards, as if she had cried all the way through.

'You shouldn't have come and upset yourself, dear, so near your delivery date,' Mary said.

'That's what I told her,' said Tom. 'But she wanted to come, so of course she did—you know what she's like. Mary, if it's a boy we've decided to call it Lionel.'

In fact it was a girl: Katharine Mary.

In 1967, when she was sixty-five, Mary retired from the Centre. But, encouraged by colleagues and her continuing good health, she decided to keep on with her Wimpole Street practice three days a week.

'Do you really think I ought?' she asked Joanna anxiously. She had seen a lot of Joanna and Tom since Lionel's death. She hoped they did not just do it out of a sense of duty. She did not think that Joanna was dutiful, but Tom, the well-brought-up son of a powerful Yorkshire woman, certainly was. They had bought a cavernous old house in Camden Town, and Mary often walked across Regents Park to Sunday lunch or to baby-sit for them—the very thing she had recommended to Myriam Hershey. (Myriam had not moved to

Islington. She was said to be drinking heavily. Mary had a permanent feeling of guilt over Myriam. But what, indeed, could she or anyone do? She remembered John Hershey's own remark: 'Women rot.') So—

'Do you really think I ought to go on treating young women?' she asked Joanna. 'Please tell me; I want an honest answer.'

'Why shouldn't you? I should have thought your years and years of experience would be reassuring.'

'But perhaps—well, perhaps young women don't much want to be touched by an old woman.'

'Oh—taboos and things, you mean,' said Joanna dismissively. That wasn't what had been in Mary's mind, but she at once began to wonder if that was what she meant: all sorts of psychological aspects of the female function were being explored these days. Joanna went on:

'I should think it might work the other way as well. Couldn't young women see you as a sort of kind old witch figure—I mean a white witch,' she added hastily.

Mary was amused. Tact had never been Joanna's strong point. But, on reflection, she thought that the white-witch image appealed to her, particularly when Joanna amended it to 'like a nice old fairy godmother'. After all, what could be more fairy godmotherly than producing babies for those yearning for them? The new developments in hormone therapy for infertility were the most exciting thing to happen in her field for many years, she thought, and it was interesting that they had emerged as a by-product of the same research that had produced the contraceptive pill. The pill was bringing in great changes, not all of them for the best, in girls' attitudes to their own behaviour; all gynaecologists were noticing it. For years now she had welcomed in her consulting room young women who believed in being responsible for their own actions and did not want to marry yet, but now mini-skirted girls were presenting themselves who seemed to have no notion of a steady sexual partnership, no notion of love or commitment or even—Mary suspected—of the power of sexual passion. They seemed squeamish and ignorant about their own bodies, glad to swallow a pill rather than to get to know how they themselves were constructed. They were promiscuous, she guessed, not from that simple, un-inhibited desire of which John Hershey had once spoken in praise, but from social pressure and the fear of being left out of things. Dear John, thought Mary nostalgically; what a pity he isn't here to see his sexual revolution in action: I would like to hear his further views.

She would also have been interested in Joanna's views on the new sexual freedom but, because of Joanna's own past history, she hesitated to ask. Joanna and Tom seemed happy together, and certainly did not give the impression of being part of that frenetic new London world of grati-fication and experiment that the newspapers went on about so. Sexual experimentation and drugs—psychedelic mush-rooms or whatever—must surely take up a lot of time and energy. Tom and Joanna's time and energies were amply absorbed by the magazine of which he was editor (and for which Joanna did lay-outs and small drawings), by Kate, and by the gradual repairing and renewing of their Camden Town home.

Summoned one day to admire the newly stripped wooden cupboards in the upstairs living room and the uncovered hob-grate, Mary said truthfully:

'It does look nice, dears. But it's so funny to think that this is just the sort of house and street that Lionel and I and all our friends used to think ought to be pulled down.'

'A lot of people still do, it seems,' said Tom vigorously. He was active in the local anti-motorway group, and an opponent of various council development schemes.

'Surely you and Lionel didn't?' said Joanna, shocked.

'Oh yes, we did. I remember I used to bicycle through these streets long before the war and think how awful they were—of course I thought that, you see, because of the awful lives so many people lived in them, and they were *much* dirtier in those days. And then in the war, when one saw blitz-damage, one thought, "at least something good will come out of evil—all this will be swept away". It isn't just evils that go out of date, it seems, it's remedies too. We all dreamed that our grandchildren would live in white, modern boxes with streamlined kitchens where everything could be done by pressing buttons: that was Progressive. We never dreamed that the progressive thing by the late 1960s would be to live in a Victorian house with a coal fire and a big family kitchen full of delicious smells of stew—or that it would be progressive to fight *against* the local council's schemes for building new flats.' She grinned at Tom, who said manfully:

'May I quote you at length in my current editorial on the pitfalls of Brave New Worldism?'

'Please do, I should be most flattered . . . Seriously, you know, Tom, it's odd to have been someone who, all her adult life, has considered herself rather advanced—"modern" as we used to say—in her outlook, and who then suddenly finds that she isn't in the vanguard after all because the procession is no longer marching that way.'

'Oh, it'll march back again,' said Tom thoughtfully.

'Do you think so? I don't think history ever returns on itself. Look at the way, when the Second World War came, we all thought it was going to be a repeat of the first one. But it wasn't, and nor were its effects. This time we're living in now—it's unprecedented. It's never happened before, a period like this. So many established concepts being called in question.'

'Yes, that's what I mean,' said Tom eagerly. 'This present period—it's unreal. Look at the property market, and the way it's been booming in the last years. Why? It isn't because more people need houses than ever before, whatever the posh Sunday papers like to imagine; it's because the money's *there*, in the system, slopping about, seeking an outlet. Take this house: two and a half years ago, when we bought it, it was priced at seven thousand, and I got the agent down to six and a half by having a go at him about the derelict house on the opposite corner bringing down the tone of the street. (Well, he wasn't to know we didn't care about that sort of thing.) Today that derelict house has had God knows how much spent on it, and has just been sold for twenty thousand—yes, *twenty*. So we reckon ours would now be about the same. Okay, we've devoted some more money, and a lot of time, to improving it, but that isn't why the value's gone up. And there's every sign of it going much higher still, without us lifting another finger.'

'You sound like David Hershey,' said Joanna, teasing.

'No, I bloody don't. Because I'm saying it's ridiculous, in fact—purely notional. David Hershey boasts about how he bought that bit of gracious Canonbury for twice nothing in 1950-something and now it's worth a bomb, as if he expected everyone to congratulate him. All it actually means is that he and Penny are older than us, so got on to the gravy-train at an earlier stage.'

'Just because you don't like David Hershey,' said Joanna.

'No, I *don't* much like the way he ignored me the first two or three times he met me, and has now decided all at once that I'm a person of power and influence after all and so worth inviting to dinner . . . Anyway, you don't like Penny.'

'That's because she imagines she can patronise me because she went to university,' said Joanna, her normally warm voice going hard. 'She's a prig, too. And underneath all that running playgroups and collecting for the handicapped and proselytising for natural childbirth, I think she's *une mauvaise fille* . . .'

'Oh really, you two!' said Mary. She was amused, and not in disagreement with their sharp judgment, but it saddened her a little. David, she thought, I saw him as a baby at Olive's breast, in that garden by the river, the day that Lionel first took me to meet Charlie, the day when he asked me to come to Brittany with him . . .

The old are vulnerable, she thought, as she walked home in the dusk past the newly restored Nash terraces. Because what the young just take to be part of the plot is, for us, the end of the story, and so we want everything to turn out well. *I* want a Dickensian idyll for my old age: to be surrounded by grandchildren—well, step- and surrogate grandchildren—all of whom love me and love each other as well. Of course I know this is a fatuous piece of sentimentality. Why should Joanna and David Hershey—or David and Charlie, rather— necessarily have anything in common today just because, in another world, they played in a garden on the Isle of Wight or were children together round a Christmas tree? I should be glad, simply, that they have grown up capable of going their own separate ways, with their own stubborn perceptions about life. As Lionel did; as I tried to; as Willie did. As poor Dodie tried to, and failed.

. . . At least Dodie never took to drink. When the sources of life had dried for her and she knew she could look forward to nothing further, she ended it. She *did* have a core of cold perception, Dodie, somewhere down there under all that hysteria and fantasy. She knew when there was nothing more for her short of a total change. Whereas Myriam Hershey, by all accounts . . .

I wonder what David is doing about his stepmother? I wonder what he *can* do? Nothing, I suppose. But perhaps I'd better ring up and have a word with him, all the same.

. . . If *I* took to the bottle, would I expect Charlie to come down to London and attempt to rescue me? No, of course I wouldn't, and he wouldn't have the impertinence to try! But that's very different. Charlie has never seen me as being in any way his responsibility. Quite right too.

I'm going up there next month. I'm rather looking forward to it. I'll stay in that hot, comfortable house of theirs where the television is on all the time, and go out for walks in the wind that comes off the Firth, because truth to tell (not that I tell it to them, of course) that house is too warm for me, and Maureen feeds me too much. I shall read aloud new books—that I shall bring with me—to those dear, funny little Scottish girls, who otherwise have an unmixed diet of Enid Blyton. And that darling little Paul, who reminds me more and more of Lionel, will ask me persistent questions about stick insects and his pet ball of mercury, and Maureen will say once again: 'It's ever so nice for him to have you to answer his funny questions. I don't know where he gets all these ideas.'

Dear girl, she is generous; she means it. And they are proud of me, their distinguished elderly relative whom they mention to neighbours: I was oddly touched when I found they had that view of me. I had assumed till then that they knew nothing about my work and cared less. But Maureen also, I know, likes to think that she's being a good wife in having Granny London (as they will call me) to stay. And I am suitably grateful and appreciative, and wouldn't for worlds let her know that, lovely as it is overall to be with the children, in detail and at any one moment I do find their company a little boring. When I was younger, of course, I should have found the whole household boring, almost embarrassingly so. But it is as Lionel once said: the old need to see the best in the young; and so I do.

It's odd: when I haven't seen them for months I yearn to be there again, afraid that the children will be growing tall and forgetting what I look like. Yet when I am actually there I soon start fretting to be back in London. More than ever before in my life I wonder how my patients are. Has Mrs B managed to conceive this month, now I've got her on Clomiphene? Has poor Mr C, unknown to me except as an indifferent test-tube specimen, managed to perform this time on the day I suggested? Is Mrs F still avoiding a miscarriage? Will I soon have another photo of a loved and wanted baby to add to the montage I prop against the wall for supine patients to look at? 'My children', I call them in my proprietary way: they are *all* my children, my stakes in the future where I shall never go.

I feel that time—time for this—is so short. That's why I don't like to be away from London for long. Only a few years more, and I shall have to retire altogether. Only—what? Five years, perhaps, nine or ten at the very most, in which to go on producing this miracle of life. And I want to see my own results: I don't want just to hand patients over to other, younger practitioners, competent as they may be. This, at the end of my life, is the career I always wanted. All the rest, all that contraception, useful and valid as it may have been, was just a detour, a long road back to the beginning.

Funny, in those two years before Lionel died, when we both knew it was only a matter of *when*, I had this same sense of urgency, of time pressing on me, but for a different reason. I thought, then, that when he was gone I would find myself standing alone with empty hands on the brink of a great vacancy. And yet now after all, because of 'my' children, it is not so, not yet. Instead, I feel more than ever that time is precious to me: that every month, every week matters.

In 1974, in the middle of the oil crisis long predicted by Tom Webber, Willie at last died, in a nursing home where he had been for some months.

'Thank God for that,' said Mary, wiping her eyes, to Joanna. 'The poor thing told me only last month that he'd been living off capital for years and that it was practically gone. He was terrified.'

'Pretty amazing and disgusting, when you come to think of it,' said Joanna sternly. 'That he never had a job, I mean. Fancy an able-bodied, highly educated man imagining that he could live out his entire life on the proceeds of jute sold in 1890 or whenever it was.'

'Ah, but it wasn't so unrealistic for him to envisage that when he was a young man, Jo. We didn't have inflation in those days—in fact in the 1930s prices fell.'

'I daresay, but even so. What a pointless life.'

'Well, there was his great work on oriental china or whatever it was. It must have been a blow to him, you know, when that peculiar accident with a paperweight happened, though he did put a good face on it. He was even quite funny about it, afterwards.'

'I'm not sure I actually believe in that great work,' said Joanna, after a pause.

'Mmm, I know what you mean. So like Willie to pick on a subject none of us was in a position to check up on. He was a most pathologically secretive man, I'm afraid.' Now I should tell her, *now*: find some formula, broach the subject in a way that will seem natural . . . What better opportunity than his dying—there will never come another one. I could even do it by showing her those letters from Dodie that I found put away in an envelope when I cleared his house last week. So many letters and papers; he'd obviously never thrown anything away for decades, the old fool: I nearly threw these away myself before I realised what they were. Such pitiful, transparent, naïvely romantic letters, as if she'd invented a quite other Willie in her mind, but nothing to shock, nothing to disgust. *Joanna—*

No. No, I can't. Not just now. She's pregnant again, she told me so last Sunday. She has one every few years, as if it were not so much an occupation as a condition of life. She doesn't make a great thing about them once they're there. It's an oddly traditional pattern in some ways; and they seem to thrive on it, Kate and those dear, busy little boys who are just like Tom, but who for me, skipping generations, merge in dreams with the Boys, my boys, quintessential boys . . .

361

No, I can't tell her today, she looks pale and tired. That inconvenient house with all those stairs—all the people Tom brings home for meals . . .

'I hated him when I was little,' said Joanna suddenly.

'Really? I wonder why?' Joanna almost never mentioned her childhood. Mary was wary, even at Joanna's invitation, of stepping into this devastated, fenced-off territory.

'I'm honestly not sure. I don't remember. I think I didn't like the way he smiled at me, sort of supercilious and knowing. And Mummy—my mother—seemed to get upset and rattled every time he came. I remember that I used to have the feeling he was laughing at us.'

'Yes, I think a lot of people got that feeling about him,' said Mary carefully. 'He was no good with children, of course; I think they alarmed him. He was a crucially shy person, you know, Jo. That awful fat little dog of his was the only creature I ever heard him speak of affectionately. He defended himself against life all along. There was a lot of fear in Willie. The First World War . . . It didn't only affect for ever the ones who fought in it, I believe. It even blighted in some way the lives of those who avoided it. Sometimes I think that all my adult life England has been working through the effects of that war. It was far more traumatic than the second one. Only now the survivors are finally dying off are we beginning at last to get clear of it.'

Joanna looked as if she were digesting this, but she did not comment. After a while she said; 'Actually, we never thought *you* liked Uncle Willie much. I remember, one Christmas, you being frightfully sharp with him about his silly ideas on the Welfare State.'

'Oh yes, ghastly ideas, I used to get furious with him when we were young. But my dear, when you get to my age—to our age, for Willie and I were the same generation—all that sort of disagreement simply doesn't matter any more, beside the fact that you've known each other almost all your lives. Perhaps it should, but it doesn't. Instead of getting angry at that stupid, selfish, reactionary old man, I remember him as he was when I was a child.'

'He must have been a most peculiar child. I simply can't imagine . . . Was he interested in china then?'

362

'No, but he did collect things obsessively, as far as I remember. But boys did that a lot in those days. The others— my cousins, your uncles—had terrific collections of birds' eggs and butterflies. Particularly Roland, the one I always say you take after. Of course, it wouldn't be considered right to collect in that destructive way today . . . Yes, Willie: he was rather a dear little boy, actually, looking back on it. Bookish, you know, and sometimes thought up interesting ideas. Including pacifist ideas, incidentally—and the others used to be horrid to him about them! Oh dear. I expect I should find them dreadfully xenophobic and philistine now.'

—Who was it said: *the tragedy of life is not that people die, but that they die to you?* We were spared that.

And I with Laurie, too.

Pursuing this train of thought, she presently asked if Joanna ever saw the young Hersheys.

'Not me,' said Joanna. 'But Tom ran into Penny Hershey at some publisher's party the other month . . . Did you know they were getting divorced?'

'No! No, I'd no idea. Why? Or is that a naïve question these days, now that people seem to get divorced so easily?'

'I've no idea, but Tom said she's gone all feminist. You know—baggy dungarees and banging on about MCPs and women's workshops. Tom said he got the impression she'd become a lesbian—he hates dungarees, for some reason. But I said I thought that would just be her showing off.'

'Well, I'm very sorry to hear it,' said Mary firmly, vaguely disapproving of Joanna's flippancy. 'I never cared for her myself, but after all, when there are children . . . How old are they now, by the way?'

'The elder two must be quite big—teenagers. But the other two are younger. She's left them, incidentally, Tom said. She's living in a women's commune, apparently.'

'Really, I must say I *do* feel . . . No, it's no good, Jo. I'm showing my age I know, but I *cannot* get up much sympathy for this new wave of feminism we've got. So odd—all my life I've considered myself a feminist. Almost as a matter of course, you might say: all concerned, intelligent people of my generation were. That was one of the main forces behind the Family Planning Movement, after all. But all this new anti-child, anti-family, anti-husband bitterness . . . And they *complain* so. I get them in my consulting room sometimes. Not complaining about brutal husbands or anything, but complaining really about nature, about being women at all. Such a pity.'

'Yes, I know what you mean, and it's a load of neurotic female rubbish disguised as a new awareness, if you ask me,' said Joanna. 'I *loathe* women who go on about what a hard time women have.' She spoke with a passion that, Mary could see, was fuelled from memory. She could guess where.

'Yes,' she said slowly, 'it's all right for *you* to say that, Joanna. You're in a position to have views on the matter that people will respect. But I feel that if I say it people will just think I'm an old fuddy-duddy or Puritan. It's most uncomfortable, you know, for someone like me to feel that she's not a feminist any more if this is what feminism now means. And look what's happened to the Labour movement, with the new left. As I said to you and Tom once before, one finds one has moved from left to right simply by staying in the same place . . . I miss crusading, rather.'

Joanna smiled, and said: 'I'm sure you could find a crusade if you really wanted one. Perhaps you don't want one much any more?'

She's right, thought Mary, after they had parted: she's right. I don't want a crusade. I don't really believe any longer that life works like that. But till she said it I hadn't noticed I didn't believe it any more. How strange.

When I give my lectures people come up to me and say how wonderful it must have been to have participated in the beginnings of the Movement and to see everything we worked for come to pass. Dr Mary Denvers, the venerated institution. So nice and harmless now. And I say, yes, oh yes, most satisfactory . . . But it didn't work like that at all, I see that now. History could have gone very differently, and yet we would still have reached the same point by another route. Individual resolution and endeavour don't matter nearly as much as people think they do, at the time. We are all children of our own time, and can only move with the tides of that time. The best people, the clearest minds—people like

364

Lionel, like Tom, like Eric Evans long ago—have some small scope for individual thought and manoeuvre within a given construct. But not much. All the rest is Vanity. Saith the Preacher.

When I was young—and middle-aged, which I call young now—I used to think how awful it was going to be, being old and feeling that nothing more of significance was going to happen to me, or be done by me. What I didn't realise is that you don't want anything more of any significance because you don't *mind* about things in the same way. You become childishly pleased—or I do—about small things: a patient getting pregnant, Kate winning that art competition, a lovely show of early crocuses in the park. But, in a way, like crocuses, they're all just events sufficient unto themselves; you are pleased with them *now*, for what they are, not for what they may mean for the years to come. You don't live in hopes any more. I miss the intensity of hope, in a way. But in another way it is a relief. The relief of so many things, for good or ill, just being over.

For a life without hope is also a life without fear. That ended for ever for me, I think, after Laurie and Lionel were both dead. Oh, I do realise that I am not immune from tragedy: no one who has a life worth living can be. I know that something could still strike a mortal blow—a small child dying—Joanna—Charlie . . . But even if it was a 'mortal' blow, so what? Really, so what? My effective life is complete anyway. Lionel used to say that everything over seventy is just a bonus. He was perfectly right.

I no longer live, as I did for such a lot of my life, with a constant background of vague fear and foreboding. For decades it seemed to me normal to exist like that: I believe I thought it was a natural part of the human condition. Now this surprises me a little. I don't believe I saw life in those terms when I was a child. From where then did it come, this formless dread, this sense of doom postponed, even in times of greatest happiness, of the fragility of things? From the Great War, that great black barrier across all our lives? . . . I believe myself that it did, in my case, and perhaps in many others' also, but I do not know for sure. Perhaps, if I were to live a whole other life, I would discover.

. . . Of course I think about death. At my age, it is surely improvident not to. Or feeble, anyway. And I have tried, all my life, not to be feeble. 'Girls are *feeble*,' the Boys used to say, when I had bored them or they wanted to go off on their own. How furious and miserable I used to get! 'I love you because you're not a poor, weak woman,' Lionel would say to me. He pretended he was joking, but he meant it too, I could tell. I liked him saying that, most of the time. I tried to live up to it. I have always tried to please the boys or men I loved and to be what they wanted me to be. Perhaps that is a paradox, in the circumstances. But it is the only way I could be.

Occasionally I feel completely desolate. Empty. There are mornings when I wake like that. But then some tiny thing happens—a letter, a phone call, a chat with the man on the greengrocery barrow, one of my avocado plants putting out a leaf—and the depression disappears. Only temporarily, perhaps. But then everything is temporary, now.

Sometimes I look at my clothes, at the expensive, good quality clothes I have bought in the last few years, the sort of thing I could not afford when I was young; and I think, this fine tweed—this thick silk—these will still be good a few years from now: maybe they will outlast me. It's an odd feeling but not, after all, unpleasant.

Sometimes I look at the body of this stiffening, ageing woman I have become and, although I am not particularly keen on it, I find I don't mind so very much after all. Oh, I have moments when my courage fails me, when I think: which bit of this trusted mechanism will finally betray me— heart, lungs, digestion, bladder, womb, memory . . .? But then I think: *you* are only temporary, only a sort of chrysalis. It's all right really. I know that my real self, Mary, is really in there, unchanged, all the time. She will emerge again.

What on earth do I mean? I really do not, logically, know. I don't believe in any sort of afterlife, much less in a heaven. But I do feel, profoundly, that this—this brief time—is not the end.

Epilogue

When, a month after Mary's death, Charlie came down to London to look through what remained of her belongings, he found the bureau drawers almost untouched.

'We have sorted through masses of other stuff, though it may not look like it.' Joanna was slightly defensive because she felt chronically, unnecessarily guilty about Mary's things, mourning in Mary the real mother she had never mourned. 'There's just so much. We gave the First World War letters to someone Tom knows who's working on an anthology. And we got rid of all the china and stuff because you said you didn't want it.' She and Charlie, ten years apart in age, had never known each other well.

'No, well, Maureen likes modern stuff,' he said easily. 'Anyway, you don't want antiques around with kids. I expect you find that too.'

She left him to it.

The bulk of the neatly kept files contained obsolete medical notes. In one were a lot of typewritten letters in American airmail envelopes; in another were a stack of brief notes headed 'Manningham', in what Charlie recognised as his father's hand. Joanna was right; there was far too much to look at in detail.

Presently he came across a buff envelope with a few letters in it in a flamboyant writing he did not know. Skimming through them, he realised they were letters from a woman. Apparently to that old geezer, cousin of a cousin or something, they called 'Uncle Willie'. He settled down to read them with more application.

His grasp of Mary's family connections—which were not his own—was so sketchy that only after he'd digested the letters in the buff envelope with mild surprise and interest did he realise that they must have been written by Joanna's mother, of all people. The one who'd killed herself. Years and years ago, of course.

He sat and thought for a few minutes, the letters in his lap. But he decided on balance that they were not his business. Or anyone else's, now.

He gathered together the buff envelope and its contents, the letters in Lionel's hand, the American airmail letters and some of the medical notes, and began to build an efficient fire with them in the empty grate.